BOOKS BY HEATHER LYNN

BOOK 1: *A Shadow in Time*
BOOK 2: *Déjà-Vu*
BOOK 3: *Between the Shadows*
BOOK 4: *Empty Shadows*

SKY WATCHER

EMPTY SHADOWS

HEATHER LYNN

www.heatherlynnbooks.com

ISBN
978-1-7381-5561-3 (Hardcover)
978-1-7381-5560-6 (Paperback)
978-1-7381-5562-0 (eBook)

For my biggest fan.
xox

Time...
is always progressing.
It doesn't slow or wait,
it doesn't meander.
Instead,
it flows,
moving endlessly,
on a path
straight forward.

What if it were to make a turn,
and circle back around from behind?

Would we see the loop?

Or would it be lost in time's shadow?

Prologue

I had been there,
waiting,
between the shadows,
every Samhain
for the past eight years
—she hadn't come.

What could possibly have happened to prevent Jessica from being there?

PART I

Thunder and Lightning

I lay my head on my pillow, and I think of her . . .

I can see November's full moon and watch absentmindedly as the clouds slowly blow across, dulling its glow. The last time I "met" with Jessica was just before Holly was born.

Every year since, I have set up my altar and decorated it with the colours of the season—with pumpkins, apples, or a cob of corn. Each year, I have performed my Samhain ritual with great care, hoping that *this time*, we'd be together, that *this time*, that special window would open, and she would be there. But no . . .

I do see her in my sleep sometimes but always in the unreality of a dream. We haven't had the opportunity to commune, to experience a connection of souls, as we have in the past.

I miss her so much . . .

Something isn't right, but I have no idea what and no way to find out. Well, that's not true; I could return to her time, which would be 2028, and see what happened, but I promised Ben I would never attempt time travel again. It's too dangerous. Nothing is guaranteed, and if I'm honest, I, no *we*, were both lucky to have made it back the last time. No, I belong here in 1834, and here is where I will stay . . . with my family.

My sleepy thoughts turned to plans for tomorrow—Holly's birthday. We didn't do birthday parties, but we did celebrate. Our family and best friends will visit tomorrow afternoon for a meal of Holly's choice and cake. Holly chose hamburgers with all the fixins—she would eat them every day if she could. I prepared everything today. By now, we had burger-making down to an art, but the birthday cake—it was a bit lopsided.

It had been a tiring day; I didn't last long after tucking the children into their beds. Robbie, now fifteen years old, still liked a hug and kiss goodnight from his mum and dad, while Sabel was quite adamant that it wasn't necessary, but she never turned us away. Phillip had reached the ripe old age of twelve and always asked for a kiss on the other cheek; for Jessie. He still spoke of her every single day, unwilling to let her memory fade. The attachment they'd had for one another was something he still felt strongly. Often, he would tell us of dreams he'd had—dreams of her beckoning him to come closer, to share her secrets.

I fell into a strange dream, and Jessica was in it; she was bent forward, walking toward me through some kind of dark tunnel. It reminded me of something you might find at an amusement park, where the tunnel wall was lit with little lights and slowly spinning clockwise, while you tried to walk through to the other side. She was calling my name. "Charlotte, are you there? Can you hear me, Char?" I was waving at her, trying to call out, to let her know I could hear her, but no sound was coming from my mouth. She stopped walking and looked around. "Whoa, it just got cold here," she said under her breath.

I felt it, too. At the same time, I could almost feel a presence in the cold, thick air, but nothing was visible in the dim light. Jessie's voice was calling, "Mummy?"

Something brushed past me. I gasped.

Then there was another voice. It was coming from a bedroom down the hall, and it was loud enough to enter my dream. "Jessie! Jessie, be careful!" It was Phillip. I watched Jessica turn toward his voice. "Come in! Come in!" he said, and she smiled.

Rolling onto my back, I awoke feeling goosebumps crawling over my body. Phillip's voice sounded eerie. Startled by a loud crashing sound directly overhead, Hazel sprung straight up from where she was sleeping on the bed. The house shook for several seconds; at the same time, a bright flash of light filled the upper level.

"I heard it," Ben said, sitting up.

The bedroom door creaked open. "What was that, Daddy?" Sabel asked, standing in the doorway. "It was really loud."

"Was it an earthquake?" my sleepy voice asked.

Phillip came to stand beside Sabel with tears running down his cheeks. "I saw Jessie. She was coming to see me and then . . . there was a loud noise and a flash, and she was gone," he said, wiping his eyes. "She's gone," he added in a whisper.

I could hear the rain hitting the windows as Ben met them in the hall. "That was just some thunder and lightning. I'm sorry it interrupted your dream. Maybe you can get it back when you fall asleep again." He put his arm over Phillip's shoulders. "Come on, you two, and I'll tuck you back into bed."

When Ben returned to bed, I snuggled into his warmth, promptly falling back to sleep. It could have been ten minutes later, or an hour, I'm not sure, but something roused me from my slumber. Unsure what had awakened me, I whispered, "Did you hear something, Benny?"

He was sliding into his slippers and reaching for his robe. "I'll be back. Stay here."

Yeah right! I slipped on my robe and followed him down the stairs. I could hear the rain hitting the roof and pelting the windows, while rumbles of thunder echoed in the background. The flashing helped illuminate the staircase and sitting room. Together, the wind and lightning were creating moving shadows outside the door. No, that's not what it was. There was a rattle at the door. "Is someone trying to get in, Ben?" I whispered.

He glanced at me over his shoulder. "I don't know. Grab the poker from the wood-burning stove and stay behind me."

I came up behind him holding the poker as he reached for the door in what felt like slow motion. Hazel slinked around my ankles. Another flash, and two figures stood on the doorstep, silhouetted on the curtains. I lifted the poker.

Ben turned the knob and opened the door.

"Ben?" said a female voice. "Char?"

Groggy

I opened my eyes to find myself lying on the settee. I slowly looked around the candlelit room, trying to get my bearings. The clock on the mantle ticked; it said said 12:50.

"You fainted, Moxie." Ben's voice sounded distant.

"I did? Why? I remember you opening the door and a flash of light . . ." My voice was groggy as I pushed myself up to sitting. There was some shuffling beside the settee. I turned my head. "What the—"

"Hey, Charlotte," she said.

"Jessica? Holy crap, Jess! What are you doing here?" I turned to her companion. "Michael! What's happening?" I looked at Ben. "Am I dreaming, Ben?" The look on his face might have been comical if I didn't feel so disoriented. I turned and found them still standing there.

I shook my head to trying to lose the foggy feeling.

"We're here, Char. You're not dreaming." Jessica smiled.

"Why? Why are you here?" I asked. After taking in their appearances, I added, "Oh, look at you, you're soaking." Each had a woolen blanket around their shoulders, but their clothing underneath was dripping wet, as was their hair.

"I had a coat on, but it didn't do much for me while I lay in the pouring rain," Jess said and hugged me hard. "God, it's good to see you, Char."

I'd always liked the way she shortened my name to Char with a hard "ch" sound, short for Charlie instead of Charlotte. She was the only one who ever called me that.

I didn't know what to do first. "Okay, we need to get you out of those clothes. Come upstairs, and I'll get you something to sleep in, then we can have a warm drink while you take whatever needs to dry out of your bags."

As we headed up the stairs, I put my finger to my lips, reminding them we had children sleeping up here. I left them in the bedroom with some sleep clothes and a candle.

Back downstairs, I hugged Ben. "You're shaking, Sweets."

"I think it's the shock of seeing their faces. Is this really happening, Benny?"

"Oh, it's happening," he replied.

"Why do you think they've come?" I asked as I took down some teacups. "Oh, who am I kidding? This is not an occasion for tea; I think we'll need to take out the whiskey." He nodded and reached up into the cupboard, while I went to take out some blankets and pillows; for tonight, they would have to make do with the settee and chair.

When they came back down, Jess and I hung their wet clothing by the wood-burning stove for the night. "How's your head?"

"It's okay. We took a couple of Tylenols before we left."

I nodded. "Please, have a seat guys," I said, indicating the settee. Hazel jumped up onto Jessica's lap and curled into a ball. "This is Hazel. Looks like she's happy to meet you, Jess."

"How sweet," she said, brushing her hand lightly over the cat's head and back.

Ben came with drinks. "Here you go. This will warm you," he said. "Michael—your eye."

His hand went to the side of his face. "Oh, that. I thought it might have been a dream . . . I was trying to sit up. The rain was pouring down on me, and I was looking for Jess. She was lying about twenty feet away. There was someone leaning over her. I don't know what he was doing, but I called out, 'Hey, get away from her!' and got onto my feet. I could only see the person's back. He had on something with a hood. I grabbed the back of him and pulled upwards. I didn't know if he was checking to see if she was all right? He turned and swung at me and hit me. I lost my balance and fell back, and he took off. Jess seemed okay. Then she came to, and I temporarily forgot him as we looked for the house. We were glad for the lightning. It helped us find it."

I got him a cold wet towel to use as a compress for the time being and some arnica cream to apply before bed.

We sat looking at one another in a long moment of disbelief. I broke the silence. "So . . . as much as I love having you here, I know there's a reason you've come. Can y—"

I heard the creak of the staircase behind the settee and immediately stood. There would need to be some sort of explanation about these two. "I'm sorry, sweetie, did we wake you?" I asked. She nodded and then her eyes opened wide as she saw the strangers in her sitting room.

Jess set Hazel on the settee and stood, turning toward the staircase. "Hello. I'm your mom's friend, Jessica, and this is Michael." As she glanced at him, he smiled. "You must be Sabel?"

Her eyes flicked from Jess's to mine before she answered, "No. I'm Holly. Sabel's sleeping."

"Oh, I'm sorry," Jessica responded, the colour draining from her face.

"Sweetheart, get back to your bed; I'll come tuck you in."

Holly nodded and, rubbing her eyes, said, "Goodnight," to the room.

When I came back down the stairs, Jess looked at me, white as a ghost. "I'm confused, Char. Sabel should be six years old. Holly should be a newborn. How was that not her?"

Eight Years

I felt a sinking sensation in my stomach at her words. "Holly is eight years old. Actually, today is her birthday. November 16th." Why would Jess think Sabel was six? She was six, eight years ago. "Jess?" I heard the waver in my voice.

Jessica and Michael were looking at one another, utterly bewildered.

"I don't understand. We left on the night of November 15th. We arrived on the right day, but why . . . why am I off? Holly was born in 1826, right? We were supposed to arrive the day she was born. How is she eight?"

I looked at them in disbelief. It was shocking enough that they were here, but the idea that they didn't arrive when they expected to was too much. "Okay, wait . . . what year did you leave home?"

"2020," Jess answered.

After a rather large sip of my drink, I said, "Let me get this straight, you left home in 2020 expecting to arrive in 1826—that's 194 years. That number of years, that gap, has been constant since I first came here. All of our communication, and when we went to see you, it's always been *that* space of time. What changed? And wait . . . I haven't been able to reach you in eight years. I've tried over and over, but you haven't been there. All I've seen are empty shadows. There was no one there, no sound, only shadows; it was as if you *had* been there and were gone, and all that remained was your shadow."

Jessica swallowed hard. "What?" Still pale, she glanced at Michael. "But we were just together on Samhain. It was only two weeks ago. You showed me the last few months of your time in Scotland, your homecoming . . . I saw your beautiful children. At the time, you looked as if you were about to burst because you were expecting Holly." She smiled. "I remember wishing so badly that I could meet them." Her smile faded.

"That was the last time I saw you, Jess. You were sitting cross-legged on the floor facing me. There was light shining from your eyes, your smile, the ends of your hair, your fingertips—you looked like an angel. I saw you and Michael walking the grounds of twenty-first century Slains Castle, Moxie surrounded by a bunch of puppies, you as a surgical nurse at the hospital. Something happened then, didn't it? We were interrupted."

"Yes. Someone came up behind you and—"

I felt the tears burning in my eyes. "That's right, it was Jessie," I said quietly, tipping my head downwards.

"And then you disappeared," she said.

"Jessie thought she heard me calling—said it woke her up. I've wondered about that many times because I never said a word; I always speak to you in my head." I swallowed hard before continuing. "So, you left there two weeks after that? Why?"

She turned to Michael momentarily. Her voice was soft as she said, "To warn you . . . about Jessie."

I felt Ben's arm come around my shoulders and did my best to stay composed. "We lost her a few weeks later, on December the 10th." My voice was barely a whisper.

Jess's eyes were wet as she looked at us. "I'm so sorry. We came to tell you, hoping we could try to take measures to prevent her death." Her voice cracked, and she hung her head.

Michael looked at Ben and asked, "What do you think could have happened?"

"I can't begin to guess," he answered, shaking his head.

"Here's to Jessie," Jess said, raising her glass.

After a short and restless night, I came down the stairs to find Jessica standing in front of the fireplace, looking at the wall over the mantle. "Morning, Char. This must be the painting Gifted Hands made for you after your wedding. Am I right?"

I smiled. "You are. Isn't it pretty? The view hasn't changed in the years since. And this one over here"—I pointed at the wall by the stairs—"was painted by Running Cub at the same time. He has a talent, too, though I haven't seen any painting from him since."

"They're beautiful. It must make you so happy to look at them every day, knowing the love that went into them." She was absolutely right!

We introduced the children to Jessica and Michael before they left to meet Gracie and the others for church. Robbie and Sabel were happy to meet the friends they had heard mentioned so often. Holly, after meeting them last night, just smiled and said good morning.

"Happy birthday, Holly," Jessica said.

Holly smiled. "Thank you."

When Phillip came down for his breakfast, he looked at the two strangers on the settee and came to stand in front of them. "*You* are Jessica," he said, quite sure of himself.

"I am." She smiled. "And this is Michael. You must be Phillip?" He nodded.

"I knew it was you." I saw Jess's eyebrows come down briefly. "You have the same name as her, too."

"Too?" I asked.

"Yep," he said and sat to have his breakfast. Jess and I shrugged at each other.

"We'll meet you at the store after church, before we come back home with everyone." I told the four of them.

Once the children left, I found my papers with the moon phases from the day I arrived here in 1818, through most of the twenty-first century. Jess's new moon in 2020 matched up with our full moon in 1826, so why were they not able to arrive then?

"For whatever reason, it looks like you were bumped to the next time the moons lined up on that date, Jess."

"So the next full moon on this day was last night? Weird. Wait, how old are you now, Char, thirty-eight?"

"Oh my God, I hadn't thought of that," I laughed. "You're thirty, right? I'm older than you now." I turned to look at Michael, expecting to see a smirk, but he just looked confused. The arnica may have helped the bruising, but it still looked like someone had punched him in the eye. "And I see you still have the crystal dragonfly. It looks pretty hanging there."

She was right. It used to hang in my bedroom window when I lived in the twenty-first century, but when we visited them in 2013, I took it home and hung it here in the kitchen window. "I've always thought dragonflies were pretty, but after meeting Keen Wolf, I learned that they represent change and transformation, and symbolize something important unfolding in your life's journey. The dragonfly also brings messages of wisdom and enlightenment from the elemental world."

"Hmm, I didn't know all that."

I was pouring us each a second coffee when I heard Ben speaking. "You know, I've been thinking about the night you meant to arrive here. Do you remember that night, Charlotte?"

"My water broke that night," I answered and promptly felt the heat in my cheeks.

"Yes." He smiled. "We were all up because we'd heard a loud bang and the house lit up, remember?" I felt my jaw slacken.

"You're right. I hadn't thought of that. It woke us all up, well, except for Robbie. And it wasn't raining. I remember looking out and seeing the full moon clearly," I said.

For several beats, the room was silent as we absorbed and tried to assimilate this information.

Jess's eyes were wide when she asked, "Do you think that was us?"

I shrugged my shoulders and thought of what happened that night. I told them that when the children came to the bedroom to see what the noise was, Phillip told us that Jessie had fallen down. We found her on the floor beside her bed. She told us she'd seen a big flash, and it hurt her head. We thought that maybe she'd stood up out of bed too quickly and fainted. She had a bit of a bump on her head and a headache, so I cuddled with her for the rest of the night. "Now that I think about it, she was muttering about flashes of light in the darkness and shooting stars as she slept."

Jessica was looking at me with a curious expression, eyes squinted as she thought to herself. "Hm-m, so maybe that was us like, I don't know, bouncing off the time window—I don't know what else to call it. If that's what happened, we bounced straight to here, and *you* took the long way."

Interesting theory.

"That's a lot to think about," I said, mostly to myself. Ben nodded in silent agreement. "Well, church will be over soon, and everyone will want to meet these two in the flesh. What do you say we take a walk down to the store and say hello? We can talk more later."

"That sounds great! I've wanted to meet Gracie forever! Oh, but first, can we check the ground? I couldn't find my Celestite in the dark last night," Jessica said.

They had come with some clothing made to suit the time, so, after dressing, we went outside. The smell of last night's rain was in the air as we searched the area where they think they landed. There was nothing to be seen but soggy leaves that had fallen over the past weeks. "Strange. The stone is a good size. I expected it would be easy to spot," Jess said.

"We can look around again later; maybe it'll be easier to see once it's dried up a bit out here," Ben said. Jessica nodded.

"So, Ben, you grew a beard," Jess said as we started walking.

His hand went up to his chin, and he smiled. "It makes mornings easier."

She looked at me sideways with a sly smile, before adding, "It looks good on you. I've been trying to get Michael to give it a try. So far, no go."

"Maybe being here will be the perfect time to let it happen," I said and chuckled.

"Hmm, there's something about a beard . . ." Jess said under her breath.

It was quiet as we rounded the back of the store. They weren't back yet, but when I looked toward the water, who did I see? "Jess, look. It's Gifted Hands, Keen Wolf, and the children."

"Shit, Char, I feel so nervous," she said with a crooked smile.

"Looks like you'll be jumping in with both feet."

In the Woods

"Gifted Hands and Keen Wolf, let me intro—"

"Jessica and Michael," Gifted Hands interrupted, smiling brightly. "It is wonderful to meet you."

"And you," Jess said, "although we have met before."

"Yes. In between, as little Jessie once said." Keen Wolf stood quietly as the women embraced.

After releasing Gifted Hands, Jess turned to Keen Wolf. She smiled as she took in his features. He didn't break eye contact as he offered her a slight nod. Then he said, "It is good to meet you, Jessica." He looked beside her and added, "And you, Michael." He did not offer a hug or a handshake, but as his gaze returned to Jess, I watched something pass between them; she knew everything that had happened between him and me, and he understood that.

"These are our children," Gifted Hands said. "Mitenah and Dark Wolf."

"Mitenah—what a pretty name," Jessica said.

"It means 'Born at the New Moon'," Mitenah answered with a shy smile. "We used to call Sabel Mimiteh, which means 'New Moon'. We were both born at a New Moon."

"And Dark Wolf?"

"Yes. He was Sitting Deer until this past summer. Now he is called Dark Wolf," Gifted Hands clarified.

Introductions made, we entered the store's kitchen, where I started some coffee. Then, the crowd returned from church, streaming in one at a time. All eyed the strangers standing beside me. "Everyone," I began, "I am happy to introduce you to our friends Jessica and Michael Saunders."

I heard Gracie suck in a breath, then she ran up to Jessica and wrapped her arms around her. "Oh me, I never thought I'd have the chance te meet ye."

"This is Ben's sister, Gracie," I said with a chuckle. She hugged Michael next. "And this is her husband, Jimmy." I looked at the girls and waved my hand for them to come over. "And these are their daughters: Alexandra, who we call 'Sandy', Lily, and Evelyn. This is Ben's mum, Mabel. And last, but definitely not least, are Hettie and Eli. These two special people look after all of us, the household, and property."

The children were slightly curious about the strangers, but naturally, were more interested in each other. Mitenah approached her mother and asked, "En-ay, can we go for a walk on the trail with the others?"

I saw Jessica look my way as Gifted Hands answered. "Yes"—she glanced at me—"you may go as long as you stay together."

When Sabel caught my eye, I said, "You can meet us at home in a while." With that, all the children disappeared.

"En-ay is mother?" Jessica asked Gifted Hands.

"Yes. And kree-ay is father."

"Why don't we a' move te the sittin' room where we can be more comfortable," Mabel suggested.

Several years ago, Gracie and Jimmy decided that three bedrooms and a kitchen attached to the place they worked was not enough space for a family of six. They needed more room where they could all be comfortable and entertain. A two-level addition was built onto the back of the building, stretching from the kitchen door to the north-west corner of the building, creating a good-sized sitting room off the kitchen and a new bedroom upstairs.

Once we were sitting with some fresh coffee, Jessica and Michael told their "story"; a sickness had come to the town where they lived in Canada. People were getting ill, a large number severely, and the death toll was rising by the day. They left their home and travelled here, keeping to themselves so as not to pick up the illness along the way, nor pass it on if they had it. "We hope that after a couple of months it will be safe to return home. In the meantime, we want to get to know all of you." Little did we know how close to true that story was.

After a bite to eat and some chit chat, we said goodbye to Mabel, Hettie, and Eli and walked back up the little hill.

"Gracie and Gifted Hands, I'm so happy to meet you in the flesh," Jess said, walking between them, hooking their arms. "I never thought I ever would. Charlie told me all about you, of course." She looked at me then and continued. "I guess we can fill them in on the details of our trip once we're back at the house?" I nodded.

"It's lovely te meet you, too, lass," Gracie said. "Charlie's told us so much about ye, and I've seen ye once or twice in me . . . hm-m, what can I call it, dreams? But I confess, I never expected I'd meet ye."

"Yes," Gifted Hands said. "That we are all able to be together is"—she looked at me with a grin—"awesome."

I giggled and glanced back to see the men talking as they followed.

Jessica went on to say how lovely all the children were. "It must get rather busy and noisy when everyone's together, and the amount of food to feed the bunch of you—yikes."

"Oh, aye. Yer nae wrong," Gracie answered with a laugh.

"The only one missing, I think, is Running Cub. Where is he today, Gifted Hands?" Jessica asked.

Gifted Hands glanced at me before answering. "Well, first I must tell you, he is now called Running Otter. It is the name we gave him when he reached manhood. He has now seen twenty-one years, and unfortunately, no longer lives with us. Several months ago, he left to live with a woman called Aleshanee in a different clan to the west."

"What a shame. Charlotte spoke of him often; I looked forward to meeting him," Jess said.

"I think Sabel misses him, too. I believe she has a little crush on him," I said quietly. Gifted Hands gave me a knowing look.

"When you spoke of the store in the past, you mentioned Jimmy's mother working there, too. Is she away?" Jess asked.

"Oh, no. Actually, Gladys passed a few years ago, lass."

"I'm sorry," Jessica said.

"It was a sad day, but now she's wi' her Johnny again. She aye looked forward to that day."

Behind us, Jimmy must have asked about Michael's face. ". . . but when I stood and called out to him, he lunged at me. We both landed a punch, and then he ran off in the rain, and I got down on the ground to check on Jessica. I never saw his face."

"Was anything taken?" Keen Wolf asked.

"I don't think so."

Gifted Hands asked Jessica, "Tell me, what do you do at your home for work? Charlotte has said you are a nurse?"

"Yes. I'm what's called a surgical nurse. I assist the surgeon when he's performing a surgery. It's very interesting work."

"Och, I dinna think I'd be standin' if I had te see the things you must see," Gracie said,

Jess chuckled. "It's not for everyone, but I love that kinda stuff."

"And what about Michael?"

"Hmm, how to explain it? He works for a telecommunications company. They deal with different forms of communication like the telephone, television—Charlotte must have told you about the TV?" The women nodded. "Or the computer. He has been made the junior vice-president of sales and operations." She turned to me and added, "They gave him a bigger office, a nice bonus, and a Rolex when he was promoted."

"Wow," I said. "That's impressive. Good for him!" I saw Gracie's curious expression and explained, "A Rolex is a very expensive brand of wristwatch."

"He works hard. I'm proud of him." Glancing behind her, she asked, "Jimmy, do you still have the watch Charlotte and Ben brought you?"

"Aye," he answered, before returning to the men's conversation.

Once sitting comfortably back at our house, I summed up what had happened last night and what we'd learned so far about Jessica and Michael "travelling" here. The room was quiet for a few moments while my words sunk in.

"Ye mean to say, a' those years ago when ye telt me you were awakened by a bang and bright light, ye think that was Jessica and Michael trying to arrive here?"

"But why would they be unable to come? What would have stopped them?" Gifted Hands asked.

"And what was different last night?" Jimmy asked.

"We haven't figured that out yet," Ben answered. "We may never."

A bang, a flash of light; the children in the bedroom doorway; Phillip saying, "Mummy, Daddy, Jessie fell,"; little Jessie lying on the floor.

"What is it?" Keen Wolf asked, looking at me.

I gave my head a little shake before answering. "Just the image of Jessie after she fainted."

Jessica looked around the room before saying, "We tried to come to warn you, to try to save her . . . but we didn't make it. What happened to her, Char?" I felt Keen Wolf's eyes on me.

"I don't know. Later that night, she talked about seeing a big flash that hurt her head. As she slept, she muttered about flashes of light in the darkness. Just a few weeks later, she wasn't feeling well; she passed out and fell. Her nose was bleeding. She had a couple of seizures. When she came around, she told us she could see 'it' growing. She said it was like a small ball growing in her head and it hurt." I heard my voice crack and stopped momentarily.

Ben continued. "I remember Phillip calling out to us that afternoon—he'd been napping with her and had been dreaming. He was staring at his sister; tears were running down his cheeks. He said there were voices whispering all around them in the dark, and he was scared." I felt a shiver run down my spine as I looked at Ben and remembered these moments only too clearly. "He said he found her hand in the dark and held it because she was scared, too." Ben swallowed hard. "Phillip said he could see it growing, but he didn't want to tell her."

The room was quiet for a moment before I continued. "We were all in the room; no one knew what was happening. She seized again. When she came around, she asked if she'd fainted again and said she felt very tired. When she saw we were all there with her, she asked . . ." I had to stop. I couldn't say the words.

"She asked if we were there to say goodbye," Ben finished. "Robbie asked how her head felt, and she told him it still hurt, but it would be better soon. She said she would be leaving, and then it wouldn't hurt anymore. Charlotte asked, 'but you're sick—where are you going?'"

With a wobble in my voice, I continued. "She looked into my eyes and said, 'I'm going home, Mummy.' Then she fell asleep again, and she was talking to people and spoke of seeing stars. Not long after, she asked me to give her stuffed kitty to Holly. She must have seen our sad, scared faces. She said, 'Don't be sad, please. I'm going home.'"

The room was silent as *we* relived that day, and Jess and Michael envisioned it. It still brought tears to my eyes. It was eight years ago, and yet it could have been yesterday. My sweet little Jessie . . .

"I'm so sorry, Charlotte." Jess hugged me hard, clearly seeing the pain on my face.

Standing back, I wiped my tears and said, "She told me she'd seen you a couple of times." Jessica raised her eyebrows. "Well, she didn't know your name: she saw your hair but said you had no face. When I asked where she saw you, she said 'in between.'"

"Between what?" Jess asked.

"That's what I asked. Her answer was 'Between the shadows—that place you go in your circle.'" I still get goosebumps thinking of her words.

"There were times I sensed another presence or glimpsed a shadow, but I never saw her, only you ladies." She smiled at Gracie and Gifted Hands. "And your mum, of course," she added awkwardly. I still felt a thrill thinking that my mum and Gracie shared the same soul, in a different time.

"Afterwards, we thought about going back again, trying to somehow warn ourselves in the past, but . . . well, it wasn't an accident that we could try to prevent—it was her health, something within her. We couldn't have avoided that."

"That makes sense, Char. It must have been a hard decision to make," she said softly. I could only nod my agreement.

Suddenly, there were voices and the sounds of feet running through the trees toward the house. The door burst open, and Robbie came inside. He bent, leaning his forearms on his thighs while he caught his breath. "Dad, Mum, we found Mr. Haskel! He's lying in the woods."

Sabel came bustling in next. "Mr. Haskel's not moving! He's dead, Daddy!"

Ben was up on his feet, getting his coat off the hook, as the other children filtered into the room—all breathing heavily after running to share the news. "Come show me, Robbie," Ben said, as Keen Wolf and Jimmy followed him out the door.

Hazel ran out the door as I pulled it closed. There was far too much noise in here for her at the moment. I looked at Jess and said, "Simon Haskel is our wainwright. He lives just past the store with his wife, Edna."

I put some milk on the stove to warm as the children told us what they'd found in the middle of nowhere. He was wearing his coat and was lying on his side, in a puddle on the ground. He was only wearing one shoe; they didn't see the other or anything else, because at that point, they ran home.

Back in the sitting room, I joined the others. "What do we know about Simon Haskel, Gracie?"

"Well, let's see . . . he and Edna arrived here in town not long before ye left for Scotland. It's just the two of them, her two brothers, and their dog, no children. From what I've glimpsed, I'd guess they've perhaps a rocky marriage. Some days when I see her, she looks ready to take down anyone in her path, rarely smiles. That bein' said, she's aye been nice enough te me."

"I've only spoken with her a few times when she was looking for special teas. She was nice but grew a sneer when the topic of her husband came up. I've only spoken to him a few times. You?" I asked Gracie.

"Aye, a few times. It's aye Edna that comes into the shop. Usually at the town events, he's off wi' the men. I've heard Jimmy say he's a fine sense of humour, and they play cards now and again. That's all I ken."

Looking at Gracie's expression, I had to ask, "What else, Gracie?"

"Jimmy played cards last night . . . at the inn. I dinna ken if Simon was there."

Before long, Robbie and Jimmy returned to say that Ben and Keen Wolf had gone to inform Lawrence of Simon's death and return to the body with a cart. "Lawrence is the town magistrate and handles these types of matters," I said, for Jessica and Michael.

When asked if Edna had been at church today, Gracie told us that no, she had not. "Emma, that's her neighbour," she added, glancing at Jessica, "says she's been away a day or two. If she's nae home, she winna have missed 'im—not yet anyway." Gracie noticed Jess's necklace then. "Yer necklace is pretty, Jessica. It reminds me of somethin' our Charlie would wear." Her eyes flicked momentarily to me.

Jessica smiled and lifted her hand to the quaternary knot pendant. "As a matter of fact, she gave this to me the night before our wedding."

"It's Celtic, aye? It has meanin'?"

"Several. It's made up of four sections, and you know many things are represented in fours: the elements; the cardinal directions; the Celtic Fire festivals, which are the same as our Wiccan sabbats; or birth, life, death, and rebirth." She turned to me then and continued. "I looked into it after you left, Char. It's also supposed to protect the wearer from negative energy and offer a sense of confidence and protection, like 'the feeling of the earth's firmness underfoot'. At the same time, the knot has no beginning and no end, which symbolizes infinity."

Gracie nodded, taking it all in.

When the men returned, their expressions were grim. Ben told us, "Simon's coat opened up as he was lifted, and something hard in his pocket dinged my shin. I put my hand in the pocket and pulled out something blue. Keen Wolf and I immediately looked at one another. Lawrence asked what it was." Jessica's eyes opened wide as she listened.

"I told him it was Celestite—the stone that Charlotte's friend Jessica was carrying when she arrived last night. Only she dropped it on the ground somewhere. We'd been out looking for it this morning."

"Maybe Simon found it early this morning and picked it up," Gracie suggested.

"Maybe. We also found his other shoe on the way, about forty feet down the path." He shrugged before continuing. "Lawrence asked how long I thought he'd been dead," Ben went on. "He was in full rigor—his body had completely stiffened. That usually happens eight to twelve hours after death. We know that Jessica and Michael arrived here just after midnight, so I would say he couldn't have died more than twelve or thirteen hours ago." He looked at the concern on everyone's face. "Lawrence suggested, judging by the bruising on his face, we should examine his body further. That this may not have been an accident."

They went to the Haskel's cabin, hoping to examine the body there. When they arrived at the front porch, the door was open. Edna had just arrived home. "That you, Simon?" she called. Before she could come out, Lawrence stepped inside to warn her about her husband.

She came out onto the step and looked down at him with tears in her eyes. "Oh, Simon. What's happened to you? Who did this?" She took a step to the side, and Ben caught her as she teetered momentarily.

Ben said, "Lawrence told her we didn't know what happened or who did this, but we would. She looked at each of us, her eyes wide with shock, and asked if we could take him in and lay him on the settee, which we did. Then she asked if we'd give her a hand taking off his coat and said she'd do the rest. I told her I would like to examine his body if that was agreeable; perhaps I might find something to help us understand what happened. She agreed, saying, 'Of course, doctor. Of course. If someone is responsible for this, they must be found.'"

"Were either of her brothers there? Ian and what's the other one's name again?" I asked.

"It's Geoff, and no, neither were there at the time, just the dog. He had a good sniff of Simon and then went out the door," Ben said. "Also, the preacher said he would go see her later today," he continued, handing the Celestite to Jessica.

"Thanks, Ben. So, what did the body tell you about what happened?" she asked.

"Well, he had to have died before the sun came up or he wouldn't have been in full rigor. I would say probably between 1:00 and 5:00 a.m."

"What about livor mortis?" she asked. There was silence in the room; the others didn't understand this term. Jess saw the questioning eyes and said, "When the body dies and the heart stops pumping, the blood settles with time and gravity, discolouring the skin."

"Yes, I saw this on his back."

"But we found him lying on his side," Keen Wolf said.

"So his body was moved?" Michael asked.

"It would seem so," answered Ben. "He also received some punches, maybe even kicks. There were bruises on his abdomen, face and knuckles, and a bloody bump on the back of his head. Whoever did this must have some bruising, too."

"Ye've telt a' this to Lawrence, Benny?"

"I did, yes," he answered. "As a matter of fact, he's asked that I help him do some investigating."

"I can tell ye he left the inn ahead o' me last night. I got in just afore midnight, I believe," Jimmy said.

"Who was still there when you left?"

"Hmm, let me think. Edmond, but of course he had to be, one o' Scott's men from the mill, and a mannie from Seneca Lake, I believe he said. If ye dinna mind me askin', what do you suppose Lawrence will think when he sees Michael's face?" he asked.

All eyes were on Michael. "What?" he asked, a soft blush spreading across his cheeks. "You all know *I* didn't do this, don't you? I told you someone was bent over Jessica. When I stood and called out to him, he swung at me. Yes, I punched him back, but only once, and he ran away. I let him go to check on my wife."

"Do you mind?" I asked, reaching for his hand. The knuckles of his right hand were slightly bruised. "Hmm. This isn't going to look good, Michael. We believe you of course, but . . ."

"Shit, Char! Oops, sorry. What can we do about it? Even with cold compresses and arnica, his black eye is still coming out."

"Yeah, and you *know* Lawrence will come to the conclusion that Michael was the one who fought Simon and killed him," I said. "Let's hope he makes quick progress finding the truth."

Missing

Lawrence set out almost immediately to question the men who'd been at the inn Saturday night. Meanwhile, once the shock of today's discovery had passed, and the children had settled, they went to the tree house. Ben had built it several years ago on the adjoining property Audrey had left us, near the spot where her house had been. It stretched between two large, strong trees and was high enough that they needed a ladder to climb into it. The kids often spent hours there at a time.

"Why don't you guys tell us what's been going on at home," I suggested.

"Oh jeez, you won't believe it, Charlie, seriously. It's like a frikkin' sci-fi movie." Shaking her head, Jess came to sit on the settee beside me. "Last year there was an outbreak of a virus that started a pandemic. Within months, the whole world had been affected. People were passing it on without even knowing they had it, and many were dying. Countries closed their borders to travel. The Prime Minister actually called all Canadians home. We were put on what they called 'lockdown', as most countries were, only to go out if absolutely necessary. Many businesses closed, although some were able to stay open for pickup orders, but anyone who could was working from home. That meant Michael set up an office at the house. I still had to work of course; people never stop needing the hospital, and so many were coming in deathly ill. Everyone was to wear a mask and wash hands religiously to keep ourselves and others safe. All sporting events, concerts, everything was cancelled. Schools are even being taught online. It's crazy—and because people were staying home and not driving around, there were more appearances of wild animals."

"Actually," Michael started, "one morning last May, Jess and I were outside having our morning coffee and watched a bear walk straight through the neighbour's yard and climb over the back fence. I shit you not." Jessica nodded as I looked at him in disbelief.

"It became serious for us in, let's see, March, so about eight months ago and is still ongoing. They set up testing centres so people could find out if they had it. If you test positive, you are to isolate yourself for a certain number of days and everyone you've been in contact with should for a period, too. We were only able to cross the border because of Michael's work, and we had to isolate after crossing. We stayed at that same beach house for a week to be sure neither of us had it, so we wouldn't bring it here. Worldwide they're scrambling to create a vaccine. I guess that will come soon, at least I hope it does. Scary shit . . . oh shoot, sorry."

"Oh my God!"

"It's grim," Michael agreed. "Everyone knows someone who's had it by now. Every day on the news we hear about the number of hospitalizations and deaths."

Gracie's face was ashen as she sat listening to this news.

I tried to wrap my head around what they were telling us, but it was difficult.

"It's hard to imagine the effect it will have on us once it's past. I mean, we can still talk and text and video call each other, but not being able to see each other for such a long time—gah!"

"Michael, how's your mom doing?"

"She's okay, I guess. The isolation has done nothing for her spirits. We still see her, masks on, but she hasn't seen anyone else, really. Thank goodness for cell phones and internet calling. She was happy to have Moxie to look after while we're gone."

"Where did you say you were going that you wouldn't be able to talk to her over the holidays?" I asked.

"We told both her and Jen that we didn't know if we'd be able to contact them and left it at that," he answered.

"Then we prepared cards and gifts to arrive at their homes in time for Christmas. Couldn't think of any other way to handle it," Jess added. "On the bright side, I used the time we were isolating to do some online shopping. I found some things I thought you could use."

"Awesome. And Moxie had puppies, right?"

Jess smiled as she answered. "She did, four, and they were so cute. They left us one by one as their new owners came to get them. I cried—couldn't help it. They were so sweet. We got her fixed after that. There won't be any more of that."

"Aw. And how's your mom, Jess?"

"Same. Everyone's in the same boat, really. Missing their friends and family. We've been encouraged to maintain a 'bubble' of people that we come in contact with and not to mix bubbles. It's serious shit. Anyway, let's talk about something cheerier, Char. We've missed eight years of your life. How about you fill us in?" Jess asked.

Ben stood and said quietly, "I'll get some drinks."

"Okay, let's see. Well, after I last saw you, we had Holly. She is a character, much like Sabel: fun, smart, only more . . . hmm-m . . ."

"Serious?" offered Gracie.

"More of a homebody?' added Gifted Hands.

"Both of those things, yes, and more self-conscious, and so responsible, almost beyond her years. We lost Jessie a few weeks after Holly was born. Poor Jessie. She was curious and gentle, and she loved to cuddle. Unfortunately, she wasn't meant to share this life with us for long enough."

"I'm sorry. I never wanted to 'see' you"—she did air quotes— "knowing what was going to happen. I usually looked up what I could find about your next year here *after* speaking with you. I didn't learn that she'd died in time to tell you."

"It wouldn't have changed anything, Jess. It was something in her head, a tumour maybe. I don't know. We were all with her when she left us with a smile."

"Here we are," Ben said as he handed us each a warm drink.

"Thanks, Benny. After her death, it took us all quite a while to feel joy again, but in time, we were able to pick up the pieces." I paused, swallowing down the sadness. "Robbie and Sabel are very different. Robbie is easygoing and looking to please, while Sabel is more . . . stubborn, obstinate even, but each is so smart and kind. Phillip still misses his twin. He still mentions her almost every day. The bond between twins is so strong; it's something I'd never witnessed before them. I believe she will be with him always."

"Aye. Poor lad," Gracie said.

"It's so strange to think that you and Michael left your home yesterday and arrived here eight years later than you expected. It will take some time for my mind to work through the idea," Gifted Hands said.

"For all of us," Jess agreed.

We were preparing for supper when there was a knock on the door. Ben answered it. "Lawrence," he said, quickly turning to look at Michael. It was too late. Michael's face was the first he saw as he was invited in. "Allow me to introduce our friends. This is Jessica and Michael Saunders. They arrived here yesterday night."

Lawrence smiled and eyed Michael. "Did they? How nice. Might I ask what happened to your eye, Mr. Saunders? It looks as if you've been struck."

Michael looked at me uncomfortably before answering. "Yes. Last night when we arrived, someone tried to take Jessica's bag. She tripped and fell as we were walking up the hill. When I turned, there was a man reaching into it. I confronted him, and he hit me."

"I assure you, Lawrence, Michael had nothing to do with Simon's death."

"You did say that your friend lost that stone last night, the one we found on Simon's person?"

"Yes," Ben answered grudgingly.

"How do we know it wasn't Simon you confronted last night?" Lawrence asked Michael.

"I don't know who it was. I didn't see a face. I only felt the punch and returned it."

"Hmmm. Well, I came past to inform you that I have spoken to the townsmen who were present at the games last night. All appear to have gone straight home. There is one man unaccounted for. Edmond called him Isaac. Stays at the north end of Seneca Lake. He's come around once or twice. Don't know where he went when he left the inn last night—didn't have a room. According to Edmond, he did quite well at the table last night. Simon, too, from what I understand," he added, glancing at Jimmy.

Gracie's eyes followed. *Does she not know they were playing for money?*

"I was able to speak to Simon's brother-in-law, Geoff Mainer. He said he was home alone last night. He wondered what had become of Simon when he didn't return home, but he wasn't worried. I get the feeling there's no love lost there. He also told me that Ian left town late yesterday. He won't know anything, of course. Had to attend to some issues with their lawyer in Buffalo. He'll be gone a few days yet. That's all I have for now. Get back to your visit, and we will talk more tomorrow. Sorry to disturb." Lawrence turned to leave, then turned back. "Mr. Saunders, I trust you won't be leaving town in a hurry?"

Michael tried to smile. "No plans to." At that, Lawrence nodded and walked out the door.

After he left, and we were once again comfortable, I said, "Jess, maybe you should have a good look through your things to see if anything else went missing."

She nodded and walked toward her bags on the floor. "Do you mind?" she asked, lifting one onto the dining table.

"Go for it," I answered.

She dumped the contents of the first bag onto the table. Some pieces of clothing, several lighters, paper bags labelled with the names of herbs, a couple of seed packets, and some vials. "This looks good." She stuffed the clothing back into the bag, leaving the other things on the table. The next bag contained only clothing. "We'll leave all the clothes for you when we go," she said and smiled. Last was the bag her stone had been in. She emptied it onto the table. "Hmm, there's something else missing, I think. I brought you a cloak pin I'd found. I had to buy it when I saw it; it was so you. It doesn't seem to be here either."

Ben spoke now. "Please describe it so we know if we come across it, Jessica."

"Right . . . It was pewter, about this big"—she showed us with her fingers—"and the top half of the pin was a dragonfly. What a shame, it was so pretty." She looked at me and shook her head.

"It sounds pretty. Hopefully it will turn up."

"Well, we found nothing like that on or near Simon," said Ben.

"Or on the ground when we were looking for the Celestite," Jess said. "And this." She held up something narrow and silver. "I brought a set of hair pins—there were four. I thought you could have two and Gracie could have two. There's only one here. They're small though, they could have fallen out and gotten lost on the ground under the leaves.

"Celestite . . . remind me?" Gracie asked.

Jess smiled. "Ben bought it for me as a Christmas gift. It offers communication and guidance from the realm of angels. He thought it would help us to contact each other over the years."

"It also helps us to think and organize information and to reduce anxiety," I added.

"Oh, good, this is still here." She picked up three small jars, each containing something that was a different colour. "These are for you, Gifted Hands. They're paints. You just have to add water to the powder and stir it." She handed the jars to Gifted Hands.

"These are wonderful, Jessica. Thank you."

"And these are for you, Ben. I remember you liked them." She passed him a sack containing some cookies.

His jaw slackened momentarily, but when he realized he was holding some Oreos, he licked his lips and offered everybody one. "Mmm, thanks, Jess."

"You're welcome," Jess replied. Then she turned to Gracie and me. "Sorry ladies."

She came to sit beside me again and passed me the one remaining hair pin. It was quite pretty with two slim prongs about two inches long that would poke into the hair, with tiny white and grey beads rising from the top forming clusters of small flowers. "Maybe they'll turn up," I said, trying to sound optimistic. "Once it's dried up a bit, we can go out there with the rake."

In her other hand, she held several small vials. "I brought you a few things thinking it would have been a while since you'd had them. Boy, I was right about that!" She chuckled to herself. "So, here are some oils: plumeria, peppermint, and just for kicks, some lily-of-the-valley. I thought you could use it for some candles or something."

"Awesome! That's exactly what I'll do. You can help."

"Oo-oo, fun!"

"And since I like to put the plumeria in my shampoo, you and I can make some of that, too. We can start that Wednesday afternoon."

"And there are these seeds." They looked vaguely familiar. I looked at her in question. "They're Mary Jane. It has been legalized in Canada, if you can believe it. And as much as it's fun sometimes, there are many health benefits to using it. Have I mentioned Rhonda?" I shook my head. "She works in my department, funny girl. Anyway, her husband works at a plant where they grow the stuff. He brought home some seeds, and she gave me some. I thought you might want to grow some and see how it works for you here."

I looked at Ben and smiled, remembering him high by the fire that night at the cottage. "I will definitely see what I can do with it. Thank you, Rhonda!"

"Somewhere, there are instructions for growing and harvesting, and some info on ways you can use it."

"I must say, it never crossed my mind to try that here. I will plant some in the spring and see what happens."

"Oh, and here is some leather cord you can cut in lengths for your stones or hair."

"Nice. Thanks, Jess."

"Oh, there's one last thing." She looked up and smiled, digging deep into the bag. She brought up her hand three times, each time with balls of wool in different colours. "I know it's difficult to make vivid colours, so I brought you these to share." There was a luscious shade of burgundy, emerald green, and deep royal blue.

"Oo-oo, these are lovely. Thank ye, Jessica."

"My pleasure."

I was aware of Keen Wolf's eyes as they moved slowly between Jessica and me. He was taking it all in with a faint smile on his face.

The kids came back into the house just as the table was set. They were all "starving" of course, after such an eventful day. There were nine of them, so they sat at the table while the adults ate in the sitting room with plates on our laps.

Aware that our words could be easily heard, we kept the conversation light. Jess asked, "You said we would make some shampoo on Wednesday?"

"Yes. I only work until lunch Wednesdays. I usually work in my room in the afternoons. I haven't made soap in a while. Hmm . . . I'll have to start some more lye."

"I'll walk down with them after supper and put some fresh ashes and water into the barrel," Ben said.

"I'll come with you," Michael said.

"We'll make some candles soon, too, Jess. Maybe you can take a few home with you. How long do you think you'll stay?" I asked.

"Well, we *have* to stay for Christmas and the New Year, right?" She lowered her voice to an almost-whisper and continued. "But I was planning to arrive here in 1826, the date of the new moon would have been January 27th. I don't know when it will be now, in 1834." Jess glanced at Michael before continuing. "I booked the beach house back home for January 27th and 28th."

"We can have a look at my charts of the moon phases later, Jess." She nodded. "This will be an extra-special Christmas," I added with a smile.

"One we shall remember always," added Gifted Hands.

By the time the dishes were dealt with, it was getting dark. "I suppose we should call the children; it's time we go home," Gifted Hands said, looking at her husband. He nodded.

"Aye, we'll go wi' ye," Gracie added.

Before they left, both women expressed their joy at meeting Jessica, hugging both her and Michael goodbye.

"You must all come to us next Sunday," Gifted Hands said as she slipped into her coat.

"That sounds nice. Thank you," Jessica answered.

Once I'd closed the door behind them, I turned to my friend and said, "Okay, Jess, why don't we take your things upstairs and move Phillip into Robbie's room. You can stay in his room while you're here."

"If you're sure."

I smiled. "I'm sure."

"I don't mind, Jessica," Phillip said from behind us. "Come with me, I'll help you take your bags upstairs."

"Oh, thank you." She glanced at me, raised her eyebrows, and smiled. Then, turning back to Phillip, said, "Lead the way."

When the kids were in bed, we relaxed in the sitting room, each with a whiskey in hand. I found my information on moon phases and sat beside Jessica. "Okay, let's see . . . 1834, no it'll be 1835 in January." With my finger on the month and date, I said, "Look, our new moon is January 28th, just one day later than you'd planned." I flipped the pages to find 2021. "And the full moon in 2021 is January 28th—perfect! You'll get home and be able to stay at the beach house."

She took the papers to have a look. Satisfied with what she saw, she set them on the table and raised her glass. "January 28th it is."

"Now, back to the present. I will have to work tomorrow, of course, but you're welcome to sit with me behind my counter or hang out in my old room, Jess. We can leave the door open so we can talk."

She looked at Michael before answering. "Oo-oo, I'd enjoy sitting with you. Plus, that way I can meet everyone as they come in."

"Michael, you're welcome as well, unless you'd prefer to go out with Ben or stay here?" He nodded.

Ben raised his glass. "Well, it has been a long and crazy day, but I am happy that it started with the two of you. Welcome to *our* time."

"Mum, don't forget Janee's coming over after supper today to do school-work," Sabel said as she left for school with the others.

"Oh, right." I'd almost forgotten—she was coming over to work and sleep over. Janee was a sweetheart and was welcome at our house any time. "Have a good day, guys!"

Sabel popped her head back inside and whispered, "Are there any more of those cookies?"

I laughed. "I'm afraid not, love. They were too good to last."

We left the house a few minutes later. "Maybe this afternoon you can give Ben a hand moving things from Molly's old house, Michael." Two sets of eyes looked at me with questions. As we started down the hills toward the store, I filled them in. "Molly was the wife of Doc McGee. He was the town's doctor and Ben's mentor. Gracie was up late working in the store the night I arrived because she'd been busy with his funeral that day. Molly was great friends with Mabel and Gracie. When she passed away a few years ago, she left her house and property to the Williams family, as Doc McGee had wanted."

"So, why are you just moving things out of there now?" Michael asked.

Ben answered, "Actually, at the time she died, my cousin Ailsa was staying in Charlotte's old room at the store. She came home with us when we left Scotland."

I continued. "She'd been working as a nanny slash teacher there—a governess they call it—but she wanted more, so she came to live here. Once she settled in, she started to help at the school, teaching half days. Eventually, she added a sort of daycare service a few days a week to help out some of the families with young ones. She was a whole different person here, and she was happy."

Ben smiled and added, "The children all loved her. They were sad to see her go. So were we, of course."

"Did she go back home?" Michael asked.

"Actually, no." I smiled at Ben. "Wow, this is getting to be a convoluted story. Okay, Ben has a friend from Harvard—Sam—he's a lawyer in Boston. A charmer." I gave Jess a knowing smile. "You know the type: smart, handsome, engrossed in his work, and popular with the ladies. Well, when we were in Scotland, he was there on business and came to see us for a couple of nights. They briefly met then."

"Ailsa and Sam?" Jess asked.

"Yes."

"Sam often travels for his work, and when he comes anywhere near us, he comes for a visit. The first time he came to see us after that, we'd probably been home two years?" Ben asked, looking at me.

"Yes, and when he saw her that first time here, his eyes lit up in a way I hadn't seen before. He didn't even try to hide it." I smiled to myself. I had liked Sam from the moment we'd met. He was a fun, engaging character. "At the time, she seemed to enjoy his attention but was well aware of his reputation and didn't think much of it. Over a period of a couple of years, he found his way here to visit several times and always made time for Ailsa. After Molly passed, Sam helped with the will, the property ownership, and such. The little house was offered to Ailsa to live in and run her daycare out of."

"Where is this house?" Jess asked.

"Just down this road a couple of minutes," I answered. We were now in front of the store. "We can walk over at lunch. So, when Ailsa left—"

"Did she die?" Michael asked.

"No, no," Ben started. "As a matter of fact, she married Sam and moved out to Boston. They only just left here last week."

"Ah . . . so what will you do with the house now? Rent it? Sell it?" Michael asked.

"Actually, we're ready to make it 'The Doctor's House'. As much as I enjoy travelling around to visit the townsfolk who require me, many of them can come see me themselves, and like your home, we are going to encourage them to begin to do that."

"Yes. Ben can keep his supplies there and work from there as much as possible. That's what Doc McGee and Molly foresaw the house being used for, and it's a great idea."

"Well, this is us," I said as we arrived at the path to my old room. "We'll see you boys in a few hours."

"You've got a good-sized garden here, Char. There's got to be room for the seeds I brought you here somewhere!" She looked around. "Where's your sundial?"

"Aww, it toppled over in a storm a few years ago and broke into a bunch of pieces. All I have now is the gnomon. I imagine I'll stick it into something one of these days." I shrugged, remembering the tears shed at the time. "Anyway, when they added on to the store, I was able to make the garden a little bigger. I'm sure I'll have room for more. What did you bring me?"

"Let's see, beefsteak and cherry tomatoes, jalapenos, cucumber, and cantaloupe."

"Nice!" I opened the side door to my room. "After you, Jess."

She stepped in and slowly surveyed the room.

"I can totally see you working in here, Char." She walked to my shelves and picked up a blue feather. "Wow! You still have the feather you found the night you first came here?" I smiled. I'd kept it for good luck. "And this is the totem Keen Wolf made you." She picked it up and turned it in her hands. "It's beautiful—just like I pictured it. And God, you described him so well. He's so serious with those dark eyes, and so tall, and his ruggedness—whoa. Are things between you the same as they were when I saw you last?"

"Pretty much. We, the four of us, are very close friends and two happy couples, but every once in a while, there's a little spark, or gaze, or comment between us and . . . well, yeah, the love is still there." I felt my cheeks get hot and turned away.

"Does he still call you Sky Watcher?"

I thought about my answer for a moment. "Yes . . . but hardly ever. He only ever calls me that when we're alone."

"I guess that doesn't happen much anymore?"

"Not really."

"You know, once in a while I drive by The Balefire, and I think about the reading Faeryn did for you when you were with us. Faeryn said he misses you, longs for you to come home, and she drew what I would call an infinity heart." This was a heart, the right side of which was a regular heart shape, the left was a half heart, which looped back up into an infinity loop.

"I haven't thought about that in a long time. I never told him, or Ben for that matter. That stays with you, me, and Faeryn."

"Gotcha! Have you seen your mum since then?"

"Not since she said goodbye. I think it's too hard for her to come to me here, with Gracie being alive here." Jess nodded.

We entered the store through my old room and were greeted with Gracie's and Mabel's welcoming smiles. "Well, good morning," Gracie said. "Will ye be keepin' us company in the store today?" she asked Jess.

"I will," Jess answered, beaming.

After she'd had a good look around the store, I set Jess up on a chair behind my counter and prepared to face the day. "I assume Michael still has a thing for fountain pens?" I asked.

"Oh, yes. He'll definitely leave here with two or three of the ones you have here! He has set up the study with a lovely old desk and some antique bookshelves. An inkwell and some genuine fountain pens will look nice on the desk."

I was bent to reach a jar of arnica when I heard Gracie's voice. "Who'da thought when we left here Saturday afternoon, that we'd be opening up the place wi' Jessica?" She smiled.

"Right?" I answered happily. "You do know, Jess, that I'll be putting you to work while you're here?"

"I hope so. I have much to learn." She smiled back.

It was, as expected, a morning busy with chatter about the death of Simon. As Emma spoke to Gracie about it, I leaned into Jess and said, "You'll soon see that you learn most of the town's news here. People do love to talk."

"My ears are flapping, Char."

The morning was all about Simon: who found him, how they found him, where they found him, how was Edna handling it, what would she do now, etc.— it felt good to get away from it for a while when lunchtime arrived. Gracie and I took Jess into the kitchen and sat for a quick bite, while Mabel went out into the store.

"That was a busy morning," Jess started. "Is the store generally this busy?"

"Aye, most days, though we don't usually have such dismal news te spik about. Last week the talk was a' about Ailsa and Sam's weddin'. How pretty she looked. How handsome he looked. How much the town would miss her." She looked at me sadly then. "I do miss her, but I ken she'll be a happy wifie in Boston. Sam'll look after her."

At noon break, we walked down Old Trail Road to meet the men. I said, "That path leads to the cemetery."

"Oh," Jess said. "I'd like to go there with you."

I felt butterflies in my stomach at the idea; it was almost the anniversary of Jessie's death. "Sure, maybe tomorrow."

Molly's house, *jeez I need to stop calling it that*, was just a minute farther down the road. Ben and Michael met us there. "Good timing. We just got here," Ben said.

We showed them the inside of the little house where Doc McGee and Molly used to live. It had a small kitchen and eating area, a sitting room, and a bedroom. Around the east side of the house was a path leading to what had been their stable, big enough for a horse and some tools. The property behind the house was surrounded by a stone fence and perfectly suited for gardening. "Ailsa didn't plant," I started. "She preferred to have the space open for children to run around outside when the weather allowed. But we had the back portion of the yard fenced off so I could grow, harvest, and stock some herbs I don't have room for at the store. So far, I have mallow—you'll recognize it from home—lemon balm, betony, and lavender; you can never have too much lavender. I have a friend in Auburn, Malcolm Huntington, who owns a manor house with gardens upon gardens. I was able to get some decent cuttings from him several years ago. Look how well they've grown since!" I watched her look around. "Next year, or the one after, I'm hoping to add poppies so we can try to make laudanum. If it works out, we can have our own supply." I shrugged.

"Interesting," Jess said. "Don't forget the seeds I brought you. You'll have to find a place for those, too." I nodded.

"We're thinking of making the bedroom into the doctor's room, where I would meet with whoever was unwell and having the front of the house made into the apothecary," Ben said, indicating the area in front of the kitchen. "Not right away, of course."

"It sounds like the town has some changes coming," Michael said.

I saw Hettie's bright smile as I walked into the kitchen. "I've packed up supper fo' ya. I hope you have a lovely evenin'," she said.

"Thank you. I honestly don't know how you do it, Hettie. Cooking for so many people? Jeez."

She chuckled. "It's not for everyone, but I do enjoy it. Enjoy yo' company, hon."

I watched Jess and Michael listening to the children talk about their day. I had always thought the kids were an entertaining bunch, but watching their expressions confirmed it.

We had finished eating but were still seated when I saw Sabel's look of impatience—eyes wide, eyebrows raised, just waiting for me to look at her. "You're ready to get Janee, I presume?" I asked with a smirk.

"Yes. Can we go?"

I looked at Ben. "Go ahead. Michael and I can handle the dishes."

"If you're sure," I started.

Ben pointed to the door.

So, Jess, Sabel, and I walked to Rebecca's. After introducing the women, Janee came out with a bundle under each arm and a big smile. She was a good friend of Sabel's, kind and always cheery. It took years to get her to call me Charlotte, but she did now.

From somewhere behind Rebecca, a little voice called, "Goodnight, Janee. I'll miss you." It was her youngest sister, Eloise.

Janee turned back with a smile. "Me, too, Sissy. See you tomorrow. Goodnight, Francis," she called, knowing she wouldn't be too far away.

"So, what is it you're working on tonight, ladies?" I asked, as we started for home.

They started talking over each other and then started laughing. Jess got a giggle out of that. "Ahem"—Sabel cleared her voice—"we are working to memorize a poem Mrs. Dickson gave us."

"We each have a part," Janee continued.

"We have to say it to the whole class," they said in unison.

"We'll run ahead, Mum. See you at home."

After they'd gone on, it seemed so quiet. Jess said, "She's a lovely young woman, Char. There's so much of you in her. I'm not sure yet who is more mischievous, though."

"Hmm, yes, that's hard to pinpoint. God knows, she'll never have the opportunity to get up to the shit we used to." I giggled.

"Amen," she agreed. "So, now you have to remind me about Rebecca."

I told her that Rebecca was the daughter of Lawrence and Phoebe Southern. "In addition to being the town magistrate, Lawrence and his youngest son, Graham, run the grist mill. She's also Lionel's sister."

"Ah." She remembered his name very well.

Lionel had held me up to the wall with his arm across my throat when I didn't want to kiss him; Lionel had plotted to rape and kill me and almost succeeded; my friend Marshall had come to keep me safe, and Lionel had murdered him right in front of me. Ben and Gracie had found me in the nick of time, and when Ben and Lionel fought, Lionel had gone over the edge of the rock face and died. I told Jessica about all of that when I saw her last.

"I remember you felt that he and Penelope had planned to take you out. She wanted Ben, right? What ever happened to that bitch?" she asked.

"Her father, the preacher, had an opportunity to work in another town somewhere so they moved away."

"Oh, right. I remember now. Good riddance."

"Agreed. Anyway, while we were with you in 2013, a baby was left on the Southerns' doorstep with a note. It said she was Lionel's daughter, and when you look at her, there's no doubt. No one knows who her mother was, but Rebecca was happy to take on the job of being her mother. Janee knows how Rebecca and Ron came to be her parents."

"Ron? I haven't heard you mention him before."

"No, I guess not. Ron took over as the town's tanner after Marshall was killed." I paused and swallowed down the lump in my throat that, to this day, came with Marshall's memory. "Ron and Rebecca fell in love. They married while we were with you, adopted Janee into their home, and had a few babies of their own; Francis is ten, Winnie died as an infant, and Eloise, who's seven. About two years ago, Ron died suddenly. The family was devastated. Anyway, Rebecca has a loving family and Ron's best friend, Edmond, who helped her through. As a matter of fact, she used to see Edmond when I first got here. He wasn't looking for anything permanent, so they didn't stay together, but it seems to me that they may have rekindled something. Time will tell. You'll meet him sooner or later."

"Wow."

"There were rumours after Ron's passing that the tannery was cursed."

"Say what now?"

I smiled. "Let's continue this at home. That way Michael will hear it, too, and you won't have to try to remember it all."

"Yes. Now tell me what you think of Ben's beard. He looks hot! Hope you don't mind me saying so, but damn!"

I felt the blush burning my cheeks. "I agree. It took me a while to get used to but . . . well . . . you can see for yourself."

"I swear, I'd be tugging on it all the time. You know, steering him here and there." She gave me a quick elbow in the side.

"Yep," was all I was willing to admit.

As we approached the front door of the house, we could hear the girls reading their poem for Ben and Michael. When they'd finished, Michael asked, "You have to memorize all that?"

"Yep," Sabel answered.

"Good grief," Ben said.

"You'd better get upstairs and get to it," I said.

"Yes, we should. Come, Sabel," Janee said to her friend.

The children spent the evening doing their homework. In fact, we didn't see any of them until they came down to say goodnight. After that, an occasional giggle could be heard from upstairs, but soon it was quiet.

"Right, so our convo was to be continued?" Jess started, looking at me.

"I was telling you that some said the tannery was cursed. You see, not long before I got here, there was a tanner who lived here with his family. The Rosatis were from Italy. They were here a few years and then the whole family got ill and passed."

"That happened while I was away at school," Ben added. "Then Marshall took over the business."

"When I arrived, he'd been here for a while. Then he died saving my life." The room went quiet. No one knew what to say. It was up to me to break the silence. "We don't need to dwell on that. We've already talked about him." I looked at Jess and got a gentle smile. "Ron bought the business after Marshall and fell for Rebecca within months. He was here for at least ten years before he died." Ben nodded.

"The gentleman who came in next, and is still here, is Mr. Ernest Albert. He came with an apprentice, a young fellow named Frederick Cole," Ben said.

"Wow! Everything and everyone has a story, eh?" Jess asked.

"It seems that way, now that you mention it." I laughed.

"I enjoyed our first workday here, Char. Mikey, you have *got* to check out the merchandise in the general store. They have a great selection of fountain pens!" She laughed. "How about you? How was your day?"

"I had a good day, too. It was interesting walking around the town with Ben. I met quite a few people. He took me past the wood mill to meet his friend Lenny. He seems to be quite a character. His father, Scott, seemed a nice man, too. I did get some suspicious looks." He shrugged. There wasn't much to be done about that.

"Oh, yes. You'll have to meet Lenny and Lennie, Jess."

Her expression was comical. "Lenny and Lennie? Are they a couple? Why is this the first time I'm hearing of these two?"

I laughed. "They are. It's a bit of a story, but do you remember me telling you about our friend Isabel when we were with you?"

She nodded. "Let me think . . . Isabel, two children."

"Andy and Maxie," I confirmed.

"And she was married to . . . Wait! She was married to Lenny?"

"Yes. While we were in Scotland, she died giving birth to Mark."

"That's so sad."

"It was. And it was difficult not being here." I paused and found myself looking into Ben's eyes. He knew the depth of my grief. "It was hard, Jess. The only thing I could do was write a letter, and even that took a month to get to Lenny . . . Anyway, Isabel's younger sister, Lenora, came to stay at the house to help with the baby and the children, and after some time, the two fell in love. They married. It's about as good an ending as could be hoped for, I guess. I think Isabel would agree. Since then, they've had two little girls: Isabella and Adelaide."

"Life is so unpredictable," Jess said.

"Did you ever tell Jess about Gifted Hands's gift?" Ben asked.

"I don't think so." I looked from him to Jess. "Sometimes she will have um, hmm, what to call it— second sight? She will 'see' a possible event before or as it's happening."

"A premonition," Ben said.

"A premonition is just remembering in the wrong direction," Jess said with a smirk.

Ben's eyebrows came down as he tried to figure that out. I laughed.

"Oo-oo, I like that. Where's that from?"

"Doctor Who."

"Makes sense," I said. Ben still looked confused. "Anyway, I don't know when Gifted Hands experienced that last." I shrugged and gazed toward the staircase. "It sounds like everyone upstairs has fallen asleep."

"So, Char, after you left, I continued to look into your bloodline on and off." I raised my eyebrows. "Well, Elizabeth being found here and being hung for murder as a witch was the reason you came to this time in the first place. And you saved her. One of us had to get some answers, right?" I nodded. "It was probably two years after you and Ben left, when someone turned me on to this off-the-beaten-path ancestry website. I sent them some questions about the last ancestor you could trace, Sarah Gray Thomason. The info we could find at that point came from Scotland. It told us that her children were born in Scotland in the late 1870s, early 1880s, and she, herself, was born in Sault Ste. Marie, Ontario in 1857. I told them we were interested in learning about her mother. Who was she? When was she married? How many children did she have? Did she have any siblings? I asked, and I crossed my fingers." Jess crossed her fingers as she said the words. "I'd all but given up when I got a response—just last year. Apparently, it was an unmonitored mailbox. No one had used it for years, but this day someone had opened my email and done some investigating for me. Crazy right?"

"And?" I prompted.

"Well, from the records, it looks like she was actually born in a little town a hundred miles from the Sault, which wasn't officially a town yet. I guess after they'd moved away, and Sarah had reason to keep records, she chose to say that's where she was born."

I glanced at Ben before asking the obvious next questions. "So, what *was* her mother's name?

"I'm sorry, Charlie, the first name of Sarah Gray's mother was *not* Elizabeth or Caroline. I even thought it might have been Amanda, as she called herself when you first met her. I really hoped it would be one of them." I waited, trying to be patient. "Her mother's name was Margaret Sarah Peterson; Sarah was her sixth child."

"Oh . . ." I felt myself deflate. After everything, I hadn't really expected Carole-Anne to be my ancestor or to find out for certain either way. Not knowing had afforded me the opportunity to hope.

"A nickname for Margaret would be Maisie, wouldn't it?"

"What?"

"It was in brackets beside her name, as if it was what she called herself."

My heart skipped a beat. "Maisie?" I asked.

Looking at my expression, Jess said, "Yes. Why?" She furrowed her eyebrows.

I felt my eyes tear up as a huge smile spread across my face. "Jess, I guess I didn't give you all the details. When we returned from seeing you in 2013, we found that Elizabeth and Brian and their baby Caroline, had come here to live. Only, to remain incognito, they changed their names." Jess waited expectantly. "They are now Carole-Anne and Keith Crawford, and they called the little one— "

"Maisie?" she interrupted, jumping up from her seat. I nodded. "Holy shit, Char! So, it's them! It's her! I can't believe it!" She came and hugged me.

Ben looked at me with raised eyebrows and a smile, but said nothing.

"Hopefully, you'll be here long enough to meet them. They've been away for almost a month already. They went to visit the reservation where Keen Wolf took her those years ago—they've stayed in touch. Of course, they took Maisie with them. She, by the way, is sixteen years old now."

"So, she won't have Sarah Gray for another"—she bit her lip as she did the math—"twenty-three years. Jeez, she'll be thirty-nine by then."

Now, when I introduced Jessica and Michael to them, we would know that Carole-Anne, Keith, and Maisie were in fact, my ancestors.

Jess was right, *Holy Shit!*

Tour of the Town

On our noon break the next day, I took Jessica on a tour of the town, showing her the different shops, the church, and the mills. We started down Old Trail Road; our first stop today would be the cemetery.

"Here we are, Jess." We turned left and followed the path.

We entered the grounds quietly, stopping first at Marshall's grave, then Ben's father, and finally Jimmy's parents and sister. Then, we visited the one that tore at my heart. "Jessie rests here." I heard my voice catch. "Hi sweetheart," I whispered.

"What are all those, Char? Thistles? It's too bad they're past; they're so pretty."

"They were her favourite. We brought seeds from Scotland to plant at home, but when . . . well, I decided to plant them here . . . with her."

"I've got a few things at home with thistles on them; they're so vibrant and pretty."

I smiled. "Right, I remember when Michael gave you that painting of thistles in a meadow."

"I still love that painting!"

"She had a lisp; watching her try to say thistle was adorable."

"I'll bet it was. I'm so sorry for that pain, Char. I can't imagine losing someone so young and sweet that you loved so much."

"Thanks." I plucked some of the remaining seeds and scattered them over her gravesite. When I looked at Jess again, she was pale. "Jess? What's the matter?"

She turned, her eyebrows raised and drawn together. "I'm not sure. I feel like I'm gonna throw up."

"Oh man! Okay, let's go over there under the trees."

After a few minutes, the feeling passed and some colour returned to her cheeks. We left the cemetery and continued down the road. "That was strange. It came on so fast, and then it was gone."

"Well, I'm glad. It wouldn't do to have you feeling crappy."

Smiling, she asked, "Is this the school?"

"It is. The teacher is Katie Dickson. Oh, there she is. Let me introduce you."

After a brief chat, we continued on our way around the loop. "Katie is Lenny Cameron's sister."

"Lenny runs the wood mill with his father, right?" I nodded. "Did Gifted Hands's children attend the school?" she asked.

"No. Gifted Hands took time each week to teach them at home. I imagine she's a great teacher—she's so patient. Anyway, she wants them to be able to communicate in both languages."

"She did well! There's no way I could ever teach anybody anything. My patience is lacking—severely."

"Oh, me, too," I agreed with a giggle.

"Do they understand what's happening, or what's going to happen with the Indian Removal?" she asked.

"When Ben and I returned home from 2013, we warned Keen Wolf and Gifted Hands about the impending Indian Removal Act. When we started to hear whispers of 'tribes' being enticed to sell their lands and be relocated—it was time to take action. We explained that the ongoing immigration of Europeans, together with an ever-present desire of many greedy and self-important settlers to have the fruitful lands that many Native American settlements worked and lived on, was pressure the government had acted on."

These desirable lands were mostly made up of what is now Georgia, North and South Carolina, Alabama, Louisiana, Tennessee, Florida, and Southwestern Kentucky. An act had been signed to begin relocating the "Indians", as they were referred to, to designated lands west of the Mississippi. The Native Americans were living on that desirable land. In fact, they were there first and had been for hundreds of years. These facts didn't bother the people who, for some reason, thought *they* deserved the land. Treaties were being offered for purchase of the lands that in many cases, had been owned and worked by the same clans for generations. Andrew Jackson's hands were all over it. He was voted president in 1829 and pushed the Indian Removal Act through congress in 1830. It was shameful.

The first to leave their lands did so voluntarily, but soon the act was enforced. The Choctaw were the first to relocate, beginning in 1831, followed by the Seminole, Creek, Cherokee, and Chickasaw, over a period of about ten years. The Tuscarora, who had lived in North Carolina and Virginia for generations, had made their own migrations over the past hundred years, after various battles and disputes. Most had relocated to reservation lands they had purchased near Lewiston, New York and Grand River Territory in Brantford, Ontario, Canada, granted to them for their support of the Crown during the American Revolution. Only a dozen or so families remained on the land where Keen Wolf and Straight Arrow had grown up near Roanoke River in North Carolina.

At this time, of course, it was only 1834. We were less than halfway through these migrations; the Cherokee and Chickasaw had not yet been forcibly relocated, but the time was quickly approaching. During many of our visits with our Tuscarora friends, I had witnessed Keen Wolf's internal fight; he wanted to be home to support and protect his family, but he felt the guilt of not being with those who had not been as lucky as him. Were it not for Gifted Hands and the children, I felt sure he would have gone to help, to fight, to do whatever was required to make things easier for the others.

"After many conversations over the years, we made a plan with them. Ben and I would 'purchase' the properties owned by Gifted Hands and Keen Wolf, her parents, and any of their neighbours interested in our help. Their neighbours chose to make the journey toward Grand River, where Between Two Homes had taken Elizabeth, um, Carole-Anne. They felt they'd be safe there. They left several months ago. Gifted Hands and Keen Wolf purchased a parcel of land adjacent to theirs from one of them, thinking the family could use it in the future.

It was strictly on paper, but with Sam's help, we put the legal ownership of the three properties in our names."

"I had voiced my concern about the portion of their land that hadn't been built on; the area is still treed, but it is quite large, and squatters seem to have rights these days, regardless of ownership. Shortly after I first arrived here, Keen Wolf had planned to move back from North Carolina and build a home on that piece of property. The idea had been abandoned after Straight Arrow died."

"That was his brother?"

"Yes. As you know, after that, Keen Wolf joined with Gifted Hands and moved into the cabin that had belonged to her and Straight Arrow, and his parents before that. Keen Wolf assured me that I needn't worry about squatters. He said one of them walks through that area every day when they check their traps."

These areas may not have been targeted for relocation, or even on Jackson's radar, but if it came under scrutiny, these properties belonged to us and there was no way that was going to change.

"That was good thinking," Jess said. "I hope the ownership is never challenged."

"Me, too."

Soap

Jessica looked up at me over her morning coffee and asked, "So, today we make soap?"

I smiled. We had run the lye-water back through some fresh ashes in the barrel yesterday morning. "Yep. We'll test the lye with a chicken feather to be sure, but I think it'll be ready." She clapped her hands, as I stuck a vial of the plumeria oil she'd brought me into my bag.

While we walked to the store, we chatted about her work. She had taken some additional courses to become certified as a surgical nurse. She'd been working as such for a while now. "I love everything about nursing, really, but the hands-on experience I get and the things I see during surgeries is awesome! I feel like I've found my place."

When we arrived in the store kitchen, we were greeted by Hettie. "I'm going to steal some hot water, Hettie. Jessica's going to melt some wax for me."

"Help yo'self, child," Hettie answered.

I took Jess into my room. "Right, your job will be to chop enough of this wax to fill this cup." I set the wax onto my chopping block. "Then put it into this bowl and set it over this pot to melt." I lit the fire and poured the water from the kitchen into the pot on the wood-burning stove. "Just give the wax a stir now and then, and once it's melted, add in this olive oil." I poured it into my measuring cup.

"I think I can handle that," Jess answered happily.

"There's no hurry; we can't do more until after lunch. For now, let's leave the stove to warm up for a bit. Come sit with me behind my counter."

It was a regular morning—nothing much to talk about except maybe that Edna came in just before noon. I hadn't seen her since Simon had been found three days ago. He was to be buried tomorrow. She approached me first. "Good morning, Edna. I was so sorry to hear about Simon. How are you doing?"

"Och, I'm bone tired. I don't know what to do or how I will get it done. My brothers help in the shop, but it was Simon who did most of the work. I don't know if we'll be able to stay on here." I didn't know what to say. "Ian left town over the weekend. He doesn't even know what's happened. Geoff has closed the shop for now while he does his best to finish up what Simon had been working on. I believe he's off to meet a chap in Auburn this evening." She sighed loudly. "For now, I hope you can sell me something that will help me sleep. I haven't been able."

"Of course. I'll bring it over shortly."

After eating our lunch, Jess and I went around the back of the store, where my lye-barrel was kept and poured some lye-water into a bowl. Now we had everything we needed.

Back inside, we filtered that water and stirred some into the hot, melted wax/oil mixture. Once blended, we added in a few drops of the plumeria oil for scent and poured most of it into my soap mold tray. "This will be a special soap," I told Jess, adding, "It will stay in this cupboard for about six weeks."

"And what about shampoo?" she asked.

"For that we use this." I showed her the small amount of soap mixture I had reserved in a jar. "It's a little harsher than the soap we use at home, so for shampoo, we'll add some water and olive oil and one more drop of plumeria." After doing that, I put on the lid and shook it. "Voilà, shampoo."

"Fun!" She opened it up for a sniff. "Mm-m. I look forward to trying it out."

I smiled. Now it was time to make up a tea mixture. "So, I have to mix a tea for Edna to help her relax and get some sleep. What would you recommend?"

"Hmm. Well, chamomile or lavender or feverfew . . . no that's for a headache, I think."

"It is. For relaxation and sleep, I usually recommend chamomile, lavender, valerian, or a combination of them. In her case, I think we'll do that." I watched Jessica make my recipe and stir it up. Then we walked it to Edna.

The sun was out, but the air felt cool, even under my poncho. Jess tightened her borrowed shawl around herself. After knocking on her door, I could hear Edna's footsteps as they dragged across the floor. She opened the door looking pale and exhausted. "We've made you up a nice mixture. I suggest you make yourself a good strong tea about half an hour before bed, then hopefully you'll be able to have a decent sleep."

She thanked me and turned, closing the door in my face. I looked at Jess, whose eyebrows were raised. "Well done, Char. Have a nice evening," she said sarcastically. I simply shrugged.

When we walked back around the other side of the building, we could see Edna's brother Geoff working inside the shop. I wondered what would become of them.

"So, tell me about Slains," I said to Jessica.

"Well, when we finally got the insurance money after Michael's car accident, we decided we didn't really need to replace the car. He had the truck, I had a car—we didn't need three vehicles, so we put the money toward a vacation. We decided to go to Scotland, and of course, we *had* to see Slains. I walked the cliffs and imagined you there, walking in your long dress, hair blowing in the wind. It was such a pretty spot. A shame they let it go to ruin. We also walked the streets of Aberdeen, including the street your house was on—Belmont Street."

"That's wild!"

"Right?"

"And how is the house at home?"

"The house is great. We've had to paint of course, but otherwise it's exactly the same. The neighbourhood though, that's a different story. That whole stretch of forest between the motel in town and the house has been cleared and filled with houses that are like five feet apart. So-o many houses and increased traffic, and it's ongoing. You'd be disappointed to see it, and I admit, I preferred the trees, but in all honesty, the little pocket of the neighbourhood we live in is still the same."

She was right, I would be disappointed; for some reason, those in control of such things, don't care to realize the very reason many people want to live in the area is the space and the trees they are eliminating.

"So, you said Ben is going to Auburn for a day?"

"Yes, he meets with some of the doctors there for an afternoon every couple of months to compare notes. I was actually thinking I'd like to take the two of you there tomorrow. I'll see how Mabel feels about all of us going. I can't think of the last time I took a day off—hopefully she won't mind."

Auburn

The next morning, Jess and I walked into the kitchen to find Mabel and Gracie preparing for the workday. "Mabel, are you sure you don't mind if I stay away today?"

"Off ye go, lass. Best go while it's quiet. Ye never ken what'll happen next 'round here. Enjoy yerselves. We'll be here when ye return."

I gave her a hug and turned to Gracie. "Where are the lads?" she asked.

"They've gone to hook up the horses," Jess said with a bright smile.

"You lassies have a good day. See ye a bittie later." With a wink, she turned on her heels and headed into the store.

Looking at Jess, I asked, "Shall we?"

"Let's! Mm-m, I have to tell you, Char, every time I turn around, I can smell my hair. That shampoo smells terrific—light but pretty."

When I stepped outside and saw the open stable doors, my mind offered a quick flashback to the night I thought I would steal a horse and leave town in the darkness. I'd told him, told all my friends, the truth about where I'd come from and why. Naturally, they were shocked and needed a little time to digest the information. Ben had been accepting and curious about my world and my knowledge of medicine. I had denied my growing feelings for him. I'd fought them hard, but I'd lost—I'd fallen for him. I was devastated at the thought of loving Ben and losing him when I returned home and thought it would be better to just leave. What a stupid idea! If he hadn't come to find me and forced me to acknowledge my feelings, I don't know what would have become of us. Gah . . . that's not true. We would have found each other one way or another; we were meant to be together. He's my soul mate.

Then I saw the horses' noses coming through the open doors, followed by Ben at the reins of the "driver's seat" of the cart. Michael came out behind them and closed the stable doors. "Everybody in," Ben said, his breath fogging the air around his face. It was a sunny but cool morning.

Michael climbed up beside him, while Jess and I got into the backseat with a blanket over our legs. "Get comfortable, folks. Next stop, Auburn," I said.

The ride passed quickly with Jess and I quizzing each other about life, and soon I heard Ben saying, "We're coming into Auburn now."

We left Ben in front of the inn and tavern, promising to meet him inside in a couple of hours. "So, where shall we go first?" I asked.

"The glassmaker!" "The bakery!" They answered over each other.

I smiled. "We'll definitely do both, but right now, I'm with Michael. How about a scone?"

Jessica's eyes opened wide when we walked inside and saw all the lovely bakery items on display. "Looks like we're going to have to take some home. There's way too much to choose from." She giggled.

"The kids won't complain about that," I said.

Ten minutes later, we were walking up Genesee Street with our bundled pastries. We looked in all the windows and visited the cordwainer, fruit market, apothecary, and a couple of general stores that, between them, sold just about everything: fresh meat, dry goods, like teas and spices, fabric, ribbon, jewelry, hard candy, clothing items, washboards, wax, candles, and soap. When Jess saw what the first store had under glass, she fell in love—delicate glass perfume bottles. "My God, Char. I love these. I have to have one. Oh, how will I pick only one?"

I smiled, not surprised by her reaction. "Hmm, that's tough, Jess. Tell me, must you only pick one?"

She cast a humourless glance in my direction. "They're so pretty."

"Well, I can tell you Gracie sells one almost like this one here." I pointed to a delicate-looking bottle with a small cork. "So, maybe choose a different one. Also, we still have to pass the shop where the glassblower works."

"Oh boy," she said, biting her lip.

We left there with an hourglass-shaped perfume bottle wrapped in layers of fabric and some beeswax for me. "Before we go back to the tavern, let's walk by the Huntington house so you can see it. Obviously, the gardens are past, but you can get an idea of what I was talking about before."

We arrived in front of Malcolm's home and stood on the road outside of the stone fence, looking at the stone and woodwork of the house and the extent of the gardens. "Wow, Char. This is gorgeous. It's hard for me to imagine the amount of work that would go into a home and property like this in this day and age." I looked toward the windows, thinking I'd wave if I saw him, but there was no one to be seen.

"I know, right? It's really something. Okay, ready to go hit the glassblower's shop and then get back to the tavern?"

On the way back to the inn, Jessica picked another lovely perfume bottle from the glass shop. This one was a stout, wide-bottom bottle, quite intriguing. She was tickled with herself.

We entered the tavern with our small bundles and sat at a table with four chairs, ordering a warm drink while we waited for Ben. He joined us shortly after and filled us in about his time with his fellow doctors. He always enjoyed the sharing they did as a group.

Knowing we needed to be home in time for Simon's service, and not wanting to spoil the supper we knew Hettie would have for us at home, we each had a quick bowl of soup to get us through the afternoon.

The inn's groomsman was kind enough to have the horses and cart waiting for us outside.

"You get comfortable in the cart," Ben said. "I see someone I'd like to say goodbye to. I'll be right there."

While Jessica and Michael climbed up into the cart, I had my eyes on Ben and a gentleman I didn't recognize. Ben's eyebrows came down—something had caught his eye. I watched him walk toward the coach waiting behind our cart. Yes, he was looking into the window as he moved toward the door. He poked his head inside. Curious, I walked to where he stood. He was speaking. "… Williams. I am a doctor in Owasco. I couldn't help but notice the timepiece you're wearing on your wrist. Might I have a closer look?"

The gentleman smiled. "Of course. It's new—well, new to me. I only purchased it a few days ago." The gentleman held out his arm to offer Ben a better view.

Arriving at Ben's side, I asked, "Ben, who—" The disbelief I suddenly felt, cut off my words.

Seeing Ben's expression, and then mine, the man asked, "What is it?"

"Well, sir, I gave this piece to a friend of mine as a gift several years ago. Apparently, it went missing a week or two ago. He thought it was lost forever," Ben said, thinking fast.

"I beg your pardon?" the man asked with surprise.

"On the inside of the strap are small numbers 2-0-1-3. Is that correct?" The man nodded. Without a doubt, it was the watch we gave Jimmy when we returned from 2013. "Might I ask how you came to have it?"

Bringing his arm back to his side, the man tucked the watch back under his sleeve before answering. "I was walking past a peddler's cart in Cayuga and saw it. He let me have it for $4.00. I'm quite taken with it."

"I will give you $5.00 to give it back to me."

I briefly turned in time to see Jessica and Michael coming our way. Her forehead was creased, showing her curiosity, but she said nothing.

"I don't think so, doctor."

"But you must. It was stolen. You have purchased stolen property. I must know who this peddler is, and I must leave here with this wristwatch," Ben insisted.

The man looked at his companion, who shrugged her shoulders and whispered into his ear. He cleared his throat before speaking next. "Very well, I will let you have it for $8.00."

Ben reached into his bag for his coin sac and peeked inside. After adding up what he had inside, he said, "I'm afraid I only have $7.00. Will you take that? Please."

The man's mouth formed a hard line as he thought, then he nodded and reached under his sleeve. As he undid the leather strap, he said, "I will let you have it because it is a special timepiece and the man who had it stolen must miss it."

I heard Jess suck in her breath before saying, "Jimmy's watch."

"Yes," Ben said.

"Now, the seller will not have been the thief, but I can tell you when I saw him, he was heading east. He's probably in Aurelius by now. Perhaps close to here."

"Did you get his name by chance?"

"Hmm, no. But he had a brown painted cart with a name on the side. Give me a minute . . ." He closed his eyes, trying to recall what he'd read. "Yes, that's it. In golden letters it said, Tate."

The first portion of the ride home was quiet until I broke the silence. "Ben, did you know Jimmy no longer had his watch?"

"I did not."

"How do you suppose this happened?" Jess asked.

"Do you think someone stole it?" Michael asked.

"I don't want to speculate. Let's wait to talk to Jimmy," Ben said.

We arrived back in town in time to attend Simon's service, after which we went to the store with the others for supper. Hettie had planned ahead, and our meal was waiting for us. I was pouring our drinks when I noticed an odd look pass between Ben and Jimmy.

Gracie said. "The children a' had a bittie supper before the service and headed home to do their schoolwork."

"Have you eaten?" Mabel asked.

"Only some soup," I answered. "I'm hungry."

"How was yer time wi' the doctors, Benny?" Gracie asked.

"It went well. Nothing much to speak about. It was afterwards that things got interesting." Ben shot another glance at Jimmy.

"Out wi' it, lad. We havena got a' night," Gracie said. I saw Jessica smirk.

At this point, Ben told them about what had transpired as we were preparing to leave. When he'd finished his story, he stopped and looked around the room. Gracie's face was as white as a ghost. Jimmy's was pink.

"Ye lost it, Jim? Ye didna say."

All eyes were on Jimmy. I watched the sweat break out over his forehead. "Ah . . . that's nae exactly right." He looked down, trying to sort out his explanation.

I looked at Ben, who was watching me, eyebrows raised. He knew he'd started something, but he didn't know what. Jess and Michael sat silently, as did Mabel.

Jimmy started, "I didna lose . . . well, I did, but not the way ye think. The last time we played cards, the night Simon—" He paused and swallowed hard. "We'd been playing for coin, ye see. Any man who wanted to play, had to put their coins on the table. After a few games, my coins were gone. I wanted to win 'em back." Gracie sucked in a breath. "Simon'd had a slow night as well. It was 'im, me, and another mannie left playin'. I put me watch on the table. I kent it wasna a good idea, but . . ." He shook his head. "Simon won. He got the money and me watch. As he strapped it on, he gave me a wink n' said, 'Next week, Jim.' He was goin' te gi' me a chance te win it back. And then—"

"And then somebody killed him," Ben said.

"And the watch went missin'," Jimmy added.

Gracie stood up from the table, looking angrier than I'd ever seen her. "You and I will spik aboot this, Jim. But nae tenight." She left the room and walked up the stairs. He hadn't told her any of it—the betting, losing his watch, or that the man they had found dead should have had it.

"Jim, have you told Lawrence this detail? Does he know that Simon should have been in possession of your watch?"

"No." He shook his head to himself. "I didna want Gracie te ken," he said, stress thickening his accent.

Mabel stood, shaking her head to herself. "I'm nae part o' this conversation. Goodnight." She turned and walked up the stairs.

"Well, Jim, you've made your bed, I'm afraid. You will have to deal with Gracie," Ben started. "But you and I can bring this new information to Lawrence tomorrow, and maybe we can make some progress learning more."

I looked at Jess and Michael, who looked like they wished they could disappear. I said, "On the bright side, it looks like you are no longer a suspect, Michael." He nodded. "Let's get back home, you guys. It's almost time to tuck the kids into bed."

For the most part, the walk home was quiet.

"That was uncomfortable," Jess said.

"It was. I don't know what he was thinking keeping this to himself," I agreed.

"At least we have something to go on. After cards that night, someone killed Simon. Someone took the coins he'd won and the watch he had strapped on his wrist. Either Simon took Jessica's stone, or someone put it into one of his pockets," Ben said.

"*And* someone moved his body after he died," Jess added.

Ben and Jimmy left early the next morning to meet Lawrence. Together, they decided to brief the town messenger—a position no longer held by Young Henry, but by Lenny's son, Andy, now almost nineteen years old—and send him to Auburn to investigate and learn anything he could about the peddler called Tate.

Jess and I walked partway to the store with the children on their way to school. We left them with hugs and wishes for a happy Friday. "Tell me, Char, how is it that you and Ben didn't have more children? You could have had two or three more by now?" she asked with a smile.

"After Holly's birth, I bled—a scary amount, I was told. Ben did what he could, but in the end, he removed my uterus to save me." Her eyes opened wide. "Drastic, I know, but I had five children, and I'd be there to enjoy them."

"Well, that answers that," she said, hooking my arm as we walked.

With things as busy as they were, I thought perhaps it would be best to stay on this side of the lake over the weekend. I would send a message to Gifted Hands; they could come here on Sunday instead.

Before slipping behind my counter, I popped over to see Edna. "Good morning, Edna," I said as she opened the door. "I just wanted to see if the tea mixture was of help. You looked exhausted at the service yesterday."

She offered a weary smile. "I was able to get some sleep last night, yes. Thank you, Charlotte." She looked at Jessica standing beside me and smiled.

Just then, Geoff came into the room behind her. I offered him my condolences, since I hadn't spoken to him yesterday.

"Thank you. It was busy enough 'round here when Simon was with us, but now . . ." He looked at his sister, shaking his head. "And I don't know when we'll see Ian back." After a quick glance at Jessica, he excused himself and walked out the door, heading for the wainwright shop.

Later in the day, Becky came into the store looking radiant. "Good afternoon, ladies. How are you?"

"Becky, you seem to be having a wonderful day," I said.

"Oh, I am. And I hope to continue it into the night." She blushed as she said the words.

She came to stand at my counter. I smiled and whispered, "Edmond?" She nodded.

"Yes. We've been spending some time together and talking about . . . well, about a lot of things, really. We thought that tonight we might . . ." She looked around and although there was no one there but Gracie, Jess and me, she lowered her voice. "My folks will watch the kids and I will stay with him at the inn when he's finished behind the bar."

"Well, first—yay! Good for you! And second, why doesn't Janee come spend the night with us? She and Sabel can watch the younger ones with Robbie, and maybe we will go for a drink at the inn. A girls' night." I looked from Rebecca to Jess to Gracie.

"Sounds good to me," Jess said.

"Aye, the men can wait on us for a change," Gracie said with a smile.

Becky smiled. "Lovely. Thank you. I'll send her here after supper and she can walk home with the children."

The four of us, Gracie, Rebecca, Jess, and I, sat in the tavern and enjoyed a few slow drinks. We talked and we laughed. Becky told us that after Ron had died, she didn't want to do anything, see anyone, nothing. Her family had been there for her, of course, but Edmond persistently came to check on her. He hugged her when she needed to cry. He cried, too, after losing a close friend. He took her out for a walk or a ride in the cart or sleigh. He would come over after closing sometimes with some whiskey, and they would sit and talk. Over the space of two years, they had fallen in love. At first, she felt guilty, but he told her he knew Ron would want her to be happy. He would want her to be cared for by someone who loved her. And just the other day, he told her that he loved her. He wanted her. He wanted to marry her and be a part of her family. I glanced over at him and saw that he was watching us. He knew she was telling us her story, and knowing Rebecca as I do, it took a lot for her to say the things she felt, especially when they were so important. She was excited at the prospect of tonight. She blushed when she said it, but she smiled.

He came to the table with a handsome smile. Time had been good to Edmond. He had aged well; the creases in his face had deepened some with time, and his hair was beginning to show flecks of grey, but he was still a good-looking man.

"Becky, love, would ye mind running up to my room and bringing down the oil lamp? Then I can fill it and take it back up."

She smiled. "Of course."

As she pushed back her chair, I did the same and said, "We'll walk with you, Becky, then we'll be on our way."

"Take this candle with ye," Edmond added, passing her a candlestick.

"Careful," said a voice behind Gracie as her chair bumped into the next table.

"Oops. Sorry, lad. Did I spill your drink?"

"No." He scanned our faces and smiled. "You've enjoyed your ladies' night, judging by the laughter," he said, his eyes settled on Jess.

"Oh, aye," Gracie responded. "Are ye in town visitin'?"

"Just passing through."

"Ah, well, sorry to've disturbed ye."

"Not at all. Goodnight, ladies."

Gracie, Jess, and I thanked Edmond for a nice evening and said goodnight. I knew the outside stairs to Edmond's room were on the side of the building, but I'd never had the occasion to use them. At the top of the stairs, Becky opened the door. "Come on in, ladies. I'll just need a minute." She giggled as she tripped but didn't fall inside.

When Jess closed the door behind us, it was hard to see anything except the glow from the candle Rebecca carried in front of her. She set it on his small table and gasped.

All eyes were on the site now illuminated by the candle—a woman standing on the other side of the table, wearing nothing but a smile. In an exaggerated moment, Rebecca pulled herself together—well, sort of. "What the . . . who . . . what are you doing in here?"

The woman said, "Don't you recognize me, Rebecca?"

Becky's hand returned to the candlestick, and she lifted it, lighting up the woman's face.

I reached for Jess's and Gracie's hands as I felt the shock.

Rebecca's hollow voice asked, "Penelope?"

Her eyes briefly flicked to mine. "What is *she* doing here?" she asked with a sneer.

At that moment, Edmond came in through the door from the hallway on the opposite side of the room. He stopped short when he found himself standing behind a naked woman. She turned to face him.

"Penny?" He paused a moment, confused. "What the blazes are you doing here?" Taking in the sight of her, he reached for a blanket. I felt Gracie's elbow in my side. "And why are ye not dressed? Put this around yerself, lass."

"You used to enjoy seeing my body, Edmond. What's changed, love?" she mocked.

"It has been many years, Penny. *Much* has changed." He looked at Rebecca, his eyes widening. "Becky, I can't explain this."

"I can." Penelope's eyes moved from Edmond to me as she pulled the offered blanket around her shoulders and allowed one side to slip down, revealing a rather voluptuous breast. "Surely you haven't forgotten, Edmond." She allowed for a dramatic pause and looked around the room. Her eyes reflected the hatred she was feeling when she looked at me. She returned her gaze to Edmond and smiled. "I've come for my daughter."

Daughter

Saturday morning, we left Janee at our house with Sabel and the others and a list of chores. I found myself repeatedly looking out the store window, hoping to see Rebecca. We had walked her home last night while Edmond remained with Penelope. That's all we knew.

"Why do you suppose that bitch would come back now? After fifteen years?" I asked Gracie.

"I dinna ken, lass, but I canna imagine it's onythin' good."

Rebecca walked into the store at the same time as Mabel came out to relieve us. So, we sat together in the kitchen to hear her news. Jess offered to give us some privacy, feeling a little out of place, but Becky said, "Jessica, you're an old friend of Charlotte's and you know all that's happened. Please stay." She looked exhausted.

"Edmond came in some time in the middle of the night. I was in bed, but sleep was impossible, because I didn't know what was happening. He sat beside me where I lay and took my hand. He said, 'Becky, I'm so sorry. I never expected to see that woman again.' I asked if they had, you know, if they'd been together. He told me there was much he hadn't told me because it was of no consequence . . . at least he hadn't thought so. But if I wanted to know, he would tell me."

We all waited expectantly. "Years ago, after Charlie was attacked and Lionel died, the night of your wedding," Rebecca said, looking at me, "Penelope came to him in the night. She didn't tell him her reasons, only that she was lonely. Edmond learned that she and Lionel had been together. He thought that Lionel had been rough on her, hitting her and such, but was unsure of the nature of their relationship."

"I can tell you, Becky. It was me. I was the nature of their relationship. She wanted me gone so she could have Ben, and he was angry that I didn't return his affection—he felt humiliated. I am positive that they worked together to get me out of the picture."

Rebecca nodded. "I believe you're right, Charlie. Edmond said that, when she realized she was with child, she told him. He suggested she speak to you, that maybe you could help her if she didn't want to keep it. She got upset and told him, no, *you* were not to know. No one was to know. She made him promise never to tell. Then she and her father moved away. She probably didn't want to disgrace her father, being a preacher and all. After having the baby, she brought her to us knowing Lionel was dead . . . I suppose she wanted Janee to be where she would be loved."

"What do ye think she's plannin' now that she's here, lass?"

"I don't know, but Janee is her daughter. She must be told." She looked up with dark, wet eyes. "I can't lose my Janee. Lord, I wish Ron was here. He would know the best way to handle it."

I took her hand across the table and said, "Janee loves you. To her, *you* are her mother."

"But what if she wants to go with her?" she asked.

"We'll cross that bridge when we come to it, lass. Let's just take one day at a time, will we?"

Rebecca nodded and wiped her tears before continuing. "Edmond is letting her stay in his room while she's in town. He'll stay with me. I'm supposed to bring Janee to the tavern to meet her this afternoon."

"Then we best go get her at my house. She'll need some time for this all to sink in."

Jess and I walked up the little hill with Becky and watched as she walked away with Janee. This would be an emotional day for them.

When the door closed behind them, Jess asked, "What do you think the bitch wants with Janee now, after all this time?"

"It's anybody's guess, Jess."

Learning that Janee was Penelope's child was a surprise, but not a shock—it did explain things; if she and Lionel had, in fact, conspired to get me out of the picture before Ben and I were married, then her trading sexual favours made sense. She used her body to get what she wanted from him and got pregnant in the process. I had no idea that there had been any sort of relationship between her and Edmond. That is another matter.

"Jess, I'd like to take you to my spot before we go back."

"Your spot?"

"Yep. You'll see."

We walked to the rock overlooking the water. "This is my thinking spot . . . my relaxing spot. It's also where Ben and I first kissed."

"Aww." She sat on the rock and looked around, taking in a deep breath. "I can totally see why you love it."

As the day wore on, Penelope never left my thoughts. Back at home, with Jess and Gracie, I said, "I thought I was finished with her the day we saw her leave town with her father almost sixteen years ago. He was the preacher, if you can imagine that. I wonder what she told him about being pregnant. I can't imagine he would have dealt well with it, although clearly, he got her out of town before anyone knew the truth."

"Aye."

We were interrupted then by a low voice. "Mommy, I'm finished my schoolwork, I made my bed, and folded my clothes that were on the floor."

"Phillip, I didn't even have to ask. Good for you! What would you like to do now?" I asked.

He looked down at his feet for a moment, biting his lip before saying, "I was thinking I could take Jess, I mean Jessica, to see our treehouse." His cheeks were pink, but I don't think he knew that.

She looked from him to me and then answered, "I'd love that, Phillip. It sounds like a really cool place to play and hang around. I always wanted one when I was little, and my mom would have let me have one, but we didn't have the right trees." He smiled and waited as she reached for her coat.

"My dad found the perfect trees. Come with me."

Jess turned with a wink. "We'll be back soon." She put her arm around his shoulders and the two walked out the door.

Gracie looked at me with a huge smile on her face. "Aww, that's nice. He seems to've taken a real shinin' to Jessica, eh?"

"He has," I agreed. "Come have a seat, Gracie." I pointed to the settee. "Now that I've got you alone, tell me what's going on with Jimmy. Did you talk? Did you have it out?"

"Ah, Charlie. Sometimes I dinna ken what to do wi' that man. He kens how I feel about playin' cards for coin. Sure, he could come home wi' a pocketful o' coins, but more often than not, he doesna. I've telt 'im my feelins many a time, but he just willna listen. This time, o' course, he lost more than money—he lost something that was given to him as a gift. It's special and should've been treated as such. It was worth more than the money the others put in. And, if that isna enough, he tells no one, not a soul that he's lost it; that he planned to win it back; that Simon was wearing it when he died; or that it was missing when Simon was found. I'm so angry, I could spit!" She finished then, blowing out a deep breath.

When Jessica arrived back home, she sat beside me, and Phillip ran upstairs. "That's a great treehouse! You said that was your property?"

"Yes. It belonged to our friend Audrey. I must have told you about her; she suggested that after her death, we let her body burn in her old house so that we could feign Elizabeth's death." Jessica nodded as she found the memory. "She left us her property thinking we may need it for our family as it grew."

"Well, that's a wonderful way to make use of it until then."

The Peddler

Andy returned to town the next morning with news. Lawrence asked Ben and Jimmy to meet with them while the rest of town was at church. While Jess, Michael, and I waited for news, they sat around the table in Lawrence's parlour, and Andy told them what he'd learned.

It was just after noon when they arrived back at the house with Gracie, Gifted Hands, and Keen Wolf. "Good afternoon, everyone," Gifted Hands said. "We left the children with yours at the store. I hope that is okay?" She winked as she used the expression that still seemed strange to her.

"It's perfect. Let's get everyone comfortable, and I'll make some coffee. Then we can hear Andy's news," I said.

Once we were ready, Ben started his story. "When Andy reached Auburn, he stopped at the general store to inquire about the peddler Tate. The storekeeper told him the peddler had not arrived there yet. So, as per Lawrence's instruction, Andy travelled west hoping to cross his path. He found him only two miles out. He passed on a letter written by Lawrence and waited as the man read it. Of course, Mr. Tate remembered the wristwatch because it was an unusual piece and because he got it for a song and sold it for double. He did not know the name of the man who traded it, but he remembered the town he'd been in at the time—Cayuga. To the best of his recollection, the man was tall and thin, with dark eyes and long dark hair under a leather hat."

"Did the man look as though he'd been in a scuffle, Benny?" Gracie asked.

"No. Andy said there was no bruising on his face." I saw disappointment on Gracie's face. "Mr. Tate said the man wore a fancy metal belt buckle with horses engraved on it. He said he tried to get the man to trade that, too, but he wouldn't consider it." Ben glanced at Jimmy then and continued. "At that point, Lawrence saw Jim's expression and asked, 'What is it, Jim?'"

"I telt 'im I thought that man was at the card table that night—him, Simon, and me played the last round. He woulda seen Simon's winnin's. Ah, but onybody there would've."

"Then Lawrence said, 'But not anybody traded that watch. This is the man we need to find. Did you hear his name?'"

"I never did, but it seemed Edmond had met 'im. Perhaps he'll ken," Jimmy answered.

"Lawrence thinks he may be the man named Isaac, Edmond mentioned," Ben continued. "He's going to speak to him today, after seeing Geoff Mainer; apparently the storekeeper in Auburn passed on a letter for him that had been left there in error."

When Ben finished, I said, "So, inasmuch as I'm disappointed that Jimmy would make that watch a part of the pot . . ." I paused and looked at Jimmy. If he hadn't known my feelings on the subject, he did now. "At least it has given us a clue in solving the mystery of this murder."

Gracie looked at me, expressionless. I knew she was having a difficult time dealing with this herself. Jimmy's eyes were on the floor. Jessica shifted awkwardly.

We learned later that Edmond had met the man once or twice. He knew nothing about him other than he called himself Isaac and he lived at the top of Seneca Lake.

Lawrence and Andy, who was hoping to learn the ways of investigation, would leave again tomorrow morning for the Village of Geneva to see what they could discover. For now, we would have to wait.

As talk of Isaac ended, the children bustled into the house ready for supper.

After the dishes had been collected, Jessica said, "While we clean the dishes, why don't the rest of you go on outside and make sure the fire's burning nicely. I have a little treat for everyone. Everyone will need a stick about this long."

Keen Wolf's eyes met mine momentarily as he wondered what she could be talking about. I winked. "Oh, you'll like this. I promise."

"Mm-mm, will this be a sweet treat?" Phillip asked, licking his lips.

Jess smiled. "Oh yes. Would you like to give me a hand?" He nodded enthusiastically, happy to help his new friend.

Jess had found some square marshmallows at home and brought them along with some chocolate-topped wafers. We had tried *my* version of marshmallows roasted over the fire and they'd been okay; everyone had asked for seconds. But when they put these ones between the chocolate wafers, everyone made sounds of delight, and *everyone* asked for more.

"Good morning, Charlotte," Edna said as the little bells over the door rang. She walked to my counter. "I was hopin' you could give me a bit more of that tea. It's done wonders for my sleep." She looked behind me momentarily. "Hello, Jessica."

Sure," I answered. "How much would you like?"

"Maybe enough for two more nights. That'd be nice," she answered and turned to flash a smile at Gracie.

While mixing the tea I asked, "Is the shop open again?"

"Oh, yes. Geoff had expected to have to go back up to Auburn today, but his plans changed, so he's opened up this morning. I believe he can put off the journey till next weekend. When I told him I'd be seeing you, he gave me a few coins to pay for my teas. Will this do, dear?" She opened her hand, showing me the coins.

"That's great, Edna. Here you go."

After she'd left, Gracie came to stand with Jess and me. "She seems in better spirits, eh?" she asked. "Are you ladies ready for your dinner?"

"Oh, aye," Jess answered with a giggle, as Mabel came out on the floor.

"Good afternoon, Hettie," Jess said with a smile, as we entered the kitchen.

"Well, by golly that morning went fast," Hettie answered.

"What is it, Hettie? Is everything all right?" I asked.

"I don't know if it is. My Eli is feeling under the weather today. He's been in bed all morning."

"Aww. Does he have a fever?"

"Mm-hm and his head is at 'im."

I didn't even sit down. I said, "Come with me, Hettie. Let's see if I can give him something that will help."

We walked to their little house behind the store. The poor man was shaking under his covers and sweating with fever. His colour was off, and I asked if anything hurt. He said it was his head and his chest. "I can give you something for the fever now, and I'll get Ben in here to have a listen to your chest. Sip this water while I prepare your tea." I handed him a cup Hettie had left at his bedside. "Hettie will bring it in in a few minutes, all right?"

He nodded and pulled the covers under his chin.

As we walked back toward the kitchen, I said, "We'll make him some tea now, but please do your best not to get too close and be sure to wash your hands with soap whenever you've been in the house. It wouldn't do to have you ill as well."

"I'll be careful, Miss Charlotte."

Ben and Michael walked into the kitchen while I was steeping Eli's tea: white willow for his headache and fever and dried elecampane root for potential chest issues. "Benny, I'm glad you're here. Can you please see Eli? He's got a headache and fever and says his chest hurts. I'll be there shortly. I just want to steep this five minutes more."

He bent to kiss my cheek. "I'll see you there."

After listening to his chest, Ben said, "I hear phlegm in your lungs, Eli. Have you been coughing?" Eli shook his head. "The tea Charlotte made is a good start to helping you feel better." He poured out a cup. "Drink this over the next half hour. We'll give you another cup in a few hours. Meantime, I'll see what else we can do for you. I'll be back in a while, all right?" Eli tried to smile as he nodded, but it didn't work. "Don't worry, you'll feel better soon," Ben assured his friend, patting his back.

While Ben and I walked back up to the store, I asked, "Bronchitis?"

"It's possible. I'm worried about pneumonia. We'll have to keep our eyes on him and perhaps make him some garlic tea. Also, I have some eucalyptus oil we can add to a bowl of hot water. Breathing that for a while should open things up."

"Instead of the tea, I have a tincture of garlic we can give him, Ben."

He nodded as he took his plate to the table.

As I gobbled down my lunch, Michael asked, "Can I help somehow? I mean with Eli out of commission, there must be something I can do."

Ben smiled. "Oh, there is. How do you feel about filling the water barrels?" Michael's eyebrows raised. "Before I get back to work, I'll show you how we fill them and where you can find the hand truck to move them."

"That sounds fine," Michael said and smiled, happy to be able to contribute. "And then I'll go back up to the house and start supper."

Jess gave Michael a wink, and then she and I returned to work. Almost immediately, Edmond walked into the store looking very serious. "Afternoon, ladies," he said with a nod, but without his usual smile. "I need yer help, Charlotte, yours or Ben's."

"What is it, Edmond?" I asked as Gracie came to join us.

He looked around before answering. "It's Penelope." I felt the hairs on the back of my neck rise. "I popped into my room this morning and found her there on the bed." I imagined the woman naked, kneeling on his bed, ass in the air for him to take. "She was sweatin' and dizzy and she'd been pukin'. I told her I'd come talk to you, to see what you might suggest. She told me 'no' rather harshly. Told me to get her another bucket and give her some time, she'd be better soon."

"And?"

"Well, I've just come from there." His face paled and took on a greenish hue. "She's not better. She's got it coming out at both ends. It's a mess in there."

"Oh dear," Gracie said under her breath.

"And what would you like from me, Edmond?" I honestly couldn't care less, although I did feel for Edmond. It was his living space, after all.

He glanced at Gracie then back at me. "Is there somethin' that might settle her?" he asked.

"Hmm, well you can try, but she'll have to keep it down for it to do any good."

"Aye?" he asked, waiting for more.

"Peppermint?" Jessica asked.

"It sounds like she's beyond that at the moment. Maybe ginger? It's good for nausea. As for the diarrhea, she'll need to keep something down before you can deal with that." Reluctantly, I bent to see how much ginger I had.

Gracie walked back to her own counter as someone came into the store. Jess sat on the stool beside me, watching, listening, and waiting to see how I was going to handle this.

I stood with a piece of ginger root in one hand and my grater in the other. "Alright, Edmond, I will give you enough for two teas, and you can see how that goes." I began to grate. "If it helps, come back for some more, if it doesn't, I'm afraid you'll have to find help elsewhere."

"I'm not sure I understand what you're not sayin', lass." His eyes flicked to Jess. "Do ye not care for Penny? Is that it?"

"That *is* it, but it's much more than that. Please understand that I am only offering you the ginger to help *you*, because she's making a mess of *your* room. If not for you . . ." I shook my head, not finishing the sentence. "Now, put this into enough boiling water for two cups, and let it sit for ten minutes. Then strain it. She can sip it slowly over the rest of the day."

He nodded. "Thank you, Charlotte. I'll even up with ye tomorrow?"

"Sure. And Edmond, be sure to keep your hands clean. Wash with soap every time you touch her or something that she's touched or barfed or shit on."

With a frown, he turned and quickly left the store.

"I'm proud of you, Char. She doesn't deserve help from you."

"She doesn't want it either." I could hear the satisfaction in my voice.

"Could it be cholera, do you think?"

"I suppose it could. I haven't seen it before. I've heard about it though. There was an epidemic in New York a few years ago. Spread through a large area and killed thousands."

"Was Sam affected?"

"No, but we warned him at the time to get out of town if he could, to be sure to wash his hands thoroughly, and to boil any water he would drink or cook with.

Thankfully, he managed to avoid it and we were safe here. We used it as an opportunity to remind everyone in town of the importance of proper cleanliness and boiling their water."

A short time later, as we were closing for the day, Ben came in after checking on Eli.

"Well, whatever he has is settling into his chest. I'm a bit worried. I'll just go to speak to Hettie, then I'll meet you, and we can walk home together?"

"Of course. I'll get those buns Hettie set aside for us and meet you out back."

"Aww," said Jess. "He's such a kind, happy man. I hope he's feeling better tomorrow."

"Me, too." I agreed. Then my belly grumbled loudly.

Jess laughed and said, "Don't worry, soon we'll be sitting down to Michael's spaghetti."

"Mmm, I'm looking forward to it." Among the food items they'd taken with them, was a pack of spaghetti noodles and a chunk of parmesan cheese. *This is gonna be good!*

Jess demonstrated twisting the noodles around her fork before everyone dug in. The faces of the kids as they grated the parmesan and twisted up the noodles was precious. "Michael, this is delicious! Thank you," I said as I swallowed mine down.

"I'm glad you're enjoying it."

Just then a strange "oop" came from Phillip. We all looked his way. His face conveyed a look of shock, and there were flicks of tomato sauce on his nose and forehead. The girls both giggled as they saw him. "That last noodle gotcha, didn't it?" Jess asked from beside him. "That happens sometimes when you suck in a noodle fast. Seems to me you're enjoying your meal, Phillip." She handed him a napkin then and touched the spots on her face where he should wipe on his own.

After cleaning himself, he took another mouthful and promptly flicked sauce on his chin. This time, he smiled, shrugged, and kept on eating.

Retching

I was just putting on our coffee when we heard a banging on the front door. Ben opened it to Edmond, breathing heavily as he stood on the porch.

"Ben, you've got to come help me. Please. It's Penelope."

Ben, knowing I'd followed him to the door, turned to look at me. Of course, I'd filled him in yesterday about Edmond's visit to the store, so he knew what was happening.

"It hasn't stopped. She's nothing left in her and can't keep a drop down." Ben bent for his bag that he'd left near the door. "Her eyes are sunk into her head and she's mumbling nonsense." His eyes briefly found mine before he continued. "Can ye help?"

Ben told me he'd be back and left the house. I looked out the door to see them running down the hill. For a moment, I thought about the state she must be in by now. *Nope, still don't care.* I went back to the kitchen to check the coffee and start a tea for Eli. I heard Jess behind me.

"Penelope?" she asked.

"Yep."

"Ben's gone?"

"Yep."

"Hmm. Are you good with that?"

I took two of Hettie's cookies out of the tin on the table. "I would be disappointed if he didn't." I offered her a cookie. "He's a doctor, Jess. He took an oath to help wherever and whenever he can—you know the deal. I know how he feels about her, and that's enough for me. *I*, on the other hand, took no such oath, and I don't care *what* happens to that woman."

"Gotcha! So what mixture are you making Eli?" she asked.

"Horehound and mallow. The mallow helps to soothe the inflammation and irritation of the bronchi and lungs, and the horehound loosens and helps expectorate the mucous. I'll mix in a bit of honey before we give it to him though. I understand it's bitter."

"They're lucky to have you here, Char. Without antibiotics, sickness sure is harder to deal with."

"True, but if not me, there would be someone else."

"Maybe so, but no one, and I mean *no one*, has the background and knowledge you have."

After breakfast, we left the house with the kids, saying goodbye to them at the bottom of the hill. We were almost at the store when we saw someone running toward us. It was Oliver Douglas, Edmond's brother, and part owner of the inn and tavern. "Charlotte, Ben's asked that you and your friends meet him at the Doctor's House. He and Edmond are bringing Penelope there."

What? "Thank you, Oliver."

"I'll run and tell Gracie. Meet you there," Jess said and ran the other way.

Michael and I walked briskly toward the house. "We don't have any supplies there yet. What is he thinking?" I said, more to myself than Michael.

Then we saw them in the road. The two men were carrying her on a sheet, using it like a stretcher. This was going to make a mess in the house. I ran inside to prepare the bed, while Michael followed, waiting for a task. Together we took the extra towels and sheets that had been left in a crate and sorted them, layering several over the bed. "Oh, for a sheet of plastic, eh?" he said.

"And a hose!" I agreed.

They got her in and lying on the bed. She was wearing only a sleeveless shift which was far from clean, and she smelled foul. I looked at her gaunt-looking face and might have felt pity, but the sunken and flat eyes looking back at me were still hers.

"We need to clean her, Ben, or the house will soon be full of that smell." He nodded and looked at me. "Not me," I answered the question in his eyes.

Edmond, looking at the two of us, confusion on his face, said, "I'll wash her. Maybe you could go back to my room for her satchel. There'll likely be something clean for her in there."

Ben said, "I'll get you what you'll need, Edmond. And I'd better get a bucket for when she throws up again."

"Okay, I'll go to the inn," I said.

Michael immediately said, "I'll come with you."

Out on the road, we met Jess, so the three of us walked to the inn together.

"What state is she in, Char?" she asked.

"Pretty bad, I'd say. Very dehydrated."

"Hmm. Do we feel sorry for her?" she asked, trying to gauge my feelings.

"I don't know about you, but I don't. That this would happen to her when she's here, and we would be the ones who had to help, that's karma."

The smell that rushed out of Edmond's room when we opened the door was like a punch in the gut. Michael gagged. "You stay out here, Mikey. Char and I will get what we need and be right back." He nodded, glancing down the stairs— he would wait at the bottom.

Inside was a mess of dirty towels and sheets, both on the floor and the bed. "Oh man," I said.

"Fuckin' nasty," Jess blurted out.

I opened the curtains and then the windows on either side of the door. Ventilation was a must. Scanning the room, I found her bag on a chair beside her coat. "Okay, Jess, let's grab this stuff and get outta here."

"I'm with you."

As we passed the front of the inn, I ran inside to advise Victoria, Edmond's sister-in-law, of the situation. I wasn't sure what Edmond might have told her, but that room needed to be well cleaned as soon as possible. I suggested that whoever got that job tie a kerchief over their nose and mouth and wash their hands thoroughly with soap once they'd finished.

Back at the Doctor's House, Edmond had finished bathing Penelope and had draped her in a towel for the time being. Michael looked at Jess, clearly uncomfortable.

"Jess, maybe you and Michael can go back to the store and get a few of my jars. I don't have anything here yet. Ben? Thoughts?"

"Hmm?" He turned to face me. "Well, she's extremely dehydrated so we most certainly need some drinking water and salt. Also, chickweed."

I smiled. His memory always amazes me. Chickweed, also high in vitamins C and B, contains calcium, iron, magnesium, manganese, zinc, phosphorus, and potassium. Ben could begin to replenish her electrolytes if she could keep some of it down. "Should we add rosehips? In addition to vitamin C, that should help absorption of the vitamins and minerals."

"And, if I may," Jessica began, "maybe some peppermint for the nausea. The ginger doesn't seem to be working."

He looked from me to Jess, "Good idea. Can you two please go get those jars from Charlotte's counter and some hot water if they have it?"

"Sure, Ben."

As they turned to leave, I said, "Jess, the chickweed isn't there, it's in the cupboard above the mixing table in my room."

"K."

Edmond was holding the bucket for Penelope as she retched but looked up. "I'll get a fire going, Benny."

Thankfully, before Ailsa and Sam left the house, Sam had cleaned out the old wood-burning stove and left it ready to light. Knowing that Edmond wouldn't see, I took the lighter out of my pocket and lit the paper left under the stack of wood. The wood caught fairly quickly. Within minutes, the fire was roaring and ready for the pot of water Ben had retrieved from the barrel outside.

"Done. Water's on," I told him when I came back into the room.

"Thank you. We'll need to get another barrel. That's the last of the water in that pot."

Just then, there was a knock on the door. It was Janee. "Good morning, Charlotte. I heard that Penelope was here and she's ill. Can I see her?"

I turned to Ben who had come into the front room. "Janee, she's very poorly at the moment. It might be better if you give us some time to get something into her bef—"

"Let me help. I mean, can I help Doctor Ben?" she interrupted.

"Tell you what, sweetheart," I started. "Why don't you wait and see if we can help her to stop throwing up. Then maybe you can help get something into her." I raised my eyebrows and waited for her reaction. "Maybe later today, or maybe tomorrow?" I could see the disappointment on her face, but she reluctantly agreed, asking that we tell Penelope she'd been here. "I'll send Sabel over when the time is right."

I closed the door behind her and heard Penelope retching as she dry-heaved over the bucket. *Nope, still don't care.*

Jess and Michael returned with warm water and several jars of dried herbs.

"If you don't mind, Ben, I'll leave her in your care? I must get back to the tavern."

"Oh, before you go, Edmond, would you see if there's something in her bag we can put on her?"

"Of course," he answered and walked to the chair where I'd left her things. "I'll just take it out to the table where there's more room." When he lifted the bag, we heard the sound of something metallic hitting the floorboards.

Reflexively, we all turned to see what had hit the floor.

"What the fuck?" I heard Jess say behind me.

I turned to her.

Edmond, stunned by her reaction, spun to face her awaiting an explanation for her surprise.

Michael bent to pick it up. "This," he said to the room, "is something Jess brought from home for Charlotte." He then focused on Edmond. "The night we arrived here, the person who gave me this"—he pointed to his black eye—"took this from Jessica's bag while she lay on the ground." It was the pewter dragonfly cloak pin that had gone missing.

"What on Earth is *she* doing with it?" Edmond asked.

"That's a very good question. Unfortunately, I don't think we'll get an answer for a while yet," Ben said, looking down at the woman on the bed. "We'll have to get Lawrence involved."

"Ah . . . This is not my business. Let me find her something to put on and then I'll be out of your hair," Edmond said.

He found another sleeveless shift, a shorter one, and got her into it. I'll give the man credit; he had no issue with helping her and was very respectful. He left us at noon, by which time Penelope had been at it for about thirty hours.

Ben suggested I go back to the store with Jess and Michael and have some dinner. We didn't all need to be here.

"Jess, this is beautiful!" I said, turning the cloak pin in my hands as we walked. From the top it looked like a pretty pewter dragonfly; the pin slipped through the tips of the top wings. "I love everything about it! Thank you. We didn't find the hair pins, but this is gorgeous."

She smiled. "You're welcome. I'm so glad we found it. I do wonder how *she* got it though. What a clusterfuck!"

"Agreed."

Back at the store, Gracie passed me a letter that had arrived for me. I read through the note and felt the burn of tears. "What is it, lass?"

"This was written by George Callaghan's partner. He died last month; he didn't say how. He remembered my name and found our address in a drawer. He wanted me to know." I explained to Jess that George had been a fellow apothecary who lived in Canandaigua and had helped us here when Ben and I were away overseas. We wrote to each other two or three times a year. I'd miss his wisdom and his wit.

"The poor soul," Gracie said quietly.

I returned to Ben a couple of hours later to learn that the length of time between her bouts of throwing up had lengthened and the diarrhea had stopped.

Ben had propped her up on some pillows and given her a warm cup of peppermint tea to sip. I prepared a mixture of salt, rosehips, and chickweed that would help replenish the electrolytes she'd lost.

"Did Jess and Michael go back to the house?" he asked.

I looked at Penelope. I didn't want to talk about anything remotely personal in her presence. His eyes found mine: he understood. I tipped my head toward the door.

He followed me into the sitting room. "Sit for a minute, Benny. I brought you a bite to eat." As he ate, I spoke softly. "I told them they could go hang out at the house for the afternoon. Michael asked about doing some fishing. It's a nice enough day for it, I guess. I told him where he could find a couple of rods. They're hoping to catch our supper."

"Mmm. It's been a while since we had fresh fish."

As the Doctor's House wasn't actually up and running yet, we had to figure out the best way to deal with having Penelope here. At this point she was only sipping the tea mixture I'd made and was too weak to go back to Edmond's on her own. Fine, but I didn't want her to be alone in our house. Someone would have to stay here with her, but who? Ben? Gah! After some conversation, it was decided that we would ask Janee to come and stay with her into the night. She could pass her the bucket or bedpan as needed and offer her sips regularly.

Afterwards, Jess and I walked her home while Ben returned to stay with Penelope for a few hours. Janee told us that Penelope slept most of the time she was there. When she awoke, she was offered a sip and did her best to swallow it down. Once she had, she said things like 'thank you my daughter', 'you're so pretty' and once she said 'you look like your father.' "After she said that, a strange look came into her eyes. I don't know what it meant. Maybe she'll tell me one day."

After saying goodnight to Janee, Jess and I walked home. She asked, "What do you suppose is the real reason that woman has come for her daughter? Surely, it's not because she loves her. And how the fuck did she get that cloak pin?"

Geneva

With Eli out of commission, Jess and Michael were eager to contribute to the store's workload. They were briefed by Eli on what the horses needed, and Hettie showed them where things were, so they could help to brush, feed, and water them for the time being.

Collectively, the family now had three horses: Ruby, who was here when I arrived, Mocha, purchased a few years ago after Humphrey's death, and Nya, our newest addition. Walnut, who had been given to Ben by the late Doc McGee's wife Molly, had died not long after Molly.

The first morning Jess let them out to pasture, she was in awe. "They are such lovely animals, Char. What have we been missing all our lives back at home? And Nya is just so pretty. What did you say she was called again?"

"An appaloosa," I answered. Jessica was right, she was a beauty. She looked as if she was a black horse, painted over her shoulders, back, and haunches with white, leaving different sizes of black spots over those areas, and three of her four feet were white. She arrived at the store a few years ago, delivered by messenger. The man who brought her asked for me upon his arrival and handed me a letter saying only, "I wrote this letter in Mailka's words." Inside it read:

My Dear Charlotte,

It has been several years since our meeting, but I still think of your kindness every day. Without you, your husband, lovely Hettie, and Eli, I am certain I would not be here to tell this story. After I left you that winter, I made several stops before reaching Upper Canada. When I arrived, I was cold, and I was hungry, but I was free, no longer a slave on the run. I set forward to locate my husband, Mosi. He remained on the farm where I'd been told he found work. The owners of the farm kindly welcomed me in as his wife and offered me work. Mostly I cook, but sometimes I help Mosi with the animals. Well, the time came when Mosi and me were offered a horse of our own, an appaloosa. We couldn't believe our good fortune. We use her to get around, of course, but Mosi always loved an appaloosa, so he began to breed her. I had always had it in my mind to pay you for your kindness, and so I send you this spirited young mare. Thank you. Thank you all for giving me my life. I hope you will have many years of happiness with Nya. We have called her this with love, for she will be a friend and companion to you.

    Malika

After delivering the letter, the man tipped his hat, passed me the reins of the new horse, and rode away in the direction he had come from with no further words. All I could do was shout out, "Please, tell her thank you." It was unfortunate, but for her safety, the less we knew about Malika and her whereabouts, the better.

"So, Eli looks after the horses, I know that, but what happens when one of them gets sick? It must happen now and then?" Jess asked.

"Yeah, once in a while. When one of them has an ailment that Eli can't cure, he usually speaks to one of the farmers in the area and sees what they would suggest. But if it's something that has him stumped, he sends word to the horse doctor in Auburn, and he comes down to pay the horse a visit."

Later in the day, Ben and I let ourselves into Edmond's room, where Penelope had been returned. I felt nauseous; I had no desire to be face-to-face with this woman again, but it was time to get some answers. I looked around the room and was surprised to see how well the staff had cleaned it for Edmond.

"Penelope, I'm glad to see you're feeling improved. Have you been down to the tavern yet?"

"No. Victoria has been kind enough to have one of her girls bring me up soup and tea and such. I expect I'll be able to get down there in the next day or so."

I had no time to make small talk with this woman. "Where did you get that cloak pin?" I asked. I saw Ben turn to me, surprised at the tone of my voice.

"Cloak pin?" she asked, looking innocent.

"The one with the dragonfly."

"I don't want to talk to you, Charlotte. I never did."

"Believe me, it's mutual," I responded.

She looked at Ben as she gathered her thoughts. "I got it from a man in Geneva."

"What man?" Ben asked.

"I don't know his name." She paused a moment. "He had a cart. I saw it there and bought it."

"A peddler?"

She nodded her response.

"That pin was stolen. You bought stolen property. It doesn't belong to you," I said.

"But I bought it," she said, looking at Ben.

"I'm sure Lawrence will have a few questions for you when he returns," he said.

"Let him ask. I've done nothing wrong."

Ben cleared his throat before speaking again. "In the meantime, I will ask Victoria to have the kitchen make you some thin porridge and dry toast. You need to start eating again."

I smiled inwardly at the look of distaste on her face. Looking at Ben, I added, "And the agrimony tea we brought will help reduce the inflammation in your gut."

"Thank you, Ben," she said sweetly, completely ignoring me.

As he closed the door behind us, I said, "I hate the feelings she brings out in me, Benny. When I see her I just . . . I wish . . . I don't know, but I can't wait for her to be gone. She *is* planning to leave here, right?"

"To tell you the truth, I haven't asked her anything about her life, only questions pertaining to her health. I have no idea what her plans are."

Lawrence returned to town Saturday evening. He came to see us the following morning, arriving just after the kids left to meet their grandmother, Auntie Gracie, and cousins for church. Jimmy came up to the house to hear the news and of course, Jess and Michael were permitted to join us because they were involved.

I served coffee as Lawrence began his story. Once he and Andy were in the village of Geneva, they didn't have much trouble identifying the man in question. After giving his description to three different individuals in town, the same name came up—Isaac Barrett. Where to find him? That was a different story. "I was told he lived in the back of a printer's shop on Castle Street. So, me and Andy went to pay him a visit. When we got no answer at the door, we spoke to the printer, again offering a description of the person we were looking for. He confirmed Isaac's name and that he lived in the back. Said he comes and goes, often staying away for days at a time. He had no clue where we might find him. So, Andy and I got a room at a nearby inn. We didn't go all that way to come home with nothing."

"I assume Mr. Barrett came home?" Ben asked.

"Not exactly." He paused to sip his coffee. "The next day we saw a woman from the neighbourhood go to his door with a basket over her arm. Shortly after, she came out with a bucket and disappeared behind the shop. When she came back, we were there. She told us she was a friend and had stopped with some fresh bread. Unfortunately, she'd found him quite ill. Apparently, he'd been spewing all day. Quite a mess, she said. I decided to return the next day and give him some time." Lawrence stopped then, having noticed our expressions as we looked at each other. "What is it?" he asked.

"An interesting coincidence. Please, go on with your story. It can wait," Ben answered.

"Late the next morning, we knocked on his door. He told us to come in. When we did, I offered him some tea and broth we'd brought from the inn. I'll tell you this, it smelled something fierce in there. Andy had to go outside for a spell. I told him we'd heard he was ill but needed to ask him some questions. His eyes were sunken, and his face boney—this sickness had taken it out of him, but his eyes opened wide as I spoke.

"He tried to sit up, but I had to give him a hand. Then he just looked at me waiting. So, I told him about the timepiece we knew he'd sold to the peddler. I watched as he heard the question. I believe he is practiced at his expression. I learned nothing by watching his face. I explained that we knew he'd played cards at our tavern that night in November and knew he saw the timepiece won by Simon. Then I told him that we found Simon dead the next morning. Something changed in his eyes after that. 'Dead?' he asked. Then he paused.

"He said, 'He wasn't dead when I … that is to say … yes, I took the timepiece from his wrist, but he was alive.'"

The room was silent as Lawrence sipped once more and we waited. Isaac told him this: He had left the tavern that night shortly after Simon, intending to ride north, toward home. He was walking his horse across from the general store when he turned to climb onto his mare. In the distance, just past the bottom of the hill, he said he could see a man staggering and eventually falling to the ground. He rode over to see who it was—it was Simon. He said he was surprised because while Simon had taken a few ales, he didn't appear to've had enough to make him fall down. At any rate, he had, and he wasn't aware. Isaac said he couldn't help himself. He reached for the man's wrist and took off the timepiece. Then, he checked his pockets because he had won some coin, too, but they were empty. He jumped back on his horse and headed for home.

Lawrence finished and looked around the room. "Jim, you said Isaac was still there when you left the tavern that night? Did you happen to see him walk past at any time after you left?" Jimmy shook his head. "Hmm. Well, according to Edmond, he stayed for another after you left. No one seems to have seen him after that."

"Well, he admitted taking the wristwatch, that's something," Ben said.

"Yes," Lawrence said. "Now, what were the glances I saw passing between you?"

Ben began to tell him about Penelope.

"She became ill a few days ago with something that sounds exactly the same as what Isaac had. We've been helping her to get her strength back."

"That *is* a coincidence," Lawrence agreed.

"There's more. While looking in her bag for a change of clothes, we found something that had gone missing from Jessica's bag the night they arrived."

"But surely it wasn't Penelope who took those items and punched Michael's face?"

"I don't think so, no. There's no trace of bruising on her face. What about Isaac's?"

"No," Lawrence answered.

"So do we think that Isaac took both items from Simon's pockets?" Ben asked.

"It would stand to reason that if he took the wristwatch, as you call it, then he also took the pin, although he never mentioned the pin . . . or the stone for that matter."

"Penelope said she got the pin from a peddler, so I think it's safe to assume Mr. Tate received both items from Isaac," Ben said.

"That Isaac and Penelope are both sick with the same illness at the same time is also something to consider," Lawrence said and stood from his seat. "I'll leave you to think about all that. Perhaps I will pay Penelope a visit. Would you suggest I wait a day or two, Ben?"

"Yes. It wouldn't do to have you become ill as well, Lawrence. I would like to be with you when you see her. Tomorrow?"

"Very well. See you in the morning. Thank you for the coffee, Charlotte," he said, heading for the door.

It wasn't long after Lawrence left that Gracie arrived at the house. "Good morning, Gracie. How was the sermon today?"

"Och, well, the pastor makes all sermons interestin', but I'd say it was the same as usual." She smiled. "Afterwards as we were standing outside, I heard someone talkin', someone bidin' at the inn. She was tellin' Emma about a sickness that struck her town about a week ago. It seems many o' the townsfolk were ill wi' the same ailments as Penelope."

"What town was that? Did she say?" I asked.

"Oh, aye. Let me think a mo … Bridgeport. Aye, she said much o' the town'd been to a celebration, a weddin' I think, and a couple o' days afterward, many were throwin' up and such. She and her husband hadna been invited and when abody started wi' the sickness, they left town."

I looked at Ben. "So, someone in attendance was ill and passed it to everyone. It could have been anyone—guests, the cook, servers, bride and groom."

"We may never know. Let's just hope it doesn't spread here."

"Do we think they were both in Bridgeport at the same time?" I asked.

"It's something to consider."

"Where exactly is Bridgeport?" I asked.

"Actually, it's between Geneva and Cayuga … Interesting."

Coincidence

Edmond had graciously permitted Penelope to remain in his room while she was in town, but as of yet, no one knew how long she planned to stay.

Ben and Lawrence went to see her Monday morning.

"Good morning, Penelope, Janee," Lawrence said as they entered the room.

"Oh, Mr. Southern, good morning, and Ben," she answered.

"Janee," Lawrence began, "we'd like to speak to Penelope alone for a few minutes, if you don't mind."

"Of course," she answered. "I'll go visit a friend for a short while." She slipped into her coat and left.

Lawrence spoke to Penelope now. "I understand you're feeling some better. That's good to hear."

"Yes. Thank you."

"I'd like to ask you a few questions." She nodded and he continued. "Do you have any idea where you may have picked up this sickness? Has anyone else you know or been in contact with had it that you're aware of?"

"No, I don't know where it came from. And I don't know anyone else who's been ill."

"Hmm. I also heard that you were in possession of a particular pin."

With a quick glance at Ben, she had answered, "Yes. I purchased it from a peddler in Geneva."

"Ben made you aware that the pin was stolen? Apparently, it was taken from someone's bag as they lay on the ground after having a fall."

Ben told us that, at that point, her eyebrows lifted high. "I was not aware of that detail." She looked at both men for a moment. "Surely you don't think it was me who took it?"

Lawrence levelled a serious look at her and inhaled deeply. "No. I don't think so. What's troubling me is that the pin was taken on the same night as another article was taken from a man who was killed here in town." Penelope's eyes were wide. "It would appear that both articles were sold to a peddler in Geneva. I think it's safe to assume that the peddler received both articles from the same person." He turned to Ben for support.

"I should think so," Ben agreed.

"Is there anything that has come back to you now that might help us learn who this man is?"

Ben told us she swallowed hard before shaking her head.

"I see," Lawrence said. "So, you are not acquainted with Mr. Isaac Barrett?" Penelope coughed after hearing the name, paling visibly as she looked back at Lawrence. He only looked at her with eyebrows raised. Again, she shook her head, but Ben said she was not at all convincing. "Are you certain? Because, while we believe that Mr. Barrett brought these items to the peddler, Mr. Tate, we know that he is suffering the same illness as you. In fact, it started on the same day."

"Perhaps Mr. Barrett and I were in the same place on the same day. At church, a shop, a tavern?"

"Perhaps," Lawrence agreed with a nod. Then he added, looking at Ben, "I suppose I will have to pay Isaac another visit. I was unaware of this coincidence when I saw him last."

Ben told us that they left Penelope sitting up in bed, pale and discontented.

While the men were with Penelope, Janee came to visit Sabel. I told them I didn't think it was a good idea for her to come in, until we knew that she hadn't caught the bug from Penelope, and suggested they go for a walk. They weren't gone very long, maybe twenty minutes, before Sabel returned. "How was your walk?" I asked.

"It was nice." At the tone in her voice, I turned to her.

"But?"

She hung her coat on the hook by the door and walked to where I stood. "Well, Janee just seems so sad. This . . . situation is troubling her."

"I'm sure it would. That woman coming back like that, surprising everyone, and then admitting she's Janee's mother, that's a lot to take in."

"Can I ask you something, Mum?"

"Of course," I answered.

"It seems like whenever you mention Penelope, the look in your eyes changes or the tone of your voice. You don't like her, do you?" One eyebrow arched up as she asked.

"Well, no. I don't care for her. Never have."

"Why? What are you not telling me?"

I hadn't foreseen this moment coming. Until a couple of weeks ago, I didn't expect to ever see her again. It never needed to be talked about again. "Why don't you go upstairs and change into something more comfortable? We can talk in a while."

Sabel looked across at me and started to say something but thought the better of it and turned to go upstairs. Jess, who had been sitting quietly on the settee, came into the kitchen area. "Will you tell her, Char?"

"I think I should talk to Ben about it first." Jessica nodded. "But yes, I think I will. I don't want her thinking that woman is any kind of a good person. On the other hand, I don't want to put her in an awkward position with her friend." I looked again at my friend. "You feel okay?"

"Gah, it's just PMS; it'll pass. Hey, at least if I feel like biting someone's head off, I know where to go, right?"

"Yep. Pretty sure she'd leave a bitter taste in your mouth though," I said with a chuckle. "Did you bring the things you'll need to deal with all that?"

"I did."

My conversation with Ben was brief. He told me, "Sweets, you will only tell her the truth. Yes, it will be shocking for her to hear the details of what happened to you, but if you feel it would be a benefit for her to understand what Penelope and Lionel did, then tell her."

So, later in the day, I asked Sabel if she'd like to come with me to the Doctor's House to straighten some things up. While we walked, I summarized my early days here. Some of it she'd heard before, but some details hadn't been necessary to share before now. "I need you to understand up front you will have to keep this to yourself. It might be difficult because this involves the mother of your friend. Do you feel like you can do that?" I asked. She looked at me, eyes wide, and nodded. "Okay. Your Aunt Gracie told me shortly after your dad arrived home from medical school that both Penelope and Rebecca had had their eye on him. I couldn't blame them of course; he was a very handsome man. He still is."

She smiled and turned to me, waiting for more. "And you?"

"I thought he was a nice-looking man, and I liked his personality, but I wasn't planning to stay in town, so it didn't cross my mind to think about him that way." I left out all details of my relationship with Keen Wolf at the time. That was something she didn't need to think about. "There was also something that happened with Rebecca's brother Lionel. We were at Katie and Gregory's wedding. I had gone with your father, as a friend, and we were dancing, when Lionel and Penelope came up to us together, asking to switch partners. As we danced, he started pulling me closer and . . . well, when I tried to pull back he got upset. He said some very rude things to me, a—"

"What kind of things?"

I remembered his words quite clearly, but I was not about to repeat them to my daughter who was still very innocent. "Let me just say, they were sexual comments about things he'd like to do to me, and they were quite rude. When I heard his words, I stepped back and walked out of the room. He followed me and came to where I was standing. He started to make an apology, but it turned into more sexual stuff. I reacted and tried to slap his face, but he caught my hand. Then your dad was there, and it was over." Sabel was trying to visualize this scene. "The next day, he came by while I was working in the garden. He wanted to apologize. He explained that he'd been getting some severe headaches and said that sometimes he heard himself say things, but it wasn't really him. It sounded like he was having some type of problem in his head, and I told him he should talk to your dad about it. Then, he told me that he'd wanted to get to know me better. He wanted to kiss me. I tried to explain again that I wasn't looking for anyone—I wasn't staying in town and didn't want any attachment. He snapped. He shoved me into my room, back up against the wall with his arm across my throat. Thankfully, your dad came around the corner in time and heard him talking. He pulled Lionel back and they punched each other. It was nuts. After that day, Lionel left town for a while.

"As time went on, your dad and I started to spend more time together. Rebecca seemed to accept it, but Penelope . . . well, let me put it this way, I found rude words written on my door in mud, and a pile of let's call it 'poop' on my doorstep. Then one day while we were with Gracie, Jimmy, Gifted Hands, and Keen Wolf, someone broke into my room at the store and sliced through my clothing, tossed my drawers around, broke many of my jars and some trinkets I'd had on my shelves. It was horrible. I always felt it was her, but there was no way to prove it. The only person I told at the time was my friend Marshall. You've heard me mention him, haven't you?"

"Once or twice. He was a good friend of yours?"

"He was. He was kind and caring and I liked him a lot. I told him what had been happening and that I thought it was Penelope. I also told him about Lionel, who he'd known quite well. He was worried about me and told me not to walk in the woods alone. Come get him if I needed to. He was sweet.

"Then one day, your dad got word from Sam that he would be in The Flats on the weekend and hoped they could meet there. Dad and I were together by then. When he came into the store and told Gracie and me about the letter, Penelope was there. The next day, he received another letter saying Sam would be there earlier than expected. Not wanting to miss the chance to see his friend, dad left for The Flats. After he left, I found the corn dolly I'd had on my shelf, the one that had gone missing after the break-in, on the stoop: her head was cut off and she'd been burned. That day, Rebecca came into the store and told us that Mrs. Everett, who lived south of the Southerns, was in need of Ben. Since dad was away for a couple of days, I told Gracie I'd go. I went to see Marshall first, because I knew I'd be safer if he was with me. I didn't want to walk past the mill where I knew Lionel would be working. He wanted me to wait a couple of minutes for him, but I . . ." I was starting to slip as the memory came back in full force.

We arrived at the Doctor's House and let ourselves in. "You look a little pale, Mum, can I make you a tea? Valerian?" I nodded and let her. Using the time it took to make the tea, I sat and tried to compose myself. "Here you are. Have a sip," she said.

"Thanks, honey." I sipped. "So, where was I? Oh, right . . . Marshall. We saw Lionel walk the opposite direction down the road, so I left. Marshall said he would be right behind me." I could see the anticipation on her face. Of course, she had heard a vague, edited version of what happened that day, but now she was going to hear it unabridged. "I got to a certain point on the trail and heard something. I still couldn't see Marshall anywhere, but Lionel was there. The next thing I knew I was lying in the rain, my head was throbbing, and Lionel was looking down at me. He'd tied my hands together above my head, tethered to a tree and he had the knife I kept strapped to my leg. He started talking—he was getting angry, and I thought he was going to punch me. Then I heard Marshall's voice." I could feel the tears on my cheeks and wiped them away. "When I arrived in town, they were the best of friends. Everyone said so. But something happened to change that. Marshall started trying to talk sense to Lionel, said something about 'her' poisoning Lionel's mind. It looked like it was working. He was calming down. He walked to Marshall and put his arms around him. They were talking. Marshall whispered something to him as he looked at me. Then, in the blink of an eye, Lionel stabbed Marshall. It was brutal. He sliced him open and left him lying on the ground. I had to watch my good friend die. It took me a long time to stop blaming myself. He was there because of me."

Sabel had her hands over her heart, and there were tears on her cheeks. "Mum, that's so sad. I'm so sorry."

"It doesn't end there. He punched me, he raped me, and I'm quite sure he would have killed me with that knife, but your dad and Gracie found us in time. They figured out that it was Lionel who told Rebecca that Mrs. Everett needed to see the doctor, and since I hadn't come back home, they went to search for me. Lionel had tricked me; he walked down the road away from the mill, knowing I would see him . . . He died that night, too.

"Sometime later, we learned that Sam's first letter had been found in Lionel's house. The second was found in the road, as if it had been dropped by the person transporting the mail. We looked at the two letters—they were written in a different hand. The best that we could figure out, Penelope took the first one after Gracie had put it in dad's mail slot in the store and Lionel had written the second one knowing that your dad would go, and I'd be alone for a couple of days.

"You're wondering why I just told you all of that about Lionel, when we're supposed to be talking about Penelope?" Sabel smiled. "Well, I told you that because I always thought that the two of them were scheming together. Now that we know Janee is Penelope's daughter, I'm even more convinced. She wanted me dead because she wanted your dad. Her plan for years had been to marry him. I arrived and messed her up. I might have felt for her. I know sometimes there's something you really want, and circumstances just don't work out. But her response . . . not acceptable."

Sabel took a deep breath and a tear trickled down her cheek. She quickly swiped it away and flung her arms around me. "Oh, Mum . . . I'm so sorry."

"The morning after our wedding, your father and I were making our bed, something I know you understand was a thing, since I didn't make my bed back then." I paused and offered a smile. "When I pulled up the covers and saw a lump underneath, I reached in to pull out what I thought would be a sock or something like that. It was a woman's undergarment, and it wasn't mine. Dad had left the window open a crack when he left for the wedding. Someone came into the house after he'd left and put it into the bed. I presume I was meant to find it that night. It was meant to ruin our wedding night. It almost ruined the next morning, but I know your father, and I believed what he told me. I thought it was her then, and I still do. She came back for her daughter for whatever reason, but I want you to keep in mind what I've told you. She is *not* what she may seem."

"And you helped her when she was sick?"

"No. I'm not that kind or forgiving." I shook my head. It was true. I could have left her there to dehydrate in her own stench. "I was only there to help your father. As a doctor, he must help where he can, regardless of who and how he feels about the person."

"Hmm." I could see her thinking about that.

DarkHeart

"Mum, can I talk to you for a minute?" Sabel asked, poking her head into the bedroom. I patted a spot on the bed beside me. After closing the door behind her, she had a seat.

"Janee was talking to me today about her mother—about Penelope." She paused, taking a deep breath. "I think she's going to go with her—" Her voice cracked as she said the words. "She says she loves her parents, Rebecca and Ron, that is, but thinks she wants to get to know her real mother better."

"Oh."

"The thing is, she doesn't know that Penelope has a dark heart."

"I understand what you're feeling, honey, but this is the sort of thing she may have to learn on her own. If I told her, or even if it was Rebecca, there would always be doubt in her mind. I don't think Rebecca even knows some of the things I told you."

"I'll miss her if she goes."

I put my arm over her shoulders and pulled her in. "I know you will."

When I told Jess about my conversations with Sabel she asked, "What does she even want with that poor child? Does anyone know why she came yet?"

"Not that I'm aware of."

Lawrence and Andy left to revisit Isaac Barrett. Ben would have liked to accompany them, but as he was needed in town, he had no choice but to stay. This time, they were gone for three days. During that time, Janee spent a few hours a day with her mother. Most of this time was spent in Edmond's room, but the last day Penelope ventured outside for a walk with Janee. I could see them walking arm-in-arm from where I stood by my counter in the store, and it gave me a sick feeling in my stomach.

When Lawrence returned Friday afternoon, he told us that he approached Isaac more sternly this time. Now, the man was accused of stealing not only from Simon, whom he claimed he'd come across lying on the ground, but also from Jessica. Lawrence asked, "What a strange coincidence that both of the victims were lying on the ground at the same time that night, wouldn't you say?"

Isaac had answered, "That pin was on the ground beside the path; there was no one lying there. I took the timepiece from the man's arm, yes, but the pin I found. I did not take that from anyone."

"If I'm honest," Lawrence continued, "I believed him."

"And this man showed no signs of having been punched in the face?" I asked Lawrence. He shook his head.

"Right, so where does this leave us?" Ben asked.

Out of the corner of my eye, I saw Jess and Michael look at each other. Then Michael said, "Wait, so, not only was there more than one body lying on the ground that night, but there was more than one thief?"

"It would appear so," Lawrence answered. "But that is not the end of this strange story." He had our attention. "He did not sell the pin to a peddler."

"But Penelope said she bought it from a peddler," I said.

Lawrence offered a wry smile, "Yes. That's what she said."

"She lied?" Jessica asked.

"It would appear so. Either she or Isaac is not telling the truth."

"What do you mean?" Ben asked.

"Isaac told me that he gave the pin to Penelope, or sold it, I'm not altogether sure of that detail."

"What?" Ben and Jess asked in unison.

"Why would Penelope lie about how she got the pin?" I asked.

"A good question, Charlotte. And while the answer does nothing to help us learn what happened to Simon, it is interesting."

"Please continue, Lawrence. I would love to understand how Penelope ended up with my pin," Jessica said.

"From what Isaac has told me, some time ago, Penelope engaged him to learn the name and whereabouts of her daughter. He was here in town that Saturday for *that* purpose and as it happened, took in the poker game that night."

As none of us expected to hear this, we sat looking blankly at each other.

"So, if we believe Isaac," Ben began, "then we have learned nothing about who killed Simon. Only that whoever it was, took the stone and pin from Jessica's bag, dropping the pin as they left the scene, and placing the stone in Simon's pocket."

"That is correct," Lawrence agreed and sighed. "We're no further ahead."

After spending the night with Janee, Sabel arrived home Saturday afternoon, her eyes pink with tears. Jess and I were talking over coffee in the sitting room. "Hello, Sabel," I said. "I thought you would have gone fishing with the others. Robbie said he was going to go and invite you."

"He did."

"And you didn't want to go with them?"

"No," she said, looking to the ground.

Jess stood up from the table. "I have something I've been meaning to do upstairs, ladies. BRB."

Sabel looked at me confused. "It's short for 'be right back', love." Then I looked at Jess and added, "It's okay, Jess. You don't need to leave." She raised her eyebrows and shrugged. "What is it, Sweetheart? Come sit down. Tell us."

Sabel took a visibly deep breath before she began. "Today, Janee said she's decided she's going to leave. She wants to know her real mother. She said she knows it will hurt Rebecca, but she wants to do this for herself . . . I told her it made me sad to think of her going, and I knew her mother—and I meant Rebecca—would be very sad to see her leave. I said Rebecca is so kind and such a good mother.

"She looked at me like I'd slapped her. She said, 'I know my mother is a nice person and she loves me, but I want to know the woman that gave birth to me. I want to know if she is kind and loving, too.' I couldn't help myself, Mum. I told her she's not."

I felt the colour drain from my face. "You said that?" I asked.

"I did. But I didn't mean to, so I added 'she couldn't possibly be as nice as Rebecca.' She looked angry and turned and left me standing there. I called her back. I wanted to explain what I meant, but she didn't turn around."

I put my arm around her shoulders. "Aww, sweetie, I'm sorry. I'm sure once she's thought about it some, she'll be all right. She knows you're her friend and you care about her."

"Janee is a lovely young woman, Sabel. And smart," Jess added. "I'm sure she'll come around."

Sabel looked up. She nodded and wiped her eyes. "They're leaving Monday . . . I'm going to go upstairs. I'll be down later."

"Okay, love."

Once she'd gone, I looked at Jess sadly. "Maybe I shouldn't have told her. This is exactly what I was afraid of."

"Char, it will be fine. A good girlfriend knows a good girlfriend. This will work itself out."

"I hope so. Monday's only two days away."

When the men arrived home with the kids, they did so with three good-sized trout. Ben and Michael prepared the fish for cooking while Jess and I got to work on today's vegetables. Sabel remained quiet and I think everyone had an idea it was about Janee. I hoped when they saw each other at church in the morning they would talk it out.

Jess and I prepared breakfast as the children dressed for church. It was a cool morning, but the sun was shining. Sabel remained pensive. I offered her what I hoped was a reassuring smile as they left the house.

"I'll just wash up these mugs, and we can be on our way," I said, walking to the basin. "Looks like the door didn't close properly, Jess. Would you mind?"

"Sure." From behind me, I heard Jess exclaim, "Oh!"

I turned. There on the doorstep, sat Hazel with a freshly caught mouse in her teeth. I giggled at Jess's surprise and walked to the kitty. "What a good girl you are, Hazel. A fresh mouse for us." Once she dropped it, I patted her head and smiled as she moved closer for some lovin'. When she'd had enough praise, she walked over to the wood-burning stove and curled up for a nap.

"Eew, does she do that often?" Jess asked.

"Once in a while," I answered with a smile.

Shortly after, we walked down to my room at the store to top up my jars and Ben's supply. The men came with us: they were planning to fill the water barrels for Eli. He was feeling well enough for church, but Ben didn't want him exerting himself just yet. Then, they would return home to chop wood for the wood pile.

I closed up Ben's bag and was about to start on my own jars when I asked, "Would you like a drink, Jess?"

"I'm good for now, Char. Let's get your jars done first," she answered, smiling. "Will we be making any mixes today or—" She was interrupted by a knock on the back door. I glanced at my little clock. *Church won't have finished yet; who can this be?*

I opened the door. "Oh, Rebecca, Edmond, this is a surprise. Come on in."

"Good morning, Charlie," Rebecca started. "I hope you don't mind the intrusion, but I . . . we, had to talk to you."

"Of course. I hope you don't mind if Jessica is here?" Rebecca shook her head and smiled at Jess, but her eyes showed her weariness. "Please, heave a seat." I indicated the chairs that sat around the table. "You're not at church today."

"Thank you, Charlie," Edmond said. "No. Today we sent the girls off and thought we would take advantage and come speak to you privately."

I saw Jess look my way before I asked, "What can I do for you?"

"Well, it's not news that Penelope came to town for her daughter and that she wants to take her back home with her," Rebecca started. Jess and I watched as she dropped her chin to her chest, unable to continue.

Edmond looked from her to me and said, "It looks as though Janee wants to go with her. Not because she doesn't love her mother, Becky I mean, but because she wants to know the mother who birthed her."

I felt my mouth form a grim line. "Sabel told me. What are your thoughts?" I asked.

"To be honest," Rebecca started, "I completely understand why she would want to know the woman who gave her life. And I have encouraged her to spend time with Penelope to get to know her. She has been welcomed into our home. She has eaten with us and the whole family since she's been here. But—"

"But," Edmond interrupted, "there is more to her story than she is telling, and judging from the way I've seen you react to her, well, let me put it this way, I know that you are a good person, Charlotte, and for someone to set you off the way she does, there has to have been something bad that happened."

"Tell me, Edmond. You and she had a relationship before she left, right?" He looked at Rebecca before saying yes. "Did she strike you as a good person back then?"

His eyebrows came down as he considered his answer. "Why yes, she did. She seemed to be lonely, not many friends, unsure of herself, but ready for something new. I believed she'd had a bad relationship with Lionel, one in which he hit her."

"Did she tell you that?"

"Hmmm. No, I don't suppose she did. Now that I think on it, she admitted she'd had a relationship with Lionel when I asked. One time she flinched as I raised my hand in the air, like she thought I was going to hit her. When I asked if Lionel had hit her, she nodded."

"Did she ever mention Ben?"

"No."

"Me?"

"No, but when she told me about the baby, she was upset. I suggested she speak to you about it if she didn't want it. She was very clear you were to know nothing about it. In the end, she made me promise to tell no one. I kept that promise. When Janee arrived on the Southerns' doorstep, I thought she might have been Penelope's, but she could have been someone else's. I presume Lionel got out and saw women? One never knows."

"She used to have her cap set for Ben," Rebecca told him. "We both did. But he just wasn't interested." She smiled. "Bu—" Another knock on the door.

"Who can this be?" I asked under my breath as I headed for the door. I opened it a crack. "What are *you* doing here?" I asked, with a tone that matched my feelings.

I stepped outside pulling the door almost closed behind me. She didn't need to know who I had in my room at the moment. "What do you want, Penelope?"

"It's lovely to see you, too, Charlotte," she said with a snarl, contorting a face that used to look pretty. Having nothing to say, I stood with my arms crossed and waited for her to speak. "I must admit though, I haven't missed you. Not one bit."

"Why are you here?"

"To tell you to mind your business. It would seem your *wretched* daughter has been trying to dissuade my Janee from leaving here with me."

"She's hardly *your* Janee, is she? You didn't want her, remember? You left her on their doorstep and disappeared. You didn't even claim she was yours. I can't even imagine what lies you must have told your poor father."

"You leave my father out of this!" Her voice was getting louder as her frustration increased. "None of that matters now." She paused for a breath. "I'm here, and she's my daughter. She wants to come with me. She wants us to get to know each other better."

I chuckled sarcastically. "She *thinks* she wants to get to know you, but you won't let her *really* know you, will you? Because if she knew the truth about the things that you've done, she'd want nothing to do with you."

"You think you know things, Charlotte, but you don't." I had hit a nerve. Her face flushed.

"Don't I? You think I don't know all the nasty little messages you left me on my porch, on my doorstep, or written on my door? You think I don't know that you broke into my room and tore through my clothes, my jars, the things I had on my shelves? You think I don't know that you snuck into my house on my wedding day and placed your undergarment in my bed, so I'd think Ben was messing around? You think I don't know that you stole a letter that was written to Ben and gave it to Lionel so he would know that Ben would be out of town?" She was smiling, pleased that I knew she'd been the culprit. "You traded your body and conspired with Lionel to have me killed. You thought without me around, you could have Ben." I thought my heart would burst out of my chest, but I continued. "You know that an innocent man was killed as a result? I hope that weighs on your conscience, you bitch." I could feel my eyes narrowing and my voice getting low. I was on the verge of losing my cool.

I could see in her eyes that she was calculating her next words. "It should have been you that died that day, not Marshall. Believe me, I'm sorry about *that*." She was seething; spit was forming threads between her lips. "You came here, just strolled into town, and claimed him." Then, catching me by surprise, she slapped my face. "Ben was supposed to be mine!" Her last words came as a growl.

With my hand on my cheek, I smiled and said, "I'm sure he didn't know that."

"Maybe not, but if not for you, he would have been mine . . . in time. *MINE.* Mine to love, to marry, to make a family with. Lionel was a beast! He was brutal, but he was my way to get rid of you—you shameless trollop. You whore. Such a shame you didn't—" Before she finished her thought, the door opened behind me. Rebecca and Edmond stood in the open door, eyes wide, mouths slack, Jess behind them in similar form.

"Penelope, how could you?" Rebecca asked in words barely louder than a whisper.

"I can't believe what I just heard. I never did know ye, did I, Penny?" Edmond added.

"Edmond, I . . ." Penelope's eyes turned to mine. She was pissed. "You knew they were in there."

"You didn't ask. Besides, I didn't make you do or say anything, Penelope. Never. Now if you don't mind, actually, even if you do, get the fuck off my property!"

"Well, I—" She turned in time to see Janee coming around the corner of the building. From the look in her eyes, she'd heard the whole conversation. "Janee, honey, are you ready to leave this place?" she asked, putting on a smile and reaching for her daughter's hand.

Janee pulled her hand away, looking at the woman in disgust. "I can't believe you would do any of those things. But you did them *all* didn't you? You almost made a fool out of me." Janee paused then and shook her head. "You are evil. I was wrong to think anything different." Her eyes found her mother's for a moment before she continued. "You should leave this town, Penelope, and never come back. This town doesn't need the likes of you."

The colour in Penelope's cheeks drained completely. She stood for a moment, fighting back tears. It had all been for nothing.

She turned back to the path, but we didn't watch her leave. Janee clung to Rebecca, hugging her as tears ran down her cheeks. "I'm so sorry, Mama. I'm sorry I hurt you."

Rebecca kissed the top of her head and hugged Janee back. "I'm fine, love. I'm sorry you had to hear that."

Janee looked up at her mother and smiled. "I'm not. I was starting to feel like there was something she wasn't telling me. When I saw her leave church early, I did, too. I followed her. I'm glad I did." Then she turned to me. "Charlotte, I'm sorry for those horrid things she did to you and your friend. It's hard to imagine her father was a man of God."

"Thank you, Janee. I'm glad you know the truth, even though it hurts. I'm also glad you're going to stay, and I know someone else who will be, too."

Her eyes opened wide. "Sabel!" she exclaimed. "Mama, I've got to find her. I need to apologize."

Rebecca smiled, happy tears shining in her eyes, and said, "Off you go, love."

Jess came to stand beside me and slid her arm around my back. "That went well," she said.

I couldn't help but giggle. "Well, at least we all understand what she did and what she's capable of."

"True. Any questions I may have had have been answered," Rebecca said, smiling up at Edmond. "Tomorrow, we can get your room cleaned up."

His eyes sparkled as he looked down into hers and winked. "Even though I won't be using it much anymore."

An Injury

"Have you got any new gossip this morning, Gracie?" I asked as we sat to eat.

She gave me a wink. "Well, there's almost always somethin', eh? Hmm, let's see. The preacher told us this mornin' that he'll be with us another week only. Seems *our* preacher will be returning to town. Looks like you'll get to meet them after all, Jessica."

"Oh, yay!" Jess said.

"Oh, and Ian Mainer's back in town. I heard he got in last evening."

"So, he will only just have learned of Simon's death. That will be a shock for him."

"I expect so," Gracie agreed.

"Was he at church?"

"No. Nor Geoff neither. Edna was, though we didna spik."

After we'd finished lunch, oops, dinner, we headed for the canoes, with the exception of Sabel, who was spending the afternoon with Janee, and Robbie who wanted to stay home and do some reading.

Before we were even at their door, Mitenah and Dark Wolf were outside, pulling on their coats, ready to usher the kids away for a walk on the beach.

We arrived cool, ready for a warm drink. As Gifted Hands took our coats, Kohana came to see what new ankles she could snuggle around. "Hello," I said, sitting on the settee.

When Jessica came to sit beside me, Kohana jumped up onto her lap. "Well, hello there," she said and patted her head.

"Kohana is one of Hazel's kittens. She was born when we were in Scotland; my little friend Running Cub wrote to me to ask if he could have her."

"Aww. So, she's how old now?"

109

"She's nine."

"Yikes! That was nine years ago for you, but only one year ago for me. Still weird, right?"

"Oh, yes," Gifted Hands agreed.

Jess told everyone how impressed she'd been with my reaction to Penelope. Gracie had been shocked that Penelope had actually come to my door and was disappointed she hadn't been there.

"What is it with Penelope?" Gifted Hands asked. "Does she not know that the people she's been fooling are learning who she really is?"

"Well, I think she knows that now!" I said happily. "What comes around, goes around. We all have to deal with the consequences of our actions eventually."

"Aye. She may well be damned for her loathsome behavior," Gracie said seriously.

"You mean eternal punishment?" I asked. "Hmm, as good as that sounds, I don't believe that. I just hope she gets what she deserves and is a better person next time around." Jess nodded her agreement, but I could see the others had to think about what I meant. "Now, please . . . let's talk about something else."

"How is your p—" Gracie started.

"En-ay, En-ay, it's Dark Wolf! He's hurt!" Mitenah called, bustling in the door.

"What has happened?" Gifted Hands and Keen Wolf asked together, jumping out of their seats.

"We were running and jumping to see who could jump higher. Then he fell to the ground with his hand on his belly. He said it hurt too much to get up."

We were all running for the door. As Ben bent to pick up his bag, he said, "Mitenah, you should stay here. Maybe Gracie can stay with you." Looking at both of the ladies, he continued, "Please put another pot of water on the fire and get some towels—we may need to lie him down."

"Aye. Off ye go."

We found Dark Wolf lying in the fetal position, surrounded by the other children. When they saw us running toward them, they all started shouting at the same time. Keen Wolf arrived first and dropped down beside his son. He said, "Too many voices. Dark Wolf, please tell us what happened."

His sweaty pallor was immediately noticeable; his arms cradled his belly. "I was jumping. Feels like something inside split. It hurts. It hurts." He answered on the verge of tears.

Ben was at his side now. "Dark Wolf, do you think you can straighten your legs so I can see where it hurts?" he asked gently.

The boy tried, but it hurt too much. Keen Wolf turned to Ben and said, "We should take him to the house. There we can make him comfortable and look at him." He didn't wait for Ben to answer. Instead, he scooped his son into his arms and began to walk back to the house.

Jessica walked beside Ben and me. She said quietly, "It sounds like a hernia."

"I agree," Ben said. "We will know better when we examine him."

Gifted Hands kept up with us but walked quietly.

The group clamoured into the house, kicking off their boots. "Lay 'im here. There's lots o' room," Gracie said, indicating the dining table. They had layered towels over it to cushion Dark Wolf as he lay. Keen Wolf and Gifted Hands removed his coat and boots, and then he was laid on the table. While the others got comfortable in the sitting room, Ben lifted Dark Wolf's long shirt to expose his abdomen and began to gently prod the area with his fingers.

"It's lower," Dark Wolf moaned. "Here." He pointed to an area under his breechcloth.

Ben undid the belt holding the cloth and lowered it slightly. He turned to look at me. There was a small bulge down low on his abdomen, on his left side. "Definitely a hernia," Ben said to no one in particular.

He explained what that meant to the boy's parents. "The only way to fix it is to do a small surgical repair," he said. Gifted Hands looked at her husband and nodded.

"If that is what we must do, do it, Ben," said Keen Wolf. "How can we help?"

Ben smiled and said, "Actually all you can do is be patient, my friend. I have two wonderful helpers with me today. Surgery is what Jessica does at home, and you know Charlotte knows her stuff."

Ben turned and looked at the blank faces of the others in the sitting room. "I think it would be best if you all did something outside for a while and gave us some space."

"Aye. We'll do that, Ben," Jimmy said. "Coats on everyone—outside we go."

"Here's your bag, Ben." I set it on the table. "I'll make a wash to cleanse the area."

"Thanks. Jessica, will you take out my surgical tools while I give him some laudanum, please?" She nodded.

I passed her his bag with a wink. "You're up, Jess."

Gifted Hands stood beside me while I prepared a lavender wash. She looked scared. I gave her hand a squeeze and said, "He'll be fine, I promise. Maybe you can get the white willow from Ben's bag, and we can start a tea for Dark Wolf to drink afterwards." She nodded and poured some water into a small pot.

As I cleaned the area where the incision would be made, Ben and Jessica washed their hands. Then Ben looked down into the young man's terrified face and spoke softly. "This will hurt a bit, but it will only take a few minutes. All right?" Dark Wolf nodded. Ben looked at Gifted Hands and asked, "En-ay, would you like to hold his hand?" She grasped it immediately. Then Ben looked at Jess and asked, "Ready?"

"Ready," she answered before smiling down at Dark Wolf.

Ben and Jessica worked together cutting the skin just above the crease in Dark Wolf's groin and opening the incision. I unwrapped the previously sterilized and threaded needle and waited for Ben to ask for it. He gently tucked the small bulge beneath the muscle tissue and looked at me for the needle.

Within minutes, the surgery was complete, and the wound was neatly stitched. Once again, I cleansed the area, and once it had dried, Ben covered it with a bandage. Dark Wolf's eyes were glossy with a combination of laudanum, fear, and discomfort. "We're finished," Ben told him.

Dark Wolf exhaled deeply and closed his eyes. The next minute, he let out a little snore. This brought a smile to both his en-ay and kree-ay.

"I will put him into his bed," Keen Wolf said, before slipping his arms under the boy's neck and knees. Gifted Hands walked ahead of him to fold down the covers.

I looked at Ben and Jess and smiled. "That was a once in a lifetime, guys!"

"Yeah. I'm glad I was able to be a part of it. Thanks, Ben."

"No, thank you."

When Gifted Hands and Keen Wolf returned, Ben told them to have a seat. "All we did was repair a small tear in the muscle. He will be fine. But he will be quite sore for two or three days." They listened carefully while he gave them instructions for how to deal with the wound.

"He needs to heal on the inside as well as the outside so it's important he get his nutrients," I started. "For at least the first day, he should have liquids— meat and vegetable broth, juice, tea. Then soft foods like soup, mashed vegetables, particularly carrots and squash, or cooked and mashed fruits for a day. After that, he can eat whatever he likes." I smiled. "As for teas, I would recommend white willow for the first couple of days for pain and inflammation, lemon balm will help his appetite and help him rest, and echinacea will help boost his immune system. You can add basil or dill to anything for some extra vitamins. What have I missed?" I asked.

"What about some kind of antibiotic?" Jessica asked.

"Yes. To anything you can, add garlic, thyme, oregano, lavender, or honey to help prevent infection."

Keen Wolf was looking at me blankly. I couldn't help but smile. "Should I write it down?"

"I think you should, Charlotte. Thank you," Gifted Hands answered.

The others came quietly back into the house a few minutes later.

Jess put on some coffee and milk to warm, while I made sure Gifted Hands had the herbs she would need for the next week. When Ben finished wrapping up his instruments, he came to where we stood. "I would leave him to rest for today, but tomorrow you can encourage him to get up and walk just a little bit. He'll be sore, but it will help him heal. Then he can gradually walk a little more every day. No heavy lifting. Also, keep the area dry and covered for a few days, until I come back and have a look."

She turned and hugged him. "Thank you, Ben," she said. "Thank you all."

There were many questions as we rowed back home. The children were amazed at what had transpired today—to know what their father/uncle had done was something they wouldn't soon forget.

When I came downstairs this morning, I saw Jessica was already up and looking out the front window. "Morning, Char. Look! Our first snow in 1834." She smiled as I walked toward her.

"It looks so pretty, doesn't it?" I asked.

"Jeez, you remember the fun we used to have in the snow when we were little? Oh, good morning, Ben," she said, seeing him coming down the stairs. "We used to have snowball fights, make snowmen, build forts and quinzhees. God, it was fun being a kid."

"Quin-what?" he asked, looking confused.

"A quinzhee. You make a big pile of snow and shape it into a dome, then you hollow it out like a cave."

"Ahh, like a cave," he said and smiled.

"You mean to say you and Michael don't play in the snow?" I asked her. I immediately felt myself blush as I noticed Ben smirk.

"No, not really. Although occasionally I get him with a snowball. But I don't really like it when he gets me back."

"Then you're not doing it right," I giggled and elbowed her in the ribs. "Ready for some coffee?"

Only a few minutes later, we were on our way to the store. Although there was a sprinkling of snow covering the ground, it didn't feel very cold. It was unlikely this snow would be here for long.

The bells over the door rang soon after Gracie opened the store. "Well, good mornin', Edna," Gracie said. "I hear ye've Ian back home wi' ye. Ye must be pleased."

"Oh, yes. That I am. And so is Geoff. He's missed the extra hands in the shop."

Edna turned to me. "Charlotte, Jessica, good morning. Ian's had trouble sleeping. Of course, he didn't learn about Simon until he got home on Saturday. He's beside himself with guilt. Thinks if he'd been here, things might have been different. I can see dark circles under his eyes. I've come hoping to get some more of that tea mixture you made for me."

"Of course." I glanced down at my jars. "Hmm. I don't have the mixture made up at the moment. Can I bring it over to you this afternoon?"

She nodded. "He won't need it until tonight. Thank you." With that, she put some coins on the counter and left the store.

"We can take a little walk over at lunch," I said to Jess.

Just before our noon break, I took out the lavender, chamomile, and valerian for Edna's mix. "Oo-oo, let me," Jess said with a smile. "How many days?"

"I think three will do."

She added the herbs to a bowl, mixed and mashed them up before putting it all into a small jar. "Done," she said, handing me the jar.

After eating with Gracie, the three of us walked to Edna's house behind the wainwright shop. Edna opened the door immediately. "Oh, my, you've all come. Good afternoon."

"Here's Ian's tea. I hope it—"

"Did I hear my name?" I heard an unfamiliar voice ask, before a man crossed my field of view.

"Ya did. I asked Charlotte to make you up a tea so you can get a better sleep tonight."

He stood in profile as he took the jar from Edna. "Why, thank you," he said with a nod before walking away.

"Hopefully that'll help him some," Edna said. "You haven't seen our dog anywhere, have you? I haven't seen him since Lawrence and Ben brought poor Simon home."

"No, but we'll be sure to tell ye if we do," Gracie answered.

Walking back to the store, Gracie was the first to speak. "She wasna wrong about the dark circles under his eyes."

"I did see that, but I didn't see his full face," I said.

"Aye. He wasn't for chitchat."

When I mentioned our visit to Ben later in the day, he said that Lawrence planned to visit the man this evening to discuss Simon's death. "In fact, he asked me to accompany him."

Ben came through the door around eight o'clock that evening, and he wasn't alone. "Lawrence, it's good to see you. Come on in," I said, wondering why he would have returned here with Ben. "We were just about to sit down for some tea. Would you like some?"

"That sounds good, Charlotte. Thank you."

Ben took his coat and the men joined Jess and Michael in the sitting room while I poured out two more cups of tea. I set the tray on the table in front of the settee. "So, what's the news?"

Lawrence lifted his hand to Ben. "Edna invited us in, and we all sat down. Larry expressed his condolences to Ian, saying it must have been quite a shock to come home to this news. Ian agreed. Said he didn't understand what could have happened. Simon was a gentle sort."

Lawrence continued. "Ian told us he left town in the early evening of the night Simon was killed. He said neither Edna or Simon were home at the time, only Geoff. He assumed Simon went to the tavern since Edna wasn't home to tell him not to."

"So, when was the last time he saw him?" Michael asked.

"He said Edna had left them food cooking over the fire, and they'd eaten together. Then Simon told them he was going to pay a visit to Edmond," Lawrence said. "Geoff said something to him like, 'don't lose the shop, old man' as he left. He knew full well what Simon would be doing at the tavern."

"In fact, he sounded angry just telling us about it," Ben added.

"I asked Edna if Simon often gambled and lost. Her answer was, 'he didn't gamble often, and he didn't win.'"

"I had a good look at Ian, remembering that Edna said he hadn't been sleeping and had dark circles under his eyes."

"And?" Jess asked.

"He did, one side was darker than the other."

"I thought that, too," Lawrence added, glancing at Ben.

"Then, as we stood to leave, the light from the fire caught something on the table by the door. It was crystal I think, about two inches tall and one across. It had some little silver flowers standing inside it." Ben looked at Jessica before continuing. "Jess, could you please show Lawrence that hair pin you brought?"

Her eyes found mine briefly and then she went up to the bedroom to get it. When she returned, she put it into Lawrence's hand. "This is interesting. I believe you're right, Ben. This is definitely part of the set we saw there."

"Did you ask about them?" Michael asked.

"I commented that the trinket looked pretty," Ben answered. "Edna smiled and said that Ian had given it to her when he returned home." Jess stood with her mouth slightly open, eyes round. "When I asked Ian where he'd found them, he answered that he'd seen them in a shop window in Cayuga."

"What?" Jess and I asked in unison.

"So, what do we think happened here? Do you think what he said is true? Could Isaac have taken these, too, and sold them to a shopkeeper?" Michael asked.

"I suppose he could have. But in all honesty, I believe what he told me to be true. I don't think he took anything from Jessica."

"The only trail we have right now leads to Ian?" Ben asked.

"It would appear so. I will return tomorrow and ask the name of the shop he found them in. Phoebe would have a nice place to put those . . . what are they, Jessica?" Lawrence asked. She took the one he was holding and after moving a section of her hair from front to back, secured it by pushing in the pin. "Ah. I see."

He smiled. "Well, I'll be off. I'll find you tomorrow, Ben, and I'll let you know what shop we will visit next."

The next day was quite chilly, although yesterday's snow had disappeared. Inside the store was nice and cozy; Jimmy had been keeping the wood-burning stove well supplied. It was almost lunch time when Lawrence walked into the store. "Morning, ladies. Do you know where I might find your husband?" he asked me.

I smiled and answered, "I do," just before the bells rang again and Ben and Michael stepped in. Lawrence glanced around the store and, seeing that Gracie was with a customer, asked if we could talk somewhere. I ushered them into my room and went to the kitchen to ask Mabel to come out so Gracie could join us.

"So, I visited the Mainer brothers just now. They were surprised to see me I suppose. I explained that I'd come to ask Ian in what shop he found those pins in Cayuga. I told him I'd like to find something similar for my wife. He seemed surprised at my request but answered quickly. He said, 'Ah, it was Duffy's on Genesee, or hmm, maybe it was McGuire's.' Then I thanked him and was on my way."

"What now?" Ben asked.

"Well, if I'm not mistaken, the man either got those pins in Cayuga or he took them from Jessica's bag. If he got them from a shop, I will know soon enough. I will travel there later today. However, if he did not, then we have more to consider."

"Such as?" Gracie asked.

"Well, if he took them from Jessica, did he also take the cloak pin and the stone? It stands to reason that one person took all of the items."

"But the stone was in Simon's pocket," I said, not liking where this was going.

"Precisely," he said with a nod.

Just then my belly let out a loud grumble. I felt the heat in my cheeks as everyone turned to look at me. I shrugged. "Thank goodness it's time for dinner," I said with an embarrassed grin.

"Would ye care to join us for a bite, Larry?" Gracie asked, heading for the back door.

"Oh, no, thank you, Gracie. My own meal will be waiting for me at home. I'll follow you out this way, though," he answered.

We stepped outside and, after saying goodbye to Lawrence, headed straight into the kitchen. It was only a minute later when the kitchen door opened, and Lawrence stuck his head in. "When I got to the path, I saw Ian passing on his horse. He was headed north. Andy and I will follow. I will find you when we return."

It was the following evening, Tuesday, just after seven o'clock, when Jessica said, "I hope the weather stays this good for the meteor showers, Char. Never thought we'd have the chance to watch together again."

"Fingers crossed," I answered. "But you know, the showers at this time of year aren't what we had at home in December. We've seen some, but they're not as impressive now for some reason."

There was a knock at the door. "I'll get it," said Michael. "Hello, Lawrence," he said, standing back from the door.

"Good evening. I've brought Jimmy and Gracie, as you can see. I would like everyone to hear what I learned."

"Come on in," I said as Ben collected their coats. "Warm drink?"

"No. Thank you. "

"Have a seat, Larry," Ben said.

He sat and started talking immediately. "This last trip was very interesting. Andy and I followed Ian all the way to Cayuga yesterday. He didn't stop until he arrived at Duffy's General Store. He was inside for nearly ten minutes, and when he came out, the shopkeeper, presumably Duffy, turned the sign in the door. He was closing up. Andy and I looked at each other; it would have to wait until morning. Ian came out of the shop, looked around briefly before getting back on his horse. Leaving a respectable distance between us, we followed him for a few minutes. He left the main road, meandered down a laneway, and stopped at a door we later realized belonged to a milliner named McGuire. He stood outside knocking for several minutes before he was let in and returned to his horse only five minutes later. At this point, I expected he would go to the inn or the tavern, but no. He rode back toward Aurelius. I didn't want to follow him too far, because it was my intention to visit those shops in the morning. But then he stopped in front of a row house and went in. After a minute or two, he and another gentleman stepped outside and walked to the tavern down the road. I rather expected he would be in there for the night, but to our surprise, Ian came out only an hour later and got on his horse."

"Yes, he was in the shop when I walked by earlier today," Ben said.

"Well, by this time, Andy and I were hungry and tired. We went in and had some supper." He paused and smiled. "Andy is becoming quite the investigator. He bumped into the man Ian had accompanied into the tavern and while apologizing, inquired about a place to stay. After he recommended an inn down the road, Andy invited him to join us for an ale."

"You don't say," Ben said, eager for what would come next.

"To get to the point, this man, Harry was his name, told us that he'd come in with an acquaintance of his, Ian, who'd been passing through town. He'd already had several ales, so information came easily. They had met several years ago when Ian had been in town, and every time he passed through, they would spend some time at the tavern together. Here's where it gets interesting . . ." Lawrence stopped talking to be sure we were all listening.

"Harry said that mid-November, Ian came into town and stayed for two or three weeks. He wasn't certain why he was there, or even how he spent his time while he was there; he only knew that he'd been in a scuffle early on, as he had a blackened eye. Each night they met for an ale or two, until a few days ago, when

Ian told him he was returning home. Said he had to get back and help his brother at work. Harry was surprised to see him again today."

"Did he tell Harry why he was back?" I asked.

"Told him he'd forgotten to pay Richard Duffy for something—he's the owner of the general store in Cayuga."

"Interesting," Michael said to himself.

"I said I was going to get to the point." Lawrence shook his head before continuing. "Andy went home the next morning, and I returned to the two shops we'd seen Ian go into. Mr. Duffy showed me the hair pins he had in the store. They were nothing like Jessica's. When I described what I was looking for, he told me that Ian had been in the day before asking the same questions. He also said he'd never seen anything like what I was describing and had certainly never sold any. Then I went to see Adam McGuire, the milliner. This man was altogether a different sort. I inquired about pins, and he showed me his small selection—he sold hats, but often pins were required to hold the hat or the hair under the hat. At any rate, there was nothing like what I was looking for. I pulled Jessica's pin out to show him, explaining I'd like something like this. His surprise showed for a moment. Then he took it into his hand, and while examining it, told me he'd sold a set almost exactly like it a while ago, to a man from out of town."

"Did you believe 'im?" Gracie asked.

"I did not. I said, 'Let me ask you this. Did this man come in and buy these pins? Or did this man come in, say yesterday, and ask you to say he did?' I watched him as he listened to my words. 'Did Ian give you money to say you had sold him the pins?' His complexion turned ashen. I knew then. I told him who I was and that these pins were related to a death that I was investigating. He was in no way implicated, I simply needed to know where the man had picked up the pins. At this, he let out a deep breath and admitted that he had been given money in exchange for his story."

"So, you're saying that Ian did not purchase those pins?" Jimmy asked.

"That means . . ." Jess started.

"I think it does," I continued.

Hair Pins

The next morning, Ben, Jessica, and Michael waited for Lawrence in the store's kitchen. Mabel knew what was happening, as did Hettie and Eli. When Lawrence arrived, the group left to go speak to Ian.

Gracie and I opened the store, taking turns peeking out the window down the road. I was surprised when Edna came in. "Charlotte," she said as she approached my counter. Her face was flushed, her eyes panicked. "Do either of you know what is happening across the road?"

"What do ye mean, Edna?" Gracie asked.

"I mean Lawrence, Ben, and your friends went into the shop this morning to speak privately with Ian. Lawrence asked me to leave for the time being. Why would I have to leave my own shop? Why are your friends there? What is happening?" She was becoming more distressed by the minute.

Gracie looked at me as I tried to think how to answer her. "Well, I believe it has to do with some items of Jessica's that went missing."

"I don't understand," she said.

Gracie spoke next. "Ye see, somethin' of Jessica's was seen in your home, Edna."

"Huh? What would that be? And what does it have to do with Ian?"

Turning to my friend, I said, "Let's get Mabel out here, Gracie, so you and I can walk over with Edna." She nodded and disappeared into the kitchen.

Mabel came out not a minute later, and Gracie and I got into our coats. We walked to the wainwright shop slowly and tried to prepare Edna for what was coming. "Well?" she asked, clearly frustrated.

"Um, well you remember those pins Ian gave you when he came home? The ones with the flowers on top? I believe you put them into a sma—"

"Yes, yes, I know what you're speaking of. What about them?"

"When Jessica and Michael arrived, it was the same night as Simon . . ."

"The night he died?" she asked.

"Yes. You see, when my friends arrived that night, Jessica fell in the dark and dropped her bag. Someone took several items from her bag while she lay on the ground."

"And?" Edna pressed.

"And those hair pins were gifts Jessica had brought for Gracie and me. She brought four with her, and when she tried to find them to give them to us, there was only one. She has it with her now."

"And you think it was Ian who took them?"

"He's the one who gave them to you, Edna, aye?"

Edna was quiet as we approached the wainwright shop. We could see no one inside as we walked around to the back door. There, we could hear their voices through the door and stood outside momentarily.

"So, you admit that you took the hair pins from this woman as she lay on the ground?" Lawrence was saying. "Now, what about the cloak pin and the blue stone?" Edna looked at me, eyes wide, instantly aware of the significance of the question. We could not hear a reply.

"She was lying on the ground beside her bag. I assume you didn't see Michael there as well?" Ben asked.

"Not until he dragged me up and swung at me," Ian answered.

"And you hit him in return. His face was bruised until recently. I must assume yours was as well." We could hear nothing.

Edna looked like she was about to speak, and I put my finger up over my lips, *sh-sh*.

"So let me understand. Geoff told us that you left early that evening. You were headed for Buffalo to see a lawyer, was it? So, how is it that we now know you were still here at midnight? Geoff? . . . Ian?"

Edna pushed the door open and entered the room. All eyes turned to her as Gracie and I stood behind her. "What did you boys do? Why did you mislead us all?"

"Edna, you should leave," Geoff said.

"I think not." She stood firm, raising her hands to her hips. "Now, you'd better tell us what happened and why it's come to this?"

Lawrence turned from Edna back to Ian. "Did you or did you not also take the cloak pin and the stone?"

Ian's eyes flicked to his brother's before he answered. "Cloak pin?"

"Yes, it was also taken, only it was dropped somewhere on the ground between Ben's house and the road up the hill." Ian looked at his feet. It was obvious he didn't know where to go from here.

"Stone?" Ian's voice cracked.

"The one we found in Simon's pocket, yes."

"It was also missing from my bag," Jessica added.

In that moment, something came together for Edna. "You didn't try to help a woman you found lying on the ground in the dark? Instead, you stole from her? What in the name of God were you thinking, Ian?"

"I don't suppose I was, Edna."

"And my poor Simon?" Her voice wobbled as she said his name. "What of him?"

Once again, a glance was exchanged between the brothers. "When I came down the hill, I found him lying on the side of the road. I tried to shake 'im, figured he'd had one too many ales and fallen down. I stuck the stone in 'is pocket for luck, and—"

"And left 'im lyin' there?" Edna asked.

Ian's mouth formed a tight line. He was walking a tightrope.

"Okay, wait," Jessica couldn't take it any longer. "What were you even doing up there by Ben and Charlotte's house in the middle of the night?"

Ian stared at Jessica for a long moment before he began. "I'd been talkin' to Geoff when there was a thundering bang and a bright flash of light. It came from up the hill."

Geoff nodded his agreement, adding, "Only it wasn't thunder and lightning."

"I ran up there to see what had happened. When I got there, I saw her lying on the ground in the rain." He pointed at Jess. "There were things spilling out of her bag onto the ground. I bent down to see what they were and couldn't help myself. I had just put them into my pocket when someone grabbed me from behind and lifted me. I hadn't seen him there, and I swung at him. After he swung back, I ran. I ran back down the hill to where I'd left Geoff, only he wasn't there. He'd returned home."

"Was I supposed to stand waiting in the rain?" he asked, annoyed.

Ian glared at him.

"So," Lawrence began, "the two of you were standing together at the bottom of the hill that night at midnight? Whatever for?"

The room was quiet as we awaited an answer. Then Edna said, "Boys? What the devil were you doing out there in the rain at that time of night? And where was Simon?"

"Hmm, well, he was there," Geoff said.

"What?" several voices asked at once.

Again, the brothers looked at each other before Geoff said, "We were out on the road talkin', me and Ian, when Simon came past after the game."

"You were out on the road? In the rain? At midnight?" Lawrence asked.

Ian, who'd been looking at his feet, looked up at Lawrence. "Mm-hm. Ya see, we knew he was gamblin'. We'd asked him many times to stop playin' with money we needed for the business." As Edna listened, her cheeks were pinking.

"He was surprised to see us waitin' there. I said, 'How many times have we all asked ya not to spend our hard-earned money, Simon? As soon as Edna goes away for a day or two, you're off losin' it,'" Geoff said.

"He told us he'd won some money. Put his hand in his pocket and took out a handful of coins. Proud of himself, he was," Ian said. "Then he turned angry and said, 'I'm not a child, boys, and you ain't my mama. Move on. I'm ready for my bed.' And he shoved me. I shoved 'im back."

Geoff said, "Then he took a swing at me. He missed, but mine hit him."

"That's when we heard the bang and saw the flash. I left them and ran up toward it."

"After Ian left, I walked home, left Simon holdin' 'is head. That was the last time I saw 'im," Geoff said.

"Ian?" Lawrence said, turning to the other man.

"I told ya, I picked up a few items that had fallen on the ground, got punched, and then went back down the hill. When I got to the bottom of the hill, Simon was lying there. I must have dropped the cloak pin you spoke of, but I stuck the stone in his pocket for good luck, as I said, and went home."

"For good luck, or so he'd be blamed for stealing from Jessica?" Edna asked angrily.

Ian had no answer. "Well, when I awoke and he hadn't come in, I woke Geoff, and we went out to find 'im." Geoff sat down heavily on the stool at the workbench. "The sun had yet to come up, so we didn't see him right away. Then we saw him, where I'd left 'im, lying there, soaked with rain." I heard a sob from Edna and put my arm around her shoulders. "We tried to rouse him but . . . he was gone. We panicked and dragged 'im up the hill a ways and left him."

"You mean to say, you left poor Simon there on the ground in the rain to die and to then be blamed for stealing?" There were tears in her eyes as the brothers lowered their heads.

"You left that morning so we wouldn't see your blackened eye, is that it?" Lawrence asked. Ian only looked back at him. "Did you, in fact, visit a lawyer while you were away?" He would use what he'd learned while investigating now. "Did you go spend some time in Aurelius and communicate with your brother with letters and a visit or two?"

Both men appeared surprised that Lawrence knew this. "We didn't know what to do," Ian said.

"Poor Simon," Edna said with a wobble in her voice. "The poor man. He gave you his winnings, and you killed him. I no longer know you." She turned and spoke to Lawrence next. "Please come see me when you've dealt with these two, so I can get matters in order."

Lawrence nodded as she left the building. "It's just as well you didn't know about the timepiece he'd won that night, or we might never have got to the bottom of all this." The men looked at each other briefly, regret written all over their faces—for not treating Simon better or for getting caught, I couldn't tell. "Now, I'll have you gentlemen come with me to the gaol while we determine what to do with you. Ben, would you mind accompanying me?"

They returned to the store, shocked at the turn of events. I felt for Edna; the men she had trusted all her life had caused her husband's death. Whether it was deliberate made little difference in this case.

She came into the store only a few minutes later and approached me and Jessica where we stood behind the counter. "Jessica, I believe these belong to you," she said, handing her the three hair pins. "I'm sorry for what my brothers did."

Jessica walked around to the front of the counter. "I am, too, Edna. I'm so sorry," she said and embraced her.

"I expect I'll get the word out that the wainwright shop is for sale and move on . . . somewhere."

"If there's anything we can do to help, please let us know," I said softly. "Has your dog come home?"

"No. I don't expect he will. He knows Simon's gone." With a slight frown, Edna nodded and left the store.

Ben arrived in time to share dinner with Jess, Michael, Gracie, and me. "Well, that was a turn I didn't see coming," I started.

"Aye," Gracie agreed grimly. "So, what will you do this afternoon?"

"I'd like to check on Dark Wolf," Ben answered.

"We can all go," I added.

We only stayed long enough for Ben to check Dark Wolf's incision and to share a warm drink. The stitches looked good, and there was no sign of infection. The bandage was taken off, and the wound was cleaned with a lavender wash. Ben told them he would return in four or five days to remove the stitches. Dark Wolf paled at the words, but Ben assured him it wouldn't hurt. "I want you to take things slowly for the next while. No running or jumping or lifting until after Yule. We don't want to have to do all of this again." The boy nodded his agreement and Ben looked at his parents to be sure everyone understood.

Yule

During the week that followed, Edna, with help from Hank and Lawrence, packed up a cart and prepared to leave town. Lawrence purchased the house and shop so that she could buy a home elsewhere; he would sell them to the town's next wainwright. We were surprised to hear one morning soon after that Edna had left in the night. She didn't say goodbye and told no one where she was going. As for the Mainer brothers, they were taken to Auburn and left to be dealt with by the justice system. I never heard of them again.

Ben and Michael rowed across the lake Tuesday morning to check on Dark Wolf and remove his stitches. Ben informed me that the wound looked good, and he had reminded Dark Wolf to take things slowly. Dark Wolf crinkled up his nose at hearing that he shouldn't run around, but Ben reassured him that it was only for a couple of more weeks.

The meteor showers didn't pan out; even if there had been something to see, the night skies had been cloudy for days on end. On the bright side, Jess and I still had something to look forward to. We started planning our once-in-a-lifetime Yule ritual—it had to be perfect.

My family had become accustomed to me celebrating the Sun, the Moon, the Earth, and the sabbats. They understood that my beliefs were a little different from what they were learning in church, and although they frequently asked questions, and we often went back and forth with our differing ideas, they understood we were all allowed our own beliefs. I celebrated on my own every year, and that was the way I liked it.

This year, when I celebrated the winter solstice, I would NOT be alone. This year, Jess and I would prepare an altar together. We would compose the words of our ritual together. And we would sit and speak to the Goddess and God together.

We were working in the store when the coach stopped out front with the town mail. The driver came in with a bright smile and placed the sac, laden with notes and letters, in front of Gracie. "Oh me, but there's a lot of mail here today. Thank ye, Tommy." He emptied the contents onto the counter before leaving with a wave.

Gracie started to sort the mail into the slots on the wall near the kitchen door. "Oo-oo, Charlie, this is for you, lass."

"Who's it from?" I asked.

She squinted at the name scribbled on the back. "Looks like it's from Ronnie."

After tearing open the top, I gave Jess a wink. "It looks like we'll have some holly for our altar." I smiled, remembering my friend. "Ronnie, well, her name is Veronica, is the English girl I met when I was in Scotland. She was staying at Slains at the time."

"She's not anymore?" Jess asked.

"No, she and Ewen, he is the castle's groom, have a little cabin a short distance from the castle, with a view of the North Sea. Anyway, she also celebrates as we do, and every year since I was there, she sends me some holly and mistletoe in December. I usually add it into my wreath, but first I use it to decorate my altar."

Jess smiled. "That's perfect! Holly is said to ward off evil spirits, is that right?"

"Yes. They also say that holly leaves brought inside during the winter offer faeries shelter from the cold; they will then be kind to those who live there."

Jess smiled. "Fun!" she said.

At home, I put the package together with the red and green candles Jess had brought. It all went into the small chest I keep in the bedroom cupboard to be used for Yule.

The weather over the past couple of weeks had chilled right down—it was Christmas weather. I was pleased that we had extra coats and footwear for Jess and Michael to use, because they needed it, especially today. Overnight, about three inches of snow had fallen.

This year, I wanted to have the family at our home on Christmas day. On Christmas Eve, we would visit Gifted Hands and Keen Wolf. There was food preparation to do and some decorating, because I'm me and I love Christmas decorations.

On the day before Yule, Jess and I returned home from the store mid-afternoon to find our Christmas tree set up in the sitting room. "Oh!" Jess exclaimed. "I didn't expect such a big tree." She smiled at the men who stood by the dining table waiting to be noticed. "It's a good thing you two are in such good shape!" She offered them a wink.

"It's perfect, guys. Thank you," I said. "Jess, are you ready to decorate?"

"Sure? What about the kids? Don't they like to help?"

"They used to when they were younger, but now, it's mostly just me."

"Right then. Let's get to it!" she said happily.

"But first, a tree blessing," I reminded her, heading to the kitchen. I returned with a bowl of salt and set my watering can on the floor, near the tree.

"Should we do a short one or a long one?" I asked.

"I want to immerse myself thoroughly in this Yule, Char. Let's go long."

"In that case, let's get a candle burning as well," I said.

Then I walked slowly around the tree, sprinkling salt at its base, while Jess followed with a burning candle. "By the powers of Earth, I bless this tree," I began, "that it remains a sacred symbol of life through the days of Yule."

Jess continued, "By the powers of Air, I bless this tree. As the cooler gusts of winter blow away the hindrances of the old year, we welcome a new bright year into our hearts."

"By the powers of Fire, I bless this tree. As the days have grown shorter and the nights darker, the sun returns, bringing warmth and light."

"By the powers of Water, I bless this tree." As Jess said the final words of ritual, I reached for the watering can and slowly let some water trickle into the small barrel the tree sat within. "I give this gift, that it will remain bright and green for us, and we can enjoy the peace and harmony Yule brings." As she said her final words, Jess turned to look at me with shining eyes.

After returning the watering can to the kitchen, I opened the box of decorations that Ben had set out for me. Smiling at my friend, I said, "Let's decorate this beautiful tree."

"Wow, you've accumulated quite a few decorations, Char."

"I have. Remember these?" I showed her the pair of little snowmen I had taken home after our time spent in 2013.

She laughed. "I do. These are pretty. Where did you get these?" she asked, holding up a couple of tin stars.

"Ben had a friend make them along with a tree topper our first Christmas together. His name was Walter. He was a sweet man."

"Aww. Well, he did lovely work."

I saw Ben smile as he remembered his father's friend fondly.

"And last but not least, our Christmas painting."

I slid the fabric cover off the canvas and held it up to show Jess and Michael. Her hand came up to her mouth as she sucked in her breath. "Oh, Charlotte. This is gorgeous. Gifted Hands?"

"Yes. A few years ago, she sat in front of our tree and painted this. Her talent is amazing, isn't it?"

The children came in one by one, as they arrived home from their various activities, and soon the sitting room was full of chatter, laughter, and the smell of dinner cooking while our Christmas tree stood shining with colour and promise at the front window.

The following afternoon, everyone came up to the house after church carrying contributions to a meal, with the exception of Robbie, who was spending the afternoon with his friends Tim and Diedrich, the Tuscarora, who were celebrating this day at home, and Hettie and Eli who had travelled up to Auburn for a few days, as they did at this time every year.

Gracie set her bowl onto the dining table and walked into the sitting room. "The tree looks lovely, Charlie. You ladies did a fine job wi' the decorations," she said, sliding out of her coat.

"And I see you've hung Gifted Hands's paintin'," Mabel added as she came to stand beside her daughter. "So pretty."

"How long until we eat?" Phillip asked. "I'm hungry."

"Your father is going outside to check on the meat now, Phillip. It won't be long."

Jess laughed and said, "I'm hungry, too. How about you and I get out the plates and cutlery?"

The men disappeared outside, but Jimmy came back in almost immediately. "It's ready," he said. "Ben's askin' for a platter."

After a delicious meal of rabbit and a variety of vegetables, Sabel, Holly, and their cousins went up to Sabel's room, closing the door behind themselves. Phillip had declined an invitation to go upstairs with the girls in favour of helping Jess, Gracie, and me wash the dishes.

With the four of us working at it, it wasn't long before we were able to join Mabel and the men with a glass of whiskey. "To a lovely Yule spent with friends, old and new," Mabel said, raising her glass.

We could hear the girls' giggles as they floated down the stairs. When he could take it no more, Phillip ran up to join them.

As the daylight began to fade, everyone donned their coats to walk the Moffatts back down the hill, leaving Jess and me alone. I immediately lit the plants I'd left in a dish to burn as a purification incense: pine needles, cedar, and rosemary. "I'll purify the house, Char. You can prepare the altar," Jess said, leaving the room. An aroma that was both cleansing and Christmassy trailed behind her.

I took out my altar and the items we'd chosen to use as decoration. First the evergreens: some small branches of pine (symbolizing healing and joy), mistletoe (healing and protection), and holly (fertility and eternal life), then, both of our Celestite stones, two candles, one red, the other green; and finally, a bowl of melted snow.

Ben had pushed our bed to the wall to give us more room to set up our circle; I set up the altar in the centre of the floor.

When Jessica returned, she placed what was left of the smoking incense onto my dresser and turned to me with a smile. "Are you ready?" she asked. I nodded.

We stood on opposite sides of the altar, arms opened slightly to the sides, palms turned out and began . . .

After calling the quarters, we welcomed the Goddess and God to our circle, which was now fixed between the two worlds.

I began,

"Blessed is the Goddess, the loving Mother,
lying still, resting from her labour.
Blessed is the young God, reborn on this night,
the longest night of the year.
Together, we celebrate you."

Jess continued,

"On this night, the Earth lies cold and dark,
beneath a frozen surface.
awaiting the sun's return
and with it, hope, promise, and life."

We continued, taking turns speaking.

"With the return of the morning's sun,
the days will grow longer.
All that has been hidden will soon begin to emerge.

Let us celebrate the sun.
Let us celebrate rebirth and renewal.
Let us celebrate the continuation of life,
as the Wheel of the Year turns.

So mote it be . . ."

We sat for several moments, returning our excess energy to the Earth and then stood quietly in contemplation, breathing in and out. After thanking and saying farewell to the Goddess and God, the quarters were released, and Jessica and I took up the circle we'd laid out.

When everything was put away, Jess came and stood in front of me with her arms open wide and an even wider smile. That was wonderful, Char," she said, wrapping her arms around me. "To be able to share this with you is . . . it's . . . well, celebrating the wheel of the year with a kindred spirit makes it that much better."

"You *are* a kindred spirit, Jess. I'm sure of that."

"Kindred; never one without the other," she began. "But soon we *will* be without each other." We were quiet for a moment before she added, "If we *did* choose this life together as kindred spirits, we sure made it complicated, didn't we?"

"That we did, but think of how lucky we've been; we've shared our lifetime in two different eras, two hundred years apart. Who can say that?"

"Well, probably no one." She smiled now.

"And remember, we'll always have Samhain's window."

"I like that. It is like a window, isn't it?"

I felt my heart constrict. She would be leaving me again soon, and this time it would be forever.

Christmas

The holiday this year was outstanding! We visited with family and closest friends of course, but we also got to spend some time with some of our other friends—Lenny and Lenora, Rosey and Daniel, Rebecca and Edmond—and we brought in the new year with most of the town at the Southerns' home.

The absolute highlight of the season came on Christmas Eve, when Gracie and Jimmy, Ben and I, Jess and Michael, and all the kids, rowed across the lake in four canoes. It was a cold trip, but after a vote, it was decided we would all rather take the faster route across the not-yet-frozen lake, than the longer one by horse around the bottom of the lake.

We arrived at the cabin, cold and rosy cheeked. Gifted Hands opened the door for us with a smile, as she always did, but wait, this smile looked extra happy. *What's going on?*

My question was answered as soon as I walked in. "Running Otter! What brings you home, my friend?" I asked, reaching up to hug him.

"Charlotte, Ben, it's good to see you," he said with a smile before glancing quickly behind me, taking in the others.

"I would like you to meet my friends, Jessica and Michael," I said as they both stepped forward to shake Running Otter's hand.

"It's lovely to meet you," Jessica started. "I was worried I wouldn't get the chance when your mom said you'd moved away."

His eyes creased into a smile as he answered. "Yes. I am living quite a distance away, somewhere I think we are still safe." His eyes darted to Keen Wolf before he continued. "I have come for a visit. I spent the solstice with Aleshanee and her clan, but I wanted to be home . . . here, while you celebrated your holiday."

While I stepped out of the way for the others to enter, I saw Sabel standing quite still, surprised to see him, a flush on her cheeks. "You didn't say goodbye," she said.

His mouth formed a tight line as he realized this was true.

Then Mitenah came to Sabel's side and tugged at her arm. "Come. I have something I want to show you and Sandy." Sabel allowed herself to be led away, but I was sure she didn't want to miss anything.

Once we were all in and comfortable, I asked how Running Otter liked living with Aleshanee and her clan. He told us he was still learning to make adjustments; as much as his mother and Keen Wolf lived with their beliefs and traditions, living as one of her clan required changes to his lifestyle. He looked happy, and for that I was pleased. I felt for Sabel. Though he was six years her senior, they had grown up together, learning, playing, and as they matured, talking. Her crush on him had hit hard this past spring, and only months later, he had met a woman and moved away. The day Gifted Hands told us he had left— without saying goodbye to us—Sabel had cried her heart out. She cried that he was gone, and she cried that he saw her as a child.

These feelings were ones I was familiar with, and I told her so. There was a time when I had a crush on someone a little older than me. He didn't know I felt that way—I never told him—but I knew that to him I was just a girl. When he up and married, I was heartbroken. A feeling that lasted some time, but eventually I got past it. I knew she would, too, and I told her so as gently as I could.

"I will stay a few days, but I was made to promise I would be back to celebrate the coming new year," Running Otter said and smiled. When the girls returned to the sitting room, he said, "I am sorry I left so quickly. I did not enjoy leaving without saying goodbye." He looked at Sabel as he continued. "I hope you will forgive me."

"You're a grown man, Running Otter. You're allowed to go wherever you want," she replied tartly.

"Yes," he answered with a smirk.

At this point, Gracie asked, "Running Otter, how many people are there where you're living now?"

Grateful for the change in conversation, he turned to Gracie. "As you know, we live with the family of the mother, so in our longhouse there is Aleshanee, her parents, her two sisters and their husbands and children, her aunts and uncles, one cousin, and her grandmother. Altogether, there are nineteen of us."

"Oh, me! And do ye not feel crowded wi' so many folks under one roof?"

"There are times, yes, but mostly we work together, so we are not under each other's feet."

Keen Wolf and Running Otter had rearranged the sitting room so that there was space for the outdoor table to be brought in. Gifted hands wanted us all to be sitting in the dining area on this day of celebration. When all the food had been set out and everyone was seated, Gifted Hands raised her glass of cranberry wine. The room was quiet as we awaited her toast.

"We are so pleased to be able to spend this holiday with all of you, a day made more special because Jessica and Michael are here with us." She paused and smiled at them. "Thank you all for sharing this life's journey with us."

I could see that Ben was planning to add to the toast, but then Jess spoke up. "It has truly been a pleasure meeting all of you. Thank you for letting us in and . . ." She swallowed hard, choosing her words. "And thank you for being here for Charlotte when I could not. We will leave knowing that she's happy and will live out her life in the company of wonderful friends and family." Her eyes were wet as she finished, but she smiled before sipping her drink.

"Let us not think of that day now," Ben said, smiling gently at Jessica. "Today, we celebrate love and friendship; may it remain forever strong."

I looked at each of the smiling faces in turn, sitting around the table and felt blessed. As my gaze reached Keen Wolf, I saw the love we still shared in the depths of his dark eyes, just waiting to be noticed.

The room was full of the sounds of chattering voices and laughter as we enjoyed a wonderful feast. It was after we had cleaned up and were seated for a warm drink that it happened. I shouldn't have been surprised.

"Charlie, now that ye've got your singing partner wi' ye, how about some of your Christmas songs?"

I immediately flashed back to the Christmas after returning from Jessica and Michael in 2013, when Ben and I had started to sing, and I'd lost it—crying, thinking of how much I missed Jessica. Well, she was here now! I looked at her and raised my eyebrows. She had a huge smile on her face when she nodded.

"So, what'll it be, Jess?" I asked.

"You know the one," she answered with a wink.

We began with Baby It's Cold Outside, taking turns singing the parts like we always used to do. I saw Ben nod and grin at Michael; they knew how much we were loving this. This was followed by some Christmas carols, songs which the others had learned over the years. It was great fun!

When it came time to leave for home, we all walked down to the water. Sabel and Mitenah walked arm-in-arm ahead of us. I hooked my arm through Gifted Hands's in similar fashion. "Thank you for a lovely evening. Enjoy your time with Running Otter." I heard my voice catch as I said the words. He had been such a big part of my life since I came here. He was only little then. It was hard to think of him living somewhere else, with people we didn't know, not knowing when we'd see him again.

"It is a gift I will cherish, Charlotte."

While the men pulled the canoes toward the water, I watched Sabel say goodbye to Running Otter. She hugged him and said something I couldn't hear, then he pulled back and looked into her face. His words I was able to hear. "Go in peace, Mimiteh. Be happy."

Without another word, she turned and walked toward the canoe. She didn't look back. *God, she is so like me.*

"Goodbye, my friend," I said and hugged him hard. "I wish you much happiness in your new life, but I will miss you . . . We all will."

"Thank you, Charlotte. I will miss you all, too. But this is not goodbye. We will see each other again."

Christmas morning, I was the first one up. I went straight to the kitchen to put on the coffee. I was thinking of last night's dream and being awoken by Phillip's sleeping voice. He was calling to his sister, something he hadn't done in a while. I was startled by Sabel's voice. "Good morning, Mum."

"Oh! Good morning, honey. Merry Christmas. Did you sleep well?"

"I had a strange dream." I turned to her and waited for more. "You may think I'm crazy, I don't know. Okay, here it is . . . I was sitting at the outside table, facing the water. It wasn't cold like it is now. I don't know if I was waiting for something; I was just staring at the lake. Then, all of a sudden, there was this little body on the table in front of me." She paused.

My stomach did a flop. "Little body?"

She cleared her throat. "Yes. She was smiling. She moved her lips, but no sound came out, then she put her hand on her chest, like she was going to tell me her name. It sounds strange now, but in my dream, it made sense. She raised her hands over her head and looked up at the—"

"Sky?" I interrupted.

"Yes. How did you know?"

"Please go on. What happened next?"

"Once I said her name, it seemed she found her voice. She told me she and her friend wanted to say hello. They hadn't seen me in a long time. I didn't know what she was talking about. Then I saw another little face pop up from under the table."

"Jossie," I said, breathless.

"Yes!" Her face paled. "They stood side by side holding hands. Then Jossie said, 'Jessie says be happy.'"

From behind us, I heard Jessica suck in a breath. "Okay, what? Did all three of us have this dream?"

"You, too?" I asked her.

"Well, mine wasn't exactly the same; I was watching Sabel and the two, um, whatever they were. I saw that exact scene and I felt incredibly happy."

"What about your dream, Mum?" Sabel asked.

"Mine was different. I was at my rock, looking out over the water and something bounced off my ankle. When I looked down, I saw an acorn on the ground. Beside it, was a small pile of acorns. Skye and Jossie stepped out from behind it. I was surprised and asked what they were doing there. They both made the shape of a heart with their hands, then crossed their hands over their hearts, like a thank you, and disappeared."

"Okay, Char. Please explain."

I glanced at Sabel and decided I could be honest. I told them about when we were in Scotland, and Jessie and I had seen both Skye and Jossie. "Sounds crazy, I know, but I think they're faeries. Skye visited me two or three times in the garden. She warned, 'There is danger; there is sadness. It is coming.' You came out into the garden looking for me one of those times, Sabel. I guess they saw you then."

"Hmm. So that's where Jessie got the name for her stuffed kitty?"

I smiled. "Yes. Shortly after, things went bad with Cynthia." Sabel looked confused. Now was not the time to tell her about Cynthia's late-night visit to Ben's bed while I slept with her, sick in the other room. "You remember when I took you kids to visit Ronnie at Slains?" She squinted, trying to remember. "Well, you were little. We left because your father and I had had a falling out, and I needed to get away. Do you remember the last day we were there? We took the horses for a ride and visited the Twa Een. We went into a cave and found two men inside. One threatened us with a gun, and the other, Charlie, had been shot. He fell over the edge of the rocks into the sea." I shook my head to myself remembering all too well the surprise of losing him. With him, he had taken the rainbow moonstone I'd given him to hold on to. "A while after that, I went missing for a couple of weeks, and your dad was looking for me." Sabel nodded. "During that time, Jessie had a dream . . . Jossie was in it. She helped us understand that Cynthia had put a strong herb into my drinks."

Jess nodded. She, too, had been in that Samhain "dream". "Boy, that was a long time ago, Char. I wonder why they'd come to you here . . . now."

"I don't know, but there was no warning this time."

"You did say something about when you take holly into the home in the winter it offers the faeries shelter from the cold. Maybe they came with Ronnie's holly," Jess added with a wink.

I hugged Sabel and quietly said, "Jessie loves you and wants you to be happy, sweetheart."

Phillip came down the stairs then. "Did you just mention Jessie? I dreamed of her last night. I didn't see her, but I heard her voice. She was telling me to be happy."

"She's wishing us all love and happiness on Christmas." My heart swelled at the thought, a feeling that stayed with me for the rest of the day. We enjoyed a late afternoon meal at our home, with contributions by Gracie, Mabel, and Hettie. There was turkey, stuffing, potatoes, carrots, cabbage, and cranberry sauce for dinner, and Hettie's special Christmas cake with custard for dessert. By the time we were finished eating, I could barely move.

The children and their cousins disappeared upstairs, while the rest of us reflected on the past year. It had been good, for the most part. Ailsa and Sam had married and moved away. Running Otter had found a woman and moved away. My suspicions about Penelope were proven to be correct after all these years, and she'd left here with her tail between her legs. Jessica and Michael had come to see us, ending the year in the best possible way, and I'd learned that Maisie, and therefore Carole-Anne and Keith, are, in fact, my ancestors.

The week following Christmas passed quickly. Before I knew it, we were preparing for New Year's Eve celebrations around town. The older kids had their own celebration at Rosey and Daniel's home, where they would spend the night. The rest of us walked to the Southerns' home, behind the grist mill, where we brought in the New Year.

After being welcomed into the Southerns' home, the first faces we saw were Carole-Anne's and Keith's. Surprised, I gave them each a hug and beckoned Jess and Michael over. "We didn't know when we would see you again. I'm so happy you made it home to celebrate the New Year with us," I said.

"It's good to be back, Charlie. We had hoped to be sooner, but the weather did not cooperate."

"It certainly did not," Keith agreed.

"And where's Maisie?" I asked.

"Well, she heard that the older kids were celebrating at Rosey's tonight, so off she went." Her mother smiled before continuing. "She's been looking forward to seeing Jeffery again."

"Aww, well, she'll be happy then. Now, I must introduce my friends, Jessica and Michael Saunders. They've come from Upper Canada for a visit. We haven't seen each other in years."

"Isn't that nice!" Carole-Anne answered. "It's good to meet you both. How long will you be here?"

Jess answered, "Just a few more weeks. We've enjoyed your town very much."

Carole-Anne glanced at her husband and said, "It is a lovely place to be."

I saw the men being passed drinks where they stood behind us. "Well, I suppose we must mingle just now, but why don't you ladies and Gracie come for a bite on your noon break Saturday?"

"That sounds nice. Thank you," I answered.

"Thank you. We'll see you then," Jessica said with a bright smile.

Bringing in 1835 was great fun! Sharing the celebration with Jessica made it perfect.

After leaving Gracie, Jimmy, Mabel, and the two youngest girls at the store, Phillip and Holly ran home ahead of us. "Oh, to have that kind of energy, eh, Jess?" I asked.

"It would be nice. Wouldn't be a good idea tonight though. I might land on my face if I tried that right now," she said and giggled.

"We'd better remember to drink some water before hitting the pillow tonight."

"I can't believe we just brought in 1835. That is just fuckin' nuts!"

Michael smirked. "It really is," he agreed.

The kids were already dressed for bed when we arrived at the house. "Goodnight," they said from the top of the stairs.

After tucking them in, I joined the others in the sitting room. "It's been so much fun having you guys here," I said. "I wish you could stay."

"I know," Jess answered. "Part of me would really like to."

"If I'm honest, part of me would like that, too," Michael added.

My eyes met Ben's then, and all other thoughts left me. He looked good. He always did, but right now I felt the sexy in his eyes in a very special place. His smile told me that he'd seen my reaction. We needed to get upstairs.

I stood up. "I'm so happy we were able to bring in 1835 with you guys. Happy New Year." I hugged them both. "Time for me to get to bed."

"Yeah, we'd better, too," Jessica said.

Ben followed me into the bedroom and closed the door. He looked into my eyes, smiled, and whispered, "We'll have to be quiet, are you sure?"

"Oh, I'm sure," I said, pulling his face to mine while I went for the buttons of his shirt.

Three Sister Stew

"Welcome, welcome. Please come in," Carole-Anne said, ushering us in from the cold.

"Oo-oo, it's nippy out there teday," Gracie said, hanging her coat on a hook by the door.

"It is that," Carole-Anne agreed. "Follow me," she said, leading us toward the dining table. "It's nice and cozy in here. Dinner will be ready in a few minutes. Tea?"

While she poured our tea, I said, "So, tell us about your visit."

She turned with a smile. "It was very nice." She glanced toward Maisie's room before continuing. "I do have news," she began, her voice lower than before. "I'll just wait until Maisie's left."

Just then the bedroom door opened, and Maisie came into the dining area. "Hello everyone. It's good to see you."

"You, too, Maisie," I answered. "I'd like you to meet my friend Jessica."

"Hello," Jess said. "It's nice to meet you."

"You as well," Maisie answered. "I'll be off now, Mother. See you at supper." She grabbed a roll from the plate her mother held and headed for the door.

Carol-Anne nodded as she began to serve our meal. "Oh, this smells delicious," Gracie said.

"It really does," Jess agreed.

"It almost smells like I'm in Gifted Hands's kitchen. What is this?" I asked.

"Ah, it's Three Sister Stew. While we were away, Lovella made this for us. It's so hearty and tasty, I wanted to try it myself."

"Mm-mm, it's really good!" I told her.

"So, what's yer news, lass?"

Carole-Anne looked up from her spoon and offered a smile that spoke of sadness. "I've told you of the reservation in Grand River. It's a place Keith and I love to be, a place where we can do our part, where we can contribute to the good of the clan as a whole. I believe Maisie feels quite at home when we're there, too. Well, they have invited us to come and live with them and teach them the ways of our Holy Father."

Gracie looked up from her bowl with wide eyes. She hadn't expected this. I saw Jess's eyes flick my way. "Will you go?" I asked, although in my heart I knew the answer.

"We have been discussing it. Keith and I believe it is an opportunity to spread the words of the bible, to teach people who might otherwise remain ignorant to our beliefs."

"And Maisie?" asked Gracie.

"Maisie? She's not delighted at the idea. She would like to remain here with her friends and with Jeffery. These feelings I understand, of course, but I'm also aware that she is only sixteen years old. She still has growing to do. I don't think she is old enough to make the decision to stay here on her own."

I didn't know what to say. On one hand, I could offer to let her stay with us; we have the room. On the other, she became—no, will become—one of my ancestors without my interference in her life. I could not make the offer.

"We have been invited, but it is up to us to decide if we will go and when. We are not in a hurry."

"I'm sure you will make the best choice for yourselves, but if you choose to go, we will miss you."

She smiled. "And we will miss you."

In my mind, this response was answer enough. They had already made their choice.

"So, tell me, Jessica, how have you enjoyed your stay here? I understand there was some excitement when you first arrived."

"Yes, Simon Haskel. That was unfortunate."

"The poor soul," Carole-Anne added.

"Once the cause of his death was determined, and Michael was no longer suspected in any way, things improved." Jess smiled. "I love this town."

"Is there a reason you must leave so soon?"

"Well, our mothers are both at home. We left them with help, but after two months I think it's best we return to them."

While the three of us walked back to the store, Gracie said, "I must admit, I'm a bittie surprised at what Carole-Anne said teday. In me mind, I saw them stayin' here."

"She's always enjoyed being there," I reminded her.

"And think about it," Jess added, "At some point, Maisie Peterson lives north-west of the Grand River Reservation."

"Aye." I had to smile seeing the faraway look in Gracie's eyes.

The next few weeks passed far too quickly. Jess and I worked on the words of her ritual on and off; there was still time to tweak them. I tried not to think about them leaving. I knew how hard it was going to be—we'd done this before—but I had to enjoy every single minute I had with her, well, them.

"It's hard to believe this is the last Saturday I'll be spending with you here in the store," Jess said sadly. "It's been great hanging out with you at work, learning what you do, and seeing you in action. Oh, that reminds me, will we check on that soap today?"

"Yep. It must be ready by now. We'll take it out of the cupboard and cut it up. I'll give you some to take home, some candles, too. You'll have the oldest fresh bar of soap ever." I laughed.

As we walked home, she asked, "Char, are you sure when I get home I can't talk to you for eight years? I mean, that's a long fuckin' time."

"I know it is, Jess. And believe me, the eight years I didn't talk to you were horrible. It sucked not knowing why you weren't there and what happened to you. At least you know that at the end of it, I'll be here waiting for you."

"I just can't believe I won't talk to you for so long."

"Just remember, we can't change anything during that eight years or this time spent won't be the visit we both remember."

"I know," she said, sounding disheartened. "Besides, I agree, we don't want to risk having different memories of being together. Once was enough."

"I still think about that sometimes. It's hard to believe it even happened." I chuckled. "You should have seen everyone's faces when we tried to tell them about it. It was crazy trying to explain how we went to your time and Michael died, then Ben and I went back in time and were able to save Michael, but the time we'd spent together when he was dead, never happened for you. For you, in your memories, those two weeks together were spent *very* differently."

"It's fuckin' nuts, Char."

"Yeah. So, for me, those eight years of no contact have already happened. Now it will be your turn. I guess you'll have a ton of news for me when I see you at Samhain—eight years of news."

"Eight years and nine months. What will I do?"

"Enjoy your life, Jess. And remember all the things you want to tell me about." I took her hand and gave it a squeeze.

Ben and Michael came in the front door then, arms full of wood. Seeing Jess's face, Michael asked, "Talking about the eight missing years again?"

"Yeah," Jess answered, pouting.

He stacked the wood he was carrying and then hugged her. "We'll get through it. I know there will be tough times ahead, but we'll get through. And, when it's over, Charlie will be here waiting to hear from you."

"With bells on!"

Farewell

Tuesday, the day before they were to leave, everyone came up to the house for supper. Gracie and Jimmy, Mabel, Hettie and Eli, Gifted Hands, Keen Wolf, and all the children. For those who didn't realize the finality of the upcoming goodbye, there were wishes of love and happiness. But, for those of us who understood, there were undertones of sadness behind every smile.

As usual, the kids disappeared upstairs for a large part of the visit, except Phillip. He sat beside Jessica much of the evening—something that made me feel both happy and sad. She smiled and put her arm around his shoulders, pulling him in. Then she spoke to him in a low voice. "I'm so glad I had the chance to become your friend. You are a fine young man . . . and so handsome," she added with a smile. He blushed.

We talked, we laughed, and everyone expressed their pleasure at meeting Jess and Michael. Before we were ready, it was well past dark. It was time for our visitors to get to their beds.

The lot of us left the house to walk the others down to the store. As usual, the kids ran ahead, racing to the canoes. Gifted Hands put her arm through Jessica's, and they walked together, talking quietly. Gracie took my arm and smiled, saying softly, "It was a lovely evening, lass. I'll see them tomorrow, o' course, but for now, I believe those two ladies need this last opportunity to speak quietly."

"When she leaves, I'm gonna be a mess all over again, Gracie."

"I ken that, love. Dinna forget, it'll be worse for her. She'll have to pass all those years wi' out ye."

"Yeah."

"And I'll aye be here for ye, love. And, Benny—ye canna feel unhappy in the arms o' yer soul mate, can ye?"

Leaning my head onto her shoulder, I whispered, "Thanks, Gracie."

We saw Gifted Hands pop in the store's kitchen door momentarily and come out with something which she handed to Jessica. Then they walked toward the water.

I gave them some space to speak privately and watched Gifted Hands take Jessica's hands and say some final words. As Michael shook Keen Wolf's hand, Gifted Hands hugged Jessica. Then Jessica turned to Keen Wolf. They hadn't said a lot to each other in her time here, but they understood each other's relationship with me, and in that, they shared a mutual appreciation and respect. She hugged him and said goodbye.

I felt Keen Wolf's eyes as I said goodnight to his wife. He knew what tomorrow would mean to me; he'd seen it before. Gifted Hands hugged me hard and whispered, "Enjoy tomorrow, Charlotte—every second of it." I could only nod in response, my emotions close to the surface. She smiled in understanding. "We will see you soon." She walked toward Gracie then.

I was surprised to turn and find Keen Wolf at my side. "Good night, Keen Wolf," I said, raising my arms to hug him.

"Stay strong, Sky Watcher," he said softly, hot breath in my ear.

Dark Wolf and Mitenah sat up front, ready to break up the thin layer of ice that had formed since they'd arrived. This would be the last canoe trip for a while.

The walk home was chilly. The kids didn't run ahead. This time they walked with us, chatting about their friends and school—cheery sounds that kept us from getting stuck in our heads. Once back home, they said goodnight one by one.

Before going up to bed, Phillip asked Jessica, "Do you really have to leave? I wish you would stay."

Her affection for him shone in her eyes as she answered. "We have loved being here with you so much, but we have family at home who are missing us. We *do* have to go, sweetheart. But remember, I will always be right here," she said, putting her hand over his heart. He nodded, sad eyes full of unshed tears, and went up the stairs.

Ben poured the four of us a stiff drink while Michael stoked the fire. Jess and I sat together on the settee.

"I never expected to feel like this again, Char. It so sucks!"

"It really does. It's been so good to see you, especially considering we never thought it would happen again, but knowing this is it . . . I can barely take it." I leaned my head onto her shoulder. "I will miss you forever, Jess."

"Me, too," she answered, with a wobble in her voice.

"Hey! What did Gifted Hands give you?" I asked.

"I'm not sure. She told me to open it when I get back home."

Ben cleared his voice and I lifted my head to look at him. "I think I'll go up to bed and leave you to—"

"That's okay, Benny. Jess and Michael will need a good sleep so they'll have some good energy tomorrow. I'll come up, too," I said.

"Good idea," Michael agreed.

I hugged them both goodnight outside the bedroom door, before slipping into bed beside Ben. I snuggled into him and said softly, "Oh, Benny."

"I know." He kissed me gently and added, "I love you, Moxie." His hand felt warm as it slid down the side of my shift. I felt the length of the fabric being tugged upward and then his hands were on my skin. "Roll onto your back," he said hoarsely. "There's something I've been thinking about all day."

I was the first one up Wednesday morning and went straight to the task of making coffee. I put the pot on the wood-burning stove and turned to see Jessica standing there. Her eyes looked sad, but she was holding it together. Déjà-vu . . .

"Good morning, Char. Coffee then work?"

"Yep—until noon. Then we can go over your ritual again, if you like?" She nodded.

Then the kitchen was full of voices and clanging dishes as everyone got something to eat before heading out to school or work.

We had a busy morning at the store, which was good because it kept Jess and me in the present. Several of our friends, aware that Jess and Michael were leaving tonight, popped in to wish them a good trip. Emma came in with Rosey and Lenora. When Rebecca came in it was just before noon. Gracie invited her to join us for our meal.

"You certainly came at a hectic time, Jessica, what, with Simon's death and the return of Penelope."

"That's for sure," she answered. "There hasn't been a dull moment since I arrived."

I smiled and added, "We wouldn't want it any other way, right?"

Once we'd finished eating, Rebecca stood to excuse herself. "Thank you, Gracie. That was nice. I suppose I'd better get back." She turned to Jess then. "It's been lovely meeting you, Jessica."

"You, too. Be happy, Rebecca."

"Jess and I are going back up to the house, Gracie. See you later on?"

"Aye."

I said little as we walked up the little hill. I didn't want to upset or distract Jess in any way. She would have to be entirely focused on tonight's task. I know what that entails—complete concentration.

"So, we'll go over the words and then you can help me pack?" she asked.

"Sure."

I opened the front door and immediately felt the warmth of the wood-burning stove. "It looks like Ben has already put two big pots of water on to heat. Good, your bath tonight must be warm to be relaxing."

We got comfortable at the table and took out the paper where we'd written her travelling words. After perfecting them, we were left with this:

"Blessed is the Goddess, our Mother, our provider
and the Sun God, the Lord of Light.
On this night only days before Imbolc,

we are nearly half-way
between the winter solstice
and the spring equinox.
We celebrate the return of light after winter's darkness,
a time to reconnect with nature.

I draw upon Earth's energy,
To take us home, it is my fate;
I must travel ahead through time,
Together with my heart's mate.

I ask the new moon to guide me
As we leave on this cold, winter night;
To arrive beneath a moon that is full,
Once home, our path it will light.

We must return to the time we are from,
Though a piece of my heart will remain,
In the care of a kindred spirit,
Whose love will never wane.

So mote it be."

With tears in my eyes, I put my arms around her. "I love you, Jess—always."

"Me, too, Char."

"Let's go get you packed up," I said with a sniff.

Their bags were less full going home since they were leaving their nineteenth century clothing here. In their place would be the few trinkets they had picked up while they were here—reminders of their time spent with us: perfume bottles; several fountain pens and an inkwell; Gifted Hands's gift; and a bottle of whiskey.

"Jess, thank you for coming. Trying to warn us about Jessie was kind and so-oo risky. I appreciate it more than you can know. It's a shame we'll never know what happened, why you couldn't come when you wanted to, but I don't suppose it matters. She's gone, but we still love her." I heard myself sigh. "There may be times in the future when we can't reach each other, but no matter what happens, always remember I love you, through time and space." I hugged her hard, no longer able to hold back the tears.

"Oh, Charlotte." Her arms came around me as we sat on the bed together, sobbing.

When the children arrived home from school, I was preparing supper. We had decided that the four children would eat supper at the store with Mabel and their cousins. Gracie and Jimmy would eat here with us. I asked Jess and Michael what they'd like to eat on their last evening with us. Jess couldn't have cared less—she didn't want to think about it. Michael, however, requested ribs, and they were seasoned and waiting for Ben.

Gracie arrived as Ben and Michael were getting the outside fire going. She stepped inside with a basket over her arm. "Evening ladies," she said with a smile. Her cheeks were rosy with the cold. "Jimmy's helpin' the men wi' the fire. Hettie sent some rolls and pie." She set the basket on the table. "And I brought us this." It was a bottle of wine. I immediately took out three wine glasses and a corkscrew.

"Would you please do the honours, Gracie?"

She was pouring as the kids came down the stairs, each with a bag for the evening. They came to stand in front of Jess. Robbie spoke first. "I'm glad we got to meet you and Michael. I hope we see you again one day." He hugged her.

"Yes," Sabel said, looking awkward. "I was going to say that." She smiled and added, "Best wishes to you both." She hugged Jess.

"Goodbye," Holly said and offered a hug.

"It's been lovely meeting you all. Your parents are lucky to have you," Jess said.

Then Phillip was standing before her. The others were in various stages of getting into their coats and boots. I said, "You guys go say bye to Michael outside and wait for Phillip. He'll be out in a minute."

The sad was oozing out of him as he stood facing her. "I feel like I'm never going to see you again."

Jess's eyes found mine for a moment before she answered. "You may be right, Phillip, this might be it." She forced a smile. "But I am so happy that I got to meet you. I hope you will be very happy always." She hugged him then, teary-eyed.

He stood back and wiped his eyes. Nodding, he said, "Goodbye, Jess." His words echoed in my head for a long time after that.

As we started supper, the conversation was lacking. Should we talk about it? Should we ignore it? No one seemed to know. Then Jess raised her glass and said, "Thank you for making us feel like a part of the family. It has been so nice to spend time with you all and to get to know you." Her voice wavered at the end and she put her glass to her lips for a sip.

"Aye. It's something I'll cherish always."

"We'll miss ye both. Best wishes to ye," Jimmy added.

After that, we spoke about what would happen here after Gracie and Jimmy left. Jessica would go upstairs and have a quiet candle-lit bath, using the time to let go of any negative energy and focus on the task of taking them home.

Once we'd finished our meal, the men enjoyed a whiskey in the sitting room while Gracie and Jess helped me with the dishes.

Before they left, Gracie took Jessica away to speak to her privately, during which time she gave her something wrapped in fabric. Jessica opened it up to find a lovely grey and off-white patterned shawl. "Did you make this, Gracie?"

She smiled and said, "I did. Just a little something to remember me." Her voice caught and the two embraced. "I hope you pass the next few years well, lass. We'll be waitin' te hear how yer doin'."

Ben and Michael carried the last of the hot water to the tub for Jessica, before we left the house to allow Jess privacy for her ritual bath. The time was drawing near.

We walked Gracie and Jimmy to the store and turned back for home. I walked between the men, but my arm was hooked through Michael's. "It's been such a pleasure having you with us, Michael. I'm so happy you were able to see our happy life and meet our kids." I squeezed his arm and bent to lean my head against him. "Look after Jess and don't ever forget us." I stopped speaking when my voice cracked.

"How could I?" he answered softly.

When we arrived, the house was very quiet, but I could hear her footsteps upstairs. Michael went up to get their bags and returned wearing a solemn expression. He set the bags on the floor and quietly said, "She's holding it together, but barely."

I didn't want to say or do anything. What she needed most right now was to focus within herself.

She came down the stairs quietly, clearly concentrating. She looked at us each in turn. "We should go," she said.

A quick look at the clock on the mantle told me it was 11:40. She was right—time to go.

We slipped out into the darkness. I said nothing but took her arm as we walked toward the spot we had marked earlier. She pointed to a spot on the ground and Michael set their bags down. Our eyes met then. We embraced one last time. I whispered, "Always remember."

She answered, "You, too."

I didn't look at her again. I simply turned away and walked a few paces. When Ben arrived at my side, I turned quickly for one last peek. She was preparing the ground where her circle would soon sit. When Jess looked up, I blew her a kiss, and then Ben and I walked back to the house. I cried the whole way.

As the door closed behind us, I looked at the clock, it was midnight. I ran up to the bedroom and peered out the window toward the place where we'd left them.

Samhain 1835

Sitting cross-legged on the bedroom floor before my altar, I thought of my dear friend and felt excited. I had little news, really. For me, it had only been nine months since we'd been together, but I knew she would be desperate to see me after what would be eight years of silence in her time, 2029.

I thought back to the night they left, the night of our final goodbye. After leaving them in the woods, I ran up to my bedroom window, wondering if there would be anything to see. I saw nothing in the moonless night.

Gracie'd had similar thoughts. The next morning, she told me at midnight she'd looked toward our house from Sandy's bedroom window. "I didna see a thin'. Funny though, when I came back, I heard Phillip's voice—he was asleep, mind—he said, 'Don't go, Jess' and then, 'I understand. I'll miss you. Goodbye.' It gave me gooseflesh up and down me arms."

I hadn't asked him about it. He would sort it out in his own time, his own way.

And now, here I was waiting . . .

I closed my eyes and began the words of my Samhain ritual, welcoming the quarters and the Goddess and God. I had just finished when I saw a bright light, fuzzy in the middle with a glare around the outside. "Jess?" I asked quietly.

At the same time, I heard, "Charlotte? Oh, Charlotte! I can't believe the time has come."

"Tell me everything," I thought-asked, as her image sharpened.

She looked at me with wide, wet eyes. "Michael is well. He's no longer a junior VP, now he's *the* VP, and he loves it. His mother passed away six years ago in her sleep. Her stroke was a shock, but she went peacefully. My mom . . . I don't know where to begin. She has Alzheimer's. She started showing signs about two years after I got home. Much of the time she doesn't know me. She's in a nice home not far away and is well looked after, but it's so hard." Her chin dropped to her chest momentarily, but she remembered time was limited and perked back up. A bright light shone around her, a beautiful aura, and I knew there was more. "And Charlotte? I had a baby!"

"What?!" I was shocked. Neither of them had wanted to have children. In fact, Michael had had a vasectomy years ago. Jess smiled and continued.

"I left there pregnant. I couldn't believe it! Michael almost fell over when I told him; it happened against the odds. But then . . . well, we both warmed up to the idea quickly enough. We had a baby boy in October of 2021, seven pounds, ten ounces. We named him after Michael's parents, Charles Christian Saunders, but we call him Charlie. Can you see his face?"

In my mind I could see the little face of a baby boy and images of him as he grew to eight years old. "Oh, Jess," I choked out. "Congratulations!"

"Thank you! I'm so happy I was finally able to tell you about him. It's been sooo long. I had to resist contacting you over the years—it was hard! Now, tell me what I've missed."

"Not much. Let's see, Robbie has decided he wants to be a doctor like his father. He will begin to accompany Ben at work part-time and work some hours while he waits to hear from Harvard. We'll see how that goes. Sabel's friend Janee lost her sister; remember Rebecca's youngest daughter, Eloise? She died suddenly just after you left. We don't know what happened or why. It hit the family hard, and it really affected Sabel. Eli passed away a few months ago. Poor Hettie misses him so much." Charlotte shook her head to herself. "Rebecca and Edmond married. The others are just as you left them."

"Poor Eli. He was such a nice man. And poor Rebecca, but now she has Edmond with her. That's nice." Charlotte nodded. "And how about The Doctor's House?"

Charlotte smiled. "We opened the doors last spring. Everyone is getting used to the changes. It's going well."

"It's so good to have you back, Char. Eight years was s . . . we . . . no . ." Her words were getting lost, our window was closing.

"Goodbye for now, Jess. Love you." With that, she was gone. Whether she heard my final words, I don't know. This visit wasn't followed with the usual feeling of sadness when it was over—this time I'd had a sweet surprise that warmed my heart.

Dressed only in a shift, I wrapped a blanket around myself and walked down the stairs to join Ben. He was waiting, seated in our new cozy chair with a book, and . . . he had shaved. He looked up when he heard my steps. "Oo-oo, look at you. You look like a baby."

"How is she?" he asked with a smile as I walked toward him.

I don't know why tears sprang to my eyes when he asked, but they did. "They had a baby, Benny. When they left here, she was pregnant." I stopped in front of him.

"What?"

"Yep. The chances of getting pregnant after a vasectomy are less than one per cent, but, well, they had a baby in October of 2021, or 1827 for us. He's eight now." Ben scrunched up his face as he thought about that. "Now *that's* frikkin' crazy, right?!"

"It is." He reached for my hands and pulled me down toward him. "Come here, Moxie." With the blanket still around my back, I straddled him on the chair, and gently ran my fingers over his smooth chin. He looked soo good! "What do you say *you* and *I* go make a baby?" He whispered into my ear.

As soon as he said the words, I felt his reaction beneath me. I put my lips on his in a way that answered his question and some. I lifted my face for a breath and heard, "Ahem . . ." I turned to see Holly standing at the top of the stairs.

I felt the heat in my face instantly, but said, "Just kissing Daddy goodnight, sweetheart. What's up?"

"I was coming down for a drink."

"Back to bed, love. I'll bring you some water. Just be a minute."

Holly looked at her father and giggled. "You look funny, Daddy." Then she turned back toward her room.

Ben raised his eyebrows twice, quickly, as I got up off his lap. "Upstairs then?" he asked.

I whacked his arm before walking to the jug on the counter.

After pouring her drink, I found Ben already gone. I blew out the candle in the sitting room and took the glass up to Holly. "Here you go, honey. Have a good sleep."

"Thanks, Mommy," she said, sitting up for a sip. "Goodnight. I know Daddy'll have a good night after all those kisses." She giggled and rolled over, already half asleep.

Thankfully, she couldn't see the blush I felt across my cheeks. "Night, love."

I closed her door and headed for my own room. It was dark in there—couldn't see a thing. I pulled the door closed behind me. There were no sounds. I knew he was waiting for me, so I found the bottom of my shift, and lifted it off over my head, tossing it, hopefully, onto the chair. I walked around to Ben's side of the bed and listened. He was lying on his back. I felt for the wall behind the headboard, then I found him with my hand, immediately taking him into my mouth. I love the sound he makes when I do that. He was so ready for me. I licked, taking my time, finding the nooks and under-spots. Then I got serious. I could hear his need, and I wanted him to feel it. He was close. I stopped and got up on the bed, straddling him. God, I wanted him something fierce. In the blink of an eye, I was on my back, legs spread just enough for his tongue to be on me, in me, all the places it needed to be. He knew what I liked, and he was ready. I could hear his smile when he lifted his face and whispered, "Best cover your mouth, Moxie. I'm not going to stop until you have nothing left. Only then will I allow you to mount me."

Hearing Ben's sleepy snores, I rolled onto my side. As tired and fulfilled as I was, talking to Jess had left my mind reeling.

Jessica had left here only ten months ago, and, in that time, she had a baby who was now eight years old. *What?*

I understand the logistics of it all, I mean for her, it had been over eight years since we were together. But . . . wrapping my head around the fact that it had only been nine months for me, is almost beyond belief. I must keep in mind that when she was here with us, we were out of sync, I was eight years older than her, and now things are as they were.

As I drifted closer to sleep, I felt a renewed sympathy for Rebecca. She had been through many hard times in her life. Her oldest brother became a psychotic murderer; she lost an infant, only months old, to crib death; her husband died suddenly after ten years of marriage, leaving her with Janee, Francis, and Eloise; and then Eloise died at seven years old. It would be a lot for anyone to take. When Sabel heard the news from Janee, she was devastated. She had always liked Eloise—said she was a mischievous little rascal with dimples no one could resist. Sabel couldn't understand how God would have such a plan—young innocents like Jessie and Eloise had died for no reason, and families made to suffer. "Why would God make such a plan, Mum?" she asked through tears one day.

"I don't know, honey," I'd answered.

"You don't believe in God—well, I don't either. If he's real, then he's mean and thoughtless and makes good people suffer for no reason. Who would do that? He can't be real."

She attended the ceremony for Eloise with the rest of us; it was held in the church because it was winter, and the ground was still too difficult to dig. That was the last time she walked into the church. Her exact words were, "I cannot show him any kind of love when he shows good people no mercy. I won't go to church anymore."

She hasn't been since—she can't be convinced. Of course, people tried to change her mind—even Preacher Keith tried. She won't have it.

After a night of tossing and turning, I awoke feeling exactly as I had when I'd fallen asleep.

Gracie looked at her brother the next morning and reached for his chin. "Ah, smooth as a baby's bottom." Once the laughter died down, she added, "It looks good on ye, lad." There was no argument there. He looked even more handsome without the beard. That didn't stop each and every one of the children from giggling when they first saw this new man with a chin.

When I told the others about Jess and the baby, I watched their expressions as they tried to understand. "Me mind's boggled, Charlie. That's a lot te muddle through," Gracie said, eyebrows knitted together in thought.

"Aye," added Jimmy.

Gifted Hands said little, but I could see her eyes darting back and forth, as she made the calculations in her head.

Keen Wolf looked at me solemnly. "He has now seen eight winters? Interesting."

Ben smirked at me—he had already admitted that this was indeed mind-bending.

Part II

Fire

With only a few weeks of school remaining, the students were more than ready for summer. The warmer temperatures often made for disagreeable, sweaty children, but not this day—this day was altogether different.

"What do you think this is about, Ben? Why do you think this guy would want to talk to me?" Charlotte asked as they walked toward the grist mill.

"I have no idea. We just have to wait and see."

Larry met them at the door, looking very serious. "I won't beat around the bush. Lenny and Greg caught this man coming out of the schoolhouse this morning. Long story short, when they approached him, he was holding a tin of turpentine and a striker. It looked as if he was trying to start a fire."

"What? With the children inside?"

"Yes. They each grabbed an arm and held him while they sent one of the children to find me." He looked at Charlotte now. "Calls himself Carl. He was asking for you, Charlotte, you and Ben. Don't know why. Would you care to speak to him?"

She looked at Ben; they'd never know what it was about if they didn't see him. As far as she knew, neither of them knew a Carl, but Charlotte was curious to learn his interest in them. "Yes," Ben said. He began walking toward the door of the gaol. Larry reminded them he was just outside if needed.

Charlotte followed her husband into the cell and heard the door close behind them. Inside was a man sitting on the edge of the thin pallet—elbows on knees, chin in hands—who glanced up as the door locked. He appeared to be of medium height and build, with short, tousled light-brown hair, and looked to be about forty years old.

"Carl, is it? We were told you wanted to see us?" Ben began.

Carl nodded and offered a nervous smile. "I was not trying to burn down the schoolhouse, not at all. In fact, I was trying to stop what would have become a fire. I tried to tell them, but they didn't want to listen."

"I don't follow," Ben responded.

Charlotte had been looking at this man's face, feeling as if she should know who he was, and yet she did not. "I'm sorry," she started, "but have we met?"

He looked from Ben to her and smiled. "Many years ago." Her mind was searching, trying to remember. "And not for many years to come."

What the hell does that *mean?* "I don't understand."

His smile seemed kind and familiar. Without knowing why, Charlotte felt she could trust this man's words. "You might want to sit down, Charlotte. What I'm about to tell you will come as a shock." She glanced at her husband before deciding Carl was probably right and sat beside him on the cot. "Right . . . in many years from now, after the death of my father, my mother will share the biggest secret she has ever kept in her life. She will tell me about the brave and wonderful thing her best friend had tried to do and succeeded, too, I might add. She will introduce me to a world I would never have known could exist, and she will give me the tools I will need to explore it."

He reached into his pocket. Ben stepped toward his wife, trying to get between them in case he was reaching for a weapon. Carl pulled out his hand and opened it. Lying in his palm was a shiny, almost-heart-shaped moonstone, one she recognized. Charlotte blinked slowly before bringing her eyes back up to his. "Jessica?" she asked.

He smiled and nodded, waiting.

When Charlotte first left home all those years ago, she'd left Jessica a note and a moonstone, thinking she could hold it or wear it—use it to remember her friend. *This* was the very same stone. "But how?" she asked, her voice a whisper.

"My mother gave it to me," he answered with a smile that now looked exactly like his father's. Acknowledging the look of shock in her eyes, he continued. "She gave it to me when she told me about you."

Ben wore an odd expression of amusement and confusion. Charlotte had so many questions, she didn't know where to start. "Charlie?" He nodded. "But you should only be—" she bit her lip, as she did the math. "You should be eight years old. I spoke to your mom last October, and you had just celebrated your eighth birthday, and for her it was 2029."

"I understand why you would say that. You have maintained the span of time you passed when you first came from 2012 to 1818—one hundred and ninety-four years. Right?" She nodded. "I have much to tell you."

"How old are you now?"

"Forty-three. I left in 2064." He let that sink in for a minute. "The first time I left there, I was twenty-seven."

"The first time?"

"Do you not remember meeting me before? Think about it for a moment." He shifted his gaze between them.

He did look familiar, but she was having a hard time recalling from where or when. "At the house of your parents," Ben stated. "You came to the door the day they had a summer Christmas for us. That was 2013."

Charlie smiled. Charlotte picked up where Ben left off. "So, was that you we saw on TV a few days later saving a mother and daughter from getting hit by a car?"

He was smiling. "That was me. After hearing so much about you, I had to meet you both and thought it would be nice to see all of you together. When I researched the events of that week, I saw that the woman and the girl were killed and thought I could help. I knew mom's kidnapping ended well, for her anyway, so I stayed out of that."

"So, how many times have you 'travelled'?" Charlotte asked, doing air quotes.

"I—"

"I hate to interrupt," Ben started, "but at the moment, you are in this cell. Are you not worried about what will become of you?"

Charlie's expression got serious. "Someone had dropped that tin of turpentine; it wasn't sealed properly. The cupboard behind the schoolhouse filled with fumes over the weekend, fumes that leaked into the classroom through the cracks. When the teacher lit the first candle . . ."

Charlotte felt the tears burning her eyes. "You saved the children? Two of them were ours."

"Two?" He seemed surprised but continued. "Unfortunately, someone saw me enter the schoolhouse. They found me inside with the turpentine and the striker in my hands. I didn't even have time to open the windows."

"I'm sure this will all get straightened out."

"I'm afraid I don't have time for that." Charlie forced a smile. "I have to leave here tonight. I need to be somewhere else."

"Where is that?" Charlotte asked, confused.

"I don't mean a place. I mean a time."

"But we just met . . . will we ever see you again?"

The answer was in his smile. "I feel certain that we will see one another again, but keep in mind, for me, this day may not have happened yet."

What? That was a strange thing to say!

"I was hoping you could bring me some candles and perhaps a stick to mark my circle? I will do my ritual here tonight."

"Of course. Right, tonight's a full moon."

"Tonight is a *blue* moon, Charlotte. It's extra special."

She smiled. "Anything else?"

"I don't think so. I have my stones with me. That's all I'll need."

"I think you've had enough time," came Lawrence's voice. "Ben, Charlotte, please come with me."

Charlotte whispered, "I'll be back when it's dark." Charlie nodded.

They told Lawrence that "Carl" had been passing the schoolhouse and smelled the turpentine. After searching, he found it in the storage cupboard behind the schoolhouse. He removed it and went in for the striker so Katie wouldn't use it and spark the fumes.

"That's what he told me as well. And to be honest, the first thing Katie did when she walked in after sending for help was open up all the windows because she, too, could smell it. If I may, how is it he came to ask for the two of you?" he asked.

Ben was quick on his feet. "He said someone in Moravia gave him our names when he asked about some kind of tea."

Charlotte added, "He was interested in a special mix for his mother's ailments."

That appeared to be good enough for Larry. He thanked them for their help and said, "Perhaps I will give him the night in the gaol and we'll be done with this in the morning."

"Why not this evening, Lawrence? It seems you believe the man."

"In the morning, Charlotte."

Charlotte and Ben wondered what Charlie could have told them if there had been more time.

They walked straight to the general store to share what they'd learned with Gracie and Jimmy. They had many questions, but there were few answers to give. "I will try to learn more when I see him tonight."

"Ah, be careful, lass. Ye dinna want Lawrence seeing ye keekin' 'round the place at night."

"We'll be careful, Gracie," Ben answered.

When the children arrived home from school, they were bursting to tell their parents about the man with the turpentine. When they'd finished their story, Ben put it to rest. He explained what had really happened and how, in fact, this man had saved the schoolhouse and everyone in it.

"Some of us thought we saw someone else sneaking around the classroom this morning, too," Holly said. Her brother looked at her and shook his head to himself. "You know it's true, Phillip. It looked like someone or more than one, was moving around the room, making shadows on the walls. Missus Dickson told us that the light coming through the windows was playing tricks with our imaginations because of what happened earlier."

"Did you see the tricky shadows, Phillip?" his mother asked. He didn't speak, but nodded grudgingly as Holly smiled smugly beside him.

Once the younger ones were settled and ready for bed, Charlotte asked Robbie and Sabel to keep their eye on things. "Your father and I are going for a little walk. We'll be back soon."

"Oo-oo, can I come?" Sabel asked.

"Not tonight, sweetheart. Next time, all right?" Sabel crinkled her eyebrows in surprise before nodding. Then Charlotte slipped into a light coat, and they were on their way.

When they arrived at the little bridge over the grist mill's pond, Ben put his finger over his lips. Watching their steps, they walked to the gaol's door. Charlie, who'd been listening for their footsteps, was at the door in an instant.

"Charlie?" Charlotte whispered.

"I'm here," he answered, as his face appeared behind the bars in the door's window.

"Here, take these." She passed him two candles, a stick, and her bloodstone. "Oh, and I brought a lighter. I didn't know if you had one."

Charlie took the items and whispered, "Thank you. I wish we had more time."

She reached for his hand on the bar and squeezed his fingers. "I do, too." She swallowed down the lump in her throat.

"I should get started."

"Stay safe, my friend," Ben said.

"Until we will meet again." Charlie smiled and walked toward the back of the room to begin his ritual.

The gaol was found empty the next morning. The gossip coming home from school was that Lawrence had released the man and sent him on his way— it died down after a couple of days.

Moving On

The end of the school year was only days away when Charlotte and Gracie received an invitation to Carole-Anne's for their noon meal. When they arrived at her door, Gracie said, "Ah, thank ye, Carole-Anne. This is a lovely change."

She smiled in answer, and said, "I thought it best to do this before school lets out. Everything gets a little busier and noisier then."

"That's the truth," Charlotte said with a giggle.

They sat down to a nice cool lunch and Carole-Anne started right away. "Do you remember when I told you that we'd been invited to the reservation in Upper Canada?"

With a sinking feeling in her stomach, Charlotte answered, "Yes."

"Yer leavin' us?" Gracie asked.

Carole-Anne nodded. "The decision was made with much consideration . . . I think that it would be a wonderful experience for Maisie, although she doesn't feel that way at the moment. She wants to stay here with Jeffery. She wants to believe they have a future together."

Charlotte noticed Gracie flick her eyes her way. "Don't get me wrong, he's a lovely young man, and they do appear happy with one another, but I can't help but feel if they are meant to be together, they will be."

"Aye."

"That's a hard thing to understand when you're young. It's definitely something you understand better with age, when you have some hindsight."

Carole-Anne nodded. "Moving away to live such a different life, with people who have very different beliefs, but who are willing to listen to ours is . . . well, I feel it is where we belong now. Keith has been waiting for me to come to it for quite some time. He's ready."

"When will ye go?"

"He would like to leave at the end of the month."

For Charlotte, the words were echoes in the background as her mind buzzed with unwanted thoughts. *If Maisie leaves this place, will she meet her Mr. Peterson? They had not learned his first name, where, or when they met, only that they married and lived near Sault Saint Marie in the late 1850s.* She tried to get a sense of the whole picture, as she knew it. *According to what Jessica had learned in the ancestry records, Maisie's daughter was born in or near Sault Saint Marie in 1857. Did this happen before Charlotte came to this time, when Carole-Anne was called Elizabeth and was hanged, without ever seeing her lover Brian again? In that case, it was most likely that Maisie would have grown up here in town—both Gracie and Gifted Hands had offered to take her in if that's what Elizabeth had wanted . . . At* least in Charlotte's memory, it happened that way. Her head was spinning. She could not interfere in what happened next. *Surely fate would look after who Maisie met and where. But what if it wasn't Mr. Peterson? If not, then Sarah Gray would never be born—she would never marry and become the Sarah Gray Thomason found in the family tree, who continues the birth line that leads to Charlotte's birth.*

"Charlie?" Gracie's voice was breaking through Charlotte's fog. "Charlie, are ye all right, lass?"

Moving her hand from her forehead, she looked at her friend and tried to smile. "Oh, sorry, my mind wandered off for a minute there. Yes, I'm fine."

"Are you sure, Charlotte?" Carole-Anne asked. "Can I get you some more tea? Or something stronger, perhaps? You look as though you've seen a ghost."

"Some more tea sounds lovely, thanks. Just a bit of a headache. I'm sure it will clear when I get back out into the fresh air."

While Charlotte and Gracie walked back to the store, Charlotte told her friend what was on her mind. "It confuses me, Gracie. By saving Elizabeth's life, we changed the course of their whole family's life."

"Well, yes, now they have one—together. You must remember, love, Brian came back to find her, but not soon enough to change the course of events. She woulda hanged, and little Caroline would never've known 'im."

"She might have, I suppose. If you or Gifted Hands had taken the little one in, you might have told him about her when he came to town."

"Aye, it's hard te say."

"The thing that's bothering me is that we don't know if she met her husband here, or Sault Saint Marie, or somewhere in between." Gracie saw the fear in her eyes as she continued. "What if they don't meet now . . . because of me? Would I be born? Could I even be here?"

Gracie put her arm around her friend's waist as they walked. "I dinna ken, lass, but I'll tell ye this, Jessica found those records *after* Elizabeth had been saved. Remember?"

Charlotte looked at Gracie, the relief clear in her eyes. "You're right. So, all I have to do is absolutely nothing."

"Aye."

In the blink of an eye, the kids were done for the summer and the Crawfords were packed up and ready to leave town. The night before they left, Lawrence saw to it that the town saw them off with class and gratitude. A party was held on the grounds of the inn. Every family was asked to bring a dish to share with all, be it fruit, vegetables, meat, dessert, or anything else. Lawrence paid for alcoholic beverages from the tavern, and the tavern supplied warm drinks and juice for those who didn't want alcohol.

The sun shone into the evening as everyone visited, ate, laughed, and said goodbye to the preacher and his family. Before supper, Lawrence stood before the crowd and said, "Keith, Carole-Anne, and Maisie, this town thanks you for your years spent with us. You have brought us friendship and the word of our Lord like no one before you. We will miss your presence here, but will look for word from you, from time to time. Best wishes, my friends."

Carole-Anne hugged him immediately. She looked forward to the challenges ahead, but she had buried her feelings of sadness. Now she cried. She was going to miss this town, her friends, her routine, her responsibilities. In her heart she knew they were making the right choice. This was an ending of sorts, but it was a new beginning with the two people she loved most in this world.

Gracie and Charlotte were catching up with Rosey. "How is Jeffery faring, knowing Maisie'll be leavin'?"

"He's been moping around the house. He doesn't want her to go. I understand of course, but . . ."

"Aye."

"Aw, look at her, Gracie. Let's go and say hello," Charlotte said.

When they approached Maisie, she tried to smile, but found herself unable to. Charlotte felt for her, knowing she was moving so far from her love. "Well, you can write to each other, and visit during holidays," Gracie suggested with a smile.

"I know. But we'll be so far away." There was a quiver in her voice.

Charlotte put her arm around the young woman's shoulders and said softly, "It's not so far, honey. I'm sure you and Jeffery will work something out." Her eyes flicked to Gracie's.

Jeffery joined them then. "Good evening, ladies. It's a nice gathering."

"It is. How are you, Jeffery?" Charlotte asked. He was now a young man of twenty-two, but he still had freckles across his nose and cheeks and a cheeky look in his eyes.

An expression similar to Maisie's spread over his face. "Ah, we ken lad. Charlotte and I'll let ye be," she said, taking her friend's arm. "Let's go say hello to Lennie, shall we?"

He nodded. "Would you like to go for a walk, Maze?"

She smiled at the women and left on his arm.

Apprentice

The next time Charlotte saw Rosey, it was when she came into the apothecary a few weeks later. She inquired about Jeffery. "Well, he's not been the same since they left. He's quiet—keeps to himself. He doesn't seem to know what to do or how to spend his time."

"Aww. I'm sure he misses her. What are your thoughts, if you don't mind me asking? Will you encourage him to keep in touch with Maisie?"

"Oh, yes, of course. They must communicate with each other so that as things change, both are aware. Of course, they've barely settled in yet. I don't imagine there'll be much news for a while."

Charlotte listened to Rosey's words but didn't ask her to elaborate. In her opinion, Rosey had a realistic view of the situation.

The summer passed rather quickly for the Williams'. It was hot and dry. To pass the time, the whole family spent time swimming and playing in the water. Gracie hadn't become any more comfortable in the water, but thankfully for her children, they hadn't inherited that trait. They spent many an afternoon and evening at the lake.

By summer's end, the town had found a new preacher, and Charlotte prepared to harvest her gardens, which included several healthy weed plants. They had grown much better than last year, despite the dry weather. She harvested, washed, and trimmed them, leaving the buds to dry on a hanging rack in her old room. When they were ready in a week or two, she would cure them for a couple of months. Only then could she infuse some oil and make some salve. In the meantime, she collected and cut up the trimmings. She could heat these in order to decarboxylate them—a term she'd learned from Jessica—so that she could add them to some good whiskey to make a tincture. Jess had given her the instructions and recipes to do it all.

When school started back in the fall, only Phillip and Holly attended. Robbie was working with his dad every day, learning and taking notes. Sabel was doing the same with her mother; she was learning something new every day.

"Have you heard from Jonny, Sabel?" Charlotte asked as she swept the floor.

Her daughter turned to her and blushed. "I did. He sent me a note."

"Oh?"

Sabel looked uncomfortable, but explained. "He said he hoped I remembered him. He was the young man who was apprenticing at the tanner in Auburn. Then he said he would like to see me again and hoped that would be agreeable. He said he would send another note in the coming weeks and would come down to visit after that."

Charlotte and Sabel had accompanied Ben when he travelled to Auburn in August, hoping to purchase some new jars and other containers. While there, they popped in to see the tanner. Charlotte still liked to find cutoffs she could use to tie back her or the girls' hair. Inside the shop, Charlotte spoke to the tanner while Sabel looked around at the items hanging on the walls. "Hello, is there something I can help you with, Miss?" a voice said from beside her.

Sabel turned to see a young man looking her way. "Oh, hello. No, thank you. I'm just looking. I'm here with my mother."

"My name is Jonathon Gibson. Jonny," he said, and glanced toward Charlotte. "Your mother is the town's apothecary?" Sabel nodded. "I thought I'd seen her before. And you are?"

Sabel smiled as she told him her name. A boy had never approached her in this way. He looked to be about her age, friendly face, handsome smile.

Charlotte could hear them talking behind her, and she smiled at the tanner. He rolled his eyes before going into the back where he had some scraps he could offer her. "Oh, these are perfect. Thank you," she said, and placed a few coins on the counter.

"And thank you, Mrs. Williams. Always a pleasure."

"... sure. Goodbye," she heard Sabel say.

After taking care of their business, the women walked to the lakefront to pass some time in the sun while they waited for Ben. "So?" Charlotte started.

Sabel looked at her and smirked. "You mean about Jonny?"

"I do. What did I miss?"

"He asked if he could come see me one Saturday after work."

"I see."

"He said he'd sent a note."

And it begins, Charlotte thought.

It was well into the fall now, and he had visited twice. Both times, the two went for a walk to get to know each other better. Sabel seemed to like his attention, and as far as her parents were concerned, he seemed to be a nice, respectable young man.

Samhain 1836

The end of October approached, and Charlotte looked forward to her time with Jessica. Their shared Samhain rituals offered them a special window in time; allowing them to share their thoughts, feelings, and news on an intimate and spiritual level, without words.

This year, she knew something about Jessica's son that Jessica wouldn't know for years. *It feels strange to keep it from her, but I can hardly tell Jess what her son will do years from now, because of what she hasn't told him yet. Huh?*

The house had been quiet for the past hour and Charlotte used the time to her benefit—to lie back in a nice hot bath and relax. Thoughts of Jessica were strong as Charlotte envisioned her as the mother of a nine-year-old. She breathed deeply, allowing the scent of lavender oil to further relax her and help her focus. Once finished, she wrapped herself in a big towel and went to her bedroom. Ben assured her he would look after the tub while she was busy.

She slipped into her shift and lit the candles she'd left on her altar, beginning her Samhain ritual. It seemed no time at all from her welcoming the Goddess and God to when she began to see Jessica's blurry outline. "Charlotte, I see you," she thought-heard.

"Jessica! How are you? How are your boys?"

Jessica's smile glowed as she looked at her friend. "They're both well. Charlie skipped grade four—he's in grade five now and loves his teacher. He always wants to go to the cottage—he loves it as much as you and I did, I think. Everything is the same with Michael; he works hard, and he loves it. I'm enjoying part-time hours. I still love the work, but I like the extra family time I get now. Life is good."

"Wonderful. How's your mum?"

Jessica's cheerful expression disappeared. "She's only sixty-seven, but she's gone, Char. I still go see her every few days, but she hasn't recognized me in over a year. It's heart-breaking. Thank God I have Michael to lean on. Some days it's just so hard to deal with. I honestly think it would be better if she'd just pass. She wouldn't want to be what she's become." She blinked hard then and forced a smile. "Now you."

"I'm so sorry." Charlotte shook her head. "Robbie is enjoying working with his father. We expect to hear from Harvard in the coming months. Sabel has an admirer from Auburn. I think she kinda likes him, too. We shall see. The other two are enjoying school and their friends, just like kids should. Holly has learned that she likes to paint, and I don't mind saying, she's already better than I'll ever be. Gifted Hands told her she'll help her learn more about it if Holly's interested. And let me tell you, she is!"

"That's so nice and unexpected. How about my friend Phillip?"

"He is the only child I know who loves writing. He never complains when he's assigned writing homework. Funny, eh?"

"Wow, that's great. I remember thinking all the writing they used to make us do was useless. I guess his teacher's doing something right. And the Crawfords?"

"They moved away during the summer. Oh, and I'm almost ready to start making my cannabis oil and salve. I can't wait to try it out!"

Jess smiled. "I want to hear how it g......." Her form began to blur and Charlotte could no longer hear her.

"I love you, Jess. Stay happy," Charlotte thought-said, and then she was alone. She tried not to feel disappointed. She waited all year to see Jess and it was always over so quickly. It seemed their special window only opened for a minute or two—not nearly long enough, but much better than nothing.

The first flakes of snow began to fall mid-November, as Charlotte set her chopped buds to heat over the wood-burning stove. She invited Gracie in for a cup of tea while she waited.

"Oh, it didna take long to fill the room, did it?" she asked, as she came in from the back door.

Charlotte laughed. "No, it did not. I kind of like the smell, but if you don't, we can go to the kitchen."

"No, no, this is fine, lass. It's like the good old days, when it was just you and me and you were tryin' somethin' new."

Charlotte smiled. "It is, isn't it? I never told you this, Gracie, but when we were young, we used to smoke this stuff sometimes, like a cigarette or cigar."

"Ye did? Why? Just the smell alone would put me off."

"Sometimes it smells better than others. The thing is, when you smoke it, you get what we called 'high'." Gracie had no idea what her friend was talking about. "Kind of like when you have too much to drink and it goes to your head, everything is funny, and you feel relaxed. Know what I mean?" Gracie nodded and shrugged at the same time. "The last time I did that was when Ben and I went back. Jess and Michael brought some to the cottage one night and we smoked it down by the fire."

"Benny, too?"

"Yep. We all giggled that night. Anyway, what I'm going to do with it is not that. I will infuse it into some oil, then I'll use some of that to make a salve. This way we can use it as drops that we take for pain, insomnia, anxiety, or we can rub it onto our skin for rashes, eczema, arthritis, inflammation, all kinds of things."

"Without the giggles?"

"Without the giggles."

By the time she placed the last jar of salve in the cupboard, the ground outside had a covering of snow, and Ben was sitting in a chair watching her work.

"All done?" he asked, stepping up to her and encircling her with his arms.

"I will answer after a kiss."

The snow stayed on the ground from that day through to March. The lake was safely frozen by Christmas, allowing them to easily cross wearing snowshoes or working a kick-sled. Carole-Anne, Keith, and Maisie were missed as the town celebrated throughout the holidays, but Charlotte and Gracie were happy to receive a letter just before Christmas.

December 1836

Dearest Charlotte, Gracie, and families,

Greetings to all as the Christmas/Yule quickly approaches. We have settled in well. We were given a small piece of land to call our own on the inside border of the tribe's land. All the men worked to help erect a small log house for the three of us to live in. It was finished before the cold set in, thank goodness. All that remains to be done are some finishing touches.

Keith began to teach the word of our Lord soon after our arrival and it seems that most are interested in our beliefs. Mind you, we would never force our beliefs upon them. They are, of course, entitled to believe whatever they desire. After our home was finished, work began on a small building to be used as a church. At this time, it is crude, but sufficient for its purpose. Keith has begun to preach on Sundays.

Maisie has taken a long time to adjust. She has written several letters to Jeffery and received almost as many in return. For now, she is appeased. I am enjoying our time here and have no doubt that we made the best decision in coming here. We do miss you all, though.

I hope you are all doing well, and I look forward to hearing your news. You will find our location at the bottom of this letter, so you can write to us when you are able.

We send you love and our best wishes for Christmas and the coming New Year.

Carole-Anne

Jonny came down to visit Sabel just before Christmas. The two spent their time together cozy by the outside fire, talking and laughing. He would spend his holiday with his parents who lived outside of Auburn, and while he would have loved to bring her to meet them, he knew it was too early for that. Before he left however, he made plans to come back to see her at the end of January.

The Williams and Moffatt families spent Christmas Eve with Gifted Hands, Keen Wolf, and the children, on the other side of the lake. Before the evening was over, they toasted Running Otter and Aleshanee, hoping they were happy, Jessica, Michael, and Charlie, who were never far from their thoughts, and the Crawfords, who were spending their first Christmas in their new home.

Spring

The snow was just beginning to melt when Gracie handed Robbie a letter. "I received this for ye in the post today." Robbie wanted to wait until the family was together to open it, so he stuck it in his pocket and waited for suppertime.

His parents were surprised when he pulled it out at the supper table. "It's from Harvard Medical School," he started.

"Open it, open it!" Charlotte said, feeling the excitement and hoping the news was good. "Dear Master Robert Williams, we are writing today to welcome you into our School of Medicine."

"Oh, Robbie, I'm so happy for you," his mother said excitedly.

"Wonderful!" said Ben. "It will be hard work, but you're up to it. Congratulations, son."

Sabel jumped up from her seat and wrapped her arms around his neck. "Good for you, big brother!" She kissed his cheek.

Robbie rolled his eyes, but inside he was excited and a little nervous. He would begin in the fall. After reading the rest of the letter, and after the whooping ended, they began to make arrangements. Knowing that Robbie would be accepted, Ailsa and Sam had graciously offered him their home while in Boston. He sent them a note the very next day. He would see them at the end of the summer.

In the meantime, he continued to work with Ben, questioning what he didn't understand and writing it all down. He also questioned Charlotte about the effectiveness of various herbs and the reasons for them. He was smart and curious and had the ability to easily assimilate new knowledge, a trait he got from his father. As he tucked his notebook into his bag, Charlotte reached up and hugged him. "I'm very proud of you, Robbie. And I want you to know, your mother would be, too." Her eyes were wet as she finished speaking.

He hugged her back, and whispered, "Thank you."

That year, they had a particularly wet spring. Charlotte did her best to control her hair in the humidity, but it was difficult without modern-day products. Most days, she tied a kerchief over her head and left it at that. Gracie, on the other hand, wore her bonnet most days, and the little hairs that poked out at the sides curled onto her cheeks. Charlotte thought she looked lovely, but Gracie had had about enough.

Mabel suffered from arthritis in her knees, especially in the fall and spring, although she complained little. When it hit her this year, the pain was visible on her face. After discussing it with Ben and Robbie, and then Mabel, Charlotte's salve was applied to both knees. "Give it an hour, and see how you feel," Ben said as Charlotte rubbed it in.

A couple of hours had passed when Charlotte popped into the store to check on her mother-in-law. "Charlie! Ma knees are feelin' improved. Thank ye."

"Excellent! And thank you for being the first to try it. Here's the jar; when the pain starts to come back, rub on some more. Hopefully this will get you through to the nicer weather." She was happy to report back to Ben that the salve was working for his mother. Now he could add it to his treatment inventory. She looked forward to telling Jessica.

To everyone's delight, with the onset of May, the drier weather arrived.

"Sabel, Mitenah has invited you to sleep over tomorrow. Gifted Hands asked if we'd like to go Saturday this week instead of Sunday."

"She did? Oh . . . I didn't realize. I received a note today. Jonny's coming down tomorrow, Mum. He asked if I would like to spend the evening with him. I thought I would. We can go for a ride or a walk or something like that."

"I see," Charlotte answered with a smile. Jonny, as an apprentice tanner, lived in a small room attached to the tanner's home in Auburn. Before getting the job, he lived in a village north of there with his parents. He tried to see them about once a month.

He and Sabel had continued to see each other once or twice a month over the winter and early spring. He seemed quite fond of her, and who could blame him? "I'm sure she'll understand. Maybe next time."

Sabel had just celebrated her seventeenth birthday—she was a big girl now. She and her mother had had many talks about boys and men and sex and babies. She understood certain actions had consequences. While Sabel enjoyed Jonny's company, she certainly didn't seem to be in a rush to marry and have a family; something that made her parents happy. There was lots of time for that. For now, Charlotte wanted to work with her to hone her knowledge and instincts on something she enjoyed doing and could use to make a living—plants and herbs.

Sabel now worked with Charlotte, both behind the counter and in the garden. Once or twice a week, she would spend the evening at the "Doctor's House", sorting, grinding, and mixing plants and herbs. She was a natural, and it was obvious that the work offered her a sort of calm.

Because they no longer worked out of the general store, they had extended their hours. On Wednesdays, they were now available all day, rather than a half day, and on Saturdays, they worked until mid-afternoon instead of noon. With the two of them working, it was easy to make themselves more available.

As much as Charlotte loved the progress they'd made in the apothecary, she missed working with Gracie and Mabel at the store every day; the chit chat, the gossip, the cheekiness, and just sharing the time together. After Gladys's passing several years ago, Mabel lost some of her spark. Losing her closest friend, and realizing that age was creeping up, had dimmed her outlook. She was approaching seventy years old, and while she still had her wits about her, she was visibly slowing down. She had friends of course, often spending time with Phoebe and Shirley, or sitting with Hettie, talking the night away. Last month, she received an offer she couldn't refuse.

It started a few months ago when Ailsa and Sam came to town. Sam had work in the west and Ailsa wanted to come with the children and stay with us while he was there. She and Sam had had twins, a boy and a girl. He was a changed man after meeting Aisla, but after becoming a father, he truly fell in love. He was a devoted husband and father, and it looked good on him.

While the family enjoyed a lovely visit with Ailsa, Sam was offered an opportunity to go overseas with work for a few months, more specifically, to France.

When Sam returned to town, he told everyone over supper. Ailsa was thrilled when she heard the news. She would not only get to see France, but she would be close to her family, who still lived in Aberdeen. "Sam, maybe I can spend some of our time away in Scotland with the children? I would love to see Mum and Morag and her family, and they would love to meet our children."

"That's exactly what I was thinking!" He smiled. "I can work in France, and you can visit with them. I will miss you, of course, but when will we have another opportunity like this?"

Ailsa's smile was dazzling as she looked across the table and asked, "Mabel, why don't you come with us?"

Mabel's face paled as she heard the words. "Me? Go back to Scotland? I . . . I . . . never thought I'd see it again." She looked at Gracie and then Ben. "What do you think?' she asked them.

"Yes," they answered in unison. The table laughed, but Mabel was very serious.

She nodded. "I do believe I will take this opportunity. That is, if that will work for everyone?" Her gaze rested on Sam. He could not have known how much she needed something like this.

He walked to where she was sitting at the table and bent to her ear. A smile spread across her face as she looked at each of us in turn. "I'll do it. I'll go wi' ye." She turned slightly and caught Sam's head, landing a kiss on his cheek.

Sam blushed as he stood. "It's settled then. We leave in two weeks. Let's celebrate tonight, for tomorrow we must head for Boston to organize ourselves."

"Best wishes for a safe and happy journey," Ben said, raising his glass.

"Oo-oo, I canna mind the last time I looked forward te somethin' so much," Mabel said, pink in the cheeks. That night, she went to sleep with a big smile on her face. Thoughts of seeing cousin Sheila and the family again swirling happily in her mind.

In the morning, when she hadn't come down for breakfast, Gracie said, "I'll wager she's started her packin'. I'll just run up and see." She came back down a minute later, tears running down her cheeks. "She's gone."

"Gone where? She's not leaving for a few days yet," Charlotte said.

Gracie looked at her brother and hugged him. "No, she's gone; in her sleep, wi' a smile on 'er face."

Charlotte's hand came up over her mouth. "Oh, no." She hugged Gracie.

"She's back wi' Da. I'm happy for that," Gracie said.

The store's open sign didn't get turned that day. Instead, they each took a turn visiting Mabel and saying goodbye.

Ailsa and Sam left town with heavy hearts after the service two days later. They'd liked the idea of making the trip together. It wouldn't be the same without her.

Together, they decided Sabel would help Gracie and Sandy in the store a few days a week while they tried to work out how best to proceed.

It was just after 2:00 p.m. when the two girls, well, young women actually, walked into the apothecary at the "Doctor's House" giggling. "Auntie Gracie let us go for the weekend, Mum. Sandy is going to come home with me and help me decide which dress to wear when I see Jonny later. Okay?"

She had picked up many of her mother's expressions, but "okay" always made Charlotte smile. "Sure, honey. I'll see you in a little while."

Ben, Phillip, Holly, and Charlotte were to meet in the store at 2:45. After closing the shop, Charlotte ran home to freshen up, pick up some fresh clothes for Ben, and wish Sabel a nice evening.

As she left the house, she reminded Sabel of the rules—no boys in the house when there was no one home. Sabel assured her, adding that after Jonny left, she would spend the night at Sandy's. She hugged her mother goodbye as she left for the store.

When they pushed off the canoe, Charlotte heard herself sigh. It was time to relax and see their friends. They still saw them most weekends, sometimes with the children, sometimes not. Mitenah, Sabel, and Sandy were thick as thieves—each very different from the next, but the three fit together perfectly.

Mitenah was disappointed when they arrived and Sabel was not with them, but she understood the situation and smiled as she welcomed them in. Gifted Hands was standing just inside the door, her smile as lovely as ever. "Chweh'n everyone. Come on in," she said.

"Chweh'n!" Charlotte said, walking into the sitting room. She slipped her poncho over her head and turned to lay it over the back of the settee. "So, wh— " Her words cut off as she turned toward the kitchen.

"Running Otter!" Ben exclaimed, moving in to shake his hand.

"What a surprise!" Charlotte exclaimed, wrapping him in a hug. "How are you? When did you get home?"

Holly and Phillip looked at each other and rolled their eyes. There had always been enough of an age gap between them and him that they hadn't been as close as the others. They didn't remember him playing with them when they were small and couldn't understand the depth of their parents' relationship with him.

"Holly, Phillip, come with me. Dark Wolf is waiting for you in his room," Mitenah said.

"Why don't we have a seat, and I will get some drinks," Gifted Hands said.

Charlotte smiled at her friend. They hadn't seen him in almost three years. He had been living with Aleshanee's people all this time. Now, she took a good look at him; his hair was styled differently, and although he was smiling, the shine that was always in his eyes was absent. "What brings you home, Running Otter?"

He looked around the room, his eyes resting on his mother. "I have come home."

"You mean to stay?" Charlotte asked.

Kohana jumped onto his lap. He patted her absentmindedly as he answered. "Yes. I am no longer bonded with Aleshanee. I chose to come home." His tone was flat.

"Oh," Charlotte replied, unsure how to respond. Clearly, he was saddened by this.

She moved to sit beside him and put her hand over his. "What changed?" He looked at his hand under hers and tried a smile, but it was flimsy. "I'm sorry. You probably don't want to talk about it," she added.

"I do not. You are right . . . but it has happened, and I cannot escape it." He took a deep breath before continuing. "Aleshanee and I, we . . . well, we enjoyed each other's company. I got on well with the members of the clan there. I did my part, and to be honest, I was mostly happy. But Aleshanee wants more. She says that she wants children, but I believe what she wants is more than one man. That is not what I want." He dropped his head as he finished speaking.

Charlotte looked across the room at Ben. "I'm so sorry. I'm sure she will regret giving you up. You are a wonderful man. You know that, right?"

He smiled now. "That is what En-ay tells me. I have had some time to consider all that has happened. It is a long walk from where they are." He took a deep breath. "I will move on. I will be happy again without her."

Charlotte gave his hand a squeeze and looked at his mother with a grim smile. "Well, I, for one, will be happy to have you back in my life, my friend."

"Sorry, Running Otter," Ben said. "Sometimes life doesn't go the way we expect, but it always goes the way it's supposed to. What was that expression of Sheila's, Charlotte?"

"It's a Scottish expression, Running Cu—oops, Otter. It goes, 'Whit's fur ye'll no go by ye!'" He smiled, hearing her attempt at the accent and waited for the translation. "Meaning what's meant to happen will happen." He simply nodded. He understood, but he wasn't quite there yet.

A Fresh Start

Sabel arrived home as her family was enjoying coffee and pancakes. "Good morning!" she said to the room.

"Good morning, love. How was your evening?"

"It was fun. Jonny and I started on a walk and bumped into Timmy. While we were talking, he invited us to join him and some schoolmates for a fire at his place. He said we should ask Sandy, too, so that's what we did. We sat around the fire talking and laughing. Then we went back to the store. Jonny was invited to stay in your room, but he preferred to ride home."

"Sounds like a fun night," Charlotte said.

"Yep. How was yours?"

Ben smiled before answering. "Ours was nice, too. Of course, it always is when we see our friends."

"And we had a bit of a surprise," Charlotte added.

"What was that?"

"Running Otter was there." She watched her daughter's expression change from surprise to disappointment.

"He's been gone a long time. How long will he be home?" she asked, trying to appear indifferent.

"Mum, can we be excused?" Phillip interrupted. "We're finished, and we know the story."

Ben chuckled. "Off you go. Take your plates to the counter."

Sabel was watching Charlotte, waiting for her answer. "Well, he told us he and Aleshanee are no longer bonded. He will no longer be living there. So, I suppose he's home for a while."

"Hmm," she mumbled, turning to pour herself some coffee. "I guess I'll see him next week. Will they be coming here?"

"They will."

With a nod, she excused herself, taking her bag up to her room.

Once she was safely out of hearing distance, Ben whispered, "This will be interesting."

"That it will."

The next week passed like any other. Sabel worked at the Doctor's House for three days and with Gracie and Sandy, three days. Her mother thought she was a little quieter than usual, pensive even, but perhaps she was looking too closely. When she asked on Friday if Sabel was going to see Jonny this weekend, her answer was, "No. Maybe next weekend."

Everyone arrived at the Williams house Sunday around noon. Charlotte was arranging food on a platter when she heard the door. Gifted Hands stepped in first, as Hazel ran up the stairs for the quiet of the bedroom; she was getting too old for all the noise.

They all arrived together! There was a lot of bustling going on with shawls and coats and shoes. Phillip and Holly pushed through the crowd, ready to disappear with Lily, Evelyn, and Dark Wolf.

"Bye, Mum. We'll be in the treehouse," Phillip called behind him.

The last one in the door was Running Otter. He stepped in with a smile, looking around.

Charlotte saw his eyes widen and settle on something behind her and knew he'd seen Sabel. She had come down the stairs and was saying hello to everyone, looking lovely. Her mother noted how nicely she'd done her long, dark hair and smiled inwardly. "Chweh'n, Sabel," he said. "It is good to see you again."

She smiled brightly and answered, "You as well. Mum and Dad said you've come home?"

The brightness left his eyes momentarily as he nodded, but it returned quickly. "Yes, I am home to start a new life."

"A fresh start." He nodded. "I'm sure everyone is happy about that," she said.

"Yes, especially En-ay." His smile was bright.

"Your hair looks nice this way." This was an understatement. She *liked* the way he wore his hair—it was still quite long, but the top section was fixed into two braids that ran on either side of a centre part, with the tied ends hanging over the front of his shoulders; the lower portion of hair, from just above his ears, had been shaved and was very short as it grew in.

"Come on in and sit," she said, leading him to the settee. "Can you tell me about it?"

Charlotte watched as they sat together talking, and it warmed her heart. That he was able to relieve himself of some of his troubles with her was a good start to their renewed friendship.

The following Friday, the women were preparing to close the Doctor's House for the day. Charlotte asked, "Did you hear from Jonny this week, honey?"

"Yes. He's coming down tomorrow afternoon. I was going to ask if he could eat supper with us?"

"Of course he can." As the little bells above the apothecary door rang out, Charlotte saw the happy surprise register on Sabel's face—it was Running Otter.

"Chweh'n," he said, walking in. "En-ay wanted to return this to you, Charlotte, and after hearing about your 'Doctor's House', I wanted to come see for myself."

"Of course. Sabel, would you like to show him around while I clean up this counter?"

"Sure." She smiled brightly and said, "Come through here, Running Otter."

A couple of minutes later, the two returned to the counter. "This is a good way for Ben to see his patients, Charlotte. Do many come to you?"

"Well, it took a while for the townspeople to catch on to the idea, but they have realized this is the place to come when they need the doctor, as long as they are able. We stay pretty busy. And, of course, the apothecary counter from the store has moved here, so there is a constant flow of customers coming for herbs and medicines and such. We're doing well."

"Very good." He turned to Sabel and asked, "If you're finished here, maybe you can walk me back to my canoe?"

Looking at her mother, Sabel briefly widened her eyes. Having no idea what she was trying to say, Charlotte simply smiled; it was her choice.

"Um, sure," Sabel answered.

"I'll see you at the store, hon, then we can walk home together." She nodded and turned to leave with Running Otter.

"See you Sunday, Charlotte," he said, before the door closed behind them.

Jonny came to town the next afternoon, walking into the Doctor's House as they were closing up. "Good afternoon, ladies. Lovely day."

"Jonny, it's good to see you. Yes, the sun's been shining all morning," Charlotte answered.

"Oh, hello, Jonny," Sabel said, coming into the front area.

"Are you closing up for the day?" he asked. She nodded. "Would you care to go for a walk? I thought maybe today you can show me this 'drop' you keep talking about."

She giggled. "Sure. Are you okay if I go now, Mum?"

"Off you go. I'll see you at home later."

Once the counter was cleaned up, Charlotte walked into the back room. "How is the doctor making out? Almost ready to go home?"

He looked up with an expression she knew well. "I'm finished with my patients, yes. I do have one stop to make later, though."

"Let me help you get this cleaned up and we can get out of here for the weekend," she said, reaching for the cloth. "Jonny came in to meet Sabel. The two of them went for a walk to the drop." Just saying the name brought her happy memories of when she and Ben were getting to know each other—he took her to the drop, and she surprised him by jumping.

Charlotte wondered if Sabel would jump if Jonny was there cheering her on.

As she set the table for supper, she heard the wind picking up outside. Then there was a loud clap of thunder. "Wow! Where did that come from? It was such a beautiful day?" Charlotte asked. She hoped the kids would make it home before the rain.

During supper, the rain started coming down. It poured. Ben suggested Jonny stay to avoid getting soaked on the back of a horse. "You can stay down here on the settee."

He looked from Charlotte to Sabel. "If you don't mind, I'd appreciate that."

"You can go to church with the others in the morning, if you like," Charlotte offered.

He looked at Sabel, who said, "Or, I can walk you to the stable when the others go to church—I don't go there anymore." He raised his eyebrows—this was news to him. "We can talk on the way."

They spent the evening playing cards while the rain pelted the windows and roof. When it was time for bed, Sabel brought Jonny a pillow and blanket and gave him a little hug goodnight.

When her parents peeked into her room to say goodnight, Ben said, "He seems to be a nice young man."

"He *is* nice, and thoughtful, and funny," she said as a blush spread across her cheeks.

The next morning, Ben and Charlotte met Sabel, who was already there, and the others at the store after church. Today they would go across the lake; except for Robbie, who had other plans. After saying goodbye to Jonny, Sabel joined Sandy and Lily in Jimmy's canoe. After a stormy night, the air was thick. Charlotte's hair was big with the humidity, but the sun was shining with the promise of summer.

They enjoyed their visit and were delighted to eat outside again—it had been ages. When Holly mentioned Sabel's friend had been over for supper last night, she made kissing noises, teasing her sister. "Stop it, Holly," Sabel said, blushing fiercely.

"That's enough, Holly," her mother said, but inwardly, she smiled.

Jonny sent Sabel a note when his boss asked him to deliver something to Ernest Albert, the town's tanner. He expected to be down Wednesday afternoon and wondered if she could spare an hour to "visit". Her mother was usually able to let her leave a little early on Wednesdays, so this worked out nicely.

Or maybe it didn't . . . Sabel left the shop with Jonny at two o'clock and at two fifteen who should walk in but Running Otter. "Chweh'n, Charlotte. En-ay told me that Sabel often finishes early on Wednesday. I wondered if she'd like to go out in the canoe."

She looked into his eyes. *God, he is a good-looking young man, so much like his father and uncle!* "I'm afraid she's already left. She's gone for a walk with a friend."

His face contorted momentarily. "The kissy friend?" he asked.

It took everything she had not to laugh. "Um, yes."

"Perhaps I am too late," he said under his breath.

"It's never too late, Running Otter," she offered, hoping he would feel encouraged.

He turned to go back out the door and heard their voices. ". . . so I won't be down this weekend." Then he found himself face-to-face with Sabel and Jonny. "Oh, chweh'n, Running Otter. This is my friend, Jonny," she said, cool as a cucumber.

The men smiled at one another and shook hands, but neither was looking to be friends.

"I will see you on Sunday, Sabel." Running Otter nodded at Jonny and left.

Later, she said, "That was awkward. Why do things have to happen that way, Mum? Why did they have to bump into each other?"

"I'm not sure, sweetheart, but at least now they both know there's another man interested in you."

"You think Running Otter is interested in me?"

"He came in asking for you. He wondered if you'd like to go out in the canoe." The flashbacks to Keen Wolf taking Charlotte out in the canoe all those years ago, hit her hard. The feelings she'd had at the time were not buried too deep.

Sabel told her mother she wouldn't be seeing Jonny this weekend; his parents expected him home. So, when Saturday afternoon came around and Charlotte saw Running Otter coming down the road, she smiled. "What is it?" Sabel asked, seeing Charlotte's face.

"Look out the window."

"Oh, sh—" She stopped herself and looked at her mother.

Then he was in the doorway. "Chweh'n, Charlotte. Chweh'n, Mimiteh."

"Chweh'n." Sabel answered. "I haven't heard that name for a long time." She smiled. "What are you doing here today? Aren't we going to see you tomorrow?" Charlotte made herself busy under the counter.

"En-ay thought Charlotte might want this dish back for tomorrow." Sabel eyed it as he passed it to her.

"Ah, yes, thank you," Charlotte said, setting it on the counter.

"I wonder, since I'm here, would you like to come out in the canoe with me for a while?"

"Um . . ." She didn't know what to say. When their eyes met, her mother gave her a reassuring wink. "Sure. I'll be finished in a few minutes."

"That's all right, love. I can manage here. You two go ahead. I'll see you at home for supper."

It was a lovely spring afternoon, so rather than heading straight home, Ben and Charlotte walked to the store. Gracie and Sandy had just closed up and joined them outside while some fresh tea steeped. "Where's Sabel today, Auntie Charlotte?"

"She was invited out in the canoe with Running Otter. That'll be them out there." She pointed.

Sandy's eyes opened wide. "That's nice," she eventually said. "Well, I'm going inside for now. See you tomorrow."

It was about an hour later when the canoe returned. From her seat, Charlotte could see Running Otter get out and pull the canoe in some, and offer his hand to Sabel to help her out. Then he waved, got back in, and rowed off.

"Nice and sunny out there on the water?" she asked.

"It was beautiful."

Gracie smiled before standing and said, "Well, I s'ppose I should help Hettie wi' supper. See ye tomorrow."

As they walked home, Ben asked, "You went out in the canoe, and you didn't catch us supper?"

"Dad!" she said with a laugh. "Maybe next time."

"Oo-oo, there will be a next time?" her mum teased.

She got serious then. "Maybe . . . I guess. It was nice to be out there with him. He told me more about Aleshanee and why he'd come home. He saw her coming out of another man's bed. Did he tell you that?"

"The first time we saw him after he returned, he told me she wanted more," Charlotte said.

"Yes . . . I have a hard time understanding that. How could she turn away such a good man?"

"I can't answer that. Good men are not always easy to find, and he is certainly one of the good ones." Charlotte glanced at Ben who was listening intently.

"He seems to have accepted that it's over, and he seems happy," Sabel said.

"Of course, he was happy, sweetheart. He was with you."

She looked up at her mother with wonder, and a slow smile spread across her face.

When they arrived home, Charlotte called for Hazel. Most days, as soon as she heard them at the door, she waited for it to open and went outside. "That's different. Where's Hazel today?" she asked.

She called her again and when she didn't come, started to look around. Charlotte found her curled up on their bed. She sat beside her and patted her gently. Hazel had become much thinner over the past months, but of course she would, she was nineteen years old. "Hello, sweetheart. Don't want to go outside today?"

Hazel looked at her and blinked, a soft mewing sound escaping. "Oh, Hazel. You're not feeling it today, are you? Poor baby." She picked her up and carried her downstairs, setting her on her bed by the fire. "She was on the bed. She doesn't look too good, Benny," Charlotte said, teary eyed.

He looked down at her and smiled. "Aww, she'll be cozy by the fire."

Charlotte gave her a fresh bowl of water where she lay and went about the business of getting supper on the table. When the cat leaned over to drink some water, she felt a bit of relief. Hazel stayed by the fire all night.

The next morning, Charlotte was the first one up. Aware that Hazel hadn't come up to their bed during the night, she went straight to where she'd left her. She found her curled up in a cozy ball. "Here you are. Did you have a good sleep?" She bent to pat her and immediately knew—Hazel had passed away in the night.

Their friends arrived that afternoon with Gracie, Jimmy, and all the kids who had just come from church, except for Sandy, who had stayed home with a headache. Drinks were offered and everyone got comfortable at the outdoor tables overlooking the lake. Almost immediately, Charlotte heard, "We're going for a walk, Mum." She turned to see Sabel standing with Mitenah and Running Otter. Over her shoulder, she saw a gleam in Keen Wolf's eye, and smiled.

"We're going to the tree house, Mum," Holly said.

"Okay, everyone. We eat in two hours."

When Charlotte asked about Sandy, Gracie said she'd seemed fine this morning, but when they got home from church, she said her head ached, and she'd prefer to stay home and lie down.

"We were sorry to hear about Hazel, Charlotte. She was your pet for many years," Gifted Hands said.

Charlotte swallowed down the lump in her throat. "Thank you. We'll miss her, but I know she had a long and happy life."

"Holly said ye'd buried her?" Gracie asked.

"Yes. Before they left for church, we wrapped her in her favourite blanket and buried her out the side." She blinked away her unshed tears.

"It's a feelin' that takes a while te pass, lass."

Charlotte nodded and changed the subject. "So, what's the news this week, Gifted Hands?"

She smiled. "Well, since Running Otter has come back home, we have told him he can have the house my parents lived in. He was touched. It has been empty for some time now, as you know, and some walls need repair, but he is eager to get to it."

"I can help. Just say the word," Ben said happily.

Keen Wolf nodded and smiled just a little. Charlotte remembered way back, when he told her that he was going to return here, to his family's land. He had a portion of land just south of the house they're in now, that he'd been planning to build on. That was before Straight Arrow died—before Keen Wolf bonded with his brother's wife. She wondered why they didn't offer that land to Running Otter to build on, but kept her thoughts to herself.

"Also, we received word today from some friends to the west. We met them several years summers ago. You may remember they have a son, Swan Song, who was quite taken with Mitenah. I did not feel that she was ready for a man at that time. But now . . ." She smiled. "I have invited them to come and stay with us later in the summer. I think that would be the safest choice. I would prefer not to travel, knowing there are those out there who would do us harm simply because we are Tuscarora."

Charlotte offered a grim smile. It was only too true. "Have you told Mitenah?" she asked.

Gifted Hand smiled again. "Yes, and she is looking forward to it."

After walking their company back to their canoes and seeing them off, Sabel ran upstairs to Sandy's room and knocked on the door. "Sandy, it's me. Can I come in?" she asked and pushed the door open a crack. Seeing Sandy reading by the window, she asked how her friend was feeling.

"I feel fine, thanks. How was your visit?" she asked with a smile.

"It was nice. Hey"—she paused, seeing her cousin's expression—"did you really have a headache?"

Sandy scrunched up her nose and slowly shook her head. "I wanted to give you time with Running Otter."

"What? I didn't ask for that!"

"Are you angry with me?"

"No. You really didn't need to do that, but thank you for thinking of me. We had a good visit. Mitenah and me and him went for a walk in the woods and sat and talked at the drop."

"Didn't you take Jonny to the drop a few days ago?"

"I did. Am I an awful person?"

"I don't think so. Have you and Jonny talked about, you know, being the only one for each other?" Sabel shook her head. "And did you do anything besides talk with Running Otter?" She shook her head again. "There, you see? You did nothing wrong."

Sabel smiled, but it was fleeting. "The thing is, I care about Jonny, but I never expected Running Otter to come back, and the feelings I used to have for him as a girl are still there, only now their grown-up feelings. I really like him, Sandy. Of course, we haven't talked about anything like that, and I'm not sure I want *him* to know that. I'm just telling you. He asked me if I'd like to go fishing with him on Thursday afternoon."

"Fishing?" Sandy asked, laughing.

"Yeah, well, after we went out in the canoe last time, Dad teased me about not catching our supper while we were out there. I told Running Otter and Mitenah, then he asked if I'd like to do that." She shrugged. She was her mother's daughter.

Midsummer

As Charlotte walked up the hill after work, she was distracted, not entirely hearing her daughter's words. "Mum? Mum, are you even listening to me?" Sabel asked. Charlotte stopped dead in her tracks. She had no idea what Sabel had been saying. "Auntie Gracie said that she expects Maisie any day now. Did she tell you? She received a letter today."

"I'm sorry, honey. I was thinking about today being the Summer Solstice. Yes, she did tell me about Maisie. I offered my old room for her to sleep in while she's here."

Sabel nodded. "The Summer Solstice, that's Midsummer, the longest day of the year, right? I've heard you call it something else, too."

Charlotte smiled. "Yes, Litha. It—"

"Let me see what I can remember. Your Goddess is full with child, and the God is at his most vital." Charlotte nodded and waited to see what else Sabel recalled. "Together, they celebrate fertility, strength, and growth."

"Well said." She took her daughter's arm as they walked. "It is a day for us to recognize our inner power and brightness, and a reminder that change, as we can see in nature, is inevitable."

"Hmm . . . change. Sometimes it's good, but sometimes it's scary."

They walked the remainder of the way home quietly, both in their own thoughts.

Over the years, Charlotte had let her children know bits and pieces of her beliefs. She didn't expect anyone to believe as she did; for the most part, she felt that their belief in God would help them make good choices in life. To date, Sabel was the only one who'd expressed any interest.

It was close to midnight when she sat before her altar. Charlotte performed her ritual, celebrating a time when the Earth ripens as mother with child, and the Sun God is at his longest, lightest, and brightest point. She celebrated the flourishing, fruitful gardens, and trees covered with green leaves. She celebrated the light for tomorrow, saying farewell to the waxing year and welcoming the waning year, the season of harvest and wisdom.

In the past, she had tucked a stone or two under her pillow on this night, a night when dreams are more lucid and vivid. She thought to herself for a moment, *what the heck,* and tonight, before crawling into bed, found her velvet sac and pulled out the amethyst and agate, sliding them under her pillow.

After several busy days in a row, she fell asleep almost instantly.

She had just finished saying the words that would take her and Ben back to the past, back home. They were sitting in front of her altar, hands held tightly together, stones between them. There was a bright flash, immediately followed by a loud boom. Charlotte's world began to blur and then spin, before falling away. Blackness enveloped her.

Then she was lying on a bed. She turned her head toward the edge of the bed and saw Ben's smiling face. He was kneeling on the floor at her side. He had come to before her and had carried her to the bed. His eyes looked wet as the light of the flickering candle exaggerated the smile lines around his mouth and the shadows under his eyes. She looked around the bedroom, happy to see that they'd made it back home.

He lay down beside her and kissed her with a passion that blew her away. Then he made love to her the same way. It was in the morning that Charlotte noticed the sitting room and kitchen weren't the same as when they'd left; there was different furniture. When Ben came up behind her in the morning light, she could see that he looked thin and there were indeed lines around his mouth and his eyes as well. "Benny? What's going on? Please tell me, why is our house so different? Why do you look so thin? You look as if you've been worrying for months."

This dream feels familiar.

He led her to the settee, and they sat. "Moxie," he began, "that night in the woods when you performed your ritual and spell, it was last night was it not?" She nodded, a deep sinking feeling spreading through her. "I came home to the time we left, 1819, but you were not with me. Something happened, I have no idea what, but you didn't come back until last night."

Her next question was whispered. "What year is it, Ben?"

His eyes were wet. He swallowed hard as he answered, "1837."

"I came back eighteen years after you?"

Sinking feelings—fear, regret, and loss—were rooting themselves deep within her soul.

I have been here before. I've seen this. It's not real. I have to wake up.

"I have been waiting for you. Every year on this night, I sit outside and wait, hoping this would be the year you came home."

"NOOOOO!" she wanted to cry! *No,* she tried to wake herself. *No, no, nn—*

"Moxie, wake up." Ben shook her gently. "Charlotte, you're dreaming. Wake up."

As she came back to the here and now, she wrapped her arms around her husband's neck, the heat of regret still burning in her chest. "You're crying," he said softly.

"Oh, Benny." She kissed him deeply. "We're so lucky to have lived our lives the way we have. I love you."

"Midsummer, hmm?" He started, his mouth travelling down her neck. "Something about fertility "—his tongue and teeth nipped at her nipples— "and virility. Am I right?"

As Charlotte rolled onto her side sometime later, she thought back to the night she'd had that dream. It was just before Midsummer in 1819, before they left to see Jessica and Michael in 2013. At the time, she thought the dream reflected her own fears—that they would not end up in the same place at the same time. Thinking about it now, knowing the things she now knew, perhaps that had happened in a reality that had been changed. *I died here in 1819, in Jessica's reality. Michael died in 2013, in mine. Ben did not return at the same time as me when we came home after that trip. During the time Ben was missing, he saw what he thought was my future without him. At the same time, Keen Wolf saw my future without Ben. Something or someone had intervened and brought Ben back to me.*

Maybe that happened more than once.

In tonight's dream, I returned on Midsummer night, in 1837. That's tonight! Did I just see what might have been?

Charlotte watched her oldest daughter crumbling and jarring some dried herbs. She looked troubled. When asked, she told her mother she'd had a bad dream last night, one that stuck with her. Charlotte said, "I'll make you some of my famous tea tonight—lavender and valerian." Then, she suggested Sabel work outside in the garden. Sabel looked up and smiled. "That does sound nice. I'll just get my gloves and shovel. I'll be around the back." She walked to the door and almost bumped into a strange man.

"Sorry about that, Miss. Would you be Miss Sabel?"

"I would," she answered with a smile. He handed her a note and wished her a good day. She opened it and read. "It's from Jonny. He'll be coming down Saturday afternoon." She folded the paper and stuck it in the pocket of her apron and went outside.

Working in the garden always helped Sabel to clear her mind. Life's events and problems seemed to make more sense while she focused on digging and pruning. Before long, her mother popped her head around the back corner of the house. "It's quiet now, and my tummy's rumbling. Would you like to walk over to the store and get our dinner?"

Sabel stood and stretched, peeling off her gloves. "Sure, Mum. BRB." She answered with a giggle.

As they ate, Charlotte asked, "Are you looking forward to fishing this afternoon?"

She watched the blush spread across Sabel's cheeks before she answered. "I am. I'll enjoy showing Running Otter I know how to fish."

"You'll surprise him, all right!"

After eating, Sabel returned to the garden. She wanted to check on the poppies and spread the feverfew seedlings; they were too close together. This is what she was doing when she saw two moccasins stop on the path beside her. Instant butterflies. She looked up slowly, taking in the skin of his legs and the belted tunic he wore over his breechcloth; he was not wearing his leggings today. "Oh, is it that time already?"

"There is no hurry, Mimiteh." He smiled. "The garden looks very much alive. You must know what you are doing."

She stood. "Thanks. That's it for today. I just need a minute or two to wash up, then we can go." He followed Sabel into the house and spoke to Charlotte, while she washed her hands. Feeling butterflies in her stomach, she came out carrying one of her father's fishing rods. "You brought yours, right?"

He looked at her dark eyes, pink cheeks, and long hair, and thought she was the most beautiful girl he'd ever seen.

His face lit up as he answered. "I did. Are you ready to make fish for supper tonight, Charlotte?"

"No, but Ben is." She laughed. "See you later."

Running Otter took Sabel to his favourite fishing spot. They talked about silly things, and they talked about serious things. When she mentioned Aleshanee, he said, "I understand that you would be curious about her, Mimiteh, but I do not wish to talk about her. She is no longer a part of my life. I will not look back, only forward. Right now, I am here with you, fishing, and I feel happy." He paused and turned to her as she looked out over the water. "Something troubles you today. What is it?"

She didn't answer right away, and for a moment, he thought she might not have heard him. Without taking her eyes off the water, she said, "I had a bad dream last night, and I guess it's still on my mind."

"Would you like to talk about it?"

"No."

Running Otter nodded to himself. He felt strongly for this young woman and hoped she would open up to him. He wanted her to see him as a man, not a friend. He wanted her to feel for him as he felt for her. He did not know the situation with the "kissy boy", but he knew that he must use the moments they had together to make her see *him*. "I know. Why don't we make you a dream catcher." This made her smile. She turned to him. "We have the perfect tree; we call it kreh-r'yoh. Its branches bend perfectly for the circle of the dream catcher."

"That sounds nice," she replied, looking easier.

"I will come get you on Saturday after you finish your work, and we can make one together."

Her eyebrows came down and she chewed on her lip. "I can't on Saturday."

Instinctively, he knew why. He tried to think fast. "Friday then. I will pick you up after you have had your supper tomorrow."

She smiled. "Okay. Oh! I've got a bite!" She yanked on the line like a pro and hooked it—the first trout of the day.

Before long, they had two each—enough for supper in both homes.

She didn't tell her mother about Friday until the next day. They hung their wet coats on the hooks inside the door of the Doctor's House. "It's lucky it wasn't this yucky yesterday or you might not have gone fishing."

"We probably would have gone anyway, the fish like the rain. It would have been wet and sloppy, though."

"That fish was good. Your dad did a good job of preparing it. Did you do any of the filleting? I never wanted to have to fillet a fish. Yuck."

She smiled at her mother. "Agreed, but you've seen worse working with Dad."

"True." She looked at her daughter. *Hmm.* "Is everything all right?"

"I'm not sure, Mum." She took a deep breath and let it out slowly. "When Running Otter asked what was wrong yesterday, and I told him I'd had a bad dream, he suggested we make a dream catcher together."

"That sounds nice."

"Yeah. He said he'd come get me Saturday."

"Oh."

"Yeah. Obviously, I told him I couldn't on Saturday. I think he knows why."

"And what did he say?"

"He said he'd come get me Friday."

"Oh, today! That's good then, right?" Inside Charlotte was cheering Running Otter on, but she didn't want her opinion to have an effect on Sabel's choices.

"I'm just not sure what to do or how to handle things. I don't want to hurt anyone or have them upset with me. For a while, I sat up on your rock trying to think, and remembered your stones. Would one or two of them help me see things more clearly?"

Charlotte was surprised but delighted. "Well, there are no guarantees, of course, but let me see what I can put together for you."

"Thank you." Sabel hugged her mother then. "Life's hard sometimes," she said.

When the clock struck noon, Charlotte said, "Honey, why don't you run over to the store and get our dinner, while I run home to get my stones? Your dad's out and about. I'll put the sign on the door and meet you back here."

While the ladies enjoyed their meal, Charlotte set her velvet pouch on the table. Sabel raised her eyebrows. "Your stones?"

"Yep." She tipped it, letting the stones roll onto the table. "So, I've been thinking about the issues you could use a little help with." She started to pick stones one at a time and slide them to the side. "This is—"

"Quartz," Sabel interrupted.

Smiling, Charlotte answered, "Yes, Rose Quartz. It offers clarity and aids in opening your heart and releasing negative emotions. The Obsidian is helpful when your path is blocked and you can't seem to find a way around it. It acts to ground you and protect you and then, when your mind is at ease, helps you to see your choices and solve your problems."

"It's like dark glass—so mysterious looking."

"It's actually from a volcano. It's lava that cooled too quickly for crystals to form. It's quite pretty. And you know this last one," she said, sliding a dark blue stone to the side.

"Lapis."

"Right. Lapis offers the peace that comes with wisdom and healing. When you trust yourself, decisions become clear."

"Thanks, Mum"

"Would you like to tie them onto your wrist, or would you prefer to have them in your pockets?" Charlotte asked, pulling a thin leather cord out of her pouch.

Sabel lay her arm across the table in answer.

Dream Catcher

Sabel and Sandy sat at the outside table, enjoying supper in the sun. They had planned it so she would be there when Running Otter arrived to get her.

Sandy was full of questions. "When is he coming? Will you both make a dream catcher or just you? Will Mitenah make one, too? Does he know Jonny's coming tomorrow?"

The last question brought the conversation to a new level. Sabel was very serious. "I think he does. I didn't tell him, but when he asked me to go over tomorrow, I told him I couldn't. I could see in his eyes he knew the reason.

"Are you worried about that?"

"A little."

"Listen, Sabel. I have no experience with men, but I can tell you this—if he really likes you and he knows someone else does, too, he will either try to win you over or give up. He hasn't given up."

"Not yet," Sabel answered. Unconsciously, she played with the stones on her wrist.

"Try not to worry." Sandy's eyes flicked to the water behind Sabel. "Oo-oo, he's almost here. Just be honest, no one will fault you for that." Sabel felt the butterflies, but she wasn't nervous.

Sandy collected the plates and cutlery, waved at Running Otter, and whispered, "Have fun," before disappearing into the kitchen.

Sabel walked toward him as he pulled up the canoe. Once again, he was struck by her pretty face, long almost-black hair blowing behind her, dress swaying with each step. "Chweh'n," she said. "Should I bring anything?"

"Just you." He smiled and imagined catching her by her wrists and pulling her in.

They chatted as they rowed. "What did you do today?" she asked.

"Today, I helped Keen Wolf repair the smokehouse. It has been there a long time and some of it had begun to rot. When we were done, we both smelled of smoke. *A lot.* He suggested I jump in the lake to get the smell off before I saw you." He snickered.

"Yikes! You went in there? Isn't it freezing?"

"It was cold but worth it. Otherwise, you would be able to smell me from there."

"Thank you for your sacrifice."

He was helping her out when she asked about his grandparents' old house. "I am going to go in with Keen Wolf, maybe tomorrow, and we will look at every wall, door, window, the floor—everything—to see what we must replace. Then we will see. Luckily, there's no hurry. I always have a bed at En-ay's house."

"True, there's no rush."

"And I am not going anywhere."

She felt his words in the pit of her stomach, as if he was sending her a secret message.

The cabin was quiet as they approached, and she asked where everyone had gone. "They went to visit the neighbours on the other side of my mother's vegetable garden." They arrived at the door, and he asked, "Would you like to sit outside and make your dream catcher?"

"Sure," she answered. Kohana came around from the other side of the house and looked up at Sabel. "Hello," she said, bending to pet her.

"First, we must get some branches from the kreh-r'yoh tree. Come this way." He led her down the path to the swimming beach, followed closely by the cat. "Here it is. We must choose a branch that is thin enough to bend like this and long enough to make a circle this big." He showed the size with his hands.

He watched her look for just the right branch. "We call this a willow tree," she told him as she searched. "Ah, here. Is this a good one?"

"Perfect. Now I will find one for me."

Once he'd done that, they returned to the house where he had left all they would need to create their dream catchers. Setting their branches on the table outside, they went inside to get the supplies. It was clear to Sabel that he had planned ahead; there was string, beads, strips of leather, and feathers in a variety of colours, but mostly blue. She was touched. Catching sight of a feather, Kohana jumped up onto the table, trying to catch one in her mouth. Running Otter shushed her away.

"I thought I could make mine slowly, and you can do what I do. Sound good?"

"Yep!"

After declining his offer for a drink, they got comfortable at the table and began to create. She copied him as he wrapped a thin strip of leather around the willow, securing it into a circle. Then they made a web within the circle, using string spun by Gifted Hands and Mitenah. "You can pick one or two or three beads and string them on wherever you like inside the circle. And remember, you must create a hole in the centre of the web." She nodded, biting her lip as she thought about that.

Sabel looked at the beads, trying to decide which she would like. She had to pick blue, because it was her favourite colour, but what else? Purple was her mother's favourite, and . . . "What's your favourite colour, Running Otter?"

He smiled. "I like yellow. Yours is blue, yes?"

"It is."

She took her time weaving the web. She wanted it to be perfect. Once it was finished, five strings were tied on at the bottom, each with a small puff of downy feathers added half-way down its length. At the bottom of each, hung a feather with a bead over the place it was tied. Sabel chose white feathers, thinking it looked clean and fresh.

She held it up asking, "What do you think?"

"It looks good—very good. Now you must hang it in your bedroom window. Only good dreams can find their way through the hole in the centre. They will slide down the feathers to you. The bad dreams will get caught in the web and die when the first rays of sun hit them." She had a faraway look in her eyes as she envisioned that.

"Mum told me that when you were little, you made her a dream catcher."

"That was a long time ago, but I do remember." He smiled as he thought back. Then his eyebrows came down. "I don't know what happened. I was a child. She was injured; someone had hurt her, I think. I heard her say she had not been sleeping well."

"And you made it to help her sleep? To cheer her up?"

"E-heh." Hearing himself, he added, "Yes. For as long as I can remember, I have loved Charlotte. She used to be my special friend. She even helped me learn to swim."

"Aww, that's sweet. Now, hold yours up so I can see," she said. "Nice. I like the colours you chose. It looks really good." He had two black beads and one yellow in the web, and black feathers at the bottom. "They're very different, aren't they?" she asked.

"They are, and both are beautiful."

She jumped up and, without thinking, gave him a hug. *Oh, he smells good.* "Thank you. Not only do I love this, but I'm going to hang it tonight to chase those bad dreams away." His heart was happy. "Let's get this stuff back inside before it gets too dark," she said.

They set what remained of their supplies on the counter and he turned to her. "Would you like something to drink or eat before we take you back home?"

"No, thanks. I'm fine." She shivered.

"It is cooler now the sun has left the sky. Let me get you something." He disappeared and came back with a small blanket. "This will keep you warm," he said, coming to stand in front of her. He brought it around her shoulders and her hands caught the corners, pulling it around her.

"Thank you," she looked up into his dark almond-shaped eyes. They were almost touching; his face was very close. Catching herself, she looked down and snuggled the blanket around herself. "This feels nice. Is it yours?" She could smell him in it.

He smiled. "Yes. I have had it a long time."

She wore it around her shoulders as they rowed.

It was full dark when they arrived on the opposite shore. They were walking up from the water, when her eyes were drawn under the trees. "Oh, look, fireflies. Do you mind if we sit at the table and watch for a few minutes?"

He smiled inwardly. "Let us do that."

They sat quietly, and Sabel started to count them, whispering under her breath. "You are much like a firefly, Mimiteh."

She turned to him. "How do you mean?"

He met her eyes in the dim light and paused before answering. "There is light inside you, and it seems each time I see you, it is brighter. When I am with you, I can feel the hope and happiness that is inside you."

She looked at him, unsure how to respond. "What a nice thing to say."

"It is the truth."

Soon after, Running Otter walked Sabel home; every fiber of his being wanting to keep her safe. She was standing on the doorstep and turned to face him. "Thank you. I had a nice evening. That was very thoughtful of you." She looked up into his face once more, and her eyes left his for a moment, sliding to his full lips. *No.* "Thank you," she said again, before adding, "nyah-winh," remembering the Tuscarora word. She gave him a quick hug.

"You are welcome, Mimiteh. I will see you Sunday. Happy dreams." He turned and stepped down off the porch, disappearing into the darkness.

As he walked, he thought of her. She'd been right there in front of him; he would have loved to kiss her, that's all, just a kiss, but he knew she wasn't ready. He was going to have to be patient, something that didn't come naturally, not at all.

Jonny

They were walking to the store Saturday morning when Charlotte said, "You hung your new dream catcher last night. It looks pretty. Did you sleep well?"

"Thanks. Yes, I did. Running Otter made one, too. I copied what he did as he did it. It was fun."

"He's a good teacher?"

Sabel nodded. "Jonny's coming today. I don't know what he wants to do, but I feel a little nervous about it."

Charlotte hooked her arm through Sabel's. "I get that. I would be, too, I think. Remember, sweetie, no one's asking you to choose. The time may come, and then you will do what your heart tells you. It'll be fine, you'll see."

Her mum suggested they pass by the garden at the store and see how things were growing. She was curious to see what Sabel recognized as seedlings and buds. They stopped in the kitchen first. "Good mornin' to ye both. Cup o' tea?"

"Yes, thanks, Gracie. We came by to have a look at the garden before work." Gracie came back out with Sandy and a cup of tea for her friend. The two women walked toward the garden, while Sabel and Sandy lagged behind, talking in low voices. Sandy needed a quick catch-up session. When the girls arrived at the garden, Sabel was gently quizzed and had all the answers. Her mum was proud. She enjoyed the garden and herbs almost as much as her mother. Whatever happened down the road, Charlotte hoped they would be able to complement each other's work.

"Ready to go, love?"

"Yep. See you later, ladies."

Sabel worked mechanically all morning. She didn't want to talk, she just wanted to get on with this day. Both were surprised when the bells rang just after noon. Charlotte looked up. "Maisie!" She hugged the young lady. "How are you?"

"Hello," she said to both of them. "I'm well, thank you. I arrived just a little while ago and am off to say hello to Jeffery."

Sabel smiled as her friend blushed. "He'll be so happy to see you, Maze." She hugged her then. "I am, too. Have a nice visit and we'll catch up later."

When 2:00 p.m. arrived, she reached behind her neck and untied her apron. She was hanging it on her hook when Jonny came through the door. He looked spiffed up somehow. She couldn't put her finger on it. His hair? Breeks? Shirt? No, it was his face. What had he done?

"Hello, Jonny," Charlotte said, coming out of the back. "How are you today? Did you have a good run down?"

He smiled. She was always so nice. "I did, thank you." He looked back at Sabel. "You look pretty. Are you ready to go?"

"I'm not sure, where are we going?" she asked, blushing.

"Timmy invited us over. He's asked a few of your friends over for the afternoon. He wants to have a fire—said his father has some old wood he wants to burn, so he wants to make some fun out of it. I asked Fred to join us, too."

"Oh, I must tell Sandy. Do you mind?" Sandy would be happy about that.

"Not at all," he answered. "Goodbye, Mrs. Williams."

"Have fun you two."

He wasn't wrong, there were a bunch of people there, but the only ones Sabel cared about were Sandy, who had her eyes on Fred, Janee, whose boyfriend was Timmy, Maisie who was so happy to be back with Jeffery, and Jonny. The girls sat together by the fire, catching up on the news.

At some point, they became aware of raised voices across the yard. Two guys were holding someone's arms behind his back, and someone was yelling at him. It was Jonny. "Shit!" Sabel said, jumping up from her log. "What's going on? What's happening?" she asked, arriving at Jonny's side, where two guys were holding him back. Sandy and Janee immediately followed Sabel.

"It's true!" Fred yelled at him, one hand rubbing the left side of his mouth. "Ask her!" He pointed at Sabel.

"Who, me?" Sabel called out. "Ask me what?"

"Tell Jon how you went across the lake with that savage three days ago. I saw you walking with him. You left together in his canoe."

"What did you call him?" She ran at him, ready to punch him herself, but Timmy caught her arm and stopped her. Jonny felt the fight leave him. For Sabel to react so strongly to Fred's words, they had to be true.

Timmy looked down at her. "You good?" he asked.

She nodded. When he let her go, she lunged forward and slapped Fred hard enough that the whole group heard it. There were some "oo-oos" and cackles behind her as she said, "We have no time for such disrespect here. You, Fred Cole, are a son-of-a-bitch. I hope I never see your face again!" Her heart was pounding, and her face was bright pink as she turned and walked away.

What was that? What just happened? She could feel her hands shaking as she walked and was glad to have pockets to stuff them into. "Sabel, wait! Sabel!"

Sandy and Janee ran up behind her, both out of breath. "Are you all right?" Sandy asked.

"What an ass!" added Janee.

She turned to look at them feeling only a little calmer and suddenly broke out laughing. The girls looked at each other, confused. "Did I seriously just slap that fool and call him a son-of-a-bitch?" More laughing.

"Yeah, you did!" Sandy said, giggling. "I can't believe I thought I liked him."

"Is what he said true, Sabel? Have you seen Running Otter as something *other than* a friend?" Janee asked.

"It's true." She sighed. "I don't know what I'm doing right now, Janee. I like them both."

"Well, good Lord, Running Otter is so kind and handsome!" Janee said.

"Yeah," she agreed. "I guess I forgot there are people who judge a person by their colour or how they live. It's so ignorant."

"C'mon back to the store, ladies. Hettie will have something there to cheer us up."

"What about the boys? I guess we left them. Poor Jonny, I hope I didn't embarrass him too much."

"Don't worry, sweetie. I think he already knew he had a rival for your attention. Fred just said it in such a rude way," Sandy said.

"He's such a dick!" Sabel said. The other girls laughed; Sabel sometimes came out with funny expressions, but this one seemed accurate.

Sensing there was some level of distress, Hettie whipped up a pitcher of lemonade. The girls took a glass each and went to sit by the water. "This is better, isn't it?" Sandy asked.

"Thank you both. You're good friends," Sabel said with a wobble in her voice.

"We love you, Sabel," Sandy said quietly.

"We do," Janee agreed.

They sat this way for a while before Janee stood, saying she should get home. As she walked away, Jonny appeared, standing beside Charlotte's garden.

Sandy whispered, "Jonny's here, love. I'll leave you to it. You know where to find me if you want to talk later." She patted her friend's hand and walked back up toward the kitchen with their empty glasses. She smiled at Jonny and tipped her head toward Sabel.

He sat down beside her. No words were said for a few minutes. "I'm sorry I embarrassed you, Jonny."

"Well, you did, I suppose, but that's not why I'm here. I knew there was someone else who had eyes on you. And when I met him that day, I knew it was him. Can you tell me?"

She took a deep breath and blew some loose hair off her face. "Our families have been friends since before I was born. He met someone and moved away a few years ago. That was it. They didn't stay together, and he came back home just over a month ago, I guess. I didn't know I had feelings for him, but then I spent a little time with him and realized . . . gah . . . this is hard. I realized that I like you both. I don't know what to do." She turned to look at him with tears in her eyes. "I'm sorry."

"Don't be sorry. We can't plan how we feel about someone." Jonny tried to smile. "You said you don't know what to do? Does that mean I still have a chance?"

"You still want to be with me?"

"Sabel, I think you're a wonderful girl. Yes, I want to be with you. For now, I guess I can give you some time to see how you feel. Please, just . . . don't make a fool of me."

She put her arms around his neck where they sat and sighed deeply.

Sabel told her parents what had happened at Timmy's and what happened afterward. That she stood up to the prejudice Fred was spewing made them proud. But they hurt for her, knowing her feelings. She told them she wanted to stay home this Sunday. Seeing Running Otter so soon after what just happened would not help her sort herself. So, they left her at home with some leftovers and spent the afternoon across the lake.

Sabel didn't know what to do with herself. She went to her father's bookshelves and looked through his books. Nope. She got a pencil and paper, went outside, and found a flower; it was some type of salvia, she couldn't remember which. She tried to sketch it. Nope. She looked at her mum's stack of books: herbs, herbals, recipes. Nope. She picked up her mum's knitting needles and a ball of yarn—a new scarf maybe? Nope. "I know," she said aloud to no one. "I'll have a nice bath while there's no one to disturb me." There was always water warming on the wood-burning stove, so she made a plan. She went into the "wash closet" and pulled the hinged bathtub down from its cupboard. Then, she carried in a pot of hot water, then another, then another. After refilling the pots on the stove, she picked up a bar of her mum's nice lavender soap and some shampoo and climbed in. She slid down, sinking her head under the water, enjoying the warmth and allowing herself a few minutes to soak before washing. Sabel had just finished rinsing her hair when she heard something. Unsure of what she'd heard, she jumped out of the tub, wrapping herself in a towel, and peeked out of the room. Everything was quiet.

While Sabel stepped into a fresh dress, there was a sound at the front door. *Is someone trying to get in?* Glad that she'd locked it, she tip-toed to where she could see the door, but not be seen if someone was looking in the window. There was definitely someone at the door, but she couldn't see who it was. *Should I ask who it is? If I do that, they'll know I'm alone! Maybe I can sneak out the back door and see who it is. Or run down the hill. To get who? Everyone's across the lake?*

"Pull yourself together, Sabel. You are not afraid. You can do this," she whispered to herself. She went to the back door and put her ear against it. Nothing. She opened it and slipped outside. All she could hear were the birds. She walked carefully around the side of the house and peeked around the corner. *Shit! Double shit!* It was Fred. *Now what? Go back inside!*

Sabel ran back inside, locking the door behind her. "Sabel Williams, I know you're in there. Why won't you answer the door? I just want to talk," he called.

Her heart was pounding; she didn't know what to do next. He was banging on the door. She was scared. He knew she was alone. "If you want to talk, Fred, talk. I'm listening."

It went quiet. "I want to talk about yesterday. Open the damn door."

"No," she cried.

"I swear, I'll break it down."

"Don't do that!" There was a loud bang as he kicked it. "Stop! Don't!"

He kicked it again, only this time the wood cracked. One more time and he broke through. Fred stood in the doorway, the cracked door hanging on one hinge. She had to get outside. There was no one here to hear or help her. She scrambled for the door. He caught her arm.

"What are you afraid of, Sabel? What do you think I'm going to do to you?"

"How would I know? You just kicked in the door to my house! How do I know what you're capable of?" She tugged her arm, but he had a good grip.

He stepped closer to her, talking right into her face. "You slapped my face yesterday, hard, in front of everyone!" He was angry.

"You deserved it. You don't know what you're talking about. People should keep their mouths shut when they don't know what they're saying."

He slapped her then, across the right cheek. "You dirty whore."

"I'm no whore!"

"But you are, and not very clever at hiding it."

"I have nothing to hide."

He was twisting her wrist and slowly moving them back toward the eating area. "I know that Jonny has been workin' on you for a while now. And I know I saw you get into a canoe with that Indian savage and disappear for hours."

"Oh, so I must be whoring. There's nothing else I might be doing . . . like fishing!" He lowered his eyebrows and squinted. "What I do is not for you to know."

"It is when you humiliate me in front of my friends." She tried to smack him with her other hand, but he caught it. "I am going to teach you a lesson you little harlot." He smacked her again. "You want to be a whore? Why don't you try this!" He threw her backwards onto the dining table and reached into his pants. The back of Sabel's head smacked the table. She struggled, swinging her arms, trying to land a punch. She was slowing him down as he was forced to protect himself.

He grabbed the front of her dress, tearing it as he pulled her up to standing. Fred's arm came forward, his open hand connecting with Sabel's face again, causing her to reel sideways.

"You are such an ass! You think you're better than somebody else because, why, because your skin is white? Look at what you're doing. Are you a better man? That man you have such distaste for would never, NEVER, behave like this! You should be—" Sabel's next words were cut off as Fred punched her in the stomach. Breathless, she fell to her knees, gasping. It took everything she had to stand back up, and then he grabbed her hair. He was pulling her head to the side when she kicked him—right in the crotch. He went down.

She collapsed to her knees. Adrenalin had kept her going, but now she was spent. She heard a scuffle and muffled voices as her heart pounded in her ears. Then, someone took her face into their hands. She opened her eyes fearing the worst. She was looking into Running Otter's worried face.

"I'm going to help you onto the settee."

She nodded.

He set her down gently with a cushion behind her. "What can I get you?"

"Running Otter," her voice cracked. "Hold me."

He took her into his arms and cradled her gently, cooing gentle words as he gently ran his fingers through her wet hair. After a couple of minutes he said, "Now, please, Mimiteh, tell me how I can help. Did he punch you? Are you wounded? What do you need?"

"I don't think I'm bleeding." She stuck her arms straight out and turned them. "No, just bruises." Running Otter saw the bruises that were already coming out on her arms and wanted to run after that man. How dare he!

"Did he—"

"No. Can you put some hot water into the smallest pot you can find and put it back on the stove? I will try to find the arnica."

After steeping some arnica, they made a compress, and he helped her hold it in various places on her face. "Your eye is swelling, can we put this over it?"

"I'm not sure. Better just do the rest of it." Her voice was indifferent. "Why are you here?"

"When you didn't come, I asked Sandy if it was because of me; maybe I am too much." He shook his head. "She told me what happened yesterday. You stood up for me to someone who—"

"Who's an ass," Sabel finished his sentence.

He smiled. "Yes. Thank you. That was brave of you. You never know who might feel that way until you're in a situation like that." He took her face in his hands and gently kissed her eyes. "Thank you, Mimiteh." Then he kissed her cheeks, first the right, then the left. "You brave girl." He lightly brushed his lips on hers, but there was no response. He understood. What had he been thinking? He took her back into his arms and held her. She let him.

They were quiet for a long time, before Sabel asked, "Did Sandy tell you about Jonny coming to see me afterward?" He shook his head. Sabel told him about the conversation they'd had.

"I understand." He was quiet then, even though every part of his being was aching to pick her up and take her home with him. "I must say this . . . I care for you very much. I can imagine living the rest of my life loving you, making a family with you, growing old with you. I will do what you ask of me, but I need you to say the words."

She turned to look at him with tears in her eyes. "I don't want you to give up on me. Please."

He smiled. Those words would do.

Sometime later, the family's voices could be heard approaching the house. "What happened here? Sabel! Sabel!"

What was left of the door opened. Ben came in first, followed by Charlotte. "Sabel! My God, Sabel! What happened?" They were all around her, asking questions, wanting to know. Running Otter stayed where he was. He was a part of this, and he wasn't going to leave. He wanted to deal with that man, but now was not the time.

She told them what happened—all of it.

"You said he was on his knees when you came in?" Charlotte asked Running Otter.

"He was. I grabbed him up and pushed him out of here. Told him he'd be smart to get out of town. My only concern was for Sabel."

"But what was he doing on his knees?" Charlotte asked again.

"I kicked him in the balls," Sabel answered. It caught on slowly, one person at a time, but soon the room was laughing. Sabel was a bit bashed up, but she would be fine. This girl was a fighter.

Ben and Running Otter walked down to tell Lawrence what had happened and visit the tannery where Fred stayed. Lawrence had heard about the events of Saturday; his granddaughter had told him when she arrived home. He was not impressed, he had little tolerance for bigots, but now this? They knocked on the door of Fred's room. There was no answer. Lawrence went to the main door, hoping to speak to his boss, Ernest. The man answered his door feeling rather perturbed, it was Sunday evening after all. But, when Lawrence explained why they were there, he quickly got the spare key and walked around to the door.

They opened up the room and were not surprised to find it empty. All that remained were the sheets on the bed. "I don't know when he did this. I was home all day, didn't hear a thing. Sorry I can't help ye further. Guess I'll be looking for a new apprentice."

"Good riddance!" Ben said as they walked away.

As much as Running Otter wanted to return to the house to check on her, he knew that what Sabel didn't need right now was to see him. He said as much to Ben, who completely understood, having been in somewhat of a similar situation years ago. "Thank you, Running Otter. Who knows what he might have done had you not been there."

Charlotte held her daughter in her arms and cried for what this young man had done to her. She didn't deserve that from him. Thank God she was okay. The two talked about the next few days at work and agreed she would work in the garden and avoid showing her face.

Jonny would surely hear that Ernest Albert was looking for a new apprentice and ask questions. He would either hear what happened or come to find out for himself. As much as Charlotte knew both he and Running Otter were in love with her daughter, she hoped they had the sense to give her some space for a few days.

When Sabel went up to bed that night, she wrapped herself in Running Otter's blanket, breathing him in. She tossed and turned for a while; it took some time to get comfortable and to stop replaying the day's events.

Monday went by without a hitch. Sandy passed on a message from Running Otter, who had delivered it personally. He and Keen Wolf were going hunting for a few days. He hoped to be home by Sunday. That was it, end of message.

Sabel worked peacefully in the garden most of the day, appreciating the space. Only when Janee and Maisie came by at dinner break was she not alone with her thoughts. The girls weren't looking for gossip; they simply wanted to check on their friend. "You're very brave, Sabel," Maisie started. "I can't think what I would have done."

"Me either," added Janee. "I'm just so glad you're all right."

After saying goodbye, she smiled to herself—she had good friends. Her thoughts caught up with her then. She also had two good men who wanted her and who she cared for very much. She wondered if she would actually be able to figure this situation out. Her mother had been right, no one was asking her to choose . . . but the time was approaching, she could feel it.

Tuesday was a different day. It was close to noon when Charlotte heard the bells. She looked up to see Jonny in the doorway. "Is it true?"

"Is what true, Jonny?" she asked.

"Did that jackass Fred attack Sabel?"

"He did. I'm not sure she'll want to talk about it, but she's out in the garden."

He nodded and followed the path around the back.

"Sabel, love, how are you?"

She looked up from her work. "Jonny, hello. I'm all right."

"You don't look it, if you don't mind me sayin'."

"I know." She stuck the shovel into the ground and went to stand closer to him. "I didn't go with the family on Sunday. I stayed home by myself. He came to the door. He knew I was there." She told him the whole story. Everything. Including the part where Running Otter had come to see her because of what he'd heard about Saturday.

"Thank goodness he got there before . . . well, it could have been worse."

"It could have. He disappeared, the weasel."

"I'm so sorry."

"It's not your fault."

He thought about the job he knew was now available. A job that would allow him to be closer to her. A job he would have taken in the blink of an eye if Running Otter hadn't come back to town. But he had, and Jonny knew it was possible she might not pick him. He didn't want to be here in that situation. He would wait and give it some time.

"Listen, Jonny, I know you came all the way down here to check on me, and I appreciate that, but could we maybe wait until the weekend to see each other and talk?"

"Of course. I'll see you Saturday." He leaned over and pecked her cheek before leaving.

Distracted

Sabel spent the remainder of the week working in the sun, tending to the growing plants. All that visibly remained from last Sunday's attack, was a small amount of bruising on her left eye. She felt fine. Even the front door of the house had been replaced. No longer would she arrive home and see the broken door and be reminded of Fred.

She stopped in at the store before work on Saturday morning. Maisie was leaving today and she wanted to say goodbye. She found her sitting at the dining table with Sandy, eyes teary.

"Oh, Maisie, why so sad?"

"I was just telling Sandy how much I'd like to stay," Maisie answered.

"Ah. I understand. Jeffery?"

Maisie nodded. "Yes . . . but also you, Sandy, and Janee. You have always been such good friends. I have friends there, too, but I can't help missing you all."

Sabel gave her a hug. "We miss you, too," she said, glancing at her cousin. "Write to us whenever you feel like it and we'll write to you." Maisie nodded. "How are things with Jeffery?"

"He told me that he loves me, and he misses me, but he wants me to be happy wherever I am."

"Does he plan to go see you?" Sandy asked.

"I don't know . . . I hope so."

"Try not to be sad, Maze. We love you, whether you're here or there. And we'll see each other again." Sabel hugged her then. "Let us know when you get back home?"

"I will," Maisie said, trying to smile.

"Good. I hope the journey home is easy. See you again soon."

"Goodbye, Sabel."

She walked the short distance to the Doctor's House, thinking about Maisie, and felt a sharp pang of guilt—Maisie had been here a week, and she'd hardly spent any time with her. She'd been too wrapped up in her own problems. That's not being a very good friend. She would talk to Sandy about that when she got the chance.

Sabel knew Jonny would be coming to see her today and thought a walk and talk would be a good thing. He met her just after two o'clock, as he usually did on a Saturday, only today he arrived with a bunch of flowers. His look of concern disappeared as soon as he saw her smile.

"Oh, how pretty, thank you. Let me get some water for them. She disappeared into the back and came out with a vase and water. There we are. Pretty."

"Shall we walk today?" he asked.

"Sounds nice. See you later, Mum."

He asked about Sabel's week. "It was quiet. Just what I needed. I worked outside on my own most days." He wanted to ask if she'd seen Running Otter but dared not.

When they got to the place in the woods they liked to sit and talk, they sat facing the water. Sabel leaned back on her arms, lifting her face to the sky.

He watched, thinking how pretty she looked.

"How are you feeling, Sabel? I mean *really* feeling."

"Fine. I don't understand what you're asking."

"Hmm. I'm just going to say it." He took her hand. "I love you, Sabel. I love you, and I want you to choose me."

"Oh—" Her hand came up to her mouth, and tears stung her eyes. She looked into his eyes, unsure how to answer. She didn't have to; he was leaning in for a kiss. When his lips met hers, she kissed him quickly, dismissively.

"You don't want to kiss me? I thought you liked kissing me." He was hurt, but she couldn't help herself.

"I did, I do, I just . . ."

"Do you like kissing him?"

"What? I haven't kissed him." Jonny didn't know how to respond. "Look, I'm sorry. I'm just, I'm not ready."

At that he stood up. He had just confessed his love for her and still nothing. How much longer could he take this? "I don't know what to do to help you be ready, Sabel. I've done the things you've asked, but it doesn't seem like anything's changing." She hung her head. She knew he was right. "Let me walk you home. We can talk again another day." She nodded.

When she got home, she threw herself on her bed and had a cry. This had gone on long enough. Where were her answers?

Sabel awoke Sunday morning feeling refreshed. Today their friends were coming for a visit. She didn't know if he would be here, but she hoped so. Knowing that she wasn't going to see him all week had made things easier in some ways, but she did find herself looking forward to seeing him. After Sandy got home from church, the two girls sat in the sun behind the store and Sabel waited to see the canoes. It wasn't long before she saw two coming toward her. She tried to count the number of people inside, but they were too far away. When they got close enough, she counted—five. She felt herself smile.

She walked down to meet them. When she saw him jump out and walk toward her, her stomach did a somersault.

The others came out from the kitchen, joining the group, and they all headed up the hill. Sabel let herself fall behind so she could walk with him. "How are you feeling, Sabel?" he asked with a crooked smile. She saw Sandy give her a sideways smile.

"I feel good. I had a quiet week, working in the garden mostly."

"That is good to hear."

They arrived at the house and enjoyed the happy chaos that comes with having so many people in one place. The men prepared the fire to cook the meat, the women worked on the vegetables in the kitchen while they caught up on their week, and the "kids" went to hang out at the tree house. Sabel went out to the fire to offer the men some drinks. When Running Otter looked her way, she felt it again. It was a feeling that shook her. She smiled and walked to the outdoor table to sit. Shortly after, he joined her.

"How did the hunting trip go?"

He smiled. "Keen Wolf did better than I, but we brought home some meat."

"That's good. I think I'd like to go hunting one day—I've never been." With a smirk, he turned to look at her. "What? I think I'd be good at it."

"Perhaps."

"What would you be good at?" Robbie asked, joining them, totally unaware of their desire to speak alone.

Sabel looked at Running Otter and rolled her eyes. "I was saying I think I'd be a good hunter. I just need someone to teach me."

"I can teach you," both men said together.

She laughed. "Well, we'll see who's willing when the time comes."

When Sandy and Mitenah joined them, Sabel looked at Running Otter and shrugged.

"Mitenah, I hear that you will be having some company this summer," Sabel said, rubbing shoulders with her friend.

Mitenah's cheeks pinked slightly. "Yes. Swan Song's family is coming to stay. I hope I will like them as much as I remember."

"Where will they stay?" Sandy asked.

"Do you remember our neighbours we used to celebrate our rituals with?"

Sandy nodded. "Yes, the ones that moved away."

"Well, the house has been empty since they left, but it is now ours. Kree-ay and Running Otter will make some repairs, and they will stay there."

Sabel looked at Running Otter, putting things together. *That's why there's no rush to repair his grandparents' house—this one must be ready first.*

When Running Otter excused himself and left to join the men at the fire, Sabel didn't know what to think, but there was no use in following him. Today would not bring the opportunity to talk. *It's just as well,* she thought, *what would I even say?*

She could hear them talking from where she sat; they were sharing news about the "Indian Removal".

A voice said, "There is speak of the Cherokee beginning to move."

"I have heard that, too. I understand some are going of their own free will."

"That way they will not be shackled and forced to bed in pens."

Dark Wolf came to stand near Sabel, listening to the men from where he stood.

As the evening came to a close, and their guests prepared to leave, Charlotte said, "Goodnight, all. I will stay and finish in the kitchen, mosquitoes be damned!"

Ben smiled her way, with a glint in his eyes.

While the others walked down the little hill, Gracie stopped and waited for Sabel, who she noticed lagging behind. "Yer quiet tonight, lass."

"I've just been listening to everyone else chat today, Auntie Gracie."

Gracie looked ahead and saw Running Otter glance their way. She gave him a wink. He stopped walking. "Ah well, as long as yer all right."

Then he was there beside her, and Gracie had moved on. Sabel looked up at him in the evening light. *He looks so handsome, but distant. What is he thinking?* "Did you have a nice day?" she asked.

"I did. We were not able to talk."

"No." They had reached the beach. Gracie and her group were saying goodnight.

"I did learn that you would like to learn to hunt," he teased.

"And I learned that you could teach me. Will you?"

He took her hand in the dark and in a low voice said, "I will teach you anything you want to learn and give you all that I am able, including myself"— he paused—"if you will have me."

He heard her suck in her breath.

Sabel looked up into his eyes and wanted to dive into them. She found herself unable to find words.

"Tomorrow?" he asked.

She nodded.

And then the canoes were gone.

Charlotte didn't know what was going on in her daughter's mind, but she knew it had everything to do with Running Otter. Sabel was clearly distracted and seemed to be locked in her own head. "What's going on, honey? Something on your mind?"

Sabel looked up at her mother with a goofy smile. "I'm sorry, I guess I'm a little distracted today."

"A little?" Charlotte laughed. Sabel's eyes grew wide, and she felt the heat in her cheeks. "Is it Running Otter?" Sabel nodded, not trusting her voice. *Why do I suddenly feel like I'm going to cry?*

"Were you able to talk yesterday? Ah, who am I kidding, of course not. There was far too much going on."

"He's coming today."

"I see. Well, I've said this before, but it bears repeating. There are choices to be made in life that cannot be rushed or forced. You will know when you are ready, and we will always be here to love and support you."

Sabel wrapped her arms around her mother then and said, "Thank you."

"I think you'd best work outside today; that way you can think, and I don't have to worry about what herb ends up in what jar." Charlotte laughed.

"Good thinking, Mama!"

Sabel used her time wisely. As she weeded and watered, she let her thoughts take form: *Running Otter is tall and strong, smart and funny, ruggedly handsome, and he smells so good. He is a good person. He had been the equivalent of married. He would teach me about love. It didn't work out with Aleshanee. She had hurt him. Had she left scars? Time would tell . . . Then there is Jonny. He is fun and thoughtful, cute and determined. He punched a guy when he accused me of seeing someone else, even though he knew it to be true. And he is a good kisser. He and I would learn about love together.* Sabel knew that if Running Otter hadn't returned, she would be with

Jonny, and they would be happy. But Running Otter *had* returned, and she has feelings for him, too. Was that fair? Absolutely not.

Lost as she was in the struggles of love, Sabel was unaware of time passing. It was only when she overheard his voice and the bells inside the store that she looked up. She was still on her knees when he came around the corner. *Wow! Butterflies!* He wore a sleeveless tunic belted at the waist, leggings of the same buckskin and moccasins. Today his hair was tied into one braid down the back, the sides freshly shorn. He was a sight for sore eyes.

"Chweh'n, Running Otter. I didn't realize it was the end of the day already."

He offered his hand to help her up. "I may be early."

"That's okay. Come on inside and let me put these things away."

He walked behind her to the door, hoping this day would end the way he'd dreamed and not the way he feared.

She looked at the clock. "You are early. I have another half hour to go."

"I can wait. Will I sit in here?" he asked, pointing to a chair.

Charlotte smiled at her daughter. *These two are adorable. If only they would get it together.* "Go on, you two. It's quiet here today. I'll clean up while I wait to see what your father needs for Hank. I'll see you later at home."

"Thanks, Mum," Sabel said, giving Charlotte a quick hug.

Running Otter looked at her with a serious expression and nodded.

When they got out to the road, Sabel asked, "Where would you like to go today?" Any nervousness she felt during the day was fading quickly.

"I have an idea," he answered, looking straight ahead.

"You don't want to tell me?"

"I do not." Now he turned to her and smiled. "We'll be there soon."

He helped her into the canoe and pushed them off.

They rowed for the couple of minutes it took to get to the small, secluded beach area cut into the rock face. As they pulled in, Sabel thought, *I've always thought this would be a romantic spot to sit and talk or whatever.*

He jumped out to pull up the canoe. "Don't worry about me; it's a beautiful day." She left her shoes in the boat and stepped over the edge into the water, holding up the bottom of her dress. "Oo-oo, still cool!" She found a nice sandy spot and sat, tucking her feet under the edge of her dress as he sat beside her. "I love this spot. This is the perfect time of day to be here, isn't it? The sun is so warm, and it's covering the whole beach." *I'm blabbing. I need to stop.* "Last time I was here I was with Mitenah, Sandy, and Janee. When was the last time you were here? It must h—"

"Please stop, Sabel." He turned to her, gently taking her chin in his hand. "I love to listen to your voice, but I want to hear you speak about something of importance. Please."

She turned her face away slightly, his hand falling away. *He wants me to tell him how I feel. How can I possibly do that?* "That's better," he said, smiling. "But now try to say those words out loud." He took her hand and looked into her eyes in a way that made her feel like he could actually see her thoughts. His eyes were wide and dark with emotion as he waited patiently for her to say something.

"Running Otter, I . . ."

He gave her hand a gentle squeeze. "Are you still unsure?"

"No." Her eyebrows came down. "At least, I don't think so. But . . . I'm scared."

"Of what?" He let go of her hand and reached up to tuck a stray lock of hair behind her ear.

"Of love, I guess. It's big . . . I know it can be beautiful, but it can also go bad, and people get hurt." Looking out at the water, she continued. "I'm afraid of getting hurt."

"You are right. Love comes with risks. But if you do not take the chance—"

"I could be missing out on something beautiful." She looked at him now, her eyes shiny with tears.

"Please do not miss out. Take a chance with me, Mimiteh. I promise to love you with all my heart."

She smiled to herself. "There is just one thing I need to know."

His eyes were wide, eyebrows high on his face. "What is that?"

"Kiss me."

He turned toward her, hands holding her jaw lightly and his lips found hers in a gentle kiss. He pulled his head back and looked into her face. "No," she said. "*Kiss* me."

It was some time before they came up for air. She leaned back on her arms and exhaled. *Spectacular!*

He looked at her and said, "I could do that all day."

"Prove it."

That

Charlotte and Ben were enjoying a nightcap in the sitting room when they heard their muffled voices outside the door. Sabel was absolutely glowing as she stepped inside, and Running Otter looked equally happy.

Charlotte smiled and asked, "I assume you had a nice evening?"

"Yes," Sabel answered, blushing fiercely. Then she turned to Running Otter and said, "Thanks for walking me. I'll see you Wednesday."

"I will meet you on the beach," he answered. Then he looked at Charlotte and Ben and added, "Goodnight."

When Sabel closed the door behind him, she didn't turn around right away. She knew they'd want to hear what happened. On the one hand, she wanted to keep it all to herself, but on the other, she wanted to shout it to the world.

"Did you enjoy your picnic?" her mother asked.

"He told you he'd planned that, didn't he?"

"He did; in case you weren't home in time for supper." She said those words but raised her eyebrows as if she'd asked a question.

Ben watched them, enjoying the cheerful atmosphere.

Unable to wipe the smile from her face, Sabel gave into it and came into the sitting room. She sat in the chair opposite her parents. "I finally figured it out . . . you know . . . who I want to spend my time with. It's him."

"I'm happy for you, sweetie," Charlotte said.

"It took some time, but I'm glad you're settled," Ben said.

"He's going to ride up to Auburn with me Wednesday afternoon. I have to tell Jonny."

As Charlotte lay down to sleep that night, she thought about her daughter and Running Otter. *Sabel has chosen to love the little boy who stole my heart all those years ago. Running Cub/Otter has been a joy in my life from the day I met him.* She remembered making the wind-catcher with him and Keen Wolf, planning swim dates, his storytelling, him holding her hand when they walked. *I remember telling Gifted Hands I wanted one just like him.* She laughed, remembering Sabel's reaction when she learned he had a new name. She didn't understand why she couldn't call him Running Cub anymore. With her hand on her hip, she said, "Well, I don't like it!" *She was so cute! Running Otter is a remarkable young man; he's kind, responsible, fun, and as good looking as his dad and uncle. Sabel will surely have a wonderful life.*

It was just after 1:00 p.m. Wednesday afternoon when Charlotte said, "Okay, love, off you go. He'll be waiting for you."

"Thanks, Mum. Wish me luck."

After a quick hug, Charlotte said, "It'll be fine. Oh, listen, take this." Charlotte put her hand into her pocket and took out some coins. "I want you and Running Otter to have some supper at the tavern before you head home."

"Love you, Mum," Sabel said as she took the money and turned to leave.

"Love you, too, honey."

Sabel practically ran to the store, excited to see Running Otter again. She walked around the back of the building and saw him talking to Jimmy outside the stable—they were hooking the buggy up to Ruby. "Hello, gentlemen," she said, smiling ear-to-ear.

"Good afternoon, love," Jimmy answered, as he double checked the bridle. "It a' looks fine. You take the road easy now."

Running Otter smiled in a way that made her stomach do flip flops and asked, "Are you ready, Mimiteh?" She loved it when he called her that. He was the only one who still did—well, Mitenah occasionally said it, too.

"I'm ready." What she really wanted to do was wrap her arms around his neck and kiss him, but she smiled and climbed into the buggy.

Jimmy stood watching them ride away with a smile in his heart.

They were on the road through the woods about five minutes later when Running Otter stopped the horse. "What is it?" she asked, turning to look at him.

He leaned over and kissed her, long and slow. "That." He smiled.

"Oh, that." She smiled back, her heart pounding in her chest.

"I have been waiting to do that since I left you at home the other night," he said, as they started to move again. Sabel didn't think she'd ever felt happier. "You know where Jonny's shop is located?"

"I do. I've been in with Mum. If he's not there, he stays in the back."

Running Otter planned to leave her in front of the tanner's shop and take the horse and buggy to the tavern, where he could tie her to the hitching post and water her. He did not want to see or be seen by Jonny; his purpose here was simply to be sure Sabel arrived safely and was able to speak to him. After thirty minutes had passed, he started toward the tannery, crossing the road so he would not be noticed.

When he arrived in front of the shop, he saw her come out from behind the building. *She was in his room. I suppose that was necessary for privacy. She has tears on her cheeks.* Feeling his pulse increase, Running Otter crossed the road. Then he saw Jonny running out after her. He caught up to Sabel and grabbed her arm, spinning her to face him. He said something to her, and her chin dropped to her chest. Jonny's hand was under her chin as he spoke to her; it looked as if he was going to kiss her. Running Otter froze. Jonny leaned in for a kiss and Running Otter watched as her hand came up between them. She shook her head, turned, and, lifting her skirt, ran down the road. Jonny appeared deflated. He looked up and saw Running Otter. The two men walked toward each other, stopping only when they were face to face.

"You stole her from me, you mopus!" Jonny said, unexpectedly swinging and connecting with Running Otter's face.

Running Otter brought his hand to his cheek, fighting the urge to punch back. For him, the fight was over. He knew that it could have been him standing here feeling that way. "I am sorry," he said, before turning and walking away.

He caught up with her outside the tavern. She was surprised when she saw his face and was about to ask what had happened, when he said, "Are you all right?" She nodded. "Would you like to go inside? Or maybe a walk?"

"A walk sounds nice."

She told him he had been inside the shop when she arrived. His face lit up when he saw her, but his expression changed when he saw hers. The tanner excused him for a few minutes so they could speak privately. Inside his room, they sat at his little table. "Please, don't say it," he said. She looked at him, feeling nervous and awkward. "I love you, Sabel. I want to be with you. Don't you see that?"

"I'm sorry," she said, her voice shaking. "I truly am, but I'm afraid it's over between you and me, Jonny."

He came to stand in front of her, taking her hands. "Please, Sabel." His eyes filled with tears as he tried not to sound desperate. She felt horrible making him feel this way, but what could she do?

"I'm sorry, Jonny." She slipped her hands out of his and went for the door.

He reached over her and held the door closed. She turned. Suddenly, his mouth was on hers, his tongue searching. She almost kissed him back, almost. But in her mind, she saw Running Otter's face, his eyes dark with yearning. It was him, only him. She pushed Jonny back and opened the door, trying to get away as quickly as she could.

Tears sprung to her eyes. "I feel evil for what I did to him. Giving him hope and then taking it away. He deserves better."

"This is the way of life, Mimiteh. There are times when things happen that we do not expect, and they change our path. Sometimes for the better, sometimes not."

She looked up at him sideways with a little smile. "Yes . . . for me this is better." She slipped her arm through his.

"For us both," he agreed.

"Now, tell me about your face."

Running Otter explained that he had walked to the shop, wondering why she hadn't yet returned. "When he saw me . . . well, he wasn't happy. I cannot blame him." He smiled down at her. "Shall we have some supper now?"

They went inside the tavern and were seated. She immediately noticed the eyes of several diners looking her way—well, not at her, but at Running Otter. She looked at him, confused. "There are still many who would not see a young woman like you in the company of someone like me."

"Like you? You mean Tuscarora?" He nodded. "That's . . ."

"If you are uncomfortable, we do not have to stay."

"If *I'm* uncomfortable?!" She was angry. Realizing the level of her voice, she lowered it some, before continuing. "Let the narrow-minded watch us enjoy our meal *and* each other's company."

He smiled. "Enough about them." He waited for her to calm. "I have noticed you wearing these stones on your wrist the past few times I've seen you." He fumbled with them where they hung.

"Oh, yes." She looked down at her hand. "I borrowed them from Mum." He was watching; he knew there was more to it and hoped she would explain without more prodding. "You know she believes that stones have powers and energies, right?" He nodded. "Well, this past little while, my mind has been . . ." She rolled her eyes, trying to express her state of mind. "She picked these out to help me feel at peace and to trust myself to find a way around the thing that was blocking my path."

"To help you decide what would be best for you."

She smiled shyly. "Does that sound silly?"

"Not to me. We often carry small things with us for similar reasons." He looked down at the pouch he had tied around his waist and reached inside. "Look." He placed a large canine tooth on the table. "This came from a bear. When I was young and we would find a dead bear, or kill one, we would always take a tooth. I got this after I was given my new name. Your family was in Scotland then. I carry it with me for luck and protection." She was listening closely. "It seems that it has brought me the best of luck—you." Her heart melted. She had no doubt she'd made the right choice.

They were halfway through their supper when an older woman approached the table. "Sorry to disturb. I was just looking at you, love, and you look familiar. I'm Ella Hubert. Would you be a Williams?"

"Yes. I'm Sabel Williams, and this is my friend, Running Otter."

"Ah, I thought so. Doctor Ben and Charlotte's daughter. Good to meet you," she added looking at Running Otter. "I hope you've been enjoying your meal?"

"It's quite good, thank you. I do wish these patrons would mind their manners, though."

She saw the acknowledgement in Mrs. Hubert's eyes. In a low voice, she said, "I'm sorry for that. Some folks just don't see everyone the same. It's a shame." She nodded to herself then and added, "Will you be staying the night with us, Sabel?" Her eyes moved to Running Otter and back to Sabel, who was now blushing wildly.

"No, we had some business in town and came in for our supper. "

"Very well. Good to see you both," she said brightly and walked away.

Running Otter saw the colour spread across Sabel's cheeks and felt his heart swell. *I must never let this woman feel that she made the wrong choice. We were meant for one another.*

Sabel watched Running Otter climb up into the buggy. Behind him, walking toward them, was Jonny. She didn't know if he was heading for the tavern, but she was glad he hadn't come in while they were there. When they made eye contact, he stopped walking. Noticing the direction of Sabel's gaze, Running Otter turned to look. When he turned back to her, he asked, "Are you ready?"

Slowly, her eyes met his. She smiled and answered, "Yes. Let's go."

Summer

I t was mid-July when they received a short note from Carole-Anne.

July 1837

Dear Gracie and Charlotte,

> *Maisie has arrived home safely and is very happy to have seen everyone. She told us about Mabel . . . We are so sorry and want to express our deep condolences. She was a lovely woman through and through and will surely be missed. Please know that we are thinking of you all with love.*
>
> *Carole-Anne*

They also heard from Ailsa midway through summer. She and the children had arrived safely in Aberdeen. Sheila was delighted to see her daughter's face again and overjoyed to snuggle her little ones. Sam had accompanied them to Aberdeen to be sure they arrived at her mother's home safely. He'd stayed only two days before heading to work in France. She missed him, but seeing her mother and her sister and family was something she hadn't thought she'd do again. Sheila broke down in tears when she heard about Mabel's passing, but smiled to think she would have come. Morag and Duncan send their love. She said she wouldn't have known their boys, they'd grown so much. She was going to visit her father's grave in the coming days and maybe share a dram with him. That made Charlotte smile: she had been fond of Archie.

Ailsa expected to be leaving for home in late September and promised to write before then.

"Aye, Mum woulda loved seein' Sheila again. It's a shame she didna make it."

Over the next weeks, Keen Wolf, Running Otter, and Dark Wolf repaired much of the wood roof and walls of the "guest" house. The previous occupants had looked after the house, but there were areas where its age showed. Gifted Hands and Mitenah sewed new curtains for the bedrooms and did what they could to clean and repair the furniture left behind.

Mitenah was waiting for her friends when they arrived at the water's edge. She was excited to show them the house, now that she and her mother were done adding the finishing touches.

"It looks as if someone is a little excited," Sabel said with a giggle as the three girls walked toward the cabin where Swan Song's family would stay.

"When will they arrive?" Sandy asked.

"En-ay says any day now. It depends on the path they have taken."

Mitenah took them inside; it was small, with only two bedrooms, but that's all they'd need for three people.

"So, tell us again about Swan Song," Sabel said as they sat under the shade of a tree, outside the cabin.

"Well, it has been two years since I saw him and his parents, but I remember thinking he looked very   . . . um . . . interesting. He wore his long hair in two braids, his eyes were very big and dark, and I remember his voice was very low. I hope I still like him when he gets here."

"It sounds like you're off to a good start, Mitenah," Sandy said with a giggle.

"En-ay says he and his parents will stay with us for a few weeks, and if he and I like each other, he will stay. I remember his kree-ay was very quiet, more so than mine, and his mother sang to herself while she was busy and liked to tell funny stories."

"I'm looking forward to meeting them," Sabel said.

It was a full two weeks later, on a Wednesday afternoon, when Running Otter arrived at the Doctor's House with news. He sneaked a kiss from Sabel while her mother was bent behind the counter and then announced that Swan Song and his mother, Song Bird, had arrived late the night before.

"They told us Burning Oak, that is his father, grew ill as they prepared to make the journey and passed the day before they were to leave. They remained long enough to give him a proper burial. Then, with no reason to return home, they gathered their belongings and made the journey together."

"Oh, how sad," Charlotte said, knowing the family's dreams had been shattered.

Running Otter nodded, looking solemn. "Her only wish, I am told, is to be returned after her death to be buried with her husband."

"I'm so sorry," Sabel said.

"Is there anything we can do?" Ben asked.

"I'm afraid not, but thank you. En-ay asked me to pass on the news but wants you to know that they are still expecting you on Sunday, as you had planned."

He looked at Sabel now, and though he felt the family's sadness, his eyes showed his love for her. She took his hand. "Are you needed there? I mean, can you stay for a while today? Or tomorrow?" She wanted to add, "or both", but held her tongue.

He smiled at her. "I am able to stay for now, but tomorrow I will go hunting with Keen Wolf for two or three days." With a thrill, he noticed a pout form on her lips. He felt the need to restrain himself. "I will come see you when we return."

Sabel nodded.

"Honey, why don't the two of you go for a walk or go sit by the water? I'll finish up in here for today."

Sabel looked at her mother with gratitude. "Thanks, Mum."

He took her hand, and they walked back to the canoe. He knew where he wanted to take her—the spot had quickly become their favourite on this side of the lake.

She sat in the sand and almost immediately found herself lying back, with him alongside her, lips locked in a fierce kiss.

When noon struck the next day, Sabel walked to the general store to pick up lunch for her and her mother. To her surprise, she saw a familiar canoe approaching. Her heart skipped a beat. With happy thoughts, she headed to the water to welcome him.

She reached her hand out to him. "Running Otter, I didn't think I'd see you today! What changed?"

"First a kiss," he said, taking her hand and leaning to her. "Mmm, that is what I needed."

"Come with me, and we'll get our dinner."

They walked into the Doctor's House hand in hand. "I see you picked up more than our dinner," Charlotte said with a giggle.

"I did."

"Come in and have a seat."

While they ate, Running Otter told them that Song Bird had awoken unwell this morning. "En-ay went to see her and told me she had a fever and was unable to eat or drink. She gave her lemon balm and ginger, but wondered if you might suggest something else?" Charlotte nodded. "Swan Song says it is unlike his mother to be ill."

"Oh, dear. Well, I will certainly speak to Ben and put something together for you."

"Thank you, Charlotte."

"So, tell us about Swan Song. What's he like, so far, I mean?" Sabel asked.

"He is much as I remember. Amusing, but also wise. He is certainly interested in Mitenah. I could see that immediately. I believe he and I will be good friends."

Running Otter left a short time later with a tea mixture suggested by Ben. Charlotte told him, "Please tell Gifted Hands to give her this to sip as often as she can, and if she would like us to come see her, just come get us."

He returned the next morning, this time looking far more serious. "Ben, En-ay would like you to come see Song Bird. She says she is stubborn and just wants to rest, but she looks very poorly this morning."

Ben and Charlotte immediately got into their canoe, leaving the Doctor's House in Sabel's hands.

After examining Song Bird, Ben and Charlotte stepped outside the bedroom door to discuss her health. "I believe that losing her husband and then making the tiring journey here, has left her body vulnerable."

"I agree, Benny. That kind of stress lowers immunity." She paused seeing that someone had entered the house. "Chweh'n. You must be Swan Song."

"Chweh'n. Yes . . . I am him," he said with a quick nod.

"It's good to meet you," Ben offered. "We have come to look in on Song Bird." He nodded again.

"I just realized your mother and you both have 'Song' in your name," Charlotte said as Mitenah joined them.

Gifted Hands responded, "That is because Song Bird likes to sing and has a voice as pretty as a bird's song."

"And Swan Song?" Ben asked.

Mitenah answered, "Song Bird told me it is because when he opens his mouth to sing, he squawks like an angry swan." At her own words, she broke into laughter. So did the body under the covers in the bedroom. She laughed so hard that she started to choke on a cough.

Swan Song offered her water to sip.

"Gifted Hands, I'm afraid if we can't get her to drink more and take some food . . ."

"I understand, Ben. Mitenah and I will do our best to encourage her to take whatever you suggest." He nodded and proceeded to make a list of immunity-building foods: apples, oranges, potatoes, beans, nuts and seeds, fish, chicken soup with vegetables.

Gifted Hands smiled; she had started some soup cooking this morning. She would add what she could from Ben's list.

Ben and Charlotte left with a promise to return tomorrow to check Song Bird's progress and a reminder that all wash their hands with soap frequently, especially after being in the room with her.

When Ben returned the next morning, he found Song Bird in similar form. He told Gifted Hands to continue what she'd been doing and suggested they postpone this Sunday's visit. "You have enough to do here without all of us. We will wait and come next week with the Moffatts."

"Thank you, Ben. I agree, and there is no need to risk anyone getting this sickness."

As the week progressed, Song Bird's condition remained much the same. She drank most of her teas but ate little more than a bowl of soup each day. Ben worried that the strain of her body fighting this sickness and her lack of sufficient nutrition would take its toll.

As the weekend approached, Gifted Hands sent word that, although Song Bird was not yet better, she wanted everyone to come on Sunday. She herself was in need of the break, and Mitenah was eager for everyone to meet Swan Song.

Gifted Hands felt her tension lift when she heard the voices outside—they had arrived. She opened the door. "Chweh'n everyone. It is good to see you all." She and Keen Wolf were ready for this distraction.

Ben slipped away to check on Song Bird. He found her sleeping, with her son and Mitenah at her side. He quietly entered the room and asked how she was today. "The same, Ben," Mitenah said. "I am worried. Her eyes don't look like hers anymore, and her colour is not right."

"I see that, too. Unfortunately, I don't know what else we can do for her." Ben glanced at Swan Song before asking, "She is a fighter?"

"Yes. But she left her heart at our home. I do not know if she wants to go on."

Ben nodded his understanding. "It's up to her now."

"Let's leave her to sleep for now, Swan Song. I want you to meet everyone. We can return after our meal," Mitenah said.

As he bent to kiss his mother's cheek, her hand came up and caught his, giving it a gentle squeeze. He gave it a light kiss and whispered in her ear, before leaving to meet the Williams and Moffatts.

They left for home in four canoes, the younger ones rowing ahead, leaving the adults, Robbie, Sabel, and Sandy lagging behind. "So, what's abody's thoughts on Swan Song?" Gracie started the conversation.

Robbie answered first. "He seems like a good choice for Mitenah. I'm glad I was able to meet him before I go away. He was quiet, but I suppose he had a lot of people to meet."

"Aye, and he'd be worrit about 'is mother."

"I liked him, and I could tell Mitenah does, too," Sandy said.

"Oh, aye," agreed Jimmy. "She watched 'im as he spoke with abody."

"He kept his eyes on her, too," said Charlotte. "They're definitely into each other."

Hearing his mother's words, Robbie turned back to look at her. "*Into* each other, Mum?"

She smiled. "Yep."

He shook his head and turned back around. Gracie gave her friend a wink.

SongBird

September brought some new beginnings.Sabel and Mitenah waited patiently for their men to arrive back home. After Song Bird's death, Swan Song and Running Otter had borrowed a couple of horses and a cart and taken her home to be buried with Burning Oak.

Before passing, Song Bird had expressed her wish to see Swan Song and Mitenah take their vows. Swan Song conveyed his mother's wish to Mitenah and her parents, and waited patiently for their opinions. Gifted Hands and Keen Wolf exchanged a look, and Gifted Hands smiled at her daughter. The three had spoken of Swan Song's suitability for Mitenah.

Gifted Hands said, "Swan Song, this is sooner than we had expected. We hoped the two of you would have more time to get to know one another, but of course, for your mother to share in your joining, it must be now. It is understandable." She paused and nodded at her daughter.

Mitenah looked at Swan Song with wide eyes and swallowed hard.

It was done in the privacy of the family home a short time after. Song Bird was taken into the sitting room to watch, propped on the settee. She wished them both love and happiness in their future together and placed kisses on their cheeks, before being returned to the comfort of her bed. She passed away that night, happy in the knowledge that her son had become a member of this family. Her husband would have been happy to see it.

Sabel was disappointed to learn that she wouldn't see Running Otter for over a week, but she understood his wanting to accompany his new brother-in-law. It would be a time for them to get to know each other better. She spent a couple of her evenings with Sandy, one of which they rowed across to visit Mitenah.

As soon as they sat down, Sandy told them that she had spoken to Katie and Lawrence about helping at the school. What she really wanted was to work half of the time at the store and the other half in the school. She'd kept it to herself until she was sure—now, she was sure.

"Katie looked relieved when I asked. I think she's been wanting to spend less time there. She asked if I could work in the afternoons."

"That's exciting! When will you start? What does your mum say about it?" Sabel asked.

"I start next week. Mum thinks it's good for me to get out of the store and do what I was meant to do."

"I am happy for you, Sandy. You have said little to us, but we have seen it in you. You will be an excellent teacher," Mitenah said.

"Thank you."

The three young women sat down by the water talking about men, daily chores, and kissing. They were candid, they giggled, and enjoyed their time together—time that would not be the same once Swan Song returned and Mitenah was no longer on her own.

Sabel told them about the day Robbie left. "Mum was crying and hugging him, Holly, too. Phillip just smiled and wished him luck."

"And your father?" Sandy asked.

"He looked at Robbie, and you could see the pride in his eyes. He hugged him hard and told him to keep in touch."

"They have the same eyes," Mitenah said. "I always used to notice that when I was young."

"Aye, but other than his eyes and his dark hair, he's not like Uncle Ben or Auntie Charlotte."

Sabel squinted her eyes as she looked at her cousin. "I thought you knew about Robbie."

Sandy cocked her head. "Knew what?"

Sabel's eyes flicked to Mitenah before she answered. Mitenah had the look in her eyes that her mother often had, the one that said she understood. Gifted

Hands must have told her the story at some point. "Sandy, Robbie is not my mum's child."

Sandy's eyebrows came down and she tilted her head. "You know, now that you say that, I did hear something years ago, but I don't remember. Can you tell me?"

"Before my dad met my mum, when he was living in Boston, there was a girl he used to see in the summer. When he finished school and was ready to come home, he . . . they . . . well, anyway, he came home, met Mum, and the rest is history. They had been married less than a year when Robbie's grandparents showed up at the door with a baby in their arms. His mother had died, and she had wanted him to be with his father."

"Did Uncle Ben know she had a baby?"

"No. That was a complete surprise for everyone. I think Mum was expecting me at the time."

"That must have been hard for Auntie Charlotte. I mean, a baby made by your husband and another woman." Sandy's face showed her distress at the thought.

"I imagine so. I know Running Otter was with another woman for some time. I can't think about it, but if he'd had a child? Ugh . . . I don't know if I could deal with that."

Mitenah said, "That would be difficult, of course, but imagine the poor woman who died. She will not get to see her son grow up."

"Aye, and the grandparents who loved the two of them enough to give him up, knowing they would never see him again."

"It's hard to imagine, isn't it?" Sabel asked with a lump in her throat. "Well, lucky my mum has a wonderful family and friends; I'm sure they helped her deal with it. And Robbie was, is, a good person. I'm sure he made it easy. I'll miss having him around."

They were quiet for a time before Sabel asked, "Will you move to the cabin the day Swan Song comes home, Mitenah?"

"I am unsure. I knew that we would have come together in time, but I didn't expect it to be so soon. He didn't either. I do not want to hurry. I do not think I am ready to share his bed yet."

"Completely understandable," Sandy said.

"Well, there's no rush. Just take your time, and do what feels right," Sabel said, setting her hand over her friend's.

Mitenah turned to her and smiled. "That is what En-ay said."

The men arrived home a few days later, dusty from the trail and exhausted from travel. The trip had taken several days both ways, and it had been emotional. Running Otter wanted nothing more than to get in the canoe, cross the lake, and put his lips on Sabel's, but he knew he would benefit from bathing and a good night's sleep. He would see her tomorrow.

The bells rang out at noon, and Charlotte smiled. "Running Otter, how was the trip?"

"It went as well as it could, Charlotte. I know that Swan Song is happy he was able to give his mother what she wished for before her death." She nodded. "Where is Sabel?"

"She's out back doing some cutting. Go on and say hello." He lit up and turned on his heels, heading back out the door.

They came in together a few minutes later. "Mum, we're going to go get something to eat. BRB." She giggled at the puzzled expression on Running Otter's face.

Charlotte joined in. "It's short for be right back," she said.

Running Otter raised an eyebrow and gave Sabel a sideways look. There was always something more to learn with these two women.

While they walked, he told Sabel about their ride west and the ceremony they took part in for Song Bird. "Everyone was sad to know she was gone but happy that she was buried with Burning Oak. Both had wanted it to be so."

"I missed you," she said, slipping her arm under his.

"Me, too," he agreed, looking down at her with a grin.

After enjoying dinner together, Running Otter asked about taking Sabel hunting. "I've been looking forward to teaching you how to use a bow and arrow. I wondered about tomorrow?"

She started to answer, "I can meet you aft—"

"What time do you usually leave, Running Otter?" Charlotte interrupted.

He said, "At first light."

"Go ahead, honey. You can take a day away from here. Maybe you can even bring home supper." Charlotte winked at her daughter, who looked doubtful.

"That was fun! Thank you," Sabel said, getting up on her toes to kiss him. "Maybe next time I'll hit something." She set the bow and quiver on the ground, leaning it against the wall outside the door.

He chuckled. "Maybe. But I will admit you did very well for someone who has never used a bow and arrow."

"Thanks."

"We're back," he called to Gifted Hands and Keen Wolf through the door. "Let us take these rabbits to the side and prepare them for cooking. You can take one home if you like."

"Oo-oo, thanks. Mum and Dad will like that."

She watched quietly as he skinned and sectioned the meat of the first rabbit. "Yuck!"

"Would you like to try?" he asked her.

"Um . . ." She really didn't want to. "I can hardly be willing to kill the beast and then not follow through, can I?" He smiled, waiting to see what she would do. She put her hand out for the knife. He smiled at the shiver that went down her spine.

She required some instruction, but she did it. Next time she felt she could do it herself, but she hoped she wouldn't have to.

He put his mother's meat into the pan he'd brought outside, and the rest was wrapped for Sabel to take home. Running Otter stepped inside and set the pan on the table.

"Where's Kohana today? Usually, she comes to say hello."

"I'm sure she is around here somewhere. Come, let's get you home." He took her hand and they walked to the canoe.

Back at home, she told her family how she had learned to hunt using a bow and arrow. "My aim missed, but Running Otter got two. It was exciting! Then he showed me how to do this to it." She unwrapped the meat and dropped it into the pan her mother gave her.

"I remember one time when we were there visiting, Running Cub insisted I come learn how to skin a rabbit with him. Keen Wolf was a good teacher."

Ben snickered. "I remember that day, too."

It was a few days before Sabel saw Running Otter again. They met at the beach and went for a walk in the woods. "We received a letter from Robbie today. It was short, but he said that his room at Ailsa and Sam's is perfect for studying. The twins are a bit of a handful, but Ailsa knows how to handle them. And he says his lectures are very interesting. He's enjoying things so far."

"I am guessing you miss him," Running Otter said.

"I do. He's always been there, and he was, is, a good big brother. I'm going to write him tonight and tell him about hunting."

"He'll be jealous that it was me that got to teach you," he said and kissed her cheek. She blushed. "That reminds me. Remember we didn't see Kohana last time you were over?" Sabel nodded. "Well, no one saw her for three days. We have no idea where she went, but she was waiting at the door when Keen Wolf went out this morning to check the traps. She walked straight inside and curled up by the fire."

Samhain 1837

Sabel stepped into the Doctor's House, shaking the rain from her coat and hair. "Gah, October rain is miserable. It makes me feel so cold," she complained. "Auntie Gracie wants me to tell you she received a note from Carole-Anne today. She says to come by when you've got a few minutes to sit down together."

"Oh, I will, thanks. I wonder how they're doing."

"I wonder if they'll come for Christmas this year."

"It would be nice to see them, wouldn't it? It's hard to believe Christmas is right around the corner."

"Tonight is Samhain?" Sabel asked.

Charlotte nodded in answer. She'd been thinking about it for days, looking forward to her long-awaited visit with Jessica.

When the workday was over, Charlotte and Gracie read the note together. All in all, there was little news. Carole-Anne was glad to hear that Robbie got off to Harvard safely and happy for Sabel and Running Otter. She and Keith were doing well. He continued to teach and preach and had never been happier. She felt very comfortable there and had been working on some new skills. Maisie had expressed that she wanted to spend Christmas with Jeffery and her friends this year. She and Keith had some misgivings about it; Christmas was, after all, a time to be spent with family, but they had taken her away and knew she missed everyone. She would be arriving the day before Christmas Eve. Sabel and Sandy were happy to hear it and set off right away to tell Janee the news.

After cleaning the supper dishes, Charlotte excused herself to prepare her altar for tonight's ritual. The cool temperatures and the sounds of the rain seemed to have lulled everyone into a sleepy feeling. Phillip and Holly said goodnight early, and Sabel, complaining of a headache, turned in with a cup of white willow tea. The house was quiet as Charlotte relaxed in her ritual bath, thinking about Jessica and focusing on tonight's task.

She had barely finished welcoming the Goddess and God to her circle when Charlotte heard her name, almost like a sweet whisper.

"Jess!"

"Hey, Char! How are you?"

Knowing how limited their time was, Charlotte started right in . . . "Robbie has moved to Boston and is living with Ailsa and Sam, attending Harvard Medical School. So far, he's loving it. Are you ready for this? Sabel and Running Otter are now together. It's early days yet, but they are a perfect couple. We're all happy about it. Phillip is looking forward to finishing school and finding work at a paper, and Holly is enjoying school. Mabel passed away in her sleep a few months ago. It was sudden and unexpected, but as far as ways to go, not so bad. We do miss her. Sandy has started teaching part time at the school. She loves it! Gracie and Gifted Hands asked to be remembered. Now you!"

"What about you? You talked about everyone else."

"I've been working with Sabel at the Doctor's House. It's going well. We're a great team!"

"Wonderful!" Jessica started. "Let's see, I don't have much. Michael is the same and is very happy. My mother is in her own world. She hasn't recognized me in over a year. Well, not as her daughter anyway. She does say hello when she sees me. She sometimes thinks I'm a friend coming to visit. I miss her so much. Charlie is ten now. He's curious and adventurous, and I just love him to bits. I've taken on more hours now that he's a bit bigger. Still in the surgical suite at the hospital."

"Any new pets?"

"Not right now. Charlie keeps us busy enough with school and extracurricular activities. I . . . n't . . . no! Goodbye, Char! L . . . ou."

And she was gone.

Charlotte felt a tear roll down her cheek as she grounded. It always happened so quickly. She wished she knew a way to keep that window in time open a little longer and wondered if it would be any different on a full moon. The only time Samhain had coincided with a full moon was in 1830, but that was during the time when she hadn't been able to contact Jess. That wouldn't happen again until 1849.

After putting away her altar and decorations, she tiptoed down to see if Ben was still awake. He was sitting in a chair with his chin on his chest, slumped over in sleep. She shook him gently. "Come on upstairs, Benny. I'm finished. Let's get you into bed."

He looked up, momentarily confused, and putting out his hand asked, "How is she?"

She took his hand as he stood from his seat. "Good. She looked happy."

"You know, when you stand in front of the candle in that shift, I can see right through it."

She smirked. "Can you now?"

Once upstairs, he closed the bedroom door behind them and turned to her. "Take it off."

"Bu—"

"Off, Moxie."

After catching her breath, she kissed him goodnight and rolled onto her side. It wasn't long before thoughts of Charlie returned. In Jess's time, Charlie was only ten years old. He wouldn't leave home for seventeen years. It was mind-boggling to know that at that time, he would leave there to meet her twelve years ago.

She wondered when they would meet again.

Running Otter cleared his throat before speaking. "Sabel, I would like to invite you to join us for our fire ceremony on the day of the New Moon."

"A Fire Ceremony? Do tell."

Running Otter smiled and sat beside her. "A fire ceremony is something we do during a full moon or a new moon when we want to rid ourselves of something from our past and set our intentions for the future, or when we are looking to bring newness into our life."

"That sounds like something I would love to be a part of. What happens during this ceremony exactly?"

"Each of us will bring an offering to burn. We use a small stick; sometimes it will represent something that we want to let go of in our life; sometimes it acts only to convey our thoughts to the fire. We burn the offerings, turning them to smoke, releasing them into the sky."

"I think I would enjoy that. Thank you. Will the whole family be participating?"

"Yes. I asked En-ay and Keen Wolf if they would like to have a ceremony; it has been quite some time since we did one together."

Sabel smiled. "The moon was full two days ago, so the new moon will be in two weeks?" He nodded. "I look forward to it," she added with a smile.

That evening, Sabel told her parents of her invitation. "That's wonderful. I assume you'll go?" Charlotte asked.

"Definitely. Have you been to one before?"

Her father shook his head. Sabel watched him look at his wife with an expression she didn't understand. Charlotte answered. "I went once. I was invited to join Gifted Hands, Straight Arrow, and Keen Wolf." Sabel watched a memory float across her mother's eyes. "Straight Arrow had become quite ill a few days before, but he and Gifted Hands said Keen Wolf and I should still do it."

"Where were you, Dad?"

"I had been out of town that week, but your mother and I were not yet together at that time."

"We had just finished the ceremony"—a flash of a memory flickered through her mind; Keen Wolf seated beside her, they were hand-in-hand, he was leaning in for what would have been their first kiss—"when Gifted Hands called us to get your dad. Straight Arrow had taken a turn for the worse." Charlotte swallowed hard and with wet eyes continued. "He died the next day."

Sabel didn't know what to say. "That must have been so sad. Keen Wolf married Gifted Hands so she and Running Cub wouldn't be alone?"

Without looking at her husband, Charlotte answered. "Yes."

Memories of the sadness she felt at that time washed over her. Keen Wolf had been patient and persistent; he had broken through her defenses. She had fallen for him hard. When he came to tell her he would join with Gifted Hands, it tore her heart out. He had been incredibly sad when he said the words to her; he was acting from a sense of duty. The feelings of emptiness that accompanied his absence took some time to get over. Of course, Ben was there. He was a good friend and a wonderful man. She surprised herself when she then fell in love with him. Ben was the perfect man for her . . .

Sabel left with the others as they walked to church. She wanted to use some time this morning to restock some jars at the Doctor's House. The whole time, all she could think about was the Fire Ceremony next week.

As the door closed behind the group, Charlotte asked, "Would you like another coffee, Benny?"

"Coffee? No. You? Yes." He put his arms around her, and his lips brushed her neck.

"Oh, my . . ." she muttered. After setting the mugs on the table, she took his hand and led him up the stairs to their room. "What did you have in mind?" she asked mischievously.

"Well, we can start by getting you out of that dress." He turned her around and began to undo the buttons down her back, lips and tongue slowly following his fingers.

When her dress hit the floor, he pushed her down onto the bed. With fire in his eyes, he lifted the bottom of her shift, his face disappearing beneath it.

"Well, happy Sunday to me," she said, stepping back into her dress a little later. "Can you please button me back up?"

"If I must," he answered with a grin. "So, what shall we do now?"

They went back downstairs to start that coffee brewing. When they heard the knock on the door, they looked at each other. "Who can that be? We aren't seeing our friends this week and everyone else is at church."

With a shrug, Ben walked to the door.

"Running Otter! We weren't expecting to see you today. Come on in."

"Thank you." He stepped inside and gave Ben his coat. "I wanted to speak to you while Sabel is not home."

"Oh? What's up?" Charlotte asked.

He sat on the settee and smiled. "Well," he started nervously, "I want to do this properly."

"Do what?" Ben asked.

Running Otter licked his dry lips and looked from Charlotte to Ben. "I would like your permission to ask Sabel to be my wife."

Charlotte's face lit up and tears sprung to her eyes. Ben smiled and said, "Running Otter, there is no doubt in my mind that the two of you are meant to be together. You certainly have our good wishes."

Running Otter exhaled deeply and smiled. "Thank you. I will ask her after the fire ceremony on Tuesday."

Charlotte jumped up and hugged him hard. "I'm very excited for you both."

"Thank you." He smiled. "I will leave you now and meet her at the store. I have a surprise for her. Kohana had three kittens." He started for the door and turned. "Please do not tell her I was here."

Charlotte zipped her lip, instantly realizing that this man had no idea what a zipper was. "Not a word. We'll see you later in the week."

After work the next day, Sabel rowed across the lake on her own. She'd been thinking about the kittens all day and was eager to check on them. One of them didn't appear to be doing very well yesterday; it was smaller than the others and weak. She hoped that today it would be a little stronger. Both Gifted Hands and Mitenah were excited at the prospect of having a new kitten in their homes, and her mother said she would be happy to have one, too. She missed having Hazel around.

Excited, she climbed out of the canoe and ran up toward the house. Gifted Hands answered the door wearing an odd expression—serious, sad, disturbed, Sabel wasn't sure. When she looked into the sitting room, she immediately understood. The kittens were instantly forgotten.

Standing looking back at her were Running Otter and a woman that Sabel guessed was Aleshanee, and she was *very* pregnant. Sabel looked at them, speechless. She wanted to turn and run away, but her legs were frozen, her feet stuck to the floor. "Sabel," Running Otter started. That's when the adrenalin kicked in and she got the use of her legs back. She turned back toward the door. Without a word, she looked at Gifted Hands, opened the door, and ran down to the canoe. She had to get away from here—now. No amount of talking would change that.

Aleshanee was holding Running Otter's arm, in an attempt to keep him there with her, but he moved her hand away and ran to the beach. Gifted Hands saw the sly smile that crossed Aleshanee's face as Running Otter left to try to catch Sabel.

She had just dipped her oars in the water when he caught her. Standing in the lake up to his knees, he held the end of the canoe. "Sabel . . . Mimiteh . . . please . . . let me explain." She did not turn her head or do anything else to acknowledge that she'd heard him. Inside she was kicking herself for believing that this was something more that it obviously had been. He could not know how hurt she felt. "Sabel . . . please . . . look at me." Nothing. "Aleshanee arrived here this morning. No one knew she was coming. You know I haven't seen or heard of her in over six months. I no longer want to be with her, but she told me that she is carrying my baby. She said she didn't know that she was with child until after I had gone and didn't want to travel right away. She has come now to show me and ask that I return with her." Still, Sabel did not move or turn her head. He walked deeper into the water so that he could see her face. "What am I to do? I must take responsibility for my child. I must go back." His head sunk down into his chest. He did not wish to leave here; he wanted to stay here with her. "Please tell me you understand."

As he let go of the canoe she began to row away. That's when she let her tears flow. She so wanted him and the life she thought they would share. He could only watch her row away, devastated to have hurt her in this way. He wanted to swim after her, to get in his own canoe and follow her, to talk with her, but he knew that no amount of talking would change this situation. Instead, he sadly watched her row out of his life.

Sabel pulled the canoe onto the sand and flipped it. Then she blindly ran toward home. She didn't hear Sandy calling from the kitchen door, didn't hear her father calling as he approached the general store, she just ran. Once in the door, she kicked off her wet shoes.

"Sabel, honey, I didn't th—"

Sabel ran past Charlotte, up to her room.

Her mother walked quietly up the stairs. *This can't be good.* She listened at the door. What she heard was the sound of heartbreak. She opened the door and saw Sabel lying on the bed, tears streaming down her cheeks. Sitting beside her, Charlotte lay her hand on Sabel's back. "Oh, sweetheart, what happened?"

Sabel was in no condition to talk. She looked at her mother utterly devastated. Charlotte sat patiently, waiting for Sabel to calm. She heard a sound and looked to see Ben standing in the doorway, out of breath. In a low voice he said, "She ran past me. Didn't see me or hear me. Then she ran all the way home."

Charlotte nodded and patted the bed beside her. Mystified, Ben sat down. When Sabel thought she was ready, she sat up, but looking into her parents' concerned faces, she lost the moment. Charlotte opened her arms and her daughter leaned in, trying to calm herself. "Aleshanee came back today."

"What?" Charlotte and Ben asked together.

"She came back because she's pregnant with his baby." Charlotte looked over her shoulder at Ben. "He's going back with her." She started to cry all over again, her heart truly broken. Charlotte knew there was nothing they could do to make her pain go away. With tears in her eyes, she hugged her daughter and said simply, "I'm so sorry, sweetheart. We love you."

When they finally left the room, Charlotte looked at her husband sadly. "Oh, Benny, she was so happy."

They were both surprised to hear someone at the door. Ben opened it to see Sandy standing on the porch with a bag over her shoulder. "I have no idea what's happened, but I saw Sabel when she got back. She looked . . ."

Charlotte nodded, her mouth forming a grim line, and said, "You are just what she needs right now, love. Thank you."

The next day, when Charlotte walked to the store to pick up dinner, she found Gifted Hands and Keen Wolf in the kitchen. "Charlotte, oh I am so glad it is you that came for your food. We wanted to talk to you but did not want to upset Sabel. How is she?"

After a brief hug, Charlotte answered. "Not well, I'm afraid. She is utterly heartbroken. We all are."

"Yes, we feel the same."

Keen Wolf stood quietly behind his wife. His eyes reflected Charlotte's own feelings of déjà-vu.

"They left on foot this morning. It was so sad to watch him leave; he is in love with Sabel. He does not want this."

"I suppose we will all have to come to terms with it."

"I do not wish to upset Sabel further, but please let her know that if she wants to talk, she is always welcome."

For the next few weeks, Sabel lived in a fog. She understood that he and Aleshanee had been together for a few years and had planned to have a family. She also knew that Aleshanee had not appreciated the man she had. She couldn't have loved him, or she wouldn't have let him go. Running Otter had left Aleshanee and not looked back. He had moved on. Not only had he moved on, but he had fallen in love with Sabel. She had no doubt of his love. She knew he felt for her as she did for him. And now . . . now he had to go back. How could he do it? How could he leave her? But of course, he would take responsibility for his child. He is a good and decent man. And now that wonderful man was out of her life, maybe forever. How would she go on with a heart so broken? Why had she given it to him so completely?

In her mind she had created a picture of their love, their future, their family, their life . . . but it had been an illusion, and now it had been shattered.

Mitenah came to see Sabel later that week. She walked into the store just before the noon hour, surprising Charlotte and Sabel. "Chweh'n," she said softly. "I wondered if you'd like to come sit by the water with me and take your dinner?" she asked Sabel.

Seeing the love in her friend's eyes, Sabel nodded and told her mother she would return with her meal. She slipped into her coat and the two girls walked toward the general store. "Where is Swan Song today?" Sabel asked.

"He left me to do some fishing. He will return later to take me home." They sat at the water's edge. "How are you doing, Mimiteh?" Sabel turned to look into her friend's eyes. "I see your sadness. I am so sorry."

"I just . . . I can't believe this happened. Everything was perfect."

"He thought so, too."

"It's not fair. She had her chance. He was there for her to love and she chose not to. And why did she wait so long? He had moved on! And now . . ." The tears began to flow as she spoke, and she rested her head on her friend's shoulder.

Mitenah tipped her head onto Sabel's. "I'm so sorry, and I know he is, too. He would never have wanted to make you so sad. I hope you know that."

Sabel breathed deeply. "Why does he have to be so damn noble?" she asked angrily. She sat up straight and wiped her eyes. "I know why. I feel so mad at both of them. But he's going to be a father. I'm just going to have to accept that." She felt her friend's arm come around her back. "I don't know how I'll get over this . . . or him, Mitenah."

"Please remember we all love you. We are here if you want to talk, or if you just want some company. Don't stay away from us because of her."

Trying to cheer herself, Sabel asked about the kittens.

"The little one we were worried about died the day after it was born, and one of the others died a few days later. They just weren't strong enough."

"Aww, that's a shame. Poor little things."

"En-ay told me I can have the last one, but I must wait until it is a little bigger before I can take her home. I am counting the days!"

December

As the weeks passed, Sabel stayed away when Gifted Hands and Keen Wolf visited her parents. She could not bear the hurt seeing them would bring her heart.

It was December now—winter had set in. Charlotte and Ben were ready to lock up the Doctor's House after a long, wintry day. "Let's go, love," Charlotte said to Sabel.

"If it's all right with you, I think I'll stay and refill the jars. We've gone through a lot of teas the past few days."

"That we did. Seems like someone in every home is ill at the moment," said Ben.

Her mother looked into her face; she hadn't seen a shine in her eyes for nearly a month. She missed it and hoped it would return soon.

"Okay, if you're sure."

Sabel smiled. "Yeah. I'm sure."

"I'll come walk you home at seven thirty. Lock the door behind us." Ben kissed her forehead.

"Thanks, Dad."

Sabel was happy to be here alone. It was peaceful. Here she could sort, grind, and jar the herbs while letting her mind work to make sense of what had happened. She had looked at her situation from every angle and knew there would be no miraculous cure for her sadness. She thought about Jonny. If she had chosen him, what was happening now would be of no concern. She could write to him or go see him. Maybe he would . . . no, that wouldn't be fair. She had passed him over; she could hardly go back to him when it hadn't worked out with

Running Otter. Jonny deserved better than second-best. Much better. She would have to continue to muddle through until it became easier . . .

Her parents hoped she would be able to move on soon. It was difficult to watch a girl so happy and full of life pulling away, drawing into herself. "What can we do to cheer her up, Benny?" Charlotte asked as she cleaned the supper dishes.

"I don't think there's any more we can do than we've been doing. She knows we're here for her. She knows we love her, and sh—" A knock at the door interrupted him.

Ben went to the door.

For a couple of beats, there were no words. Charlotte turned to see Ben standing in the doorway. Catching himself, he said, "I'm sorry. You surprised me. Come in."

"Running Otter!" Charlotte exclaimed and hugged him hard. "Oh, you're covered in snow." She brushed it off her apron. "What are you doing here?"

"Charlotte, Ben, I was hoping to speak to Sabel. Is she here?" he asked hopefully, scanning the room behind them. Charlotte looked into his sad, worried eyes and smiled.

"I'm afraid she's not. She's down at the Doctor's House."

"I told her I would walk her home in half an hour," Ben said.

"I can do that . . . Please. I must see her."

Ben and Charlotte looked at each other before Charlotte said, "Please, just don't do anything to make this harder on her."

Looking very serious, Running Otter nodded. Then he turned and ran.

He stopped at the stoop in front of the Doctor's House, taking a moment to catch his breath. Hoping to find her alone, he knocked. He heard her footsteps as she walked to the door. She opened it a crack to see who it was. He saw the look of surprise come into her eyes. She tried to close the door, but he knew her well and was ready for that move. His foot held the door. "Chweh'n, Sabel. Please . . . can I come in?"

"I don't think so. Besides, won't your wife be upset to find you here?" The hurt was thick in her voice.

"She is not my wife, Mimiteh, and she never will be." There was no response. "You do not have to speak, but please listen to what I have to say." She stood with her foot blocking the door. "The baby is not mine." He looked at her through the crack. "Do you understand? She is not carrying *my* baby! She tried to trick me, to make me go back with her, and she used another man's baby." He had her attention. "I heard her people talking, saw the way they looked at me. I knew something was not right. I made her tell me the truth." The expression in Sabel's eyes softened. "Before and *after* I left, she went with another man and became with child. He did not want her, with or without child. She thought I would go back and be the baby's father and her husband if I thought the child was mine." The door slowly opened as Sabel stood listening. "I told her I could not do what she asked. I had only returned because of an obligation, and I am in love with you."

Sabel looked up at him with tears in her eyes. Only now did she notice how thin his face looked and the bags under his eyes. "You've come back to be with me?" she asked shyly.

He crossed the threshold and took her hands in his. "I want to be with *you*, Mimiteh. I want *you* to have my children. I want to be *your* husband." His hand went under her chin lifting her face up toward him. "Keuh-no-reh-gwah. I love you, Mimiteh."

"Keuh-no-reh-gwah, Running Otter," she said softly, before letting him kiss her for a while.

"I told your parents I would walk you home. Would that be all right?" he asked, but he already knew the answer.

She invited him in while she collected her things. When she turned to walk toward the door, he was standing there. He gazed down at her with a look she hadn't seen in his eyes before. "I am so sorry for how I must have made you feel. I—"

She put her finger over his lips and shook her head. "Please, let's put it behind us. No more looking back. Keep your eyes on me, on us, and our future.

It's over, Running Otter. . . It's over." She lifted herself up on her toes and kissed him.

"No, it's not over. It's only beginning."

The holiday this year was different than any other for several reasons. This was the first year they would spend it without their mother, mother-in-law, and grandmother. Mabel was in everyone's thoughts as they celebrated the year gone by. Also missing was Robbie, who did not come home as he had only just arrived there. They did receive a note from him the week before Christmas, expressing his love and asking to be remembered as they celebrated.

Sabel and Running Otter spent Yule together on the other side of the lake, but Christmas Day she spent with her family. She was invited, once again, to their fire ceremony on the new moon, just two days after Christmas. Her previous invitation to a ceremony that never happened was all but forgotten. They were moving on.

Maisie arrived in town two days before Christmas. She spent some time with her girlfriends, but spent the bulk of the holiday with Jeffery and the Higgins family. Sandy and Sabel said she was thrilled to be back, sharing stories about her friends and the new skills she was learning on the reservation.

Wednesday afternoon, Sabel walked home, wondering about tonight's fire ceremony with Running Otter and his family. He would pick her up later this afternoon. Right now, she wanted to freshen up and pack an overnight bag. They had spoken to her parents about her sleeping over since they would be busy into the evening, and it would get late.

When they arrived on the other side of the lake, she saw Keen Wolf piling wood by the fire pit. "Chweh'n, Keen Wolf," Sabel said and hugged him.

He smiled as he looked at her—she was so like her mother. He knew exactly why his nephew had fallen in love with her. "Gifted Hands has a warm drink for you. Go on in," he said.

"Chweh'n," she said, stepping inside. Gifted Hands and Mitenah were sitting at the table, each with a mug of something that smelled good.

"Have a seat, Sabel, and I will pour you a drink."

"Are you ready for tonight?" Mitenah asked, giving her friend a wink.

"Actually, I'm a little nervous. Running Otter has told me what will happen, but . . . well, I've never been to a Fire Ceremony before."

Gifted Hands placed a warm mug in front of her on the table. "Do not worry, Sabel. We will all be there, just do as we do." She smiled, happy to have Sabel here with them.

They went outside after dark and found the fire blazing. "The others picked their sticks earlier in the day. This is the spirit arrow I chose for you." Running Otter showed it to Sabel, then placed it on the ground in front of her. "This is mine."

"Thank you," she said, watching him moving in the firelight. He wore his hair down tonight and when he bent down, it fell forward. He tucked it behind his ears when he stood back up. He caught her watching and smiled.

"We are ready," Keen Wolf said, sitting across from Gifted Hands. Running Otter sat across from Sabel and Mitenah from Swan Song and Dark Wolf. "Let us begin."

Sabel watched as the others stood closing their eyes and opening their arms to their sides, palms turned out. They were calling the Creator. Sabel copied as best she could, hoping that their creator would accept her presence tonight. When she opened her eyes, she found Running Otter's eyes on her, his face without expression.

He gave her a simple nod, then picked up his spirit arrow, held it between his hands, and brought it up toward his face. His eyes held hers for a long moment as they stood in complete harmony. He turned his focus to the stick; he blew on it three times. Following his example, she repeated his actions, feeling joy and love in her heart. Her wish was simple—she wanted to share her life with this man. She lowered her eyes and blew her thoughts over her spirit arrow.

"You may place your spirit arrow into the fire now," said Keen Wolf as he lowered his own into the flames. Then he and the others stood, closing their eyes once again. Sabel closed her own, and in her mind, thanked the Creator for accepting her presence here tonight. Once she'd finished, she sat back on her log, hands in her lap, and waited for the others to finish. A reflection caught her eye, and Sabel saw Kohana watching silently from under some trees.

When the others finished, Keen Wolf said, "We will now watch our sticks burn into ash." He sat on his log, hands on his knees. As his eyes passed over Sabel, he was reminded of her mother sharing this ceremony with him years ago.

Only the sounds of the crackling fire could be heard as they sat, lost in their thoughts, watching as their wishes were released into the sky.

Dark Wolf stood first and left with a nod to the group. Mitenah smiled at her husband before coming to sit beside her friend. "How do you feel, Sabel?" she asked.

"That was liberating," she answered. Then, looking at each face in turn added, "Thank you all for including me."

"It is our pleasure to share our lives with you, Sabel," said Gifted Hands. Then, with a glance at her son, she said, "Enjoy the rest of your evening."

When the others had gone, Running Otter came to sit beside her. He thought she looked lovelier than ever, sitting with the fire lighting her eyes. She rested her head on his shoulder and breathed deeply. "Thank you for sharing this, Running Otter. I feel honoured."

He stood and offered his hand. "The honour is mine, Mimiteh. Now, come this way. There's something I'd like to show you."

"In the dark?"

"Yes."

They walked past the cabin, down the path toward his grandparents' old house. When they got close enough, Sabel could see light coming from inside. "Who's here, Running Otter?"

He did not answer. With her hand in his, he walked to the door and opened it. "I wanted to show you this. We have finished."

"You did? That's fantastic! You lit a fire?"

"Come in and have a look around," he said, picking up the candle he'd left on the table and lighting it in the fire.

The cabin had a small cooking and eating area, a sitting room, and two bedrooms. The walls had been rebuilt where necessary, and the furniture had been freshened up. "It looks so nice, Running Otter. This will be a new beginning. Congratulations." She turned to hug him. "When will you move in?"

Still holding her hand, he walked to the hearth and stood in front of the fire facing her. "A new beginning, yes . . . with you. I want you by my side always. Will you be my wife, Mimiteh?"

Her mouth dropped open as her eyes filled with tears. "Yes! Oh, yes!" She wrapped her arms around his neck and kissed him. When she paused sometime later, she said, "Keuh-no-reh-gwah." The smile on her face seemed to be stuck there. "Have you spent the night here yet?" she asked.

"After we have our joining ceremony, we will live here. Until then, the house will wait for us." Then, he shyly added, "We could sleep here tonight if you'd like?"

Now she took his hand and led him into the bigger of the two bedrooms. He'd lit a fire inside her, one she'd never felt before now. She got up on her toes and kissed him hard. Before long, she was reaching for the bottom of his tunic, lifting it up. He grabbed the bottom and lifted it over his head, tossing it onto the floor, before returning his lips to hers. She began to undo the buttons down the front of her dress. Now he took hold of the hair that hung behind her and gently pulled down, tilting her head back and exposing the neck he wanted to sink his teeth into. Her dress dropped to the floor, and she was left standing in her shift. He looked down at her and a groan escaped from him. "Help me," she whispered, trying to find the bottom so she could lift it over her head.

Running Otter was struggling. He wanted her something fierce, but he wanted to wait until the day she was his. Taking a deep breath in, he stepped back. "Not tonight, my love."

She looked up at him, shocked. "What? You don't want to?"

"You must believe me—I want to. I want to more than you can imagine." She didn't have to imagine, she could see his need as clear as day. She couldn't help the feeling of disappointment that washed over her. "We have spoken little about this, but y—"

"You will be my first," she interrupted.

He smiled. "And it will be even more special if we wait until the night of our joining. Do you not agree?"

Reaching for her dress, she answered, "I suppose so . . ."

She pouted, and he wanted her even more.

This was going to be the last New Year's Eve Sabel spent with her family as an unmarried woman, and she wanted to bring it in with them. Running Otter joined them as they celebrated. Most of the townsfolk gathered at the Southerns' home to bring in 1838. As Lawrence counted down, there were drinks and toasts and hugs all around.

When the party was over, the guests made their way home, some walking, some stumbling. Sabel and Running Otter lagged behind with Sandy, enjoying the cool air and the happy voices carried on it. They were saying goodnight to Sandy at the store, when they heard someone around the side. "Must be Maisie," Sandy said.

Sabel poked her head around the corner and saw her standing, leaning her forehead on the door. "Maisie?" When she didn't answer, Sabel, followed by the others, approached her. "Are you all right?"

She stood up straight then, wiping her cheeks with the back of her hand. "No."

Sable put her arms around her friend as she broke down in sobs. "Why don't we go inside, and you can tell us."

Maisie opened the door and walked inside, waiting for them to follow. Running Otter caught Sabel's arm. "I will wait here to walk you home." She nodded and went inside.

"What's happened, love?" Sandy asked. "Is it Jeffery?"

There was no answer. Sabel lay her hand gently on Maisie's shoulder and waited.

"I told him I no longer want to . . . I can't do this anymore. It hurts too much."

"You could stay, could you not?" Sandy asked.

"I suppose I could. He asked me to. But I belong with my parents. That's how I feel. I'm not ready to leave them for him or anyone else, and I just can't continue to see him and feel so sad." She looked at them, tears staining her cheeks. "He asked me to marry him."

Sabel and Sandy looked at each other, neither knowing how to respond.

"I'm not ready for that. No. And I don't want to make a promise I might not be able to keep. I told him he should look for another girl who can give him what he wants."

"Oh, dear." Sandy leaned in and hugged her friend. "I'm sorry you feel so sad. I wish I could help."

Maisie nodded. "Thanks. It will take some time I suppose . . . for us both."

She thanked them for being there and told them she would be leaving in the morning.

While Running Otter walked home with Sabel, she told him what had happened. "She is smart to act on her feelings. She is young yet, is she not?"

Sabel smiled up at him. "She's a year and a half older than me."

"Ah, but you, Miss Sabel, are older than your years." He came to a stop, wrapping his arms around her and whispered, "I cannot wait to have you all to myself." Before she knew it, his lips were on hers. She was gasping for breath as his tongue found her neck and his hands roamed behind her, under her coat. She could feel him there waiting.

She smiled and whispered into his kiss, "It won't be long." She was secretly glad that as a woman, her feelings of urgency were not so easily displayed, but she felt the desire to have him every bit as much.

Feather Dance

It was decided their joining would take place on the twenty-sixth of January, the next New Moon. After talking about the various traditions of the Tuscarora, as well as what the Williams' were accustomed to, the two families started planning a wedding ceremony.

Gifted Hands, knowing this joining was imminent, had already prepared some white deerskins to use for both Sabel's dress and Running Otter's new tunic. She starting working on those items, and Charlotte came to help when she could.

At the sound of knocking, Gifted Hands looked toward the door. Mitenah and Swan Song came in. "Chweh'n everyone," Mitenah said. "You have decided on a day?" She looked at her friend and brother. Sabel, unable to lose the smile on her face, nodded. "Wonderful. Sabel, I have something to show you. Would you mind walking to our home with me and you can tell me?"

Sabel bundled up and left with Mitenah, happy to have a few quiet moments with her.

"So, you took the kitty to your house; how does she like her new home?"

"She's so funny, Sabel. She runs around and around bumping into doors and walls, and tries to climb everything." Mitenah shook her head and laughed. "But she snuggles into bed with us at nighttime, and I like that."

"Aww, sounds cute. Did you finally decide on a name for her?"

"Yes—Pepper. Her colours remind me of pepper, and our way to say it is too long: 'you-neh-snah-gee-wah-keh'."

"You're right," Sabel giggled. "I wonder if Running Otter plans to bring Kohana when we move to the new cabin. I hope so, but I suppose he might want to leave her for your mom." She shrugged. "I'll have to ask. So, what is it you're going to show me?"

"It's better for you to see it, Mimiteh."

When they got to the house, Mitenah said, "Leave your coat on, this will just take a minute." Sabel slipped out of her boots and followed her friend to the bedroom. Mitenah opened the door and stepped in, leaving room for her friend to come in beside her. Suddenly, there was a high-pitched mewing sound coming from below. Mitenah bent to pick up the kitten. "Look, Pepper, it's Sabel." Sabel reached for her, letting her snuggle under her chin.

Sabel looked around the room with curiosity. Her eyes found it almost immediately. Her hand came up over her mouth as a happy squeak escaped. On the bed lay an object that, while unfamiliar, was definitely for a baby.

"You're going to have a baby?" she squealed.

"I am." Mitenah smiled, looking radiant. "Midsummer."

Sabel hugged her friend hard. "I'm so happy for you. Is Swan Song happy?"

A light blush covered Mitenah's cheeks before she answered. "He is. He hopes to have a boy he can name for his kree-ay. We have also started making this basket. I do not want to have him tied on a cradleboard unless I am busy working. While he is little, he will sleep in here." The basket was an oval shape, with a bottom and sides of woven grasses. "Of course, we will cover and line it with fur for the baby."

Sabel was excited for her friend. As they walked back to Gifted Hands's home, she said, "I enjoyed growing up so close in age to you and Sandy. I hope our children will have the same chance."

"But first, the joining." Mitenah elbowed her friend lightly in the side. "Then, the babies."

Sabel giggled. "So, what was that on your bed? It's not a cradle like I'm used to seeing."

"No, it is a cradleboard. En-ay had the pieces of buckskin cut some time ago, I think. Swan Song carved the board for the bottom and Kree-ay the piece that arcs over the head. En-ay sewed it together. It is not finished; we still have to make it soft inside, and you *know* En-ay will make it look beautiful."

"Does Running Otter know?"

"We told him this morning. I wanted to tell you on my own, because—" Her voice cracked and she stopped.

Sabel put her arm through her friend's and kissed her cheek. "I understand. Thank you and congratulations."

The week before their joining, Sabel brought most of her clothes and items from her room to what would soon be her new home, while her mother and Gifted Hands finished sewing the embellishments onto the dress and tunic. Everything had to be ready for Friday's ceremony.

The day of the wedding, both the Doctor's House and the general store closed mid-afternoon. Then everyone except Sabel and Charlotte, who were already there, travelled across the frozen lake. The ceremony was to begin at 6:00 p.m.

Keen Wolf and Swan Song had erected a large makeshift room for the event, using the outside wall of the house as one wall and skins for the remaining walls and roof—there was not enough room inside the house for the set-up they wanted. Gifted Hands, Mitenah, Sandy, and Hettie had spent the past few days preparing the food for later in the day.

When Running Otter came into the room and saw his bride, he was speechless. She stood before him in her full-length white deerskin dress. The sleeves were long and tapered to her wrists; white ermine fur accentuated the edges of the V-neck; below the fur hung long leather fringes to the fitted waist, beaded at the tops in turquoise and black; a matching fringe circled the lower portion of the dress from the level of the knee to the bottom; the belt around her waist tied at the back and had a circular pattern of the same beads as the front. She had pinned back the front sections of her long dark hair with her mother's hair pins, the ones Jessica had brought her, and around her neck hung her mother's moonstone on a black satin ribbon, courtesy of Auntie Gracie. On her feet, she wore new moccasins.

She gazed nervously at her groom. Running Otter looked very handsome in his new white tunic. It matched her dress with the fur-trimmed V-neck and fringes, only his fringes were shorter. His tunic, belted with a beaded sash in the same pattern as hers, was worn over plain buckskin leggings and moccasins. He had tied his hair in a half-pony, using a strip of white leather.

"Are you ready, Mimiteh?" he whispered.

The look she levelled at him spoke volumes. He felt it in the butterflies in his stomach, and the squeeze in his heart *and* loins.

His mother approached him then. "Running Otter, you look very handsome." She took his hands. "I am so proud of you as your kree-ay, gu-sood, and ree-ah-sood would be if they were here. Be happy." She hugged him and kissed his cheek.

Keen Wolf, acting as the officiant, stood near the center of the room. He wore his finest traditional clothing, looking handsome yet serious as he awaited the others. Mitenah stood at his side.

Hanging in the center of the room was the wedding wheel that Keen Wolf had made. It looked much like a dream catcher, with a branch bent into a circle and wrapped in white leather. Within the circle and held to the edge, was a piece of white leather shaped almost like a crescent moon. The webbing, similar to a dream catcher, held a bead and was attached to the leather, filling the rest of the circle. Bound together and secured to the tip of the "crescent" were three feathers with dark tips, and from the bottom, hung several dark feathers and a few beaded fringes. It looked quite lovely. Beneath the wheel sat a bench.

Gifted Hands and Keen Wolf explained that the Wedding Wheel is a symbol of the couple's hopes and dreams of their two lives joining as one. The dark feathers represent burnt sacrifices, cleansing the air and bringing good fortune.

The attendees stood in two rows, leaving a space between them for the couple and their parents to pass through. Sabel and Running Otter, each with a basket over their arm, walked side-by-side into the room, followed by Charlotte and Gifted Hands and then Ben. Sabel walked to the right around the bench, Running Otter to the left, and stood before Keen Wolf. Mitenah smiled briefly before stepping in front of them with a tight bundle of burning sage. She smudged the area around them, Keen Wolf, their mothers, and Ben, where he stood behind the bench, as they came to stand at their child's side. As she slowly moved the smoking bundle around them, she explained that the smoke would cleanse them and help carry their wedding or joining wishes and prayers to the Creator.

"Sabel, Running Otter, please sit together on the bench," Keen Wolf instructed. "Charlotte and Gifted Hands, please sit beside your child." Ben remained standing behind Sabel and Charlotte. "As the mothers of this couple, you will forever be a part of this union and the commitment Sabel and Running Otter now make to one another." Both women nodded their response.

Running Otter looked into Sabel's face, eyes very serious, and said, "Sabel, you are my reason—my reason for being. I promise to give myself to you for always." He smiled. "I will love you, our family, our people, and our Creator."

She looked nervous, but not afraid. "Running Otter, I am yours, always, whatever comes our way. I will love you, our family, our people, and our Creator."

The couple exchanged their baskets of food—spiritual and physical symbols of loving and nourishing each other.

Keen Wolf looked now at the parents. "Do you believe these two individuals are ready to commit themselves to each other and to this union?"

"Yes," Charlotte, Gifted Hands, and Ben answered in unison.

"Charlotte, do you believe your daughter capable of fulfilling this responsibility?"

"Yes."

"Are you satisfied with your daughter's choice of husband?"

"Yes."

"If hard times befall them, would you open your home to them and their children?"

"I would."

The same questions were asked of Gifted Hands. The same answers were given.

Now Keen Wolf looked at Sabel. "Are you prepared to be this man's wife for the rest of your life? Will you prepare food for him and your children? Will you care for him whether he is sick or healthy? At suppertime, when the children are out playing with their friends, you are to call them all in to eat. If their faces are dirty, you will wash them all, as if they were all your own. Do you accept this responsibility?"

"Yes."

The questions were repeated to Running Otter. Then Keen Wolf said, "This joining is a partnership. No one has authority over the other."

The couple agreed.

"Please now stand to face each other." The couple passed their baskets to their mothers and stood. He reached out to both of them, grasping a hand. "You are now joined as husband and wife." He smiled for the first time and joined their hands together. "Congratulations."

With bright eyes, Running Otter bent to kiss his new wife, resisting the urge to pick her up and run away. There were hugs and handshakes all around while Mitenah set the wedding cake on a small table to the side. Everyone received a small slice of the cake made with cornmeal, nuts, and berries. "This looks delicious, Mitenah," Hettie said, licking her lips.

"Thank you," Mitenah answered.

When they had finished the cake, Gifted Hands stood before the group. "We have one more tradition to share. It is called the Feather Dance." She smiled, seeing the looks on the faces of their guests who had not seen or heard of this before. "Because we are sharing this ceremony together, we will now teach you this dance honouring the Great Spirit."

Charlotte looked at her husband. The first time they had danced together, she stood on his feet, unsure of herself. He smiled, seeing the worry in her eyes.

Gifted Hands passed a drum to her husband while Mitenah handed everyone two feather fans. "It is not difficult. Ladies, please come to this side of the room and stand facing me. Men, to the other side and face Swan Song. Very good. Now do as we do."

Charlotte and Gracie exchanged a nervous glance, but did as they were asked. Charlotte peeked over her shoulder and saw her children and nieces ready to dance. Seeing this, Keen Wolf smiled and then began a steady beat on his drum, as did Dark Wolf. Then he, Gifted Hands, Mitenah, and Swan Song began to sing their song. At the same time, they moved their bodies and the fans held in each hand. The newly married couple stood beside each other as Sabel did her best to follow along. At first, Charlotte felt foolish—she was completely out of her comfort zone—but soon, everyone was dancing, enjoying themselves and the celebration.

When the song ended, Mitenah collected the fans, leaving only Sabel with hers. Gifted Hands addressed the group once more. "That was wonderful. Thank you all for joining." Her smile was infectious. "Gracie?"

Gracie appeared carrying the new white blanket that she had knitted. She opened it and gently draped it over the shoulders of the new couple. "This symbolizes a coverin' of the weakness and sorrow you may have lived before today. Now, you can enter your new life, joined with peace and fulfillment."

Sabel caught her aunt's wrist, drawing her in to kiss her cheek. "Thank you, Auntie Gracie." Then, with Running Otter at her side, she turned toward their family and gave a big whoop!

As their guest clapped, she wrapped her arms around Running Otter's neck and kissed him.

"And now, we feast!" Gifted Hands announced.

Charlotte and Ben left with Holly and Phillip with happy hearts. The newlyweds would now start their lives together in their new home. As happy as she was for them, she couldn't help but feel a little sad, too. She and Sabel had spent so much time together and that phase, for lack of a better word, was over. Sabel's focus was no longer on her home with her parents or her work at the apothecary; now it was on her new home and her husband. She would still work to help her mother with the growing of certain plants, but it would never be the same.

Cat Who Caught the Mouse

It was a couple of months later, on a Sunday afternoon, when the Williams and Moffatt crews rowed over for a visit. The past few weeks, there had been no visiting, as the lake was not safe to walk or boat across, but now only the edges remained frozen. Gifted Hands greeted them at the door and ushered them in.

"Oh, me, it's a chilly day!" Gracie said, finding the seat closest to the fire.

"Don't you worry, Gracie, we'll have you warm in no time," Gifted Hands said with a smile.

She was closing the door behind Ben when she said, "Oh, here comes the other two."

Sabel and Running Otter came in, kicking the snow off their boots. "Hello everyone," Sabel said to the room. "No Mitenah today?"

Gifted Hands shook her head. "She wasn't feeling well this morning. Swan Song told us they will stay home today."

"Aww, that's too bad. I'll go see her later," Sabel said. Charlotte looked at her then. She had expressed words of disappointment, but the tone of her voice was happy and light. *Hmm.*

"What's new with you, lass? Ye look like the cat who caught the mouse," Gracie said.

Hearing Gracie's words, Ben looked toward his daughter to see what he'd missed. Running Otter, who was standing beside her, smiled at Ben and shrugged.

"And?" Charlotte asked. Gracie had said just what she'd been thinking.

Sabel came into the room and sat beside her mother. "Hi, Mum." She leaned over and kissed her cheek. "Well, we're going to have a baby!"

"Oh, Sabel." Charlotte wrapped her arms around her daughter. "That's wonderful." She got up and hugged Running Otter. "How exciting! The two of you will be parents. Oh my God, that'll make me a grandmother." She scrunched up her face, not sure she liked the sound of that.

"Aye, it will!" Gracie laughed.

"Hey, your day will come, Gracie," Charlotte threatened.

"You ladies will be the best grandmothers, that much I know," Sabel said, as her father hugged her. "You, too, Dad."

"And I'll be an auntie?" exclaimed Holly.

They expected to see their little one by the end of October. Running Otter stood behind his wife where she sat on the settee, with a dumb grin on his face. Delighted, he couldn't get over the shock of it happening so quickly.

"Oh, that's lovely. And you and Mitenah will ha' yer babes only a few months apart."

While this news didn't shock Charlotte, she, like Running Otter, was surprised it had happened so quickly. She thought back to her time as a newlywed and was pleased that they'd had some time, almost a year, before Robbie came along. She wouldn't change a thing.

With the three canoes filled up on shore, the group headed toward the store. "It's hard to imagine I'll be Auntie Holly."

"And I'll be Uncle Phillip. Weird."

"What does that make me?" Evelyn asked.

"Well, you and Sabel are cousins, so her bairn would be your . . . second cousin?" Gracie asked, looking at Charlotte.

"I think so. I never could keep track of second cousins and removed cousins. What the heck does that mean, anyway?"

"Actually," Sandy started, "the baby will be our first cousin once removed."

Charlotte looked at her niece. "Really?"

Sandy smiled. "Yes. A cousin once removed is from a generation immediately before or after *you*, so your *first* cousin once removed would be your cousin's child."

"Or the parents of your second cousin," Ben added with a smirk. He enjoyed adding to the confusion.

"So, what's a second cousin?" Gracie asked her daughter.

"Your second cousin is the child of your parents' first cousin."

"Well, now I ken why I couldna keep it a' straight," Gracie said with a chuckle.

"Aye," added Jimmy. "So, let me see if I've got this right . . . Sheila was Mabel's cousin. So, she's yer first cousin once removed. So, Morag and Aisla, bein' her daughters, are yer second cousins?"

"That's right, Da," Sandy said.

"Oy!" said Holly, raising her hand to her head.

The group laughed.

As the winter faded into spring and then summer, stories of the relocation continued. The current president, Martine Van Buren, continued where Jackson left off, instructing his agents to round up the Cherokee that remained on their land. Some began the trek to "Indian Territory", but some were put into detention camps in Tennessee and Alabama. Of those who were forced to make the journey, some did so bound in chains. Each time they stopped along the trail, burials were held. People were dying of exposure, malnutrition, disease, and exhaustion.

"It's certainly not humankind's brightest hour," said Charlotte, disgusted.

"Aye. I dinna think it'll be looked back on well in the history books," Gracie agreed.

In the meantime, Sabel blossomed. She had a small tummy and looked happier than ever. Running Otter and Keen Wolf had almost finished building a cradle for the newborn, as per Sabel's wishes. Charlotte did some knitting, making a little hat, mitts and booties, several little blankets, and a couple of baby slings so she could tie the little one to her chest when she was busy. Gifted Hands made a painting for the wall in the baby's room, similar to the one she'd made for

Mitenah. It was a baby, bundled and lying in a woven bassinet on the beach near the edge of a forest. Gathered around the baby were the animals who had come to greet her. There was a deer with a pretty butterfly on its antler; a wolf; a raven sat near the baby's head as if guarding this gift from the skies; a brown bear watching from the distance; an eagle flying overhead; a turtle crawling across the sand; and perched on a branch in a tree was an owl.

Charlotte was in awe when she saw it, and tears came to her eyes. "Gifted Hands, this is . . . it's just beautiful." She looked it over carefully, noting each of the animals. "When I look at this, I see a baby who is being welcomed, embraced by nature's creatures, and I feel so much love." She put her hand on her heart. "This is amazing. Sabel must love it."

"She reacted just as you did, Charlotte." Gifted Hands smiled. "She said she knows where they will hang it."

"And how is Mitenah feeling these days?"

Gifted Hands told Charlotte that every morning Mitenah came to see her parents, she walked in the door and she said, "I hope today is the day."

"Maybe today it will be!" Charlotte said. "It's hard to believe that within a few months, there will be two new babies in the family."

"It is. We have watched them both grow up from such innocence, and I must say, we have brought up two wonderful young women."

"At first, I was a little worried because Sabel is still very young."

"She is. But she is mature and strong, and they love each other so much."

"And who could blame them?" Charlotte asked, putting her arm around her friend's back.

Later that night, Mitenah's water broke, and by morning, her son, Falling Leaf, was introduced to the world.

After several seasons of successfully cultivating poppies and making her own laudanum, Charlotte inquired if she could use some space on the other side of the lake to grow poppies; somewhere they would have more room to flourish and spread, where the only limitations would be the elements. Having plenty of space to spare, Gifted Hands happily offered to share some land with her friend. They decided on a spot near the large vegetable garden, but not attached to it.

As the heat of summer came to an end, Ben and Charlotte began to dig and turn the soil, and by the end of September, they had created and seeded the new poppy garden. They expected to be ready to harvest late next spring.

Before anyone knew, October had arrived. By now, Sabel, heavy with child, tried to be patient with the little creature kicking her from the inside. For her mother, it was a joy to watch and brought back happy memories. Their world was about to change yet again, with a new life to love.

The house was ready, the baby's room was stocked with blankets and towels and diapers. All that needed to happen now was the baby.

A Birth

It was the middle of the night when they heard the knocking. Charlotte jumped at the sound, but immediately knew what it meant. She sat up, swinging her feet over the side of the bed. "It's time, Benny."

"I wonder what time it is," he mumbled as he shuffled toward the clothes he'd left out on the chair. He pulled on his pants and made his way to the door.

Sure enough, Keen Wolf stepped across the threshold as Charlotte came down the stairs. She looked at him with raised eyebrows and his responding smile answered her question. She immediately ran back up the stairs to let Holly know where they'd be.

Sabel's water had broken, and she'd started having contractions approximately two hours ago. She didn't want Keen Wolf to rush, knowing it would likely be several hours before the baby was born.

They rowed together in the quiet of night, feeling the invigorating effects of the cold night air. "I can hardly believe our babies are about to have a baby," Charlotte said excitedly, as she tried to imagine what he or she would look like.

"How quickly it has come to pass," Keen Wolf said, mostly to himself.

As they pulled the canoes up on shore, Ben reached for his doctor's bag. Charlotte took his other hand, pulling him forward. "Step it up, Ben!" He smiled and squeezed her hand.

As they approached the cabin, they looked at one another in surprise— they could hear the sounds of a baby crying. Charlotte ran into the house. She saw no one—they were in the bedroom. Running Otter poked his head around the door frame. His smile was brilliant.

"We have a daughter," he said, his voice catching at the end.

Charlotte's hands went to her mouth in surprise. Walking past the new father, she found her daughter sitting up in bed with a baby in her arms. She smiled at Gifted Hands who said, "She came fast, but safely, Charlotte. Mitenah is just going to wash her."

Mitenah put her hands out to Sabel and gently took the little body from her. She smiled at Charlotte before laying the baby on a towel at the bottom of the bed. She washed her under Gifted Hands's watchful eyes.

Charlotte peeked at the little face and felt her eyes fill. "Oh, Sabel . . ." She took her daughter's hand and held it. "She's beautiful, just like her mummy. That happened fast. How are you feeling?"

"Like I just birthed a watermelon. I think I tore, although I can't feel it at the moment."

Charlotte's face scrunched up in sympathy. "Oo-oo, let me help with that while Mitenah cleans the little one."

"There is water over the fire," Gifted Hands informed her, as she gathered some items in need of laundering.

"Okay. Shall we invite your dad and Keen Wolf in to meet the baby, then I'll look after your lady parts?" Sabel nodded and pulled the sheets up above her breasts.

Charlotte walked out into the sitting room with happy tears in her eyes and told the men they could go in for a minute or two, then she went to get some warm water and a bowl. Knowing Sabel had what she'd need in the cupboard, Charlotte found the lavender and some cheesecloth and started a cleansing wash. Next, in a small pot, she placed some wormwood from Ben's bag, dried echinacea flowers, and dried evergreen needles, covered it all with previously boiled water and put it over the fire to simmer for a half hour. She would use this over Sabel stitches as an antibacterial, antimicrobial, and anti-inflammatory wash.

When Charlotte came back into the bedroom, she held a bowl in one hand and Ben's doctor bag in the other. He looked at his bag and asked, "Do you need me?"

"Nope." She smiled. "I've got this. We'll just need a few minutes here."

Taking the hint, the men looked at each other and left the room.

Gifted Hands suggested Mitenah put the little one to Sabel's breast. Charlotte pinched her nipple in such a way that the baby would get a good grip with her mouth. She started to suckle immediately.

Sabel laughed. "You'd think she was the one who did all that hard work."

"Right?" Charlotte agreed. "Now I'm going to get you to put your legs up like this so I can get in there to clean you up a bit." She spread Sabel's knees and positioned herself to wash her daughter's torn perineum. When that was done, she spread her legs further. "I'm going to put in a few stitches now, love." Sabel bit her lip and nodded.

Gifted Hands said, "If you don't need me, I will prepare the tub for laundry."

Charlotte nodded. As she put in four stitches, she asked, "Have you and Running Otter chosen a name, now that you've seen her little face?"

"Not yet. I think we'll give it a day or two and see how we feel." She giggled then. "Can you hear her gulping?"

"I can. She'll keep you busy."

"Oo-oo, I felt that one."

"I'm sorry. I know this is awful." She tied a couple of knots and added, "Done. Now, while we wait for the wash to infuse, it's probably best if you stay in this position and let the area dry some."

When the pot had simmered long enough, Charlotte took it off the fire and strained a small amount into a bowl to cool for a few minutes. Then she used it to rinse the entire area. "There. I would suggest doing that a few times a day and try your best to let it dry in between. It won't be too long before it's healed."

"Thank you, Mum."

"You're welcome, sweetheart." She smiled. "Oh, she seems to be done for now. Why don't you see if you can get a little burp, and I'll get Dr. Ben so he can examine her?"

As the sun came up, there was a knock at the door. Keen Wolf opened it to Gracie and Sandy. "How is she?" Sandy blurted out.

"Come on in and see for yourself," Gifted Hands said from behind her husband.

"I will go tell Swan Song the news." He kissed his wife's cheek before leaving.

Sandy kicked off her shoes and ran for the bedroom. Gracie smiled at the others. "The lass is doin' well?"

"She is," Charlotte answered. "Go on into the bedroom. She's in the with Mitenah and Running Otter."

"A lassie?" Gracie asked, looking to confirm her own feelings.

"Yep."

After some time, Gracie came out of the bedroom carrying the little one, followed by the others. "Sabel's goin' te try a wee nap."

"She'll need that," Charlotte said as Gracie passed her new granddaughter into her arms. She looked up and said softly, "She's just beautiful."

"Aye."

Gifted Hands looked at her own daughter and said, "Mitenah, I know that you have seen a baby born and had your own, but that was the first time you've helped deliver one. How do you feel?"

Mitenah couldn't help the smile on her face. "That was, what is Charlotte's word?" She glanced at her. "Awesome!"

As mid-afternoon approached, everyone headed for home and work. Charlotte poked her head into the bedroom and regarded her lovely daughter. "Congratulations, my love. I know Gifted Hands and Mitenah will look after you today, but I will come see you again tomorrow."

When Charlotte and Ben returned the next day, they found everyone in the sitting room. Gifted Hands had used some towels to fashion a donut for Sabel to sit on, and she was sipping some tea. Charlotte took the baby from her mother and kissed her cheeks before sitting down, cradling her in her arms.

"We've decided on a name," Sabel said, smiling at Running Otter. They had told no one because they wanted all the grandparents to hear it at the same time. "We will call her Tehya."

"Tay-ya," Charlotte repeated. "That's beautiful. What does it mean?"

"It means precious."

Looking down at her new granddaughter, Charlotte gently tucked the swaddling blanket under her chin. "Perfect choice, wouldn't you say, Benny?" She looked at her husband—he was beaming. Returning her gaze to the infant, she took in the shock of dark hair on the very top of her head. Her complexion, though slightly darker than Sabel's, was lighter than her father's. She had a tiny nose, and her puckered little lips were soft pink. Her eyes were closed, but they would certainly be a shade of brown. She was a lovely, plump little thing.

As she gazed across at Gifted Hands, Keen Wolf put his arm around her shoulders. Everyone was happy as could be with the new addition to the family. When Tehya began to stir, Charlotte took her and slowly paced the room, hoping to help her drift back to sleep. It soon became clear, however, that it was feeding time.

"Come on into the bedroom, ladies," Sabel said.

Charlotte waited as Sabel unbuttoned her tunic and then handed the little one to her mother. "How are your nipples feeling, love?" she asked.

"Good so far. She suckles very well . . . at least I think she does, but I have nothing to compare it to," she answered as Tehya latched on.

"Well, I hate to say it, but they will likely begin to hurt as you go along, but only temporarily. I made you a salve to rub on them between feedings when that happens."

Sabel wrinkled her nose. "I don't like the sound of that."

"It is unpleasant, Sabel, but it only lasts a short time," Gifted Hand added.

"To try avoiding it, I would suggest you express a little milk and rub it into your nipples after you finish nursing, then let it air dry. Heck, there's only Running Otter here. I'm sure he won't mind if you walk around while they dry." Charlotte winked at her daughter, who blushed brilliantly.

Gifted Hands smirked at Charlotte.

"If they get bad, you can use the salve."

Gifted Hands giggled as she heard the little one gulping. "She is a hungry one, Sabel."

"It sounds like it, doesn't it?" she laughed back.

"And how are the stitches?"

"They're just like you'd expect." She grimaced.

"Once you've finished, I'll make you a little bath to sit in; it will help soothe the area for a while. I'll go get some warm water and get it ready." She left the room in search of the large bowl she'd brought with her.

"I will leave you in peace, Sabel. We're just out there if you need anything," Gifted Hands said, leaving Sabel on her own for the moment. She found Charlotte in the kitchen area. "Can I help you with anything?" she asked her.

Charlotte turned and smiled at her friend. "I don't think so. I'm just making a salt water and lavender bath for Sabel to sit in for a while."

"I remember those days."

"Me, too. Thankfully, they're not what stays with you," Charlotte answered. "Ah, before you sit, can you open the bedroom door for me?"

Charlotte returned to the bedroom to find Sabel rocking in the chair and humming to the little one. "Good timing, Mum. Can I hand her over to you?"

"That sounds like a good trade," she said, putting the bowl down on the stationary chair. She took Tehya and put her over her shoulder as Sabel expressed a few drops of milk and rubbed it in. Then she lifted her skirt and sat as delicately as she could in the large bowl.

"Oh, that feels nice." She blinked slowly. "Thank you."

After getting a couple of little burps from the baby, Charlotte joined the others in the sitting room. "Have a hold, Grandpa," she said, passing Tehya to Ben.

"When Running Otter was young and used to talk about his grandparents, it didn't occur to me that one day I would be Goo-sood," Gifted Hands said with a smile.

"Goo-sood, I remember and Ree-ah-sood, right?" Charlotte sounded out the syllables.

Gifted Hands nodded, adding, "That is right, Goo-sood."

Samhain 1838

It was the last day of October when Charlotte and Ben delivered a package to their daughter across the lake. "Mum, Dad, I didn't expect to see you today."

"Hello, honey," Charlotte answered, giving her daughter a loose hug as she stood holding Tehya. "Where's hubby?"

"Oh, he's out somewhere with Keen Wolf. What's up?"

Ben smiled and sat while his wife handed Sabel a parcel. "This came for you today."

Sabel's eyebrows rose as she looked at it. "Who's it from?" she asked, turning it in her hands. "Ah . . . the Crawfords."

Inside, she found a pretty little knitted blanket with stripes of yellow and white. "Oh my gosh, this is so sweet! Look, there's a note. *Dear Tehya, We were so pleased to hear of your arrival. Please give your parents and grandparents our congratulations! We look forward to meeting you. With love, from Carole-Anne, Keith, and Maisie.* That was nice of them." Sabel smiled at her parents. "Can I get you a tea or coffee?"

"Just a quick one, thanks."

"Yes, tonight is Samhain, right?"

"It is," her mother answered with a smile.

Tehya slept while they sipped their warm drinks. She lay swaddled in what Charlotte would call a bassinet, woven from some type of wild grass, with a layer of soft fur above and below her. "She sure looks cozy in there," her grandmother mused.

"Doesn't she?" Sabel asked, smiling and then stifling a yawn.

"We won't stay, love; you should try to nap while she does."

They were rowing home when Charlotte said, "I often wish I could tell Sabel about why Samhain is so important to me . . . but it's such a crazy story."

"And you couldn't really tell only one of them, could you?" Ben asked.

"No, I don't suppose I could."

The candles flickered in the darkened room, as Charlotte sat waiting for a vision of Jessica to appear.

The air took on the sound and haze of static, and she heard a faraway voice calling her name. ". . . u hear me, Charlotte?"

"Jess, I'm here."

Jess's face blossomed into view. "Charlie, I'm so happy to see you. Quickly, show me what's new." She watched as Charlotte showed her Sabel and Running Otter holding hands, joined, and holding their new baby.

"Oh my gosh, Char. Imagine, after all the years you've loved them both, they married. You're a grandma! What did they call the baby?"

"Tehya, and she's beautiful. I miss working with Sabel every day, but it's good to see her so happy."

"Hard to believe the two of us are forty-two years old—I'm the mother of an eleven-year-old, and you're a grandmother! That's frikkin' nuts! And how is everyone else?"

"Everyone is well. Ben has been talking with some doctors about coordinating some type of surgery rotation that will allow people who don't live near a hospital or have an experienced surgeon nearby, to have needed surgeries. We'll see what comes of it. Also, Mitenah and Swan Song had a baby boy a few months ago, Falling Leaf. Gifted Hands and Keen Wolf became grandparents twice this year! How's Charlie? And you and Michael?" She thought-asked her friend.

"Charlie is fantastic! He keeps himself, and me, busy. He plays soccer in the summer and hockey in the winter, so there's lots of running around—it's fun. He resembles Michael's dad, I think. Look!" She thought of his face and Charlotte saw his dirty-blond hair, freshly cut, his green eyes, and his freckles.

"He's adorable! Yes, he looks like his grandpa. Who would have thought it, Jess?"

"I know!" She smiled. "Michael is still in the same position, loving it, and expecting to be there until he retires. I'm still doing part-time at the hospital. Once Charlie's in high school, I'll probably go back to full-time. My mom is the same. She seems happy enough, but I wouldn't have wished this for her. I . . . ng . . . no."

Their time together was coming to an end. Rather than try to say words that would be cut off, Charlotte made a heart with her hands and held it up. With tears in her eyes, Jessica was nodding as her apparition faded into the darkness.

After releasing the quarters, and Goddess and God, Charlotte took some time to ground.

She wished she could tell Jess about meeting Charlie. Maybe one day the time would come for that, but at this point she couldn't risk possibly changing their future. She would have to learn about him, as with all of Jess's news, during their Samhain visits.

The months that followed were cold. Charlotte stayed busy at the apothecary counter while Ben saw patients at a regular pace, and on the weekends, they would try to visit with their family and friends on the other side of the lake. Phillip and Holly accompanied them most of the time; they got a kick out of watching the two little ones and trying to make them smile.

Sabel, now in a good day/night rhythm with the baby, looked better rested, but admitted she still felt quite tired. On this day, the four grandparents were visiting Sabel and Running Otter. "How is Dark Wolf enjoying being an uncle?" Charlotte asked.

Gifted Hands glanced at her husband before answering. "He seems to enjoy the little ones, but if I am honest, it seems he is distracted by other things these days."

"What things?"

Keen Wolf answered. "A few days ago, we received word from an old neighbour about those who were forced to leave their homes." Charlotte felt her stomach sink. She had told them all she could about this, so they would be ready, but to hear about it as it was happening was still infuriating. "Broken Feather wasted no words as he spoke of the devastation of our people. He said they held some who refused to leave in stockades for many weeks, and as they grew weak, many became ill and died. Others were forced to march, with only the clothes they wore, through the cold, wet weather, watched by armed soldiers." Ben shook his head to himself, unable to understand the ignorance and heartlessness of those in command. "Dark Wolf was here when we heard this news. He feels furious about it."

Charlotte simply nodded. There were no words to express her feelings. "He smiles as he looks at Falling Leaf and Tehya, but his thoughts are somewhere else," Gifted Hands finished.

Winter's chill was eventually replaced by a cool, damp April. Everyone was ready for some warmth, but no one more than Charlotte. She was eager to celebrate spring and usher in the warmer temperatures and the approaching summer. Tonight, she would perform her Beltane ritual.

As she and Ben pulled the canoe up on shore, they looked up to see Gifted Hands and Keen Wolf coming out their door. They were going to Sabel and Running Otter's home, too. "Chweh'n, you two. Good timing," Charlotte called.

"Chweh'n," Gifted Hands answered, her lovely smile noticeably absent.

When Charlotte came up beside her, she asked if everything was alright. Gifted Hands paused before answering and Charlotte glanced at Keen Wolf, hoping for a clue. His expression was serious, the line of his mouth was held tight.

"What happened?"

"It's Dark Wolf," Gifted Hands began, her voice catching.

"Is he okay?"

She nodded and continued walking. "He has left us."

"Left?"

Gifted Hands nodded again, her eyes damp with tears.

"Where did he go?" Ben asked.

Keen Wolf answered. "He said he could listen to stories of relocation no longer. He wants to help. I do not know what he thinks he will be able to do to make things better, but he wants to try."

"Oh . . ." Charlotte didn't know what to say.

"He gave me a hug and a kiss, and then he said goodbye. I had barely enough time to remove the sky stone you gave me from my neck and put it around his," Gifted hands said.

"Does he plan to return?" Ben asked.

"We do not know," Keen Wolf answered.

"I hope he stays safe," Charlotte said.

Gifted Hands nodded but said no more.

Sabel welcomed them in, holding Tehya in one arm. She smiled but her eyes showed worry.

Once everyone was sitting, Running Otter and Sabel explained Dark Wolf had come by this morning. "He told us he feels he must go help those who are forced to march to a new home in Indian Territory," Running Otter started.

"He kissed the little one on both cheeks, hugged us both, and left." Sabel's voice shook as she spoke. Many were dying on that march, some from sickness, but some from cruelty and negligence at the hands of the army leading them.

The mood was somber; only Tehya's gurgles and giggles allowed them to smile at all.

It was two full years before there was word of Dark Wolf. It came in the form of a Cherokee who called himself Bear Creek. He befriended Dark Wolf at one of the stops on the trail to Indian Territory, which Charlotte knew was the future Oklahoma. He said Dark Wolf hunted regularly and offered food and encouragement to those making the journey. Bear Creek had been doing the same for some time. The two worked together for a while, but Bear Creek had seen enough. He chose to head north now and find others of his tribe.

He told Dark Wolf he would find his family and tell them of him. "He is in good health and will continue his work there." That was it. Two years later, and that was all Gifted Hands and Keen Wolf got. Of course, it was good to know that their son was well, but that could change at any time. They would continue to worry, despite their momentary happiness.

Sabel and Running Otter came to visit Charlotte and Ben the day they got the news. They were relieved—he was safe. Charlotte was steeping some tea at the counter when Sabel came to stand beside her. "How are you feeling, love? You've got dark circles under your eyes. Is it still morning sickness?"

Sabel's chin wobbled at the question, and her mother set everything down on the counter. "I've lost it, Mum," she cried, tears coming to her eyes.

"Oh, no. Are you bleeding?" Sabel nodded. "Oh, Sabel." She put her arms around her and quietly said, "I'm sorry, honey. Have you been taking anything?"

"No. I wanted to ask you about that."

After confirming that, yes, she had actually miscarried, Charlotte put together a tea mix for Sabel that would help slough off what remained inside, so she could resume a regular cycle. "Please, don't try again until you've had your cycles for a couple of months. Your body needs the time." Sabel nodded.

She hadn't told Gifted Hands yet. She'd wanted to speak to her own mother first. "Listen, you know I'm always here if you want to talk, but remember, Gifted Hands went through this a few times before Mitenah. Talking to her might help."

"Yeah."

Just then there was a big giggle from Tehya, who had been trying to catch her grandpa as he ran around the sitting room. When she caught him, he scooped her up over his head and onto his shoulders. She loved this game!

At almost three years old, Tehya was a happy little chatterbox. She was learning to speak in the languages of both parents. Sometimes her words were unclear to her grandparents, but with time, they would all learn some new words. By now, she had long-ish black hair that her mother and grandmother enjoyed braiding in a variety of ways—all of which were adorable, in Charlotte's opinion. Her almond-shaped eyes were a difficult colour to describe: stormy-grey around the outside and chocolate-brown in the middle—quite stunning. She and her cousin, Falling Leaf, were the best of friends, running around, playing together— and sometimes arguing—whenever they got the chance.

Sabel and Mitenah spoke often of having more children. Both were eager, but knew they had time. Sabel took her mother's advice and waited a few months after her miscarriage. By the beginning of fall, she was ready to try again. Running Otter offered no argument.

The whole Crawford family came to visit that winter, just before Christmas. Maisie was very excited to meet Tehya. As soon as she laid eyes on her, she said,

"I can't believe how much she looks like both of you, Sabel. She's got eyes like you and your dad, all mixed up, and your nose, Running Otter's lips and hair, and that skin—she's beautiful.

"Tehya, come say hello to Mummy's friend, Maisie."

She sauntered over to where they sat on the settee and said, "Hello, Mathie."

Maisie giggled. "Not Mathie, Maizie. Try May."

"May," Tehya repeated.

"Zee."

"Th-ee. Thz-ee."

"Very good. Try slowly, May-zee."

"May-thee."

"Good try, sweetie. It's very nice to meet you, Tehya."

The little one smiled, giggled, and then ran off toward her bedroom.

"The way she speaks is adorable, Sabel."

"It is. Mum says she'll likely outgrow that lisp."

Maisie spent the night at Sabel's, and the girls spent some time catching up. Sabel learned Maisie remained happily unattached. She had created a role for herself on the reservation and was quite enjoying life. She still lived in the house with her parents, but she also travelled some, acting as a sort of liaison with the nearby townsfolk, setting up exchanges of food, clothing, art, services, etc.

Carole-Anne and Keith were very proud of her work, but often worried for her safety. Not everyone was happy to have the reservation there. "There is prejudice everywhere, Sabel. I'm curious. Do any of your Tuscarora friends or the folks in town have anything to say about you and Running Otter being together?"

Sabel hadn't expected the question. One side of her mouth tweaked up as she thought about this. "Well, among the Tuscarora that I've met, no one has ever given me reason to think they disapproved. They are very welcoming. The other side of the lake . . . there were some who would look the other way when they saw us together on the road. I don't suppose it helped that they knew I'd stopped attending church services. My friends have always been friends with him and Mitenah, and none of them were offended. Once or twice, when a new family has come to town, they will look surprised to see me with him, or to see Tehya—that is their initial reaction, but most get to know us and never think about it again. There was one day, though. I was with Tehya and Janee; we were standing by the hitching post outside the Doctor's House, when someone I didn't recognize came out. She smiled at us, and when she realized I was carrying the little one, asked to take a peek. I lowered the blanket to uncover her face and saw the surprise register on the woman's face. She didn't even try to hide it! She said, 'Oh, she's a darkie.' I found myself momentarily speechless, but Janee wasn't." Sabel smiled, remembering her friend's reaction. "She said, 'A darkie? What the hell is a darkie? How rude! This little girl has been blessed with two loving parents and a wonderful family, more than many can say.' I caught up at that point adding, 'What's in a person's heart is more important than the colour of their skin, don't you think?' I turned and led Janee inside then, leaving the woman gaping on the step. Janee had seen her at church the day before and thought she might be more . . . gracious. Mum told us she was just passing through town and had come in for a tea mix."

Maisie shook her head. "I suppose much of what the church preaches depends on your interpretation. Not everyone is ready to accept people's differences."

"Tehya will grow up aware of that. I will see that she's prepared for this type of thing as she gets older. It's not likely to change."

"And although this affects nothing, I think the colour of her skin is lovely. It's like tea with milk, as if she enjoys time in the sun, and she's only slightly darker than you. She'll be a beautiful young lady, just like her mommy."

"Thank you."

"Holly has grown into a pretty young thing. How much more school does she have ahead of her?"

"Another year, I believe. She's looking forward to finishing and working with Mum, as I was doing."

"That's lucky for Charlotte. I'm sure she misses your company." Sabel nodded. She knew it was true. "Will you tell me about Dark Wolf? When I asked Mitenah where he was, she said he had left. She didn't seem to want to talk about it. What happened?"

Sabel told her what she could about him and his mission. "It's just awful what's happening, not just here either. It's so . . . Christ, I can't think of a word strong enough."

"Agreed."

"And Phillip? How is he spending his time?"

Sabel smiled proudly. "He now lives with a colleague about an hour from here. He writes articles for the newspaper or the odd broadsheet."

"I'm impressed."

"Me, too."

The Crawfords spent the week between Christmas and the New Year, enjoying the company of their old friends, but were ready to leave when the week was up. As far as Sabel knew, Maisie had corresponded with Jeffery a few times since they broke up. Last year, he told her he'd met a woman and had fallen in love, and Maisie was genuinely happy for him. She did not, however, search him out while she was in town.

Carole-Anne, Keith, and Maisie were preparing to leave on January 2nd, gathering their belongings in front of the store where they would await the northbound coach. When it came into view, they said goodbye to Gracie, Charlotte, Sandy, and Sabel. Keith was bending to pick up a couple of bags when the coach door opened. "Good morning," a young man said, stepping out onto the road. "I wonder where I might get a quick drink before the coach starts on again?"

Gracie smiled, "Right here." She looked at the driver and said, "We won't be a minute. Come along, lad. My name's Gracie."

Inside, she asked what he'd like, tea, water, or milk, and noticed his pink eyes. "A glass of water sounds lovely, thank you. I've been travelling for five hours already this morning."

She poured some into a cup. "Where are you headed?"

"Actually, I'm making my way to Upper Canada."

"Oo-oo, ye've a bit of a ride ahead o' ye, then."

"That I do, but I'm in no hurry and it's a sunny day."

They stepped back out onto the road as Maisie was sitting down inside the coach. The driver looked at Gracie impatiently as the stranger climbed in. "Thank you," he said.

"You're welcome. It was nice te meet ye . . ."

He smiled and leaned out to pull the coach door closed. "Sonny, and it was good to meet you, too, Gracie."

It was six months later when they heard from Carole-Anne again. Gracie's smile was huge as she read the letter to Charlotte. ". . . Since the last time we saw you, Maisie and Sonny Peterson (who you'll remember from the coach) have been inseparable . . ."

"Peterson?" Charlotte asked with a smile. "Well, I guess I don't have to worry about *that* anymore, Gracie."

"Aye. It looks like you'll be born after all, Charlie."

I t was an afternoon in early spring when Gracie, Jimmy, and Sandy approached Charlotte and Ben. "We've come to discuss a matter wi' ye," Gracie began. "When Audrey passed those years ago, she left her bit o' land to ye."

Ben saw his wife's eyebrows come down as she tried to imagine what was coming next. "Well, ye see, w—"

"Mum, I can do this," Sandy interrupted. "I was wondering if perhaps we could build a house for me on that property?"

"We'll pay ye for it, o' course," Jimmy added.

Ben smiled at his wife before responding. "When Audrey left us that land, she said it was 'for our family's future'. You are our family, Sandy."

"Of course. We've always considered the Doctor's House and Audrey's parcel of land family assets—the Williams *and* Moffatts," Charlotte added.

"So, yes? Can we build a house there for me?" She looked at her parents one at a time, then her aunt and uncle. "Wonderful! Thank you! You see, I'd like to live on my own, but I'd also like to have a space, aside from the schoolhouse, where I can offer extra help to teach a child who maybe doesn't learn as fast as the others or can't attend the school for some reason. Much like Audrey did, as I understand."

"Audrey would be thrilled with your choice, Sandy," her uncle said.

"I understand Katie's been ill, Sandy. Have you enjoyed having the children all to yourself this past week?" Charlotte asked.

Her smile was bright. "Oh, yes. I do enjoy them. I wouldn't wish anything bad on Katie, but I like it when she's not there, and I get to be the schoolmarm."

"It's good to know that the woman teaching our children is enjoying the task."

Plans for the building began as the 1842 school year ended—the last for the Williams clan. Holly walked straight to the Doctor's House after class was dismissed. "Hello, Mum. How was your day?"

Charlotte looked at her daughter, feeling weary. "It was busy. How about you? Glad to be finished?"

"You know I am," she said, all but jumping up and down. "Monday morning, I would like to start my new job with you."

Charlotte smiled. She'd been looking forward to this day. Having her daughter help her would free up some time, but she would also enjoy spending the time together. She expected to relish working with Holly every bit as much as she did with Sabel. They were very different people, but both were quick studies and enjoyed the learning.

"So, you're all finished school. How do you feel?"

Just then, Ben came out of the back room with a worker from the wood mill. After the man had left, Ben smiled at Holly and asked, "So? All done?"

She grinned. "Yep, and I'm starting work on Monday!"

And that is exactly what happened. Holly walked to work the first Monday after school had finished, happy as she'd ever been. She'd looked forward to spending more time with her mother and learning the craft she knew so well.

In her free time, she still enjoyed painting. The tips that Gifted Hands had shared with her allowed her to use her imagination and skill slightly differently, and the works that she had created were beautiful. Everyone who saw them encouraged her to sell them. Gracie, of course, already had a few choice scenes for sale in the general store. Indeed, there had been a couple of times over the past year when she had gone to Auburn with her father and visited a few stores with her work. On those occasions, the store owner had purchased paintings. The idea of doing something like painting for the fun of it *and* making money for it overjoyed her. As a matter of fact, when Jimmy returned from Auburn a few days ago, Gracie told Charlotte, "Jimmy sold two more paintings while he was there. He was right pleased wi' 'imself. Bugger came home shy on the molasses, though."

"Has that happened before?"

"Not molasses, no. I s'ppose it can 'appen easy enough when yer bundlin' all yer purchases up into a cart."

Holly soon realized that her genuine passion was the knowledge of herbal medicine she was now beginning to learn. Painting became her way of unwinding after a busy week, of setting her mind free after being focused on her work.

She spent much of her free time with Evelyn—they were cousins, but they were also best friends. Evelyn would finish school the following year. She told Holly that when the time came, she would take over cooking for the family and Hettie would help and guide *her*.

The first weekend in July saw the beginning of construction on Sandy's new home. The Moffatts enlisted the help of friends to get the skeleton of the structure built; it would be a small house with a good-sized office on the main floor and the master and a smaller bedroom on the second floor.

As the summer progressed, Sandy spent many hours helping with the construction of the inner walls and floors. She was competent with a hammer and nails and enjoyed the work immensely. They expected she could move in before winter.

One day, toward the end of summer, Charlotte suggested Holly run over to the general store to pick up their lunch. While there, she overheard Lily outside talking to Jimmy. "I don't know what's wrong with her, Da. She isn't eating. It's been a couple of days now—since you returned from Auburn. I think we should get the horse doctor to come see her."

"Aye. I'll run back up to Auburn and speak to 'im."

Holly stuck her head out the door. "Which horse is it, Lily?"

Lily looked at Holly and answered, "It's Nya."

"Oh, the poor girl. Let me know if I can help," Holly added, before slipping back into the kitchen to get her lunch basket.

When Jimmy returned from Auburn, he immediately went to check on Nya.

"There's been no change, Da. Will the doctor come see her?"

"He wasna there, lass." He saw the terrified look in his daughter's eyes. "But his apprentice was, and he said he'll come down later today." She nodded and leaned her forehead on Nya's nose. When she looked up, she saw her aunt Charlotte.

"I came to check on her," Charlotte said, petting Nya's muzzle in long strokes.

"Da says the horse doctor from Auburn will stop in to see her," Lily said.

Charlotte took a good look at her niece, considering the young woman she'd become. She was dressed like Charlotte would like to be, wearing an oversized men's buttoned shirt tucked inside men's belted trousers. In Charlotte's day, this would have seemed quite normal, but here, not so much. It was, however, perfect attire for dealing with horses all day. She'd tied her long dark hair into a ponytail and the shorter bits were falling over the sides of her face. She was a pretty young woman, but entirely unaware of the fact.

"Thank you, Lily." Before she left, Charlotte wrapped her arms around Nya's thick neck and whispered, "Feel better."

It was late in the afternoon when the apprentice horse doctor arrived. Lily, who'd been keeping watch, introduced herself, and escorted him to the stable. "This is Nya," she said, stopping at the stall gate. "Nya, this is . . ."

"I'm Clement Nicholls." He smiled, taking in her appearance, before looking at the horse. "Hello, Nya," he said and rubbed his palm down her shoulder.

Lily left him in the stable and went to let her father know he was here.

After examining the horse, Clement said, "Well, she doesn't appear to have any pains anywhere. That's a good sign. However, now we must find out what might have happened that has put her off her food. Tell me about her diet." Jimmy allowed Lily to explain the horse's meal plan. Clement nodded. "That sounds perfect. Has anything happened that you're aware of that made her nervous? Or has she had reason to fret over the past week or so?"

Lily looked pensive; she knew of nothing. "Not while she's been here. Father? What about when you were in Auburn?"

Jimmy looked from Lily to Clement, thinking to himself. He had only been away for the day, no overnights, no strange places. Nya was left with Harris, the groom at the stables of the general store. Jimmy and Gladys sold the general store in 1819, but to this day, he was permitted to leave his horse(s) there when he was in town. "She stayed at the general store for the day, as always."

"With Harris?" Clement asked. Jimmy nodded. "He's got a new horse. I believe his name is Raven." He saw the look of surprise on Jimmy's face. "You didn't meet him?"

"No, and he didna say. Hmm."

"Well, it could be something as simple as that. Raven is still young and . . . excitable. Perhaps he agitated Nya."

"But wouldn't she feel better now that she's at home?" Lily asked.

"I should think so. Perhaps all she needs is another day or so to realize she's back and she's safe. Why don't we try that? You can fuss over her a little, remind her she's loved, and see if she improves. I'll come back down in two or three days and see how she is."

Just then, Holly stumbled in through the stable doors. "Oh, sorry. I didn't realize someone was here."

"It's all right, Holly. This is Clement Nicholls. He came to look at Nya."

He smiled at Holly and turned to shake Jimmy's hand. "Very well. Thank ye for makin' the journey down."

"Can we offer you supper?" Lily asked and then blushed heavily.

He smiled. "Thank you, but no. I must be getting back. Doctor Roberts will wonder what's become of me."

Jimmy walked Clement and his horse back out to the road while the girls stayed with the horses. "He was so handsome, don't you think, Lily?"

Lily smiled. "He was, and nice, too. He spoke to me like a person, like I was a man. Not every man does that!"

When Charlotte walked to the store just before the noon hour a few days later, Gracie told her that Clement Nicholls had returned, accompanied by the much older Dr. Roberts. Lily told them Nya seemed to be back to herself. Happy to hear the news, and finding nothing upon examination, they were on their way. Gracie offered them their noon meal, but they'd declined, claiming they had another horse to visit on their way back.

When Charlotte told Holly, an odd expression crossed her face.

"Is something wrong, love?" Charlotte asked.

"No. I'm glad Nya's feeling better . . . I just was hoping to be there when Mr. Nicholls returned." Her face reddened in a blush.

"Ah. Was he handsome?"

"Very," Holly answered. Feeling the heat in her cheeks, she smiled.

Tehya's Stone

When Jimmy made his trip into Auburn that fall, he chanced to pass Clement Nicholls on the road in front of the jeweller. "Mr. Moffatt," he said, stretching out his hand in greeting. "What brings you to town today?"

"Hello, there. I'm pickin' up supplies for the store. Seems I came back short last time I was up."

Clement nodded. "And how is Nya?"

Jimmy smiled now. "As a matter of fact, we learned some time after we last saw ye that Raven did more than just spook our Nya." Clement tried to understand his meaning. "She's going to foal."

"No! That was a bit of a surprise, I'll bet?"

"Aye, but everyone's lookin' forward to it, now that we ken."

"So that'd be"—his eyes darted upward as he calculated—"May?"

"Aye. It'll be the first for us."

"That will be interesting for you, then. Remember, Dr. Roberts and I are here if you find you need us. Best of luck, Jim."

While they were all new to the upcoming experience, Jimmy didn't expect any problems. Horses had been foaling for thousands of years. Nya would be fine.

Meanwhile, Sandy was busy packing up her things, getting ready to move up the hill. Jimmy had Hank and Helen make her a new bed and nightstand; Gracie had Rebecca weave a pattern in blue and yellow that she sewed into a bedspread; her sisters bought her a new wash stand, bowl, and pitcher; and between her mother and aunt, she was given some odd plates, cutlery, and cups. She planned to spend the holidays with her family and move into her new home in the new year.

By this time, Nya was barely showing her pregnancy. Jimmy and Ben still used her regularly for their runs, but when Jimmy went to Auburn, he had to leave her somewhere other than the general store. It only took one visit for her to make her distaste for that stable clear—she did not want to be anywhere near Raven.

The full moon this September fell on the 19th. The Corn Moon, falling so close to the autumnal equinox, made it this year's Harvest Moon. Today, Charlotte celebrated both the moon and the equinox she calls Mabon. She decorated her altar with fresh baked cornbread, an ear of corn, her garnet and tiger's eye stones, and sprigs of rosemary and basil tied into a bundle.

Her ritual paid tribute to the end of summer, the beginning of the harvest, and the cycle of rebirth. Now was time to gather and harvest the crops in preparation for the winter that would surely follow. She gave thanks to the waning sunlight that welcomed the change of season. She thanked the Goddess and God for her family and friends.

When the ritual was over, she went outside to sit in the moonlight. She remembered a friend she had not seen in many years, with whom she once performed this ritual—Ronnie. She hoped that Ronnie, too, was celebrating tonight. The last time she heard from Ronnie, she and Ewen were living happily not far from Slains Castle and she was expecting a baby. That was this time last year. Since then, Charlotte had written three times and heard nothing back. She hoped to get some news soon.

Early in the new year, Sabel received a letter from Maisie. It had been quite some time since she'd had news, so she was excited to read it.

January 1843

Dear Sabel,

    Hello my dear friend. It has been a long time. I do apologize. To say I have been busy hardly seems acceptable. It is, however, the truth. My work has certainly kept me busy. I absolutely love it, but that's not the reason either. I have been spending every moment I can with Sonny. I know my mother has mentioned him, but I haven't told you much about him. I'd like to now. I hope you don't mind.

Well, you know that he's handsome because you saw him, however briefly. I love his face; I just love it! He is also kind and thoughtful and smart. He lives in a town about five miles from the reservation. He was living with his parents until recently when they moved back to Scotland. He works as a lawyer. When we met him that day, he was returning from a trip to Cortland, where he'd been doing some business. It was a happy coincidence that we got on the coach with someone travelling out the same way as us. The trip took us a few days and we chatted the whole way. When we arrived home, he told me he would like to see me again. The very next week, he came to visit. We've been together ever since, at least, when he's not travelling. I can honestly say I've never been happier!

I hope you are doing well with your little family. Any more on the way yet?

How is Mitenah?

I look forward to hearing from you.

Love Maisie

Sabel smiled and gently laid her hand on her belly. She couldn't feel him yet, but she knew he was there. She hadn't had her cycle in three months and expected to give birth in July. She kept it to herself this time. If anything were to happen like it did last time, she didn't want everyone to know about it. She was planning to tell her parents when they came for Sunday dinner.

Running Otter and Tehya arrived home as she was setting the lid back on the pot. Dinner was almost ready. "Mummy, Mummy, look what Goo-thood gave me."

Sable squatted down to look at the clear white stone laying in Tehya's palm. "Isn't that pretty? Do you know what it's called?" She stood back up and smiled at her husband.

"It hath a name?" Tehya asked, looking utterly perplexed.

Sabel giggled. "I think it's quartz. We'll ask Grama when we see her next."

Running Otter put his arms around her. "How was your afternoon?"

"It was nice and quiet. Thank y—"

"What is it?" he asked, instantly worried as he saw her expression change.

With a grunt, she doubled over, one hand grabbing onto the counter for support. "Oh no," she cried.

"Should you lie down?" She nodded with eyes full of tears.

A short time later, Sabel started to bleed. It was happening again. After so much time trying, it was happening again. Running Otter asked his mother to watch Tehya for a while, hoping the peace would help Sabel, who found she could do little more than cry.

"After all the trying we did," she said to him. "We tried over and over again."

He tipped her chin up to look into her eyes. "That part wasn't so bad, was it?" He smiled, hoping to cheer her some.

She tried to smile back. "No, that part was fine."

"Fine?" he asked, pretending to be devastated.

"Stop, you know what I mean." Sabel started to cry again. "I thought it was going to be fine this time. I really did."

"I know it is not what you want to hear, Mimiteh, but it *will* happen when it is meant to." He helped her wrap up some so that she could try to get some rest and held her as she cried herself to sleep.

In the morning, Running Otter suggested they cancel today's visit with her parents.

She smiled at him sadly. "No. I'm sorry if this hurts your feelings, but seeing my mum now is just what I need."

When Tehya came into the kitchen she said, "Grama and Grampa and Goothood and Ree-ah-thood are coming today! Yay!" As she danced around the kitchen, her hair spun around her.

"Before they get here, I think we'd better tie up that hair of yours. It's a little wild today," Sabel said.

"Firth-t you have to catch me!" She immediately sprang into action, running about the place.

"Oh, I'll get you, you little rascal." Her mother chased her around for a minute or two, her heart feeling momentarily lighter.

When they arrived, Running Otter said, "Don't take off your coats, we're going to make snowmen today!" Then he caught Charlotte's eye and tipped his head toward the door.

She walked inside and slipped out of her coat. "Mm-mm, it smells delicious in here. Here you go, I baked some bread. Before I forget, Sandy—" Seeing her daughter's sad eyes, she stopped. "What is it?" she asked, wrapping her in a hug.

"Oh, Mum," she cried over her mother's shoulder. "It happened again."

Charlotte pulled back to look at her. "What happened? You mean a miscarriage?" Sabel nodded. "Aw, Sweetie, I'm so sorry."

"I feel like a big baby. I can't stop crying. I'm just so sad."

Shortly after, Gifted Hands came in. "I . . . oh. Sorry to interrupt."

"It's all right," Sabel said and filled her in.

"It's a feeling I understand too well. I'm very sorry you have to go through this again, but please, look at the wonderful little girl you created and don't stop trying." She hugged her.

Sabel reached up to get the bottle of wine she had in the cupboard and poured three glasses. "Thank you for being the two best mothers."

"What were you going to say about Sandy, Mum?"

"Oh, she wanted to invite you to come see how the house is coming along."

"I look forward to it." Sabel smiled.

"Also, we heard from Robbie the other day. He said that the dean has recommended him to a hospital in New York. He said he'll let us know when he hears anything."

"Good for him," Sabel said, happy for her big brother.

Soon the door opened, and the sounds of voices filled the cabin. Tehya grabbed for her mother's hand and pulled her toward the door. "Look at the th-nowman we made." Charlotte's heart caught at hearing Tehya's sweet lisp, which so often brought thoughts of little Jessie.

Charlotte and Gifted Hands caught each other's gaze, both sad for Sabel's loss.

Not long after, Tehya stood in front of Charlotte expectantly. "Grama, Mummy th-aid you have a name for thith." She opened up her hand, showing Charlotte the stone in her palm.

"Your mummy's right. This is called Quartz." Tehya looked at her mother with a nod. "It's known for its powers of protection, healing, awareness, and psychic ability."

"I don't know what that mean-th, but it'th pretty."

Sabel continued to drink her teas and reminded herself her time would come. In the meantime, she enjoyed Tehya for the delightful little soul she was. She was teaching Tehya her numbers and letters, and on the weekend, Gifted Hands and Mitenah taught her the language of their people. Sable enjoyed sitting in for these lessons, too.

As temperatures warmed, the women started planning this year's garden. There was a time in the past when several women worked together to tend the large vegetable garden. After they had moved away, Gifted Hands wanted to continue growing. With the help of her family, she had maintained it. When Sabel moved here, she took on much of the work. They grew the same plants as always; corn, squash, beans, potatoes, and more recently, tomatoes, lettuce, and cucumber.

Every once in a while, Gifted Hands would take the little one for a day or two, and Running Otter, and perhaps Keen Wolf, would take Sabel hunting, or fishing, or to check the traps. She enjoyed learning new tricks and had become a good shot. To date, she had brought down a deer, two rabbits, and a partridge. She also enjoyed fishing, whether it be out in the canoe or through a hole in the ice. Running Otter enjoyed taking her along.

Swan Song thought it odd that Sabel accompanied Running Otter sometimes. He was not accustomed to women doing these tasks. He was constantly reminded that, while Mitenah's family celebrated their Tuscarora traditions, they had adopted a lifestyle that incorporated some of "white man's" ways. That being said, he was happy that Mitenah had no desire to hunt or fish.

While Sabel enjoyed the hunt, she did not enjoy preparing the kill for cooking or smoking; when it came time for skinning or de-boning the beasts, her word was "yuck". Every time she said it, Running Otter felt the need to get her alone as soon as possible. She was fun, and beautiful, and all his.

Poppies

Nya's belly grew large with the approaching spring, and everyone started guessing at the sex of the foal. For no reason whatsoever, most expected it would be a filly. More than once, suppertime conversation was all about baby horse names. Although Nya was shared by the whole family, she had been given to Charlotte as a gift, so she would be the one to name the foal.

Nya delivered early on a May morning. It was the first time Charlotte had been a part of a horse's labour and found it exhilarating! The delivery went off without a hitch, and Nya delivered a colt. He was mostly black, except for the lower portion of his left front leg, which was white; he had his mother's blanket of white and black over his haunches; and on the left side of his long nose, was an almost perfect circle of white. After seeing him, Charlotte suggested the name Oreo. "Oo-oo, like those cookies Jessica brought us when she came. Do you remember those?" Ben asked the kids.

"That name is perfect!" Holly said. "Those were sooo good!"

Lily was in her element after seeking advice from everyone she knew about horsemanship. She was confident and up to the task of teaching Oreo how to be their horse.

By now, the poppies on the other side of the lake were blooming. While Charlotte and Ben were visiting, Sabel and her mother went to check on them. "Oh, aren't they pretty, Sabel?" Charlotte asked.

"They are. At least we're able to enjoy them before we have to harvest them. You said we collect the heads after the petals fall from the plant?"

"Yes, between five and ten days. We can do that together. We'll collect the milky sap from the seed pods. After it's dried, your dad will do the rest. Before that though, maybe you can keep your eyes open for the strongest looking plants and we can leave them to mature and use for seed for next year's crop."

"Sure. Tehya will enjoy helping with that job."

When the time came, they harvested a decent amount of poppy resin, more than Charlotte had worked with before. Once it had properly dried, Ben would store it, mixing only small amounts in alcohol as needed for his patients' pain. Charlotte had explained the dangers of being too free with laudanum many years ago. It was a very addictive substance. At this time, it was classified as medicine, so people who wanted it could get it cheaper than wine or whiskey, because as medicine, it wasn't taxed as alcohol was. Ben only dispensed it when doing a surgery or when a patient was in severe pain. Sometimes, though rarely, a patient would return to him asking for more, but he understood the dangers and did his best to prevent this situation.

Such was the case in early autumn. Cuthbert Simmons was hired to work at the wood mill for the spring and summer. In late September, he had an accident which resulted in him losing his thumb at its base. Gregory had arrived at the Doctor's House, out of breath and frantic, explaining what had happened. Lenny had immediately sat Cuthbert down and wrapped his hand up tight, sending Gregory to fetch Ben. He had also saved the thumb, unsure what to do with it. Ben and Charlotte ran to the wood mill, leaving Holly in charge.

They took him back to the Doctor's House, where the environment was closer to sterile, and laid him out on a bed. After close examination of the thumb, there was no question about whether an attempt could be made to re-attach it— it had been cut through the bone, and the tissue below the thumb joint was torn—it could not be done. All Ben could do was cut away what was necessary and close the wound to the best of his ability.

Of course, Cuthbert was given laudanum, enough to keep him still and pain free, to allow Ben, with Charlotte's assistance, to work on his hand. Holly came in to check on their progress twice. After the wound was closed and wrapped, they left Cuthbert to sleep it off, with Holly on watch.

For the first two nights, Ben stayed with the man to be sure he was comfortable and safe. After that, he returned to the cabin he was staying in on the Cameron's property. Understanding the amount of pain the man was in, Ben kept him on laudanum for a few days, although he lowered the dose after the second day. When his medication was reduced, he felt the difference immediately. "But doctor, I feel so much pain. My hand feels like it's on fire."

Ben explained that he would adjust to the new sensations, and they would diminish as the days passed. "Unfortunately, some pain comes with healing. Continue to drink the willow bark teas I've given you. They will help."

It was two days after Ben reduced his medication when the man disappeared. Lenny went to check on him early that morning and found him preparing to leave. "He told me he could not stay here under these conditions. He was unable to work and unable to take the pain. He was going to return home, which I believe is just north of Auburn."

"Did he take the jar of tea we gave him?" Ben asked.

"He did."

"Good. He'll be all right. He just has to give himself proper time to heal."

"I told him as much. In fact, I told him to come back next spring if he's up for it. He will still be able to do the work, thumb or no thumb."

September's end came with an abrupt change in weather. The sun remained bright, but the air was cool with an almost constant breeze.

They had word from Robbie. He'd been offered a job at Bellevue Hospital, in what would become Manhattan, New York. He was very excited and was in the process of moving out of Ailsa and Sam's house in Boston and finding new accommodations.

Hettie had been under the weather, so Ben stopped in to check on her this morning, while Charlotte and Holly continued on to the Doctor's House. Holly entered the building ahead of her mother and stopped suddenly after stepping inside. "Holly? Wh—get behind me!"

Charlotte picked up the pot sitting on the counter and walked toward the back room. Shards of broken glass lay on the floor outside the open door. With no idea whether anyone was in the room, she called, "If you're in there, come out now!"

There was only quiet.

With her potted-hand raised, she peeked into the room. There was no one there.

Holly followed, her hand coming up over her mouth in surprise. Someone had broken the window into the room and a chair lay toppled beneath it. "What would anyone want in here, Mum?"

"I don't know. Let's look around and see if anything's missing."

The patient room had only a bed, chair, and linens in it at any time, there was nothing missing from there, although several folded sheets had been used over the bottom of the window where the glass would have been jagged.

The other room, with supplies of gauze, sterilized bundles of needles, and surgical tools, appeared untouched. They walked back toward their apothecary counter and saw what they'd missed when they'd entered—broken jars on the floor, jars on their sides on the shelves, and an empty laudanum bottle. Holly picked it up and showed her mother. "There were two. Is the other one there?" Charlotte asked. These bottles had been labelled, as many of them were, to prevent any errors in dispensing.

"No, just this one."

They looked at each other disappointed. "Let's see what else might be missing," Charlotte said and crouched down behind the counter. "I don't see anything else missing, just broken jars. I'll get the broom."

They had just finished cleaning the floor when Ben came in. His smile vanished the moment he laid eyes on them.

Holly let her mother explain what they'd found. "So, whoever this was only took the laudanum? And then they left out the window they came in? Well, I doubt anyone would have seen or heard anything being located where we are. Who have we given laudanum to recently who would have wanted more?"

"Who would have wanted it that badly?" Charlotte added.

"It's hard to say; I use it regularly. Holly, would you please walk over to get Lawrence? He should know about this."

"Sure, Dad." Slipping back into her coat, she turned and left.

"This is a first, Benny. Do you still have some in your bag?"

"Not enough. I was going to top it up today."

"I'll make you up some more." She got up on her tippies and kissed his cheek. "Maybe we should think about taking some precautions to avoid this happening again."

He raised his eyebrows in question. "Like bars on the windows?" His eyebrows came down again. "I don't like that idea."

"Okay, some type of alarm, something that would make a noise if someone who shouldn't be here, comes in."

"Like a dog?" Now he was smiling.

"Well, that might work, but if we had a dog, I'd want him home with me at night, not here by himself."

"I suppose. Let's think on that."

"How's Hettie?" she asked then.

"She'll be all right. It seems to be in her head. I left her with some tea, and I'll go back later."

"I'll go after we close, Benny."

Soon after, they went through the scenario with Lawrence and his son Graham, who was getting his feet wet preparing to take over as magistrate. Lawrence's mouth formed a grim line; he understood the implications of this situation. "We must determine the best way for you to store your laudanum, Ben. You need it, I understand, but this cannot happen again. Perhaps you could store it in my office for the time being?"

"I could do that. I don't think leaving it at the store would be prudent. We wouldn't want anyone breaking in there," Ben answered, looking at his wife.

"Very well, at the end of your workday, stop by with what you have, and we'll look after it. Sound good?"

Gracie came in while Ben was nailing some boards over the missing window. She had seen Holly and then Lawrence from the store window and wondered what was happening. "Oh dear. I'm glad they waited till there was naebody about."

At the end of the day, that was how each of them felt. Ben brought the fresh bottle of laudanum and the wrapped, jarred resin to Lawrence after work, only holding on to the smaller bottle he kept in his bag. "Thank you, Ben. I must travel to Auburn in the morning. While there, I'll arrange for your window to be replaced. Whenever you need this, you just come back here and Graham or myself will get it for you."

"Thanks, Larry."

Laudanum

Before going home, Charlotte stopped in to check on Hettie. She knocked lightly on her door before pushing it open. "Hettie, how are you feeling?" she asked, sitting on the bed beside her friend.

"Charlotte," Hettie said and forced a smile. "I do feel improved, but I should like to use the chamber pot, if you don't mind."

Charlotte retrieved the pot. "Here you are. While you do that, I'll make some fresh tea."

When she sat down with Hettie a few minutes later, she said, "I hate to see you feeling badly, Hettie. It's the only time you aren't smiling."

"Ah . . . well." Hettie placed her hand over Charlotte's on the bed. "Charlotte, my darling, I seldom have time alone with you anymore. Used to be we'd share tea and talk."

"Yes, before all the children. That a while ago, wasn't it?"

She smiled now. "It was, and I wouldn't change a thing. You and Gracie have raised two beautiful families. I'm happy to have been a part of it. Eli was, too."

"You sound like you're planning to leave us."

"No, but I do know my days are numbered. I'm an old girl, Charlotte." Her friend looked at her in question. "Listen, I've always wondered about ya, never wanted to ask, but if not now, when?" Charlotte raised her eyebrows. "Tell me about *you*, where ya came from, really. I know what you told us, but I also know it wasn't all exactly true."

Charlotte's mouth curled up at one side. She'd always known Hettie was intuitive, but she also had the sense and respect not to stick her nose where it didn't belong. Charlotte loved this woman—she was part of the family. Now old and frail, she asked a question she'd been holding on to for almost twenty-five years. Charlotte squeezed her hand and told her the whole story . . . everything. Coming here from 2012 to save Elizabeth, who they met as Amanda and who later became Carole-Anne. How when she and Ben had gone to visit Jessica, they had returned to 2013, and that when Jessica and Michael came here, they came from 2020. She told her they had come to warn her about Jessie's death. And then, she told Hettie that the mysterious man who had been accused of trying to burn down the schoolhouse was actually Jessica and Michael's son who had come to prevent the fire. She also explained how she "speaks" to Jessica each year on Samhain when they both perform a ritual.

Hettie listened to the whole story. Never interrupting, squinting at times, nodding at others. "Well now, I always knew there was something. I confess, that would not have been my guess. Jeepers." She smiled. "Thank you, Miss Charlotte. I do appreciate you sharing the truth with me."

"I always wanted to. It's just—"

"I understand, hon. I understand. And your secret is safe with me."

Charlotte leaned over and kissed Hettie's cheek. "Well, I'm leaving you with a lot to think about tonight, Hettie."

Hettie chuckled. "That you are."

Charlotte said good night to her friend and promised to check in the next morning.

She and Ben ate at the store that evening with Gracie, Jimmy, and the girls. Evelyn, who was now doing most of the cooking for the store, had prepared an omelette filled with vegetables and ham. "Mmm, this is delicious, Ev!" Charlotte said, licking her lips.

Her niece smiled, pleased with herself.

Laudanum and its effects, both long and short-term, was the main topic of conversation tonight. No one left the table without understanding the importance of controlling the dispensing of the liquid.

Overnight, dark clouds moved in, and during the night, it started to rain. It was around that time that Charlotte's dream became confusing. She was patting Oreo in the dim light of the otherwise empty stable, pressing her forehead to his and speaking softly. Something was moving up her leg, almost slithering. Was it a snake? She looked down and saw only her dress and feet. No, there was a hand slowly caressing her, moving upward. Then something was moving beneath her undergarments. Startled, she jumped, tripping and landing in a heap in the hay. She could hear the rain falling as awareness began to creep in . . . there *was* something touching her—it was his tongue, and he had found just the spot he was looking for.

When Ben came down the stairs in the morning, he found Charlotte at the counter. She turned to offer him a mug of coffee with a suggestive smile.

He smiled back with a glimmer in his eye. "It's still raining."

"It is. I just love the rain, don't you?"

Holly came into the room then. "You may love it, but I don't. It does nasty things to my hair."

Ben laughed, having heard the same complaint from his wife for many years.

They walked down the hill together. "I'll see you in a few minutes, Holly. I'm just going to pop in to check on Hettie."

Charlotte found Hettie pink in the face and sweaty, her breathing raspy and laboured. She made her as comfortable as she could and told her she'd send Ben with something for her chest.

Just before noon, Gracie came into the Doctor's House with dinner for Charlotte, Holly, and herself.

"Gracie! This is a pleasant surprise! And you've come with food—even better," Charlotte said with a wink.

"Auntie Gracie, I was going to come get that. You didn't need to come."

"Och, it's nae bother, lass. Besides, we received a letter from Carole-Anne today. I thought we could have a read while we eat."

"Sounds nice. Let's flip the sign in the door and have a seat." They got comfortable and Gracie opened the letter. It wasn't long, only ten lines. Carole-

Anne had news—Maisie and Sonny were to marry next week. They were planning a church wedding in town; followed by a small celebration on the reservation the next day. Maisie would move into Sonny's home after the wedding. Carole-Anne sounded very excited about it.

"Aww, isn't that lovely? I'll write a wee note to offer our congratulations and wish them the best of luck, will I?" Gracie asked.

"Thanks, Gracie."

By late-afternoon the rain had stopped, and the sun was trying to come out from behind the clouds. "Look, Holly, we won't need to worry about getting wet on the way home."

"Perfect." She walked to the window and peered out. "Oh, here comes Lawrence." She stepped back in time for him to open the door. The bells jingled.

"Hello, Lawrence."

"Good day, ladies. Is Ben in? I'd like to talk to you all."

"I'll get him," Holly said, disappearing into the back.

"Lawrence," Ben said, walking toward the counter. "What brings you in today?"

"Well, I've got news for you."

"Would you like to sit?" Ben asked, offering a chair.

"Gads, no. I've been sitting on a horse all day." He smiled awkwardly. "So, as I told you, I rode up to Auburn this morning. I was about an hour out, when I came upon a horse and cart on the road. When I came up beside them, I looked down into the cart. Inside, lay a man who appeared to be sleeping, and he was soaking with rain. The driver noticed me looking and stopped. I started to identify myself before I realized I knew him. It was Rab Hutchins from Auburn— he's the wainwright on Genesee Road and he was with his apprentice. He told me he'd been sent to collect this man who someone had come across early this morning lying near the road. Long story short, the man was Cuthbert Simmons."

"Was he alive?" Ben asked.

"I'm afraid not. Lying beside him was this." Lawrence reached into his pocket and took out a small corked bottle with a label on it. "This would belong to you, correct?"

Ben and Charlotte looked at each other before Ben answered. "Yes. Is it empty?"

"It is. Is it safe to assume it wasn't when it was taken?"

"It was nearly full," said Ben.

"If he drank all that within a short time—" Charlotte started.

"He will have taken a lethal dose?" Lawrence asked.

"It's likely," Ben replied.

When Charlotte glanced at her daughter, she saw the horror on her face. She put her arm around her back.

Lawrence told them that once they got him back to town, they took him to the doctor. "Doctor Kirby told me he knew the man. Said he'd come to him looking to ease the pain after losing his thumb in an accident. He looked at the man's hand to confirm the story and then, feeling pity for him, gave him enough laudanum to last him a week, trusting him to take the doses himself." He paused, watching Ben and Charlotte exchange a knowing look. "But that's not the end of the story. You see, the reason I went to town was to see a solicitor. While I was entering his office, I bumped into a gentleman whom I heard someone call Doctor Randle. I identified myself and asked if he'd been asked for laudanum recently by anyone. He said, 'As a matter of fact, just two or three days ago. A man came to me, showed me his hand which was missing a thumb, and asked for some laudanum to ease the pain. I did not doubt his pain, but I could tell that the surgery was at least a couple of weeks old and well on its way to being healed. I told him no. He looked agitated, but he didn't argue, just turned and left.'"

"So, he came back here where he knew I had some."

"That is what I would assume, Ben."

"What a shame," Charlotte said under her breath.

While Charlotte and Holly walked home with Ben, they caught him up on Maisie's news. "It's always nice to hear about a wedding. I'm happy for them," he said.

"How old is Maisie, Mum?"

"Um, she'd be twenty-four now."

"Hm-mm. I wonder if I'll be married by the time I'm that age," she said.

"Maybe you will. But trust me, there's no rush, honey," her mother said.

"And there's lots of time between now and then," Ben added. "You're only seventeen."

News spread around town quickly. Everyone had heard about the man who'd been working at the wood mill and lost his thumb. There were whispers outside the church after service as neighbours caught each other up on the latest gossip. Those who hadn't heard what happened to Mr. Cuthbert Simmons now knew what became of him.

Ben, Charlotte, and Holly met the group at the store after church. They were sitting outside to eat before going to see their friends across the lake— Phillip would join them today. All heads turned at the sounds of hooves coming down the path toward the stable.

When the rider came into view, they saw it was Clement Nicholls. Charlotte felt Holly's elbow hit her side. Jimmy stood and said, "Good day, Mr. Nicholls. What brings you here today?"

He tipped his hat to the group and smiled. "Hello everyone. I've come to check on your new foal. Nya must have delivered by now?"

Lily stood, a light blush covering her cheeks. "Come with me, Mr. Nicholls. Let me introduce you to Oreo." Charlotte gave Gracie a wink.

As the two walked toward the stable, he was heard to say, "Please, call me Clement."

Now Charlotte leaned toward Holly and whispered, "You were right. He is handsome."

When they came out of the stable a few minutes later, Gracie invited Clement to join them for his meal. He smiled and did just that. Over dinner, they learned a few things about the man: he was almost finished his apprenticeship, after which time he would be a full-fledged horse doctor; he expected to stay on with and eventually take over for Dr. Roberts; he loved his work; he lived in Auburn; and, in addition to being handsome, he had a good sense of humour.

When it came time for him to return home, Lily walked him out to the road. "Hmm, is she taking her role as horse guardian very seriously, or do we think she might like a certain doctor?" Sandy teased. When Lily returned to the table, she had a new sparkle in her eyes—question answered.

The next morning, Ben set his doctor's bag down by the door while Charlotte poured their coffee. Hearing Gracie's footsteps coming down the stairs, she poured another cup.

"The two o' ye are early this mornin'. Looks to be a lovely day. Thanks, Charlie," Gracie said, taking her cup.

"It does, but it's chilly out there."

"Oh, aye," Ben said with a smirk. "Ye'd best hae on yer woolies if ye plan te go oot."

Charlotte nearly spit her coffee across the table. Gracie raised an eyebrow at him but couldn't do anything else but laugh.

Then they heard the padding of feet running toward the door. Ben, who was standing closest, opened it to see who was out there.

"Ben! Good, you're here. You must come across with me—now!"

Gifted Hands

Running Otter's chest was heaving. He'd rowed hard to get here quickly.

"What is it?" Ben asked, reaching for his coat.

"When she opened her eyes this morning, she could not see."

Charlotte, slipping her arms into her coat, asked, "Will we take two canoes?"

"Yes," Ben answered. "Gracie, if anyone asks for me, I will be back as soon as I can."

"And please tell Holly," added Charlotte.

Gracie nodded. "Aye."

They ran to the canoes. "What else can you tell me, Running Otter?"

"I am not the person to ask. Keen Wolf and Sabel would know better." They climbed in and pushed off.

"Yesterday she had a bad headache," Ben said.

"Yes, and after you left, she went to her bed. Sabel made her the tea you left, but I do not know if it was of any help."

"It could be many things," Ben said. "We need more information."

The remainder of the trip passed in silence, each of them rowing hard.

When they arrived, Sabel greeted them at the door. Keen Wolf sat holding his wife's hand, where she lay in bed.

"Gifted Hands, tell me everything you can," Ben said, bursting into the room.

"Ben, thank you for coming so quickly. Did I hear Charlotte's voice, too?"

"You did. I'm here."

"After everyone left the house, it got worse. I came to my bed. It was like I could feel my pulse here." She brought her fingers to her temples. "My whole head hurt, even my jaw. I was able to sleep for a while, but I awoke in the night, and it was still very sore. I got up to get something to drink, and Keen Wolf lit a candle. When I looked across the room, everything was unclear—things almost seemed to be moving. I remembered when Mabel used to get migraines; sometimes she saw flashes of light or spots. I thought that must be what was happening to me."

Charlotte sat on the bed beside her friend and took her other hand. "Have you eaten anything?"

"Only the tea that Sabel brought me. It might have helped a little. I do not know."

"Gifted Hands also said that the skin hurt on her head where she had her hands," Keen Wolf offered.

"And when you woke this morning, you couldn't see?" Ben asked.

"Nothing at all. Everything is black. Do you think it will come back?"

"If what you have been experiencing is a migraine, then it should, yes. But it sounds like it might be something more. Does anything come to your mind, Charlotte?"

She looked at him, the worry showing in her eyes. "No."

Gifted Hands turned her face toward her friend. "I am scared, Charlotte."

Charlotte squeezed her hand. "We're all here for you, Gifted Hands, and we always will be."

Ben did his best to assess her further. He didn't want to miss anything. When he asked if she had a fever, Charlotte gently touched her friend's forehead. As her fingertips touched the skin, she looked up. "Ben?" She lifted Gifted Hands's hair and saw the blood vessels near her temples bulging slightly. He looked at his wife, wide-eyed.

"Charlotte, let's step outside and see what we can come up with." Once they were alone, he said, "I don't like this." She nodded. "What would cause the blood vessels to swell like that?"

Charlotte had to think. "Um, inflammation in the arteries . . . I would say infection or disease."

"Disease?"

"Do you remember reading about auto-immune diseases?"

"Yes, the body stops or is not able to tell the difference between its own cells and those foreign to it and begins to attack its own normal cells."

"That's right. But could this be an infection?"

"I don't think so, Moxie—she can't see."

"Ben, I want to be optimistic, but if her eyesight has been damaged to this extent, we may be too late to help her."

He took a moment to respond, as his mind covered different possibilities. "If we treat the swollen arteries, she may regain her sight." Charlotte's expression was somber, but she knew they had to try. "White willow bark—she's been taking it, but perhaps we can increase the concentration."

"In the future, this would be treated with corticosteroids, I think. We're unable to do that. We have to think about what we know acts against inflammation. There's white willow, yes, turmeric, and zinc. Herbs high in zinc are thyme, basil, poppy seed, cardamom, celery, and dill seed. There are others, but I need to see my notes at home. You know what else works as an anti-inflammatory, Ben?"

"Your oil."

"Yes."

They started an infusion of white willow bark immediately. "How can we help, Mum?" Sabel asked, coming to stand beside her mother.

"Someone has to go to the Doctor's House."

"I will go," Keen Wolf said.

"No, I will go with Sabel. You stay here," Running Otter said.

Charlotte looked at her daughter and said, "We need the turmeric, ginger, and basil, and my special oil. I keep that locked in the cabinet in the back room—Holly knows. Dad will give you the key."

"You go, I will watch Tehya," Mitenah said from somewhere behind her, "and Swan Song will get a message to Phillip."

Sabel got down on her knees to speak to Tehya while Running Otter bent to speak into his mother's ear. Then they were gone.

Gifted Hands sat up in her bed, sipping a cup of strong white willow tea; the look in her blind eyes was terrified.

Charlotte considered how she would deal with blindness if it happened to her. "I would survive of course, but I think it would take me some time to not be afraid," she said later to Ben.

"Afraid of what?"

"I feel kinda foolish saying it, but . . . I've never been a big fan of the dark. When I was young, it scared me. I used to sleep with a little light in my room, so if I woke up in the night, I would feel safe. I don't know how I'd deal with having to live the rest of my life in the dark."

Gifted Hands was put on a regimen of turmeric, ginger, and basil infusions, and drops of cannabis oil. They stayed with her most of the day, and while she appeared to calm, her headache did not clear, nor did her sight return.

Charlotte and Ben checked on her every morning for the next few days. Keen Wolf answered the door when they arrived Saturday afternoon. It had been five days since Gifted Hands lost her sight.

She was sitting on the settee with a cup of the prescribed tea in her hand and looked up at them. "Good afternoon," she said.

"Chweh'n, Gifted Hands," Charlotte said, hopefulness filling her at the sight of Gifted Hands's smile. "How are you feeling today?"

"My headache has gone. I feel well, although it may have to do with those drops I've been taking," she answered.

"She remains unable to see," Keen Wolf said, answering the real question.

Having seen the approaching canoe, Sabel, Running Otter, and Tehya arrived. Charlotte started some tea steeping and joined the others in the sitting room. Ben started the conversation. "The best way I can explain what I think happened to you, Gifted Hands, is this: for some reason, maybe an infection, maybe you were born with this and it didn't happen until now, I don't know, the blood vessels in your head became inflamed. You felt the pressure inside your head as a terrible headache, but that inflammation also put pressure on the nerves behind your eyes. When this happens, it doesn't take long for those nerves to become damaged to the point where they can no longer function and sight is lost."

"Permanently?" she asked in a weak voice.

"Unfortunately, yes," Ben answered.

With tears in her eyes, Charlotte moved to sit beside her friend, taking her hand and holding it in her lap. "I'm sorry, Gifted Hands. We did our best, but I believe when you woke up Sunday morning and couldn't see, it was already too late."

She nodded, blindly looking past the others in the room. "I understand. I will do what I must. Life will continue. I just won't be able to see it—" Her voice cracked as she broke down in tears.

Tehya came to stand in front of her grandmother and took her other hand. "Don't be sad, Goo-sood. I love you."

In the months that followed, Gifted Hands, having accepted this was how it was going to be, began to adapt to life without sight. In the beginning, she asked for guidance while attempting a task, but gradually became confident and proceeded to the next challenge.

Sabel came to the Doctor's House one afternoon midwinter, surprising her mother. She was looking for some advice on how to treat Tehya's rash. Her father suggested a salve that Charlotte had made.

"How's Gifted Hands doing this week?" Charlotte asked.

Sabel smiled before answering. "She's well. You know, Mitenah told me she walked into their house the other day and found Gifted Hands sitting at her easel with a paintbrush in her hand."

"Get outta here!" Charlotte exclaimed.

"Isn't that something?" Ben added, shaking his head.

"She did say to me, 'If this is to be my life, so be it. Not being able to see will not stop me living.'" Charlotte said. "I don't know if I could be so . . ."

"Strong?" offered Sabel.

"Persistent?" added Ben.

"Yes, both. I admire her courage and determination. She will not let blindness rule her."

"Any word from Robbie yet?" Sabel asked.

"Yesterday," her mother started. "He has found accommodation in a brownstone not far from the hospital and is enjoying his work so far."

"Good for him!" Sabel said.

As the end of winter approached, and everything in town began to melt, they lost Hettie. She had been in relatively good health and was cheery till the end. It was simply age that took her. She had lived and enjoyed her last few months, telling everyone how she felt about them and receiving their love in return. She had lived a good life, thanks to Mabel and Alec. Had they not purchased her and Eli at that slave auction and given them their freedom, they would not have truly lived. She thanked God for their kindness every day.

After learning the truth of Charlotte's adventure, Hettie knew she'd seen and heard it all. She had only been sorry she wasn't able to share it with Eli. Occasionally, when her curiosity got the better of her, she'd asked questions of Charlotte. The first of which was: "When and how does slavery end?"

It was Gracie who found her, and although she was very sad to see her go, she was happy to say that Hettie had passed peacefully with her crochet in her hands and a smile on her face.

Almost as soon as Charlotte closed her eyes, she saw a vision of Jessica. "Jess, it's been a long y—" Her sentence was left unfinished as she looked at the image before her. Usually, Jessica had a glow all around her, but today, it was absent. "Jess?"

Her face crumpled and she dropped her chin to her chest. "It's Michael. He died last month. He was in Calgary on business. He got back to the hotel after a group dinner and shortly after, had a massive heart attack. An associate found him in his room the next morning.

The tears were streaming down Charlotte's face. "Oh, Jess . . . I'm so sorry." Jess blinked hard, trying to hold back the tears. "Were there any signs?"

"Not really. He put on a few pounds over the past few years, but he wasn't overweight. He went to the gym three or four times a week. During his last checkup, the doctor said his blood pressure was a little high—said if he was a few years older, he might order some follow-up tests. They told me that even if paramedics had been called, it was unlikely he would have made it. God, he'd be so pissed off if he knew what happened! He was so young, Char. He still had so much life to live."

"I can't . . ." There were no words. "How's Charlie?"

"Well, he misses his dad, but he's been strong. He's a great support."

"I'm so sorry."

"Thank you. It's been hard, and it's still fresh. When we lost my mom, it felt like a blessing; it was easier to deal with. How is everyone there?"

"Um . . ." Charlotte couldn't remember what else she wanted to say or ask, this news catching her completely off guard. "We're fine. I told you about Gifted Hands?"

"Yes, last year. How is she doing?"

"Quite well. And we lo—" Jess's apparition began to fade. "No, not yet. I love you, Jess," Charlotte said.

Then she was alone in the dark. Her emotions being what they were, it took all of her concentration to take up her circle and ground herself. Then she sat and cried. Visions of Michael, things she hadn't thought of in years, danced through her mind. The first time he asked her out; the first time they'd kissed; the evening he proposed and the night that followed; the day before she left 2012 to come here, when he'd come into her shower; seeing him lying in a casket when he'd died in the car accident that never happened; dancing with him at his wedding to Jessica; his visit here, dressed in nineteenth century clothing and collecting fountain pens . . . *Poor Michael. He deserved so much better.*

When Ben saw his wife's face, he jumped up from his seat. "What's happened?"

The tears started all over again.

The Baker

It took some time, months in fact, to shake the sadness that lingered within Charlotte. Michael dying so young was a shock, and knowing she couldn't be there for Jessica ripped at her heart. She was glad that she and Charlie had each other.

That winter was relatively uneventful. The Williams family spent their evenings reading, playing cards, or doing puzzles by the wood-burning stove. Holly took some time to paint, and Jimmy took some of her works with him to Auburn, to sell at the general store there.

The family had seen Clement Nicholls several times over the past few months. What started as "visits to check on the new foal" became what they really were—visits to see Lily. He usually came on a Saturday or Sunday afternoon and usually sent a note earlier in the week to let her know. They always started their visit in the stable with the horses. In the stable is where he stole his first kiss and where he said, "Lily, I find myself thinking of you at all times of the day. I realize we cannot see each other every day for now, but I hope that will change in the future." She looked up at him, feeling butterflies at his words. "I wonder, when I think about you, or when I talk about you, can I call you my sweetheart?"

A smile spread across her lips. "I wish you would, Dr. Nicholls." And then she kissed him.

When she told her family at supper that night, her cheeks were pink, and her eyes were bright. "Happy New Year to me!"

"When will you meet his folks?" Sandy asked.

"Will you put on a dress that day?" Evelyn asked cheekily.

Lily shot her a look and then laughed. "I imagine I will, but he has said he likes how I look in breeks."

"Oo-oo," the girls teased in unison.

"Och, that's lovely, lass," Gracie said, setting her hand over Lily's on the table.

Some weeks later, on a bitterly cold afternoon, Holly walked to the store to get some warm soup and food for herself and her mother. She stood on the road opposite the store, waiting for the oncoming coach to pass. It was the regular coach that ran through town several times a week. As it passed, something that had been secured to the back rack broke free and fell to the ground. Of course, the driver had no way of knowing it had happened, so he didn't slow down. Holly saw it and started jumping up and down, waving her arms. When it didn't look like the coach was going to stop, she bent and scooped it up, and went straight into the store to stand by the wood-burning stove.

"Hello, lass. It's bloody cold out there teday."

"Yes, it is, Auntie Gracie."

"What happened out there?" Gracie asked. "It looked like ye were jumpin' around flappin' yer wings!"

"I was." Holly laughed and slipped her hat and hood off her head. "A parcel fell off the coach as it passed. I was trying to get the driver to see me. Of course, he was looking the wrong way!" Gracie nodded. "Well, I picked it up." She showed her aunt the bundle in her hands.

"Oh dear. What a shame. I—"

Then bells over the door jingled, and in came a man neither recognized. "Hello," he started, looking from Gracie to Holly. "If you'll excuse me. I couldn't help but notice you bouncing around when the coach rode by. You wouldn't have been waving at me, would you?" The question was directed at Holly, but he flicked his eyes to Gracie and offered a wink.

Holly smiled. "I was, well, maybe not *you*, but I was waving." She liked the way he teased her.

"Might I ask why?"

"Well, this fell off the coach as it passed." She showed him the bundle.

"Oh, thank goodness you saw it." His cheeks pinked. "That's mine. It was tied in with a bigger bundle; I wonder how it got separated." He shook his head. "I was bringing it home for my grandmother."

"Were you now?" Holly said suspiciously.

He glanced at Gracie again, looking for his next words. Feeling it was safe to return to her counter, she left them to talk.

"You don't believe me?" he asked with a smirk. "If I tell you what it is, will you believe me?"

"I suppose I'll have to—if you can tell me." Holly smiled, surprised to hear herself flirting—she had no idea she knew how.

"Where are my manners? My name is Owen, Owen Rogers. And you are?"

"I'm Holly."

"It's good to meet you, Holly. If I'm honest, when I saw you on the side of the road, I thought you looked pretty. I was watching you as we passed and when you started to jump and wave, I knocked for the driver to stop. I guess, in a way, you *were* trying to get my attention."

She blushed and felt silly. "So, what is in the parcel?" she asked him.

"It's a small painting I found in Auburn on my way south."

"A painting? Of what?"

"It's flowers; a garden with a stone wall behind it." She felt her smile fade. "Is there something wrong?"

Holly began to unwrap the painting, which had been carefully rolled and wrapped in cloth. She recognized it even before it was unrolled. It was her mother's garden at the Doctor's House. She'd painted it last summer. She wasn't sure what to answer, or if she should tell him.

"Am I correct? Will you allow me to take back my painting?"

After a momentary pause, she answered, "I will. And, because I like you, I will give you this one to go with it." She reached to where Gracie had the painting behind the counter. "They are of the same garden."

His eyebrows came down. He had no idea how that could be. "How do you know that? Did y—"

She smiled. "I did. Please, take this one as well. Give your grandmother the set."

Just then, the bells rang out again and in came the coach driver. "If you'll excuse me, Mr. Rogers, we are waiting."

Owen's mouth tightened into a line. He didn't want to leave. He grudgingly replied, "I'll be there straight away." Looking at Holly he asked. "Do you work here? Can I come back so we can finish this conversation?" He raised his eyebrows, eager to hear yes.

She smiled. "I work at the Doctor's House, just there." She pointed down the road.

"Saturday?"

"Yes." She blushed. "After two o'clock."

"Brilliant!" He rolled the second painting around the first and headed for the door. "I'll see you Saturday."

She turned to see her aunt watching from her counter with a huge smile on her face. "That appeared to go well, lass."

"It did, didn't it?" She walked straight through to the kitchen. Evelyn *had* to know about this!

After Holly came back to the store the other day and told her mother all about meeting Owen, Charlotte wondered how she would make it to Saturday. Holly was more excited than she'd ever been over a boy, well, a man.

Gracie had described the meeting to Charlotte as well. Her best guess put Owen at approximately twenty-four years of age—around five years older than Holly. That made her parents leery. He will have experienced much more of life than Holly, who was still quite innocent in the area of romance. Gracie also said in the short time she saw him, he struck her as "the honest sort", which Charlotte supposed was a good thing. She would form her own opinion soon enough.

When the clock struck two Saturday afternoon, the bells rang at the Doctor's House. Holly was nervous, but she looked toward the door with a smile. It was him. "Hello," she said. She turned to her mother and said, "Mum, I'd like you to meet Owen."

Charlotte stretched out her hand to shake his. "It's nice to meet you, Owen. I'm Charlotte." He smiled at her nervously. *I like him.* Just like that, she felt her daughter was with a good person. Ben came out from the back with Lenny, and Holly blushed. "Dad, this is Owen. Owen, this is my dad, Ben Williams, and his friend Lenny."

"Good to meet you, Owen . . .?" Ben asked.

"Rogers, sir. Owen Rogers."

After the formalities, Ben and Lenny headed for the wood mill. Charlotte looked at the young pair in front of her and asked, "So, what will the two of you be doing this afternoon?"

"Actually, if you can tell me where I can leave Lacey, I thought Holly could take me for a walk." He looked at her then.

"Very good. Enjoy yourselves. See you in time for supper, Holly."

She nodded at her mother. "Come on. Let's go see my cousin Lily. She probably won't mind if we leave Lacey with her. Bye, Mum."

"Goodbye, Mrs. Williams. It was nice to meet you."

Once they'd gone, Charlotte felt a familiar happiness. Watching them, new to each other, nervous yet eager to know more, possibly at the beginning of something very special. It made her feel warm and fuzzy.

Charlotte was setting the supper table when she heard their footsteps on the porch. She considered inviting him in for his meal, but thought it might be too much for one day. Holly came in the door alone. Her cheeks were rosy with the cold, eyes sparkling with happiness. She closed the door and leaned back on it taking a deep breath.

Her mother asked, "I take it you enjoyed yourself?"

Snapping out of it, Holly slipped out of her coat and hat. "I did. He's very nice and funny, too."

Over supper, she told them about her walk around town with Owen. "He lives between Aurelius and Auburn in a house with his grandmother. Both of his parents passed when he was very young, so his grandmother brought him up. He works as a baker—says he's very good at it, too." She paused and smiled.

"Where was he coming from when you met him?" Ben asked.

"He said he was in Moravia talking to the owner of a bakery there."

"And the paintings he took home?" Charlotte asked.

"He said she loved them! He's going to make frames for them."

While visiting their friends the next day, Charlotte told Gifted Hands about Holly meeting Owen and their subsequent walk together.

"Holly hasn't been interested in anyone before, has she?"

"No, this is a first, and she's very happy about it."

"I'm happy for her." Gifted Hands set her coffee cup on the table. "Before I forget, I wanted to tell you about a dream I had yesterday. I was sitting here with the three of you, only I could see. Sabel and Running Otter came in and joined us." She smiled brightly. "They had news to share—good news." Her words were cut short as they heard a quick knock and the door opened. "Is that them?" she whispered.

"Yes," Charlotte whispered in return.

"Chweh'n," Sabel said to the room.

"Is Tehya not with you today?" Charlotte asked.

"No. Mitenah has the little ones for a while today. How are you?" Sabel asked, leaning down to kiss her mother's cheek.

"Good. A little suspicious though," Charlotte said, squinting at her daughter.

"Oh?" Sabel asked, innocently. "Well, I'm not up to anything, but I do have something to tell you." She looked at her husband and smiled before continuing. "We're expecting again. I believe it will be June. I feel really good about it this time."

"Oh, honey, that's wonderful. Congratulations," Charlotte said, jumping up to hug her daughter and then Running Otter.

She hoped with all her heart that Sabel's feelings were right. These two deserved it.

After a quick visit, they left to pick up Tehya.

Ben said, "Gifted Hands, it would seem that your gift has not left you." Gifted Hands had had the gift of second sight for as long as she could remember. She would sometimes see an event that would happen in the future or one that was happening right now, somewhere else. It was by no means a regular occurrence, but it happened now and again.

"Yes. Thankfully, my sight has not deserted me completely."

"Do you think it helps you to navigate a life that you can't see?" Charlotte asked.

"I do, yes."

As they snowshoed home, Ben and Charlotte discussed Sabel's news before moving on to the topic of Gifted Hands. Ben was quiet for a moment before he said, "You know, every once in a while, I think about Gifted Hands seeing the future." He paused a moment. "I often wonder how many things she saw she never told us about. I guess I'll never know unless I ask her."

"And will you?" she asked.

"Probably not. If she saw something that affected us and didn't tell us, then she felt it best to keep it to herself. I trust her judgement."

She turned and looked up at him. "But it would be neat to know," she said, raising her eyebrows and smiling guiltily.

He looked at her expression and smiled, thinking, *She looks as beautiful as ever,* and then, *Oh, the things I want to do to her. I wonder if there's anyone at home . . .*

Watching thoughts cross his mind, she asked, "What?"

"Will Holly be home when we get there?" His eyes twinkled.

Ignoring him, she said, "Gracie came in this afternoon. We got a letter from Carole-Anne today, Benny."

"Oh?" He waited; he could tell there was something coming by the look in her eyes.

"Maisie and Sonny are expecting a baby in June. Isn't that a fun coincidence?"

"It is." He smiled at his wife. "Do you remember when we learned you were expecting Sabel?"

"I do. When we got home from 2013. I did a test that night while Gracie and Jimmy were with us." She smiled. "It's exciting news to learn there's a baby growing inside you. I'm almost sad that I'll never do it again." Ben squinted in thought as he looked at her. "I remember making her, too, after Jess's wedding. Oo-oh, that dress . . . those shoes . . . your lips." Ben stood from his seat on the settee, stretching his hand out toward her. He pulled her in for a very seductive kiss, one that led his tongue and teeth over her neck and collarbone. Then he ushered her upstairs and onto their bed.

"I don't know how long we have before Holly gets home, Benny." She gasped as his tongue began to work its magic.

When Holly arrived home an hour later, Charlotte was setting the table for their supper, and Ben was stoking the fire. "What have you two been up to since you got home?" she asked.

"Just getting things ready for supper, love," Charlotte answered, flicking her eyes in Ben's direction. He smiled at the blush on her cheeks.

As the weather warmed and spring arrived, any fears Sabel may have entertained about her pregnancy faded. Her belly had grown round and heavy—she and Running Otter were ecstatic. Tehya, now almost seven, was, too. She liked to sit with her mother before bed and rest her hand on her tummy. When the baby kicked, Tehya would giggle and clap her hands. She was counting the days to meet her little brother or sister.

Sabel and Maisie had written back and forth several times, comparing notes about swollen feet, achy legs, and forgetfulness. They shared their dreams of baby girls and boys, of names, and of all the things that would change once the babies had arrived. Maisie told her that Carole-Anne planned to come and stay for a while after the birth, to help out while Maisie got her strength back. Sabel was happy to hear that; she knew having her mother and Gifted Hands so close after the birth of Tehya, was both helpful and reassuring.

Then came a day in June when Running Otter rowed across the lake to fetch Charlotte, Ben, and Gracie. "It is time," he said nervously.

Strawberry Tarts

For Lily, the past several months had been delightful. Clement visited on a regular basis, generally three weekends out of four. His work kept him busy as Dr. Rogers began to give him more control in preparation for the day he would hang up his horseshoes.

It was an afternoon in early May when the two of them approached her parents. "Clement, are ye gettin' ready te make the ride back home?"

"I am," he answered with a smile. "Before I go though, I wanted to ask you something, if you don't mind. My parents have heard all about Lily and would like to meet her. They have invited her to come up for supper next Saturday and stay the night."

He waited nervously, as Gracie looked at her husband for a long moment. Jimmy cleared his throat before speaking. "I think that sounds very nice." He looked at his daughter then. "I assume ye'd like to go?"

"Da!" she said, blushing.

"Well then, I suppose that'd be fine."

"Wonderful," Clement said and turned to Lily. "I will be here for you at noon."

"Lovely, ye can share dinner wi' us afore ye leave," Gracie added.

The idea thrilled Lily. She knew it meant he truly cared for her, but it also scared her. "What if they don't like me?" she asked him.

He put his arms around her and said, "That's impossible."

After a fun but exhausting couple of days, Lily sat down to dinner with her family. "It's been a while since we've had Sunday supper just us," she said.

"Aye, it has, but I'm glad we planned it this way. Now ye can tell us about yer time wi' Clement and his family, privately."

"Well, his mother is quite the church bell. She seems nice enough, but between all her questions about us, she shared all the town folks' gossip. I felt the need to watch what I said, thinkin' she might repeat it." Gracie nodded. "As you know, they own several horses. His father works with them, much like Eli used to do."

"Ye mean like you do," Jimmy pointed out.

"Yes. He's a quiet sort of man, but he takes it all in. They already knew that's what I do—he'd told them—so they asked how I enjoyed the work. I told them I love it! I didn't really know what to say about it, so I told them about Eli, and how I learned a lot from him and Da—how I was there as Nya delivered Oreo and how I worked to teach Oreo the things we wanted him to learn."

"I'm sure they could see yer enthusiasm, love. Yer eyes light up every time ye talk about the horses."

"Clement told me that, too."

"Was his brother or sister there?"

"No, they moved away some time ago when they married. I suppose I may meet them one day." That said, she blushed fiercely.

Over those same months, Holly had regular visits by Owen. His work as a baker allowed him only Sundays off, so he came Saturday evenings and stayed the night in Phillip's old room. His grandmother could manage on her own for one night and was happy to see him smitten as he was. He was considerate, so Charlotte and Ben had no issue when this became a habit. He was crazy about her, there was no doubting it. They had fun, enjoyed each other's company, and talked about everything under the sun. One weekend, the two of them made one of his favourite bread recipes and some muffins. He was good at what he did, and when Charlotte overheard them working together, she thought he was a good teacher, too. When he left them last, it was with a promise: "Next weekend, we will make strawberry tarts."

All week, Ben talked about the strawberry tarts he was looking forward to. When he was out of hearing range, Charlotte whispered to Holly, "Maybe next time Owen won't give your father something so tasty to look forward to?"

Holly quickly agreed. "I'll ask him to keep it to himself." She giggled.

"What's so funny?" Ben asked, coming back into the room.

"Oh, nothing," his wife answered with a grin.

After closing the Doctor's House for the weekend, Charlotte and Ben were sitting out behind the general store, sharing some tea with Gracie. "Mmm, tonight they're making strawberry tarts. I'm looking forward to those," Ben said, licking his lips.

Charlotte smirked while Gracie whacked his shoulder. "Och, they're not a' for you, lad. Mind that."

He did his best to look hurt. "But . . . Oh, look." He pointed to the water and the approaching canoe.

Running Otter rowed up with Tehya. She jumped out of the canoe and ran up toward them. "Mommy says it's time to meet the baby!" She was excited as she reached up to grab Charlotte's hand. "Come, Grama, we have to go!"

Running Otter came up behind her. "She says she is sure this time."

Ben had already retrieved his bag, and Gracie was telling the others where they were going. From the kitchen, Evelyn shouted, "Give her my good wishes."

"Mine, too!" Lily called from the stable.

Jessica's concerned voice reached out from beyond. "Charlie, are you there?"

"I'm here, Jess. I'm here. How are you?"

"I thought I might have missed a step. I wasn't sure I'd find you."

"How are you?" Charlotte repeated.

"I'm fine. I mean, most of the time."

"You miss him . . ."

Charlotte could see the tears spring to Jessica's eyes. "I really do. Life just seems to be a mess without him here."

"And Charlie? How is he? How's school?"

She smiled then. "Charlie is wonderful. We just celebrated his eighteenth birthday. He can be a handful. Sometimes he's moody, and I don't know the best way to deal with it. Michael wasn't like that, you know? He has everything ready to apply to a few universities. He thinks he wants to take physics."

"And work?"

"Well, I've reduced my hours. I don't have the drive anymore. It all just feels like a lot. Michael says I shouldn't worry so much."

"You mean Charlie?"

"Oh, yes. Did I say Michael?" She shook her head.

"What are you worried about, Jess?"

She looked at Charlotte, eyes wide and wet with unshed tears, and said, "My senses, my priorities, what I'll do with myself if Charlie goes away to school."

"Aww, Jess. You've always been a strong, sensible woman; you'll be fine. Charlie's right, try not to worry so much."

"And what is your news?"

"Sabel and Running Otter had a little boy in June. They named him Tuari. It means Young Eagle. And guess what? Maisie had her first baby in June, too. They've called her Annora Elizabeth. I guess you know the names of all her babies already." She smiled. "Holly has met a young man named Owen. He lives a few hours from here, but comes to see her as much as he can. They're cute together. Phillip . . ." Their space between the shadows began to blur, time was almost up.

"You didn't get to finish, Char. I'm sorry."

Charlotte smiled at her friend. "Next time, Je—"

And just like that, Jess was gone.

It was all Charlotte could do to finish taking up her circle and ground herself. Then the tears came. Jess was not in a good place right now, and her best friend could do nothing to help.

By the third week of December, the lake had frozen. Winter had come early. Of course, they always took precautions to be sure that crossing was safe. No one wanted anyone to go through the ice. They still crossed wearing snowshoes or using their kick-sleds most of the time. And they still crossed the lake every other week or so.

This year, Gracie and Jimmy hosted a Yule celebration. Those who couldn't be with them on Christmas day would join in the festivities. Gifted Hands and Keen Wolf were there. A pregnant Mitenah and Swan Song came with Falling Leaf. Sabel and Running Otter came with the children. Charlotte and Ben were there. Phillip came and stayed a few days with his family. Holly came with Owen. And all the Moffatts were there, and that included Lily and Clement. The only one missing was Dark Wolf.

Holly introduced Owen to the Tuscarora, who had, until now, only heard about him. Phillip, she learned, had met Owen once or twice while doing business in his area of town. She'd asked her parents if it would be all right for him to join them on this day. As much as he would have liked to share Christmas with them, too, he did not want to leave his grandmother, and she was no longer up to travelling. He had a generous heart, and when you met him, you just knew that. They were the kind of young couple you knew would be together, but seemed to understand they had time; in the coming months, or maybe years, they would be together.

Before everyone took a seat, Gracie raised her glass. "Boy, we have grown into a big, lovely group." She paused and smiled before continuing. "This is the time of year for counting all our blessings. You are mine, and I thank ye."

Jimmy, now standing beside her, added, "Aye. Keep a warm heart and spread that joy and cheer around ye."

The evening was cold, but as Jimmy had wished, their hearts were warm. When it came time for the Tuscarora to head home, Gifted Hands found Gracie and Charlotte. "The two of you have been the best of friends for many years. Thank you, I love you both. I hope your Christmas celebration is as wonderful as today's." She hugged one and then the other. "Best wishes to all for the coming year."

With a tear in her eye, Charlotte hugged her friend. "And to your beautiful family as well. Let's make 1846 the best yet!"

"Wait! Let's not wish each other a happy New Year now! Why don't you all come to our home to celebrate this year?" Sabel blurted out excitedly. She looked at her husband then, realizing she hadn't given him a chance to have an opinion. He smiled, looking so like his father, and nodded.

Gifted Hands added. "A wonderful idea. Between your house and ours, there is plenty of room for those who would like to sleep there."

Charlotte was the first to reply. "I'm in!"

"Aye! Us, too," said Gracie.

"Excellent! Everyone who would like, can come over after supper on New Year's Eve. We'll do the rest."

Charlotte had invited Owen to stay the night at the house; he could ride home in the morning. He was a gracious guest. When Charlotte came down in the morning, she found the fire roaring in the stove and the water on for coffee. In addition, he had brought some biscuits for their breakfast that he'd made before leaving home.

"Mmm," Charlotte said after sinking her teeth into one. "These are delicious, Owen."

"I'm glad you're enjoying them. Thank you for a lovely evening."

Holly beamed at him. He tossed her a quick wink.

To the delight of his family, Robbie arrived home the day before Christmas Eve. Once Robbie settled into his old room, he handed Ben a bottle of whiskey he had brought from New York.

Christmas supper was held at Charlotte and Ben's. All the Moffatts and the Williams, minus Sabel, were in attendance. Holly was sad not to have Owen there, but she understood he didn't want to leave his grandmother, and as much as she would have liked to be with them, Holly didn't want to be without her family on Christmas day.

Ben watched his wife prepare supper. She was delighted to have both her boys at home for a few days. She missed Sabel, but they had spent a good amount of family time together, and it had been fun. Charlotte positively shone.

As everyone took a seat and filled their plates, Charlotte and Ben stood for a toast.

Charlotte started. "Christmas is a time to feel the magic in the air and to touch every heart with love."

Ben continued. "We are very happy to share this day with you all. We wish you all a Merry Christmas."

The conversation over supper varied, but much of it focused on Robbie, since he'd been away for so long. "Tell us, Robbie, have you met anyone?" Sandy asked, broaching the topic.

He smiled shyly at his cousin. "No, I haven't. I haven't been looking though. Work keeps me busy."

"Aye, but ye've got to live a little, too, lad," his aunt added.

"I do, Auntie, I do. I have mates I spend time with. We have fun together. That's good for me for the time being."

"You're not getting any younger, Robbie," came Holly's voice. The room broke into laughter. "I'm not joking. He's what . . . going on twenty-eight years. Do you not think this important? While you're still young and handsome?"

"Holly, I appreciate you don't want me to be lonely," he said, and she raised her eyebrows. "Right, but I am happy. Maybe not every person enjoys having someone else around all the time. Or maybe, I don't want an attachment because I want more than one. Who can tell me either of those feelings is wrong?"

Holly's mouth formed into a line. Then, she said, "I understand what you're saying, I just . . . I guess I don't like to think of you alone."

He gave her a warm smile. "Thank you, but please don't worry. I'm a big boy. I have friends, and I know where to find company if I want some." Charlotte thought he sounded much like Ben when they first met.

Charlotte and Ben made eye contact across the table. Robbie was clearly ready for an end to this conversation. "What about you, Sandy?" Phillip said from out of nowhere. "You started this conversation. Have you not met someone you'd like to spend more time with?"

"Nope. You?"

"Well, no, not yet. I don't feel rushed. It will happen when it happens. Am I right?" At this, he looked from mother to father. Both smiled.

"Right," Charlotte agreed.

From there, the conversation changed—work, friends, weather, horses. As she offered dessert, Charlotte asked what everyone's wishes were for the coming year—they all had them.

Winter

With the celebrations over, life naturally returned to normal. Ben had several slip and fall injuries to deal with, due to the ice and snow. There were strained muscles, cuts and bruises, and broken bones, as well as numerous cases of chest congestion/bronchitis/pneumonia. On those occasions, when Ben would have to visit someone's house, Holly accompanied him, while Charlotte tended to everything apothecary/medicine related.

One dark evening, as they walked home from work, Charlotte's foot slipped on some unseen ice. She was glad she'd taken Ben's arm. She said, "When it's like this, I worry about Gifted Hands walking around outside on her own. She could easily slip and hurt herself. It's dangerous enough to walk around when you *can* see the slippery ground. I know she goes outside on her own sometimes."

Smiling, Ben said, "I don't think you need to worry, Moxie. You know Keen Wolf would never let anything happen to her." He led her off the path, into the trees slightly as they talked.

"I know, but she has been known to go off and do things on her own that make the rest of us worry."

"Well . . ." Ben bent quickly and scooped a handful of snow. The look he gave her then made her heart skip a beat. "I'll give you to the count of five."

She ran toward the biggest tree she could see, scooping some snow on the way, quickly forming a snowball. When she peeked around the trunk, a snowball hit her shoulder. She looked at him in momentary shock. Then she smiled a mischievous grin and lobbed one at him. It caught him in the chin. *Déjà-vu.* She bent to make another.

When she straightened up, he was there, his doctor's bag on the ground somewhere behind him. Before she could lift her arm, he grabbed her wrists and leaned into her ear. "Do you remember how this ended last time?"

She smiled innocently. "Last time and every other time."

His lips were cold as they landed on hers and so were his hands as they reached around her back, still holding her wrists. She pulled them free and brought her hands to the buttons of his coat, opening it, and spreading her fingers across his back. His hands were already inside her coat, smoothing over her curves.

Charlotte felt her blood heat. "Benny," she said breathlessly into his mouth. Hearing the passion in her voice, he immediately began fumbling to lift the bottom of her dress. "Here?" she asked, as his lips nipped at her throat. She reached for the front of his breeks, surprised at the strength of his reaction.

He didn't answer, instead he bent slightly at the knees, taking himself in his hand long enough to find her. She gasped, wrapping her legs around him under his coat, while his hands supported her weight. Her arms wrapped around his neck and she kissed him thoroughly, feeling every inch of him deep inside her.

She moaned softly, finishing just after him. "I feel like a young woman again. It's been years since we've done that," she said as she smoothed her dress and buttoned her coat.

"You're still a young woman, Moxie."

"I'm fifty now, Benny. That's far from young."

He took her hand, and they started walking again. "It's far from old, too. You're just past halfway—there's still lots of time for that sort of thing." He smiled then; he couldn't see it, but he knew there was a blush spreading across her already rosy cheeks.

Holly, who'd left early today to start supper, greeted them when they arrived home. "It's a cold evening. I'll bet you're happy to be back by the fire," she said, setting the supper plates on the table.

"It is. Spring can't come soon enough this year. Thanks, love."

There was one wonderful thing that happened on a cold, snowy February morning—Mitenah gave birth to a healthy baby girl. She had done her best not to share her fears about this pregnancy after witnessing Sabel's two miscarriages and taking so long to become pregnant herself. But now, she was overjoyed, as was Swan Song. Her mother and Sabel were with her as she delivered, and Ben and Charlotte arrived shortly after, just as the sun was rising.

Swan Song opened the curtains to see a spectacular scene—the sun peeking through the soft, falling snow. He immediately shared the scene with Mitenah. She took her mother's hand and said, "The sun is rising, En-ay, and it is shining through the snow as it falls. It is beautiful." Charlotte watched them, wishing Gifted Hands could see the snow and the face of her little granddaughter. "Let us name our daughter Kaneihtio," Mitenah said.

"That is lovely, Mitenah," Gifted Hands said with tears in her eyes.

"Ka-nieh-tee-yo," Charlotte said. "What does that mean?"

"It means beautiful snow," Gifted Hands answered softly as Keen Wolf put his arm around her shoulders.

There were a couple of particularly cold weekends in February and March when the usual Sunday visits with their friends were cancelled—*that's* how cold it was. Last weekend had been one of those.

The cold didn't stop Owen from coming to see Holly, though. He couldn't get enough of her. When he had a quiet moment with Charlotte and Ben, he paled and asked, "I wonder, could I have your permission to take Holly up to meet my grandmother when the weather is more agreeable?"

They looked at each other briefly before Ben answered. "Owen, I think that would be fine. Just so long as we know where you'll be and when you'll return."

"Oh, and—" Charlotte started.

Blushing fiercely, he interrupted. "You need not worry about your daughter's innocence. We have spoken about it, and we will wait."

Charlotte smiled at him. "That's good to know, and I do trust you both to do what's best. But what I was going to say was, I'd like to send something for your grandmother when the time comes."

Charlotte smiled inwardly as an embarrassed Owen looked around the room, wishing Holly back.

To everyone's delight, as the end of March approached, so did warmer temperatures. Charlotte, Ben, and Holly, along with Gracie, Jimmy, and the girls, looked forward to a trip across the frozen lake on Sunday. It had been a couple of weeks since they'd all been together, and they knew that with temperatures rising, the lake would begin to thaw. It could be a while before they could cross again.

"Go on up to bed, Benny. I'll be right up. I just want to set out a couple of things to take over tomorrow. I don't want to forget them," Charlotte said before looking out the serving dish and fork that belonged to Gifted Hands.

The night air was cool. After setting Gifted Hands's things by the door, Charlotte ran up the stairs and into bed, where she knew it would be nice and warm.

She was right. Her man was waiting for her, and he was ready to go. She managed to get out of her dress, but her shift didn't make it to the floor. It got pushed up as she was completely and thoroughly ravaged by her husband.

The morning air had a chill in it, and Charlotte put her arm over Ben's side, cuddling behind him, trying to share his warmth. *Why didn't I put on my warm night dress before going to sleep? Because I was too cozy and lazy, that's why.*

"Your skin feels cold, Moxie," he said, and then, "My God, I can feel your nipples on my back." He rolled over, immediately sucking one into his mouth. "Mmm, doesn't that feel better?" he whispered, before finding the other.

She could feel his morning readiness on her thigh as she arched her chest upward, looking for more suckling. She found it . . . and much, much more.

Sometime later, and now wearing her housecoat, Charlotte started their morning coffee while Ben stoked the fire. When he looked up, she saw that glimmer in his eye, the one that said, "I could do that all day."

She was smiling back at him when Holly came down the stairs. "Good morning, parents."

"Good morning, love. I'm just starting breakfast. Are you hungry?"

"Yes." She came to sit at the table and looked at her mother. "We're going across today, right?"

"We are. Why?"

"I want you to ask me questions about herbs on the walk over. I'd like to get faster at suggesting teas when someone asks."

Her father winked and said, "You'll be faster before you know it."

"I hope so. It seems so easy for Mum and Sabel. I want it to be like that for me, too."

Charlotte set a muffin down on the table in front of Holly and returned to the counter. There was a knock on the door as she picked up two hot cups of coffee. Ben answered it. "Running Otter, I di—" He didn't finish the word. "What is it?"

Running Otter looked from him to Charlotte. "It's En-ay . . ."

Just another Sunday

Charlotte saw Running Otter's expression, and the two cups she was holding crashed down onto the floor, hot coffee splashing up on her ankles. She didn't feel the burning.

"Keen Wolf came to us not long ago. He looked very pale, and he spoke quietly. He told us that when he awoke this morning, she was gone. She died in her sleep."

"What?" she heard the shock in her own faraway voice. Charlotte's tears overflowed before she could think straight. She threw her arms around Running Otter, crying.

Holly looked up at her with dark, wet eyes. Returning to where her daughter sat, Charlotte took her hand.

There was silence for a moment, before Ben asked, "Have you seen Gracie or Jim yet?" Running Otter shook his head. "And Sabel?"

"She is with Keen Wolf and the children. She was going to Mitenah's while I came here."

Ben started for the stairs. "We will dress quickly, then we'll go. Will you tell Gracie before you leave?"

"Can I come with you, Mum?" Holly asked as they headed upstairs.

"Of course, honey. This may be your only chance to say goodbye." Her voice cracked as she said the words.

"What about Phillip?" Holly asked.

Charlotte looked at her husband. "We'll have to get a message to him."

"I'll have to look at your ankles before we go; that coffee was hot," Ben said.

They arrived at Gifted Hands's home just after Gracie, Jimmy, and the girls. The house was full of her family and friends. Charlotte made eye contact with

Gracie as she looked for Keen Wolf, her burnt and bandaged ankles the last thing on her mind.

She hugged him. "Oh, Keen Wolf, I'm so sorry." She stepped back and wiped away her tears. "Do you have any idea what happened? Was she well yesterday?" she asked as Ben came to stand beside her.

He looked back at her, his dark eyes reflecting his profound sadness. "She was well, yes. When we went to our bed, she said she had a headache and hoped it would be gone in the morning."

"Can we see her?" As she asked, someone tapped her shoulder. She turned to see Running Otter.

"I have asked a neighbour to take a message to Phillip," he said with a nod.

"Thank you."

"Come with me," Keen Wolf said, and walked with them to the bedroom. Charlotte looked for Holly, signaling her to join them. When they stepped into the room, they saw Gifted Hands lying in her bed, blankets covering her body. Holly immediately grabbed onto her mother, hugging her hard and crying.

"She's at peace, sweetheart," Charlotte said softly, rubbing her daughter's back. Holly stepped away from her then and walked to the bedside. Her parents looked on as she kissed her fingertips and gently placed them on Gifted Hands's cheek, whispering goodbye.

After Holly left the room, Charlotte sat on the bed beside her friend, taking her hand. Ben stood solemnly behind her, beside Keen Wolf. "My dear friend, I don't"—her voice cracked—"I don't understand what happened, I wish I did, but I know that you have left us for a better place. I miss you so much already. I hope you felt no pain as you left us and that you are in a place where your spirit can soar." She took several moments to regain herself. "Thank you for your friendship all these years—for all the wonderful memories—and thank you for your love. I love you, Gifted Hands, always." Then she leaned forward and tenderly kissed her friend's cheek, before lying her hand back down on the blanket and standing.

Charlotte wiped her tears as she stood up beside Keen Wolf. She hooked her arm through his and leaned her head on his shoulder while Ben bent to say a few words to Gifted Hands.

Back out in the sitting room, Charlotte found Mitenah, who stood holding her infant daughter, and hugged her, expressing her condolences. Mitenah stood quietly, eyes wide and unsettled. "Thank you, Charlotte." She blinked twice before adding, "What will we do without her?"

"It will be difficult, but we have each other, sweetheart. Remember, we are always here for you."

Next, Charlotte found Gracie, who was standing with her girls and Sabel, eyes full of tears. "Oh, Charlie," she said and shook her head. "The poor lass. I hope she's in a beautiful place."

"She has to be, Gracie. She earned it." As she looked around the open space, she could see that Gifted Hands had left the plates and cutlery stacked on the counter for today's visit, the pots sitting beside them. Charlotte crumpled then, tears flowing freely, sobs racking through her.

The younger children went to play outside, supervised by Swan Song, while the rest of the mourners spoke in low voices about their friend. It was during this time that Phillip arrived. When he came in, he looked for his mother first. She told him what she could and went with him to see Gifted Hands. When they came out of the bedroom, Phillip found Running Otter and Mitenah before settling into conversation with Holly.

Charlotte kept her eye on Keen Wolf, hoping that he would deal with this as he did with everything life dealt him. The last time he had been forced to deal with such grief, it was his brother Straight Arrow who had died, and it was Gifted Hands he mourned with. Now he had his family to lean on: Running Otter and Sabel, and Mitenah and Swan Song. Dark Wolf would have no way to know until a message could find him. However, no one knew exactly where he was, so it would likely be some time before he learned of his mother's fate.

Keen Wolf came to stand with Charlotte and Ben. "A few days before the snow, I found her in our cemetery. She had gone on her own, telling no one. She was standing at Straight Arrow's gravesite, speaking to him. I did not hear her words, nor did I ask, but when we walked home, she told me she had dreamed of him and wanted to tell him."

Charlotte had not been to the cemetery—the family wanted it kept private—but she had an idea of where it was and was surprised to hear that Gifted Hands, without her sight, would have walked there alone. "She was a mysterious and wonderful woman, Keen Wolf."

The Williamses and the Moffatts walked home together. "It's hard te think we'd planned te spend the afternoon there teday." Gracie shook her head to herself. "I canna believe she's gone."

Charlotte could hear Holly sniffing behind her as she walked with her cousins. She turned to Ben and softly said, "It was just going to be an ordinary Sunday. We were all just going to do the same things we do every Sunday. And now . . ." She choked up, unable to say more. After a moment, she felt Holly's hand take hers, and they walked the rest of the way home together in silence.

Loss

We will never spend another Sunday, or any other day, all together again.

This thought was with Charlotte constantly—she woke up with it, and she went to sleep with it. She seemed unable to escape it. The shock of losing her dear friend so unexpectedly was almost too much to bear. The discomfort of her healing ankles was a persistent reminder. She hoped the burns didn't leave scars that would forever mark the day.

It was Keen Wolf's belief that after ten days, Gifted Hands's spirit would have joined the afterworld. "After that time, her spirit dwells where happiness lives forever." Until that time, they would give him the privacy and the space he needed to accept what had happened and be with his family.

Sabel, Running Otter, and the children visited during the week. They informed Charlotte and Ben that the family had buried Gifted Hands with a few mementos, and each was offered a chance to say something.

Keen Wolf had said little since her passing, keeping mostly to himself. They were certain he was having difficulty dealing with his loss, but knew that all they could do was give him the support he needed.

Charlotte and Ben planned to go see him the following Wednesday—that would mark ten days. Gifted Hands's soul would have reached the loving freedom of the afterworld. They were taking out the kick-sleds when they saw the two figures approaching. It was Running Otter and Sabel.

Standing at the shoreline, Charlotte said, "We were just coming to see you." The smile died on her lips when she saw the darkness in her daughter's eyes.

Sabel looked at Running Otter, waiting for him to explain. He looked from Ben to Charlotte and said, "Keen Wolf has left us."

"What?!" they exclaimed in unison.

"He has gone. He left us a short time ago."

"You mean he—" Charlotte started.

"No, Mum. He came to see us and told us that he cannot remain here. He stayed long enough to be sure Gifted Hands moved on, but now he must go look for Dark Wolf."

"But we have no idea where he might be," Ben said.

"No, we don't," started Running Otter. "But he wants to tell his son about his mother. To be honest, I feel that he would have left even if Dark Wolf was here. He doesn't want to be here now."

A part of Charlotte's heart throbbed. "Oh . . . Did he say when we might return?"

Sabel shook her head. "He told us that when he left our house, he would be gone." Her voice cracked. After a brief pause, she continued. "He said Running Otter and I could have the house and call it our home; he would no longer need it, and it was what his wife would have wanted."

Charlotte's hand came up over her mouth and her tears ran over. *How could he leave like this? Now? And how could he not say goodbye?*

Gracie, seeing them conversing at the beach, came out to see what was happening. When she saw Charlotte wipe her eyes, she was instantly worried.

After filling Gracie in, the group went to the sitting room at the back of the building. Gracie and Charlotte left to make some tea. Sabel came into the kitchen only moments later. Looking at her mother and aunt, she quietly said, "Running Otter feels lost. First, he loses his En-ay, and now Keen Wolf. I don't know how to help him."

Charlotte hugged her, saying softly, "You are there for him, love. That's all you can do. Just love him."

As she said the words, she felt that part of her heart that had belonged to Keen Wolf for so long, break, shatter into tiny little pieces. How would she go on knowing he was no longer there? Not knowing when she would see him again . . . if ever.

"How are your ankles, Mum?" Sabel asked.

"Almost good as new, thanks."

Running Otter told them of a family friend. "His name is Black Feather. Our families met years ago and looked for each other at the summer festivals. Many years back, Black Feather lost his wife. He did not join another; he found his happiness in his children. When they had grown, his sons left to live with different clans, but his daughter remained and took a man. She died soon after, during childbirth. Black Feather could no longer stay in the longhouse. He simply walked away one day, saying little more than 'I am leaving'. En-ay asked for him every year after that, but no one had heard of him since that day."

"Oh me," said Gracie. "I canna think we'll not see 'im again."

Charlotte sat quietly, with her heart in her throat.

Ben watched her; it was something they did not discuss, but he had always been aware of Charlotte and Keen Wolf's love for one another. He'd always known that if Straight Arrow had not passed away, Keen Wolf would not have joined Gifted Hands; it would have been Charlotte he would have loved. Gifted Hands had known this as well. She spoke to him of it only once—on the day he and Charlotte married. But that was not what life had planned for them. They were both able to move on and love another fully, but the feelings they shared for one another remained. He knew she would feel this loss. She would miss his presence and friendship. She would miss *him*. He spoke now. "It has been an extremely sad time for us all. We have lost two very special people. Our lives will never be the same without them." He glanced at his wife and saw the sorrow in her eyes. She stood and walked to the door.

Charlotte stepped out into the cool air and took a deep breath. Both Sabel and Ben made to follow, but Gracie shook her head. She followed her friend outside and joined her at the table.

Without looking at her friend, Charlotte said, "How can I go on now, Gracie? It was hard enough to lose Gifted Hands." Her voice wavered, but she continued. "Now I don't know if I'll ever see Keen Wolf again. How will we know if he's safe? How will we know if he is even alive?" She dropped her head and gave in to her tears. "How could he do this?" *How could he have done this to her?*

"Aye, lass. I'm sure his leavin' is somethin' he needed te do, but te just leave us this way is . . . well, it doesna seem like Keen Wolf atta."

Charlotte sniffed. "Well, I guess he has every right to think about himself. Everything I've ever seen him do is for someone else."

Shortly after, the group came outside. "We've got to get home, Mum. Mitenah will want to get the children to bed, and I'd like ours in their own beds tonight."

"Of course. Give them big hugs from Grama, okay?"

"With pleasure," she answered, putting her arms around her mother. "Will you come over on Saturday after work? I'll get word to Phillip. We can have supper and talk." She looked over at the others. "You, too, Auntie Gracie."

"Thank ye, love, but not this week. I've got a lot of catching up to do and that's when I can do it."

"I'd love that, honey. What can I bring?"

"Don't worry about that. You'll have been working. I've got this one." She tried to smile, but her sadness couldn't be disguised.

On Saturday, Charlotte and Ben crossed the lake in the late afternoon sun. Both felt the strangeness of walking up from the water toward a house they had come to more times than they could count. A house where two of their best friends had lived only two weeks ago. Charlotte reminded herself, *it will never be that way again. We, I, must adjust to life* now. *When we come here from now on, it will be to see Sabel's family and Mitenah's family.* It hurt to think it, but she knew she would have to adjust, just as everyone else would.

As they walked the short distance to Sabel and Running Otter's home, she could smell their fire burning. Running Otter opened the door, and they were surrounded by the aromas of supper cooking. "Chweh'n, Running Otter. Oh, Sabel, whatever you've got cooking smells so-o good," Charlotte said, hugging one and then the other.

"Grama, Grampa," came Tehya's voice, as arms wrapped around Ben's waist.

He scooped her up and kissed her cheeks. "Tehya!" She giggled as he leaned her toward his wife, holding her in his arms.

Charlotte kissed her cheek. "I'm so happy to see you. Have you been having a fun day?"

She nodded. "I'm helping En-ay cook supper," she answered excitedly.

It was a relatively calm visit, just the six of them, as Phillip couldn't come. Sabel said, "We decided we'll move into the bigger house, but first we want to share some of the items in it with Mitenah and you and Gracie . . . if there's anything you'd like."

"That's kind of you, Sabel. Thank you. I'll have a look once you and Mitenah are ready."

It was a nice evening; the children were a little off, not comprehending death, but knowing they'd never see their goo-sood again was a lot. It would take some time for it all to sink in. Just as it would for us, and we *did* understand the finality of death. When Sabel told them it was time for their beds, Tehya asked, "Can Grama read us a story?"

Charlotte smiled and jumped at the opportunity. "Yes," Sabel said, "but just one."

The two children cuddled up in the same bed to listen, but Charlotte didn't read them a story, instead she told them one she knew.

The others could hear the children's giggles, and it helped lift their spirits. When Charlotte came out into the sitting room, she said, "Winnie the Pooh is always a hit."

"Thanks, Mum. They needed that tonight."

"I think we all could use some of that right now—feelings of love and safety."

"Losing the two of them in such a short time has been . . . just . . . horrible. I will miss them both forever." With that, Sabel lost it. She turned to Running Otter and buried her face in his neck as he pulled her close.

"We all will, sweetheart. They are two people I thought would always be in our lives. Two people who were kind, thoughtful, helpful, fun—they were everything. I can hardly imagine how I'll go on without them," Charlotte said, her words shaking at the end.

Promise

When spring finally arrived, they were more than ready for it. After a winter of cold and heartbreak, the warmer air and sprouts of greenery cheered everyone.

Charlotte walked to the general store after work to have a cup of tea with Gracie while Ben finished some paperwork. As she came around the back of the store, she noticed her friend sitting down by the water.

"Gracie, what are you doing down here all by yourself?"

Gracie looked up at her, eyes pink and wet. She sniffed, dabbing her nose with a hankie. "Charlie." She tried to smile. "Clement has asked for Lily's hand."

"How nice. You expected that, didn't you?"

"Aye." She paused to steady her voice. "She's agreed, o' course. The thin' is, he wants te tak her te Auburn te live." Her accent thickened as it did when she got emotional.

"I see," Charlotte said softly, putting her arm around Gracie's shoulders.

They sat quietly for a few minutes before Gracie said, "I ken it's nae so far, but I just canna think of 'er somewhere that isna wi' me."

"I understand, Gracie."

"Aye. I ken ye've been through this yersel', lass."

"It's one of those things that happens in life. Children grow up and have their own lives. It can be difficult to let them go, we love them so much, but it comes with the choice we made to have them."

"Aye."

"We're lucky ours haven't strayed too far. Think about poor Sheila—Ailsa moved across the ocean."

"I canna imagine her despair."

"Well, I'm happy for Lily and Clement. I suppose we have a wedding to look forward to."

When Clement proposed, Lily had dreamily answered yes. She wanted to be with him. But they hadn't discussed where they would live or what she would do as his wife until that time. When he told her he'd like her to move to Auburn with him, she'd been angry. Why wouldn't he have told her he wanted that earlier? She'd thought, wrongly, apparently, that he would move here. She could continue to work with the horses, and he could doctor from here. That was not what he had planned. He would take over Dr. Roberts's practice in the coming months, and he wanted to remain there, in town, where people knew how to find him.

He had his eye on a property in Auburn belonging to a gentleman who had engaged Dr. Roberts's services many times over the years. It had a stable big enough for four horses, a good-sized pasture, a stone house with three bedrooms, and when he heard the current occupant was planning to sell, he spoke to the man. After telling her all of this, Clement invited her to visit the house to see what she thought of it.

She hadn't told her parents about the engagement right away because she knew these questions would come up, and she needed to figure out what *she* wanted to do first. The idea of leaving her parents, her sisters, her auntie and uncle, and cousins, didn't sit well. Clement was understanding, but stubborn. After all, he had worked long and hard to get where he was, and Dr. Roberts handing over his practice was an offer he could not and would not refuse, even for Lily.

Owen arrived Friday evening to take Holly to his home for the weekend. She was looking forward to meeting his grandmother, whom Owen spoke of all the time. She was a little nervous though, because she would be alone with her for a few hours on Saturday morning while Owen worked. "Try not to worry, honey. It will work out fine. She's gonna love you, you'll see," Charlotte said, giving her daughter a hug outside the stable.

"Thanks, Mum."

Owen walked out of the stable with Lily and went to fetch his horse, Lacey, from the fenced pen. Lily passed over Nya's reins, saying with a wink, "Have a fun weekend, Holly."

"Thanks, Lil. Is Clement coming down this weekend?"

"Yes. He's taking me to see the house in Auburn tomorrow."

Holly nodded. She understood Lily's desire to leave, not because she wasn't happy here, because she was, but that Clement needed, well, *wanted,* to be in Auburn for his work. She could only imagine how difficult the decision had been to come to and hoped with all her heart, she wouldn't be faced with the same situation.

Ben closed the door behind him and set his bag on the floor. "Did Holly get away?"

"She did," Charlotte answered. "Are you ready for dinner?"

"I'm ready to devour something, but that's not what I had in mind." His eyes sparkled as he spoke. "But first, I'd like to see those ankles of yours."

Upon inspection, her ankles were declared fully healed . . . and quite delectable.

Samhain 1846

Charlotte had cast her circle and called the quarters, the Goddess, and the God. She sat still and quiet, feeling empowered and ready for her visit with Jessica. As she waited in her Samhain circle, she breathed deeply, focusing on the news she wanted to share with Jessica this year. She thought-called, "Jess, I'm here."

There was no response. She tried again. She opened her eyes, hoping to see the electricity in the air that often precedes the vision of Jessica.

The candle flickered.

"Jess, are you here?" Tears filled her eyes as the feeling of déjà-vu hit. She wasn't there: there was no sound, only vague and empty shadows. *Why isn't she here? I know she looks forward to this time as much as I do. I can't imagine what would make her miss it.*

By now, Charlotte knew their window in time had passed. All she could do now was remain calm long enough to finish and take up her circle.

After grounding, she stood to leave the bedroom, tears streaming down her cheeks.

Ben looked up from his journal when he heard his wife coming down the stairs. He was immediately on his feet. "What is it, Moxie?"

"She didn't come. She wasn't there. What could make her not be there, Benny?"

He wrapped his arms around her. "I can't imagine, sweetheart."

"I have no way of knowing if she's alive or dead. I'm scared, Benny." She sobbed into his chest.

"Don't you think she would find you if she had passed away?"

She stood back, contemplating. "I don't know. I suppose she would if she could."

"Perhaps something happened, and she just couldn't be home this time. It was bound to happen sooner or later."

"I suppose." Charlotte sniffed. "I had so much to tell her this year, too." She exhaled heavily, feeling deflated.

"Have a seat, Sweets. I'll get you a drink."

Full Flower Moon

All right, that's enough for me!" Charlotte said, jumping out of her chair and heading toward the store, slapping at her arms as the mosquitoes swarmed.

"Aye, those nasty critters've come out by the thousands," Gracie agreed, standing up.

Ben smiled at Jimmy and the two followed the ladies inside.

"What are your plans for tomorrow, Gracie?" Charlotte asked.

"After church, I'll give Evelyn a hand wi' the laundry, and then I'm hopin' te do a whole lot o' nothin'. It's been a busy week."

"That it has. Well, if we don't see you, have a nice day." Charlotte slipped into her poncho.

"You, too, lass. See ye Monday."

As they headed home, Charlotte looked up at the sky. "Looks like we won't be able to enjoy the full Flower Moon tonight. It's far too cloudy up there."

"Maybe not, but you'll know it's there," Ben answered, watching his wife. She never seemed to tire of the night sky and the moon. He took her hand as they walked. "What would you like to do tomorrow?" he asked.

"I'm with Gracie. A whole lotta nothin' sounds good to me. Actually, I should probably do some laundry, too. Maybe I'll get Holly to give me a hand when she gets home from church. I won't complain. It's a lot easier than it used to be with only three of us living here."

Back at home, Ben said, "Why don't you have a seat, Moxie, and I'll pour you a drink. Would you like a glass of wine?"

"Oh, would I!"

He poured them both a glass and sat across from her in the sitting room. He watched her expression as she sat lost in her own world.

"What are you thinking about?" he asked.

She looked at him, only now aware that her mind had been elsewhere. "Sorry, Benny." She offered a quick smile. "I guess I was thinking of them. Tomorrow is Sunday, and I still think of them when I think of Sunday."

"Cheer up, Moxie. We will always have our happy memories." He raised his glass. "To Gifted Hands and Keen Wolf, friends forever."

Charlotte raised her glass and tried to smile, wiping the single tear that rolled down her cheek.

Owen stayed home with his grandmother that weekend, so Holly left on her own to meet the others for church. Ben stoked the outside fire under a large metal pot while Charlotte cleaned up the breakfast dishes. She had the windows open. There was a lovely breeze coming in, and the sun was bright in the sky.

She was startled when she heard a knock and then two voices. She opened the door to find them talking on the porch. The man turned to her, taking the hat off his head and pressing it to his chest. "Charlotte, I'm sorry to disturb you this sunny Sunday morning. How are you?" She looked at him, taking in the short light-brown hair and familiar green eyes. "Do you not remember me?" he asked with a cheeky smile.

She blinked slowly. It took a long moment to place the face.

"Charlie?"

"It's me." His smile was so like his father's. He didn't look much like Michael, more like his grandfather Charles, but those eyes and that smile were definitely Michael's.

"Charlie!" She hugged him now. "Please come in, have a seat," she said, ushering him into the sitting room. "What brings you to . . . well, to now?"

He sat on the settee. "The last time we saw you, we didn't have time to talk."

"No. Were you able to leave safely?" she asked.

"Yes. In fact, I left there and came straight here. This may have helped." He smiled and passed Charlotte the bloodstone she'd given him through the window that night. He watched the confusion wash over their faces as they heard his words.

"Straight here? It was a full moon the night you sat in the gaol in the grist mill," Ben remembered.

"It was also a *blue* moon, the second full moon in the month. I did my homework. I studied the moon phases and the dates before I left home. I left home on a full moon, arrived in 1836 on that same date, under a full moon. I left the same day and came here . . . also May 30th and also a full moon. And tonight, I will return home to the day I left in 2064."

Huh?! "You can do that?" Charlotte asked incredulously.

"I don't see why not. The rest of the dates worked."

Charlotte looked at Ben as she thought about what he'd said. Charlie left home in 2064 at forty-three years old. He travelled to 1836, then to 1847, and his plan was to return to 2064 tonight. He will have travelled three times, over two-hundred-and-twenty-eight years and will only have spent two days of his life. Also, and this was big, he was travelling to years of his choice, there was no fixed time span.

"So, when you arrive back in your time, you'll have to cross the border and find your way home. Where are your things?" Charlotte asked.

"Actually—" He paused and smiled seeing Charlotte brace herself for what she might hear next. "Actually, when I travel from full moon to full moon, I can land in the place of my choice. I just make my intentions known in the words of my ritual." He watched her mouth slacken, and one side of his mouth twitched up in a grin. Ben tilted his head in thought.

She shook her head to herself. "Okay, so what you're saying is when you leave *and* arrive under a full moon, you can choose both the year and the location you arrive in?"

"Correct." Charlie smiled.

"Whoa! Time *and* space . . ." She was quiet for a few moments, contemplating this information. "Very interesting. So, now please tell me about your mom. How is she? When did she tell you about us? Why did she not come with you?"

"This is why I wanted time to talk, Charlotte."

"Coffee first?"

"Yes, black please."

She poured three mugs of coffee and returned to the sitting room with a plate of cookies. Charlie took two and immediately bit into one. "Mm-mm, good."

Charlotte smiled. "Not my work—I'm not much of a baker. Holly and Owen made these."

"Let's hear what you've got to tell us, Charlie," Ben said.

"Yes . . . well, if I've timed it right, you did not hear from Mom last Samhain."

"No. She didn't come through."

He nodded, choosing his next words. "Charlotte, there's no easy way to say this—Mom has Alzheimer's, as her mother did. There were subtle signs for a few years, and I'm sure dad passing away did nothing to help her frame of mind. In 2040, when she was fifty-one, things started to deteriorate. That would have been last year for you. She flat out started forgetting things, big things, some days. On *that* day, she set up her altar in the room she always used when she visited you, but as the day wore on, she forgot. It was Halloween—she and I answered the door for the trick-or-treaters, but she didn't remember what else the day meant to her and at that time, I knew nothing about all this. She and dad kept it well hidden from me. But a couple of days later, when she remembered, she got very upset and agitated. She told me everything. It was all in a jumble, and she was worried I'd think she'd hallucinated it all, given her state of mind." He paused and smiled sadly. "But over time, she and I sorted it all out. She told me where I could find all the written information to help me understand, and I learned all I could about *you* to corroborate her story."

Charlotte sat listening with tears on her cheeks. "I've known about you being here for almost twenty-five years. In that time, mom has all but forgotten us. Poor thing. Once in a while there's a flash of her, but mostly, she's gone."

Charlotte swallowed hard before speaking. "Will I ever communicate with her again?"

Charlie smiled. "You will, yes. Once I had a good understanding of your Samhain ritual, I sat with her several times while she met with you. But you should know, those days are few, Charlotte." He looked from her to Ben before continuing. "Actually, I wanted you to know about her, but I also wanted to ask you a sort of favour."

"Of course."

"I was hoping you could start to keep a journal, or something like it, that I could come back and collect later in your life and bring to Mom. I thought then she could read about your life, your adventures, on days when she could understand and remember."

Charlotte nodded but said nothing as she thought to herself.

"That's a beautiful idea, Charlie," Ben said. "When she's alert and receptive, she can read about Charlotte's life, in Charlotte's handwriting." Looking at his wife, he added, "You could tell her so much more than your brief window on Samhain allows. I imagine that would make her very happy."

"I hope so." He nodded. "I think I would bring it to her in her early sixties, when she still had full days she remembered. Those days are past now. She's living in a facility built specifically for people like her. We moved in some of her furniture and her favourite photos. When I asked about decorating her walls, she said she only wanted her two thistle paintings." He shrugged. "It's the best I could do."

"That sounds expensive. Are you managing?" Charlotte asked.

"Yes . . . it is. She gets dad's pension and her own, so that's helpful. And when I realized what had to happen, I sold the cottage. It broke her heart when she found out, mine too, to tell you the truth, but we needed to have savings to draw from." Charlotte nodded. "When I left her at seventy-four, she . . ." He stopped, aware of what he was telling them.

"So, will you be changing your own past?" Charlotte asked, mostly to herself.

"To be honest, I don't know, but I don't think so. I think I will remember what I am making happen now."

Ben could see that all this was a lot for his wife to take in. "You said you'll leave tonight. Will you spend the rest of the day with us?"

"I'd like that," Charlie answered with a smile and a glance at Charlotte. "I'm sure you will have questions."

"I know *I* do," Ben said. "When did you first travel?"

"I was twenty-seven. The first time, I just wanted to see if I could do it. I stayed at home but travelled back to 2006 and kept my eye on young Jessica and Charlotte for a few days. I tried to keep them out of trouble." He smirked at Charlotte, but of course, she had no idea when he was talking about. "After that, I tried different times and places, and different phases of the moon to see what I could learn."

"And?" Charlotte rejoined the conversation.

"Well, I learned a few things you may not have thought about. I tried several times to land somewhere, some *time,* where I was already present. For instance, I tried to go back to see myself as a kid messing around out in the backyard with my dad. I couldn't do it. I could not travel to a place where I already was." He looked at them. "Does that make sense?"

"It does," Ben answered. "You can hardly be two places at once."

"What happened when that didn't work?" Charlotte asked.

"It's hard to explain. It was like I got bounced to another time, the same day, but a different year. One where I didn't already exist."

"In the future?"

"Yes."

"So, you're saying you couldn't land in a time where you already were?"

"Never. What I did though, was start keeping track of my trips so I could try to land in a time where I *did* exist, but I was 'travelling', so I wasn't there. I wanted to see if that would work. There are several gaps of time when I am away in another time that future me can land in."

"Whoa."

"Right?" he said with a smile.

"And did that work?" Ben asked.

"It did. One time I left home on a new moon and landed at home two weeks later on the full moon. Then, a few years later, when the dates lined up, I travelled to that time and spent two weeks there. Mom never even knew." He chuckled.

"That's amazing, Charlie. She would be so proud of you. Maybe I can tell her about this visit in one of my journal entries. Would you mind if I did that?"

"I think that would be wonderful." They were all quiet for a few moments, before Charlie said, "I must ask, when I saw you in the gaol, which was years ago for you, you said two of your children were in the schoolhouse that day."

"That's right."

"I thought there would've been three: Phillip, Jessie, and Holly."

Hearing her name, Charlotte felt the tears spring to her eyes. She looked at Ben.

"We lost Jessie in 1826," Ben told him.

Now Charlie looked confused. "In Scotland?" Ben shook his head. "Oh," was all Charlie could say.

Ben eyed him. "Why oh?"

"Hmm. This will come as a shock, but in my time, in the history I found, Jessie died in Scotland in 1825." He looked at Charlotte and saw her furrowed brow. "You were visiting Slains; you were at the site of a cave."

"Oh, my God! That was you?" She looked at Ben briefly. "In the cave, that was you?" Charlotte's voice was barely a whisper as pieces began to fit for her.

Charlie nodded. "Jessie was killed in an accident that day. The man who'd been hiding in the cave shot his gun into the air to threaten you, and the horse Jessie was on bolted. She was thrown from the horse and killed. I went there that day to stop that man from shooting this gun and save Jessie. Instead, he shot me." He stood then, digging his hand into his pocket and pulling something out. He opened his hand to show Charlotte her rainbow moonstone sitting in his palm before placing it in her hand.

She gasped. "I gave you this thinking it would help you heal after being shot."

"I believe it did. It also helped me travel somewhere I was able to get help."

"You disappeared over the edge of the rocks. We thought you fell to your death in the North Sea," Ben said.

Charlie sighed. This was a lot. "Charlotte, you left me alone in the cave when you went to meet the others. I did a short ritual to take me out of there. Your stone, together with my own, some feathers, the lit candle, and my words to my deities, saved me."

"So, when we thought you'd slipped into the sea, you had travelled?" she asked.

"Yes."

"Thank you." Swallowing down the lump in her throat, she continued, "You did save Jessie that day, and because of you, we were able to enjoy another year with her."

"What happened?" he asked softly.

"She died of what we think was a brain tumour in November of 1826," Ben answered. "It was quite sudden."

"I'm so sorry."

"Thank you. And thank you for coming back to save the others from that fire." Charlotte was quiet then. Ben smiled as she bit the edge of her lip, as she did when she was thinking. He looked at her expectantly. "Wait, I'm confused. You read that she died in 1825. But your mom and dad came here in 1826 to let us know she was ill. Did you know that?" He shook his head. "How did you read a different history?"

"That is strange," Ben agreed.

The room was quiet as they all thought about these facts.

"The only thing I can think of is . . . wow, this is going to sound nuts."

"Go on," Charlotte encouraged him.

"Okay, so what if I read Jessie died in Scotland in 1825, when I was thirty, and I went back and changed that? So, when Mom read the history before coming here, the new history, Jessie had died *here* in '26."

"You changed the timeline?" Charlotte said.

"But I'm still in the one I was in when I was thirty?"

"A paradox," Ben said.

"Maybe your mom'll be able to tell you about it when you get home," Charlotte offered.

He had a faraway look in his eyes. As much as he'd got their minds spinning, his was boggled as well.

"So, you don't know about the time they spent with us here? We can happily fill you in about that."

Together, Charlotte and Ben shared the story of their time spent here with their friends. "The next time I saw her, she told me she'd left here expecting you."

"Imagine all that," he said. "Well, now that I know, I'll have to go back to that time and check up on you all somewhere down the road."

"Weird, so I may have seen you back then and not realized it was you, and you haven't even gone there yet?" Charlotte lifted her hand to her forehead. "My brain hurts."

Both men chuckled.

Eager to move on to her questions, Charlotte asked, "Now, about travelling to wherever, whenever?"

Charlie, forcing himself to think about the timeline paradox later, answered, "Yes. Well, I knew that you left home on a new moon and arrived in the same place, on that date, in a different year under a full moon. You had done that several times successfully. I thought it made sense that if you can travel through time, you should be able to travel through space or location as well. In my mind, that's a bigger leap, so I tried leaving on a full moon and landing on the same day in a year that was also a full moon, in the place of my choice. I was meticulous with my choice of words to be sure I landed where and when I wanted. With the exception of the times I tried to travel to a time where I already was, it has worked.

I left my home and travelled to Slains; I left home and came here; I left here to land here in a different time."

"Amazing. Have you tried to arrive on a full moon on a different day, not just a different year?" Ben asked.

"Not yet."

Holly came in the door then, with Evelyn in tow. "We're back," she said, coming into the sitting room. "Oh, hi." She smiled at the stranger talking to her parents.

"Honey, this is Charlie. He knows my friend Jessica. Do you remember her?" Holly nodded. "He's passing through town and popped in to say hello."

"It's nice to meet you," Holly said with a grin. Charlotte introduced her niece to Charlie, and then the girls told her they had planned to go visit Sabel and the kids this afternoon.

"Very well," her father said. "Be careful and be home before dark."

The girls each grabbed a couple of cookies and left.

"Looks like there's more lunch for us," Charlotte said. "Shall we eat outside?" Without waiting for an answer, she stacked the plates and cutlery to carry outside.

"Let me help," Charlie said, walking into the kitchen.

"So, tell me, Charlie, what was it like growing up with your parents? I know from the minute your mom told me about you, she was head-over-heels for you." She set the plates on the table. Ben followed immediately after with the tray of food.

"Well, they hadn't planned on me, I know that. I came as a complete shock, but I always felt they were happy I happened. When I was young, Mom always used to call me her Little Ace . . . she said even though they hadn't expected me to come into their lives, it must have been 'in the cards.'"

"Aww. I like that! I know about your mom, now what was your dad like?"

Ben gave her a curious glance but waited to hear Charlie's thoughts. "My dad?" He paused a moment, gathering his thoughts. "He was a great dad. He was fun and helpful. He used to take turns with Mom, reading to me at night, unless he was away, of course. He spent a fair amount of time travelling, and while I know he missed us, I also know he loved his work. I did hear Mom remind him it was just a job, once or twice." He smiled sadly. "I miss him. I miss them both."

Charlotte was about to say something, but stopped. "Look, Charlie, a dragonfly just landed on your shoulder. She is a messenger from the elemental world—maybe it's him saying hello."

Charlie smiled—he liked that idea.

They left Charlie in the woods with all he would need to get home. "Thank you for all you've done for us, Charlie. When you see your mom, please give her a hug for me. She may not understand, but it won't go wrong."

He smiled back at her. "I will." Then he turned to Ben. "Take good care of yourself, Ben." He stretched out his hand.

"We will," Ben answered, shaking his hand and patting his opposite shoulder.

Charlie hugged Charlotte then. "Goodbye for now, Charlotte."

Dear Jess

Summer 1847

Dear Jessica,

Hello, my friend. It's been so long since we were together—twelve and a half years—but I still think about you every single day. I hope as you are reading, you are well and were prepared before beginning to read, as this could come as quite a surprise.

Ben and I recently had the pleasure of meeting your Charlie—HERE! In my time (which is 2041 in your time), he is only eleven years old, but he came to us from 2064 at forty-three. It's mind-boggling, right?! No matter how many times I think about it, it's still a lot to wrap my head around. He has grown into a fine man, so brave, and so like his father. It's hard to believe the travelling he's done on his own, experimenting, learning as he goes. Turns out we've met him once or twice in the past without realizing it was him. He's been watching from there, keeping his eye on us. When he suggested I keep a journal that he could share with you, I jumped at the chance. I will write as if I'm writing letters, keeping you up to date on the goings-on around here. I expect it will be much better than two or three minutes of catching up once a year. I hope you enjoy it as much as me.

Since the last time we had the opportunity to "see" each other, a lot has changed. Our dear friend Gifted Hands passed away quite unexpectedly last March. She seemed to be healthy, aside from losing her sight, but obviously there was some underlying condition we were unaware of. We were all devastated—I still am. As you know, she was a wonderful person; everyone whose life she touched was better for it, and her absence has been hard to bear. In addition to that, Keen Wolf found he could not stay here. By that I mean that once he was assured that she was in the spirit world, he left here. He said goodbye to his children and left—he just walked away. He told Sabel and Running Otter he was going to look for Dark Wolf, who you may remember left to help those on the Trail of Tears several years ago. I understand Keen Wolf wants to inform him of his mother's passing, but I also believe he cannot face living in the home they shared together for so many years without her. I miss them both so much, Jess. As you know, and something I will say to no one else, there is a piece of my heart that will always belong to him . . . he took it with him.

Now on to brighter things . . . Robbie is still working at Bellevue hospital, in what is for you, Manhattan. He is thriving as a doctor and surgeon, and has no desire to come back home to work, only to visit. I'm so proud of him.

Sabel and Running Otter are well. They have moved into the house that once belonged to Gifted Hands and Keen Wolf. Their daughter Tehya is nine and son Tuari is two. Both are happy, lovely children. They love to curl up with their Grama or Grampa and listen to, or read, stories. Tehya is learning to read and write English together with Mitenah and Swan Song's children, spending several hours each week with Sabel, Mitenah, Sandy, or me. Of course, they are learning their native language every day, as well. Tuari is still so little and cute—very like his father when he was young.

Mitenah and Swan Song have two children now. Falling Leaf is nine and Kaniehtiio is only one. (Her name means "Beautiful Snow" and is pretty, but difficult to say, so I call her Snowy.) They're great playmates for Tehya and Tuari and are just adorable. Sabel and Mitenah share the large vegetable garden that Gifted Hands used to work, which keeps them quite busy in the warm weather. Sabel also continues to grow poppies and now lavender, too, in large amounts for me to harvest.

Phillip has a little cabin of his own on the west shore of the lake, between where Sabel lives and Auburn. Not too far away. He is enjoying regular work, getting articles into a paper or broadsheet. His future is definitely in that arena. He's happy to write about whatever they ask but has also been given the freedom to submit articles on topics of his choice. He has been doing a sort of series, spreading the word about the horrid conditions the Native Americans are in and how they are still being treated. He gets his information firsthand from Running Otter, Swan Song, and their connections.

Holly met a man named Owen Rogers—I think I told you this. He's a baker, and let me tell you, he creates some yummy treats. Until recently, he was living with and caring for his grandmother just outside of Auburn. For the past couple of years, he's come to see Holly almost every weekend, staying with us. When Holly met his grandmother, she told her privately, "You are Owen's heart, my darling. Please do look after him when I am gone." He proposed to Holly this spring, a few weeks before his grandmother passed away. He told us early on that he wanted to come live here with Holly and be a part of our family when the time came. Gracie heard the words and the gears started turning. Owen moved in with us, just last week. He got his grandmother's affairs in order, sold the house, and brought his belongings here. They will live with us for the time being—and why not, we have lots of room in the house these days—and will marry at the end of the month.

Holly continues to work with me in the apothecary. She's knowledgeable, interested, and fun. In her free time, she loves to paint and often disappears, looking for scenes she'd like to capture.

This past year, Ben has been spending a few days a month in Auburn, both giving lectures to doctors who want to expand their surgical practice and demonstrating or supervising surgeries. He is becoming known over a larger area for his practice and abilities, and has been invited to spread his knowledge outside of our area. He loves his work and seems to be happy at the way it has evolved. I often wonder if we will stay here or move somewhere with more hustle and bustle, where he could use his skills more frequently. Time will tell, I suppose.

Lily has married Dr. Clement Nicholls. You may remember he was the horse doctor that came to check on Nya before she had Oreo. There was some turmoil when he proposed. Don't get me wrong, she wanted to marry him, there was no question of that, but when she realized he wanted her to move to Auburn, she was distraught. She hadn't expected it, and they hadn't discussed it. Anyway, the doctor he apprenticed under retired, leaving him the practice. Naturally, he *wanted to stay in town where everyone knew him and where they could find him. Lily was sad to have to leave here. She'll miss her family and her horses, although I imagine she has a few to look after now. Gracie was a mess when she found out Lily would be leaving town. She said, "I just ne'er thought o' her livin' somewhere I wasna." She has had to adjust. Fortunately, Owen is here and, in addition to baking for the store, he's been helping Jimmy with the horses. Oreo seems to have taken a real shine to him.*

One last bit of news: Maisie had her second child recently, a boy this time. They have called him Christopher Brian—ten more years before we hear of Sarah Gray.

Me? I am living a great life, Jess. We see Sabel, Running Otter, and the kids most weekends, and Phillip about once a month. I am working with Holly at the Doctor's House and loving it. There was a time when I worried that, like Gracie, I would lose my daughter to Auburn, but thankfully things didn't go that way. We are as good a team as Sabel and I were. I still grow my herbs and medicinal plants, working long hours in the apothecary and the garden, especially when Ben's away. I'm still growing Mary Jane. Some years it has grown better than others, but every year gives me seeds to continue on. I've had good results with it, particularly the oil, and thank you regularly in my mind! Between the gardens we have at the store, the Doctor's House, and at Sabel's, I think this fall will be our best harvest yet!

Well, I think we're all caught up for now. I miss you Jess, and I love you till the end. Our love transcends time and space—it always will.

Charlotte

When October Comes

Last summer was hot! Almost every day of August was hot, and sometimes, but not always, humid as well. Charlotte didn't mind so much, and Holly took after her mother, only hating the effect on her hair, but poor Gracie was fit to be tied. She just couldn't get relief. She had taken to sleeping in the back room of the store. The bedrooms didn't get enough air circulation in this type of weather. She was counting the days until September, hoping it would come with some relief.

Of course, when it finally arrived, she was delighted. The days were still quite warm, but the evenings brought some cooler air. She would open all the windows to capture some cool that she could hold on to through the next day. "Charlie, a' this time I've been so desperate for September to arrive, but it's still so hot! I fear I may well melt into a sloppy puddle on the floor o' the store, ne'er te be heard from again."

Charlotte laughed. "Aww, Gracie, please don't do that. I wouldn't want to lose you down the cracks in the floorboards. What would I tell Jimmy? You just have to hang in a little longer."

"Aye," she said it with a smile, but it wasn't heartfelt. She was miserable. "I'll be happy when October comes."

"Look, Ben will be gone this weekend. Why don't you and I row across to Sabel's? It always feels a little cooler on that side of the lake. What do you say?"

The week spent without Ben was difficult. As it happened, someone had come into town with some sort of respiratory infection. The gentleman recognized he was ill and kept to himself in his room at the inn, but not before having his midday meal in the tavern and then visiting the Doctor's House.

"Good day, my dear," he started when he saw Holly standing behind the counter.

"Good afternoon," she replied, stepping back slightly as the man coughed.

Hearing the rattling sounds of his breathing as he drew in air, Charlotte came out to see a man she didn't recognize, searching for something in the pocket of his breeks.

"Well, that doesn't sound good. How long have you been coughing like that?"

"Excuse me," he said, coughing once again, but this time into his handkerchief. "Just started like this yesterday. I've come to see what the doctor might suggest."

"I'm afraid he's away today, but I'm the apothecary. I can help. Tell me, have you had a fever? Headache? Is there mucous coming up with the cough?"

Holly bent to look under the counter, predicting what her mother would suggest. She set several jars on the counter: thyme, horehound, basil, chickweed, elecampane. Charlotte smiled and tucked the basil back underneath. "Let's make Mr.?"

"Little. John Little," he said.

"Let's make Mr. Little a mixture of these; say enough for four days."

Holly started measuring the dried herbs into a fresh jar while her mother instructed Mr. Little on how best to take his teas.

After he'd left the shop, Charlotte gave the counter area a good clean and suggested Holly wash her hands well. That was that.

The next day was a different story. There were reports from the Inn that several of the guests had developed the same symptoms as Mr. Little. Charlotte made a few jars of the tea and brought them over to Victoria. In order to prevent further spread of the illness, she asked that those suffering stay in their rooms for the next couple of days and be brought their meals and teas. "I know it's a lot to ask, but it's the best way to avoid more people getting ill," Charlotte explained. "I might even go so far as to suggest, whoever goes up to the rooms wears something over their nose and mouth while they're there, so they can stay healthy. And wash their hands well afterwards, with soap and water."

Victoria shook her head but took the jars and promised to do her best. That was all that could be expected.

It was mid-afternoon when Charlotte noticed the sweat on her daughter's forehead and her pallor. "Oh, no."

Holly looked at her with wide, shiny eyes and nodded. "I think I've caught it, too, Mum."

"Well, you know what to do, love. I'll make you up a jar to take home, but before that we'll get some of that tea into you."

By the time they arrived home, Holly was spent. She had a bowl of soup and crawled into bed. Charlotte suggested Owen sleep in the spare room for the time being. Charlotte woke her in the night so that she could drink some more tea, and then again in the morning. "Here you are, sweetheart. Hopefully after another tea or two, you'll be feeling better." Holly nodded and sipped at her cup. "I'll come back at noon to see how you're doing. Have a good rest."

The day, as expected, was much like the day before as a few new patrons of the inn had developed symptoms, but she and Victoria were on top of it. By Thursday, people were beginning to feel better; the spread had ceased. Charlotte arrived home that evening to find that Holly, who felt much improved, had made supper with Owen. The three ate together, hopeful that tomorrow would be a better day.

By the end of the week, the situation at the Inn was much better. Holly was back at work and the ladies had a normal workday. They restocked the shelves and mixed a few jars of this and that, pleased that "the plague" had ended. Holly spent Friday evening with Evelyn, while Owen did some baking for the store's Saturday morning. "If you don't mind, Mum, we'll sleep there at the store, and I'll see you in the morning."

"Sure, sweetheart. I'll see you when I come for my coffee. Have a nice evening," she added, kissing her daughter's forehead.

Charlotte felt tired, and although she missed Ben, she didn't mind being alone tonight one bit. Holly would be happy to spend time with her cousin, and Ben would be home tomorrow. Charlotte could have herself a bath and a glass of wine before turning in early. It sounded perfect.

It was well after suppertime Saturday when Charlotte began to worry. Ben had yet to arrive home. He always came home on Saturday and usually with plenty of time for his supper.

Owen said, "I imagine he's likely been held up by one of the other doctors. Try not to worry, Mom." She smiled, still not used to him calling her mom.

After putting away the dishes, she sat at the table, thinking about writing to Jessica. That's when she heard footsteps on the porch. She met him at the door. "Moxie! I'm so glad to see you. What a long week." He dropped his bags to the floor, took her into his arms, and kissed her. "How are you?"

"We had a long week, too, Benny." She kissed him again. "I want to hear all about it, but first, let's get you cleaned up. Are you hungry?"

"No. Cleaned up?" he asked with a glint in his eye.

"Sh-hh." Charlotte put her finger over her lips. "The other two are upstairs." She took his hand and led him into the wash closet where a now lukewarm bathtub was waiting.

Jessica's letter would wait for another night.

The next morning began much the same as the previous night ended, only this time, Charlotte rolled on top of Ben and stayed for a while. "Looks like someone's making up for lost time," Ben said from below her.

"You know I am," she replied, riding him just so.

They were relieved to come downstairs and find Holly and Owen sitting at the dining table. "Good morning, Dad. Did you sleep well?" Holly asked.

"Morning, love," he answered, bending to kiss the top of her head. "I did. After such a tiring week, I'm glad they decided to wait a couple of months for the next session. I could use the break."

"Ah, you're getting old, Dr. Ben," Charlotte laughed, setting his coffee on the table as he sat down.

He shrugged. "Maybe I am."

Seeing the solemn expression on his face, she added, "I was just joking, honey. What's wrong?"

"I just feel a bit tired. Thank goodness it's Sunday. Do we get to stay home today?"

She smiled now. "We do. We decided that everyone would stay home today and just relax."

"That's heaven t . . . t . . . m . . . m . . ." Charlotte turned to see what had distracted Ben.

She felt immediate horror.

Ben sat looking at her, eyes wide with fear and confusion. "Ben! Can you speak?"

His lips moved, but there was no sound. Holly jumped out of her seat. "What should I do?" She went to the wood-burning stove and put some hot water into the small pot, setting it over the heat to boil.

Charlotte's mind was spinning. "Benny, do you think you can you walk? Let's get you to the settee where you'll be more comfortable."

Owen was at his side in an instant, taking his weight as he stood and appeared to lose his balance, guiding him to the sitting room. Ben's left arm hung slack at his side.

"Ben, can you smile for me?" His eyebrows came down—he understood. "I need to see if you can do it. Please try."

Her heart fell as only one side of his mouth lifted.

"Owen, please run down and get Gracie and Jimmy. They should be here." He nodded. "And perhaps you or Jimmy could get Sabel and Running Otter; the kids don't need to be here."

He ran out the door.

Charlotte sat beside her husband on the settee. "Benny, can you understand me?" He nodded. "Good. Can you say I love you?"

He blinked slowly and swallowed. "I . . . I . . . lo . . .lo . . ." He had a look of panic in his eyes. He couldn't do it.

"Now, try to raise your arms." He lifted his right arm above his head, his left, only a fraction, and then it fell.

"Holly, can you bring the willow bark tincture? It's in that cupboard, behind the mint, and a teaspoon," Charlotte said, pointing. She took Ben's hands and held them. "Okay. Tell me if you understand. You're having trouble speaking, you seemed to lose your balance earlier, and one side of your face is slack." His grey eyes widened, looking deep into hers. She could see the fear. "You might be having a stroke."

"A stroke?" Holly asked from the kitchen.

"Yes. An apoplexy." She looked back at Ben. "Do you understand?" He nodded slowly. "The best way I know to deal with this is a blood thinner."

Holly came with the glass tincture and a small cup. Charlotte poured out about two teaspoons and helped him sip so it wouldn't spill. "That's it. All of it, Benny."

She watched as he tipped his face downwards. He was thinking—or trying to. "Does anything hurt?"

"N . . . n . . ." He stopped trying and shook his head.

"I think you're either having a stroke, gah, an apoplexy, or what we call a TIA." His eyebrows came down again. "Something has happened to block the blood flow to your brain. Do you understand what that means?" He nodded slowly.

She glanced at her daughter. "Thanks, Holly. Maybe you can start some coffee for your aunt and uncle. I'll just sit with dad for a bit."

Ben looked at Charlotte with a different expression now. He understood what had most likely happened and was afraid. He tried to tell her, but the words still would not come.

"It's okay, Benny. Give it some time."

It was only a few minutes before Gracie and Jimmy came in. Gracie sat across from Ben, looking at him while Charlotte explained what happened and what she thought it meant. "He's still alive, Gracie, and he understands what's happening. Hopefully, this was just an episode that will pass."

"Aye," Gracie answered, with tears in her eyes. "We're here for ye, lad." She moved, sitting beside him and taking his hand.

It was another forty-five minutes before Sabel and Running Otter arrived. Owen borrowed a neighbour's horse and rode off to tell Phillip what had happened. By this time, Ben was much improved. He spoke slowly, but the words came now. Once again, Charlotte explained the situation.

"Dad, you've got to stay strong," Sabel said, kneeling on the floor in front of the settee and taking his hands and kissing the backs of them. "We love you."

"You got here quickly," her mother said.

"Thankfully, Mitenah and Swan Song were at our house, so we just ran to the canoe." She flashed a smile back at her father. "How can I help, Mum?"

"Well, we already gave him a double dose of willow bark tincture. I think I will give him another dose tonight and will continue him on it, maybe forever. I'd like to hear his opinion first though."

"So, what do ye think happened, lass?" Gracie asked.

Charlotte looked at Ben before answering. "I think he had what I've heard called a transient ischemic attack—a TIA. It happens when something temporarily blocks the blood flow to the brain, like a blood clot. It can be fatal. It wasn't, but we'll need to stay on top of it so it doesn't happen again. We know he's at risk now."

Gracie said no more. She sat ashen-faced and in shock.

After they had something to drink and some time had passed, Ben started to look improved. His face, though not completely back to normal, no longer looked so saggy on one side.

Ben nodded, catching Charlotte's eye. "Th-th-ank you," he said softly.

Tears sprung to her eyes. She wrapped her arms around him after hearing his voice. "How do you feel?" she asked.

"Umm . . ." He looked up at her from under his lashes, and she knew he was worried about what would happen if he tried to talk. She smiled, trying to encourage him.

"That was s-scary," he said slowly. "I knew w-what I wanted to s-say . . . I couldn't make my m-mouth say it."

"I canna imagine," Gracie said.

"Do you want to try to walk a little?" Charlotte asked.

"Let me help wi' that," Jimmy said, coming to stand beside Ben where he sat. He stood himself and wobbled a little but was able to take a few steps without the need of Jimmy's arm.

"It looks as though it's passed," Gracie said, visibly pleased.

"It does, yes," Charlotte agreed.

"Mum, how much of the tincture do you have?" Sabel asked.

Charlotte looked at the small bottle. "Enough for a couple of doses. I can make tea after that; today I didn't want to waste the time it takes to make the tea. I wanted to get it into him as quickly as possible."

"I have some. I'll bring it tomorrow, and I'll start some more."

"I can start some, Sabel, but if you can bring some that would be good," Holly said, eager to help.

By mid-afternoon, it was clear that Ben was recovered. He'd been lucky.

Owen returned and said, "Phillip wasn't home. There was no sign of him."

"Thanks for trying," Charlotte said.

"I'll go see him later on or tomorrow and let him know," Sabel said.

Leaving Ben with the others, Charlotte called Sabel and Holly to the dining table for a learning moment. "Now, you both understand that one of the things willow bark does is help to prevent blood from clotting? It can also help dissolve a clot over time. That's why I gave him a high dose today and will continue to for about a week. After that, I'll lower the dose and give him some every day, spread throughout the day to keep his blood thinner."

"Are you sure it was a clot?" Sabel asked.

"Well, pretty sure. If a blood vessel had ruptured, I think he would have had a really bad headache. He said his head didn't hurt at all. Apart from that, the symptoms are pretty much the same. I don't know yet whether his memory has been affected. Also, I don't think he would have recovered so quickly if he had a bleed."

"I see."

"Do you know what else we should be sure he's getting in his diet?" She looked from Sabel to Holly.

"I imagine certain fruits would be beneficial, maybe orange or lemon?" Holly said.

"Yes, I call it vitamin C. It's in citrus fruits, but also strawberries, peppers, tomatoes, cabbage, broccoli, things like that, and potatoes. It helps repair damage to blood vessels and reduce plaque buildup. Anything else?"

"Cod liver oil is good for a lot of things," Holly said.

Charlotte smiled. "Yes. I call this vitamin D. Cod liver oil, fatty fish, cheese, eggs, beef liver; these can help thinking and nerve impairments. If he had a stroke, this would help his recovery."

"Greens and nuts are what I would add, Mum," Sabel said.

"Excellent! This is vitamin E. Sunflower seeds and oil, almonds, peanuts, greens, pumpkin, the list goes on. This might help with any memory impairment. It does more than that, of course, but this is what we need to think about now."

"That's a lot to remember. How do you do it, Mum?" Holly asked.

"Well, in the beginning, I wrote it all down, but over time, I've remembered it. You will, too, one day." She smiled, but the worry showed in the lines on her forehead. "We have to look after him to avoid this happening again."

She got up from the table and returned to Ben's side. "How are you feeling now?"

"To be honest, I feel fine. I know that it happened. I remember most of it, I think, but I feel fine."

"Good, lad. Well, we'll leave ye for now. Be sure to rest for the balance of the day. There'll be time enough for work tomorrow."

"Would you like us to stay, Mum?" Sabel asked quietly.

"I think we'll be okay, hon. Thank you." They hugged each other hard; this could have turned out very differently.

Holly and Owen walked everyone back down to the store, leaving Charlotte and Ben in peace.

"Ben . . . I was so scared—" Her voice caught, and she started to cry.

He put his arm around her shoulders where they sat on the settee. "I was, too. I thought for a minute or two that I was going to die. I'm not sure why I didn't. Thank you for thinking so fast. I agree with your remedy."

"I hope you weren't planning to do anything alone in the near future, because I'm not letting you out of my sight," she said, kissing his cheek. "It's hard to believe our sexy morning turned into this day."

When Ben lay down for a little nap before supper, Charlotte took pen and paper upstairs where she could keep her eyes on him and wrote to Robbie detailing what had happened and her response. He was too far away for a swift reply, but this was something he needed to know and would understand. These are the times when she missed the telephone. She could let him know what happened immediately, even ask his advice, but no. She would have to wait a week at the very least, to hear back from him.

Concern

During the week that followed, Charlotte kept her eyes on Ben, but she had to admit, if she didn't know anything had happened to him, she wouldn't have guessed. He looked good, he felt fine, and he was up to all his regular tasks.

Of course, his family was very concerned for him and each checked up on him every day or two. Phillip came into the Doctor's House first thing Monday morning and greeted his father with a hug. Last night, Running Otter told him what had happened; he'd wanted to come right away, but made himself wait until the morning.

When Ben walked into the back room with a patient, Phillip approached his mother. "Mum, would you like me to stay with you for a while? I'd be happy to if I could be of help."

She reached up and hugged him. "Phillip, I don't mind telling you, I've never felt so scared as when your dad was trying to speak and couldn't, but it seems to have passed. I don't think I need you to stay, and Holly and Owen are there if I need anything. But thank you, love."

"If you're sure."

Phillip returned home feeling some relief, but no less worried about his father. He decided then that he would write a series of articles on health issues or events that were common and sometimes life-threatening, and the best responses. He had his parents and brother for all the information he would require.

Wednesday afternoon, Hank's daughter Helen came running in. She'd been at work with her father at the carpenter shop and he'd had an accident. A large piece of wood had fallen on his leg. She and Emma had managed to lift it off, but they worried about his leg and needed a doctor's help.

Charlotte glanced at Holly briefly as they listened to the story. "You go, too, Mum. I'll be fine here. Send someone if you need anything."

Ben and Charlotte arrived in the workshop to find Emma sitting on the floor holding several towels tightly around Hank's naked shin. "Emma, thank you for keeping his wound covered," Ben said, setting his bag on the floor and kneeling at Hank's side. "How are you feeling, Hank?"

"It bloody hurts, I'll tell ye that," he answered. His face was pink and beaded with sweat.

"I'll have to lift the towels and have a look. Are you ready?" Hank nodded as Charlotte opened Ben's bag and took out the alcohol.

Ben uncovered the wound to have a look. "I'm sorry, this will sting, but it needs to happen." He took the bottle from Charlotte and poured it over the three-inch gash. As Hank groaned, Charlotte guided a wobbly Emma to a chair and asked Helen to keep an eye on her. Once back at Ben's side, she assessed the situation. The bone had a lump on it. The skin was split and bleeding freely down his leg, the alcohol making the site look even worse.

"You were lucky, Hank. It doesn't look broken," Ben said and began to feel the leg around the wounded area. "You will definitely need some stitching, though."

Charlotte looked at Emma; she was pale and sweating. "Emma, do you have water on?" She nodded. "Could you please bring me a bowlful? And some fresh cloths or towels." Emma walked out the door. They helped Hank up onto a chair.

Helen came to have a closer look. "It's not so bad, Pa. Just a bit of blood." When Emma returned, Charlotte wiped the area around the still-bleeding wound with some fresh water and found her marigold salve to apply once the stitches were in.

Ben had it stitched and wrapped in no time. "Now, Hank, I'll be back the day after tomorrow to have a look. I want you to leave this bandage on until then. Also, this will likely give you some pain since your shin bone took quite a thump. You can certainly move around and put weight on it, but don't push yourself; don't overdo it."

Hank nodded. "Thanks, Ben. You as well, Charlotte."

When they arrived back at the Doctor's House, they found Holly eager to know what had happened. They told her while they cleaned and sterilized the items Ben had used while there. "He's lucky he didn't break it," Holly said, imagining the situation.

"That he is. He'd be in a bad way if he had, and he'd have to keep weight off the leg for some time as well."

Holly smiled at her mum, happy to see her father looking good and doing his thing. "I'll just put these things away, and then we can walk home?" Ben asked them.

"Sure," Charlotte answered. While he was in the back room, she said, "I think I'll invite everyone over for the afternoon next weekend. It's been too long since the whole bunch of us were together."

"That sounds nice, Mum. When we see Sabel next, we can get her to pass it on to Mitenah and Phillip."

"Yes, and we'll send a note to Lily and Clement."

For the next while, Sabel came across every other day to check on her dad; she needed to see with her own eyes that he was doing well. Gracie saw them every day, her keen eyes assessing the health of her brother. Rebecca had come into the Doctor's House while they were away with Hank, and Holly had filled her in. Rebecca, in turn, had told Lenora when she'd seen her later in the day.

It was noon the next day when Lenny visited the Doctor's House. "Lenny!" Charlotte exclaimed. "It's been a while. How have you been?"

"We're well, Charlotte, but I'm here because I heard about Ben. How is he?"

His footsteps could be heard coming from the back. "Is that Lenny's voice I hear?" he asked, joining them with a smile. "Len, how are you? Is everything all right?"

"You're asking about me? Jeez, Ben. I'm here because I heard what happened to *you*. Are you well? How do you feel?"

"Thankfully, it was something that passed. I feel fine now, and the ladies are looking out for me." He winked at his wife and daughter. Lenny didn't look convinced. "I am fine, Len."

Lenny looked from Ben to Charlotte. "Would you care to go for a walk, Ben? Sun's out today."

"Sure, let me just change this shirt."

He knew Charlotte felt uneasy letting him out of her sight. "We'll be back shortly, Moxie." He kissed her cheek and headed for the door.

Lenny followed, turning to smile at Charlotte. He could read her feelings in her eyes. "I'll keep good care of him. I promise." She nodded.

She did her best to not worry about him, but she understood the seriousness of what had happened. He could have died. *And* the incident was a warning. They had little control over it aside from the herbals he would now take every day—his diet and level of exercise had always been good. They would have to remain vigilant and continue with the herbals and vitamins for the rest of his life, there was no question about that.

At the end of the week, Ben and Charlotte paid Hank a visit. Ben gently unwrapped the bandage and lifted the gauze. "Hmm-m, this is a little pinker than I would like. I think there may be an infection starting here, Hank. We will give it a good clean today and apply another bandage."

"Charlotte, let's prepare a wash and then we'll apply more salve." She nodded and took out the mixture of marigold, St. John's wort, and goldenseal Ben kept in his bag—plants that are antimicrobial, work to speed healing, and reduce pain. Hopefully they would be able to beat the infection before it could really set in. Once the wound had been washed and dried, Charlotte applied the salve and Ben tied on a fresh bandage. "We'll let this be for a few days, Hank, then I'll have another look."

After leaving the woodworking shop, the two stopped in at the general store. "Charlie, Ben! I was hopin' te see ye. I've been thinkin' te invite the old friends for dinner here Sunday after church. Does that suit ye?"

"That sounds fun, Gracie. We haven't done that for ages," Charlotte replied.

"Sounds good to me," Ben answered, and she smiled.

"What can I bring?"

"I thought we could make hamburgers. Everyone likes 'em and it isna too much work."

"Sounds perfect. I'll bring the toppings. Anything else?"

"Just yourselves, lass."

"I'm looking forward to Sunday, Benny," Charlotte said as they walked home.

"Me, too. But I'm looking forward to tonight even more."

Hearing the tone of his voice, she turned to look at him. "What? Oh, I don't know, Benny."

"Don't worry, you will." He smiled to himself and said nothing more about it.

After saying goodnight to Holly and Owen, Charlotte and Ben retired to the bedroom. He crawled into bed nude, as usual, and waited for her. He said nothing while she slipped into a nightie and got in beside him. He turned to her before she could say a thing and planted his lips on hers. She responded tentatively, but broke away after some time. "Benny, I know what you want to do, but I'm scared. If you get your blood pumping too hard, things could happen . . . bad things."

"No—good things, Moxie."

"Bu—"

"You're worried that I'm going to die." She looked at him now, eyes full of tears, and nodded. "I admit, I'm a bit worried about that, too, but we can't let this stop us from living. I love you. I have loved you and made love to you for years. I don't plan to stop now." He smiled down at her. "Besides, I could think of many worse ways to go. Death by loving my wife wouldn't be so bad."

"For you, sure! But think about me. All of a sudden, you'd be dead lying on top of me."

"Or under you," he added, raising an eyebrow.

She smiled. "Yeah, or under me. Either way, it would be horrible to be in the act, or just finished, and have you . . . gone. It scares the crap out of me."

He held her close for a few moments, listening to her breathe, and appreciating the feel of her body against his. "I love you, Charlotte Williams. I will love you forever, here, or wherever we go when this is over." He bent and kissed her forehead, then her cheeks.

She was aware of his aroused state when the conversation began, but now, as his tongue trailed down the side of her neck and his hand ran up her leg, under her nightie, she was beginning to feel herself respond. She had no more words for him. She sat up to help him slip the garment over her head, but rather than lying back down, she bent to lick his inner thighs. When she heard him groan softly, she moved upward, licking and gently suckling her way.

It wasn't long before she heard, "Moxie . . . please . . . I need to be inside you."

She climbed on top of him, sliding onto him slowly, savouring the sensation. His hands clasped around her waist, pulling her down, forcing her to move with the rhythm of his need. Then he flipped them, now he had the control he was looking for, the control he needed to make the intensity last. He moved lower down the bed, his face disappearing between her thighs. She covered her mouth with a hand as an involuntary sound came from her. He knew just what she liked.

Then he was there, kissing her hard, her scent on his lips.

It was some time later, when Charlotte rolled onto her side, her arm lying across Ben's chest. He turned to look at her with a smirk on his lips. "See, I'm fine," he whispered.

"You're much better than fine, Benny," she said, languorously. Then she propped herself up on her elbows and kissed him. "You're sure you feel all right?"

"I'm sure." He smiled. "You did a good job of staying quiet today."

Blushing, she whacked his shoulder. "Only because I *had* to."

They arrived at the back of the store before anybody else. "Ah, Charlie, I wanted to ask. It's a nice day, do ye think we could sit outside? We'll need a coat or somethin', but it's not too cold, is it?"

"I think that would be perfect," she answered. "It's still quite mild, and there will be a fire if anyone wants to sit close."

"Aye."

"I'll help you take some chairs out."

"Dinna fash, lass. Jimmy can do that."

"Jeez, Gracie, I haven't heard that in ages, not since we lost Mabel."

"What? Fash?"

"Aye," Charlotte answered with a giggle.

"I can help Jim with the chairs," Ben said.

Gracie glanced at Charlotte before saying, "No, Benny. I've got another job for you, lad. You will cook the hamburgers. Would ye mind checkin' on the fire?"

He cocked his head at her. He knew what she was up to. She didn't want him carrying anything. He was about to say something cheeky, but when he saw her expression, hand on hip and eyebrow raised, he changed his mind. Instead, he went to check on the fire.

Soon, the yard was filled with chattering voices as old friends caught up with each other.

In attendance were Rebecca and Edmond, Rosey and Daniel, Lenny and Lenora, Katie and Gregory, Charlotte and Ben, and of course, Gracie and Jimmy.

"Well, it's been a long time since we've done this," Lenny said to the hosts.

"Aye. I s'ppose we've a' had te keep up wi' the children. That didna leave a lotta time nor energy for much else."

"That's true. The more you have, the less time. Wouldn't change it, though." He smiled as he looked around. "We're just missing Gifted Hands and Keen Wolf," he added.

"I miss them every day," Charlotte said. "Life isn't the same knowing they're not just over there." She pointed out toward the water. Lenny's mouth formed a line as he nodded his agreement.

Rebecca and Edmond approached them; she flung her arms around Ben. "Oh, Ben, I'm so happy to see you. You look good. We were so worried—" She stopped herself, afraid that the topic was not up for discussion.

Ben hugged her back. "Thanks, Becky. I know I worried everyone, but as you can see, I'm fine." She smiled. She was still a beautiful woman.

Then a voice came from behind them. "You'd better be, Doctor Ben. We love you around here, you know," Rosey said, moving in for a hug of her own. As he spoke to her, his eyes met his wife's, showing his delight at being here with everyone.

"Yes," added Edmond. "Becky had quite a scare when she spoke to Holly."

"How are the girls?" Charlotte asked.

"Ah, well, Janee is off for a few days to visit Harper in Port Byron."

"I did hear something about her having a new beau." Ben looked at Charlotte—he'd heard nothing. "It's serious, I suppose, if she's gone to stay?"

"It is. The poor girl hasn't had much luck before him, but he's a keeper," Becky said with a smile. "Although I don't much like the idea of her moving away."

"Aye," Gracie said. "Perhaps it willna come te that, lass."

One by one, each had a word with Ben, all wanting to express their concern. He felt like a king. Charlotte came up beside him at one point and elbowed him gently. "Don't get too used to all this adoration, Benny. It'll go to your head." He slipped his arm around her back, leaning over and kissing her cheek.

By the time everyone left for home, Gracie was bushed. Charlotte took in her friend's rosy cheeks and the slight dark circles under her eyes. "Come on, Gracie, I'll help you clean up. It's not too bad—no pots."

"Aye. Thanks, lass."

"We'll give you a hand, ladies," Ben said from behind Gracie.

"That'd be nice, lad. 'Haps ye can gi' us a few minutes and then ye can help te dry."

While the men finished the cleanup outside, the ladies started washing. "Gracie, you look very tired. I know you've had a busy day, but are you feeling all right?"

"Just tired. Well, and I s'ppose I've been worried about Benny. I canna help mesel'."

"I know. Me, too. I can't keep my eyes off him."

Gracie smiled then. "Ah, ye ne'er could do that, could ye?"

"True. He is a looker, aye?" Charlotte said with a giggle, remembering Gracie's words many years ago. "He seems to be doing fine, though, Gracie. And, if I'm honest, no amount of worrying will change what happened or what could happen down the road."

"Well, that doesna make me feel ony better, lass."

All Together

Holly placed the cutlery on the table and sat down with a sigh. "Wow, it's only Wednesday? It feels like Friday. What a busy week," she said.

"I agree. So many cases of stomach upset and sniffles."

"We've gone through quite a few jars of herbs and mixes. I suppose we'll have to do some restocking tomorrow morning," Charlotte said.

"Do you need more supplies? I think Jimmy's planning to go into Auburn next week?" Ben asked.

"We—"

Ben raised an eyebrow as he heard the door. When it opened, they jumped up from their seats. "Robbie!" Charlotte said, throwing her arms around his neck. "What a nice surprise!"

"Hello, Mum!" He smiled as he hugged her back.

"Robbie, I didn't think we'd see you till Christmas," Holly said, moving in.

"Hi, Holly. Well, after I got Mum's note, I decided not to wait till then." He embraced his father, the reason he had come, and said, "Good to see you, Dad."

"You, too, son. Thank you for coming."

"You're just in time for supper. Come sit," Charlotte said, turning to get out one more plate. "Good to see you, Owen," Robbie extended his hand before taking a seat.

After catching up on his father's health and sharing his own hospital news, Charlotte asked, "How long will you stay?"

"Four or five days. I thought I could work with dad while I'm here; it will be a refreshing change of atmosphere."

Ben smiled. "For me, too."

"Perfect. I've invited the whole bunch here on Sunday. We haven't done a big get together for a long time."

"I've timed it well, then."

The days following were less busy than the previous, which made Charlotte happy as she planned for Sunday's gathering. She would have help with the food of course, but she wanted this get-together to be just right. She would make a roast beef with gravy and mashed potatoes. Gracie was bringing a dessert; Sabel some venison pie; Owen was making a surprise dessert; Sandy a cabbage salad; and Mitenah a vegetable dish. She was wondering if she needed anything else when Holly said, "Robbie looks good. Life in New York seems to agree with him."

"I thought so, too."

Sabel and the children came into the store Thursday afternoon. She liked to bring them around in the daytime, and she wanted to check on her father. She was more than a little surprised to see her big brother standing at the counter.

"Robbie," she exclaimed, hugging him.

"Uncle Robbie!" Tehya said excitedly.

"Ung Wobbie," Tuari tried to echo, wrapping his arms around his uncle's legs.

"Look at the two of you!" he said, picking them up, one in each arm. He kissed each on the cheek before returning them to the floor.

After a short visit with her father, Sabel invited her brother over for supper and the evening.

"Actually, I was planning to spend the evening with Tim."

"Bring him."

Gracie had ordered Charlotte's beef through the store, so Friday after work, she and Charlotte walked to the Hill's farm to pick it up. As they pulled it home in the store's wagon, Gracie said, "It's lovely that Robbie's come te see his father."

"He's a good boy," Charlotte agreed.

"Benny's enjoyed 'is company." She paused a moment. "He seems te be doin' very well, Charlie."

"He is!"

"I dinna ken how long it'll be afore I stop thinkin' about it. It's stayed with me, ye ken?"

"I do. Me, too. We just need to do our best to move on, for ourselves and for him."

"Aye. I'll try."

Robbie was waiting for them when they returned to the store and carried the roast home for his mother. Tonight, she would season it and leave it where it would stay cool. Once they had it stored away, she gave Robbie a big hug. "Thanks for your help, honey. And thank you for coming to check on your dad— it means a lot."

"You don't have to thank me, Mum. I love him. I wanted to see him with my own eyes."

Holly, Owen, and Robbie were at church, while Charlotte and Ben prepared for company. With all of the family, their spouses and children, and Mitenah's family, there would be twenty people here today. Suddenly, a vision of Gifted Hands came to her mind; standing beside her was Keen Wolf, who had his arm around her waist, both smiling and looking radiant. *They should be here, too.*

Ben saw the faraway look come into her eyes, and then a tear. "What is it, Moxie?" he asked, coming to her side.

She leaned into his chest. "Just thinking of them." He knew who she meant. This had happened before. "I can't help it. I miss them so much."

His arms came around her. "I know. We all do, but you must try to make those thoughts happy, not sad. The memories should make you smile. You remember them with love, right?"

She wiped her cheek and tried to smile. "I know. You're right." She took a moment to compose herself. "Okay, Benny. It's your job to cook the meat. It's going to take a few hours. You should probably start that fire."

"On it," he said and kissed her cheek, then winked as he slipped out the door.

Charlotte began setting the table just before noon. "Good morning," Sabel called, coming in the door with Tehya and Tuari. She smiled at her mother. "We thought we'd come early to see if you'd like some help."

"Good morning, loves," Charlotte bent to hug the children. "Thank you, I could use it. It's been a while since we've had such a big crowd. Running Otter's outside with your father?"

"Yep, him and Phillip."

With that, she put Sabel to work while the young ones went outside with the men.

Soon, Holly, Owen, and Robbie returned home. "Auntie Gracie says she'll be ten minutes, Mum."

Charlotte looked at Sabel and smiled. "All we need is to make room for the food the others are bringing."

"You've got this, Mum." Charlotte smiled, hearing her daughter say such a modern phrase.

The next time the front door opened, it was Gracie. "Hello, Charlie. I'm here wi' most o' the Moffatt bunch. It's nice and cool out there." Her cheeks were rosy, and her eyes were sparkling. She set her dessert and a bottle of something on the side table and slipped off her coat.

"October finally came, eh, Gracie?" Charlotte asked with a chuckle.

"Aye."

One by one, the rest of the crew came into the house: Sandy, Evelyn, and soon after, Lily and Clement. Just as the door closed behind them, it opened again; now Jimmy, Ben, Running Otter, and Phillip came in with the children.

"Hello everyone. Looks like all we're missing now is Mitenah, Swan Song, and the little ones. No hurry, we have a couple of hours before we eat."

"Well, while we're waitin', I brought a bittie somethin' te share." Jimmy held up a bottle of amber liquid. "The good stuff," he added with a grin.

"Hand up if ye'd like a wee dram," Ben said, heading to the cupboard for glasses. Charlotte raised an eyebrow and looked his way; she *liked* it when he did his Scottish accent.

Jimmy poured the drinks and Sandy helped pass them out, while Sabel poured some juice for the children. Raising his glass, Jimmy looked at Ben and asked, "If I may?"

Ben raised his glass in response.

"May ye aye keep hale and hearty till ye're auld enough te dee," he said. "And may ye aye be just as happy as I wish ye aye te be."

"Now me," Gracie said. "May those who live truly, be aye believed, and those who deceive us, be aye deceived."

"It's only fitting I go last." Ben smiled and added his toast. "Here's to men of all classes, who, through lasses and glasses, will make themselves asses." The room exploded with laughter.

Charlotte looked around the room and felt suddenly emotional. She loved these people . . . every single one of them. She watched them swig or sip their drink, happy to be together again. Ben raised his glass again. "This may sound maudlin after that, but I thank you all for making my life complete." She smiled at him; his energy was positive, happy, and contagious. And, at fifty-four, he was still a stunner. "I lo—" As she watched, the smile left his face; his eyes opened wide and caught hers, and he collapsed to the floor.

There was the sound of glass shattering and high, loud voices that blurred into the background as Charlotte dropped to her knees beside him.

November

This can't be real!

He can't really be gone ...

December

Why?
Why Ben?
Why now?

I must have missed something.
What else should I have done?

420

January

I should have done more . . .

What if I had given him a larger dose of white willow?
What if I had given him something else?

I miss him so much.

422

Letters

January 1848

Dear Jessica,

I hardly know where to begin, Jess. Three months ago, at the end of October, Ben passed away. I suppose if you've seen the dates, you already knew that. Earlier that month he had what I suspect was a TIA. When it was happening, I thought he was having a stroke, and for a few moments, I thought we'd lost him. We put him on a regimen of white willow bark to thin his blood, to try and prevent another event, and he seemed to recover well. What I did wasn't enough. Maybe it wouldn't have made a difference what I did—I don't know. It was almost a month later, at a family gathering, that he collapsed.

I know that, for a split second, he felt it happening. He was making a toast. There was no time for words; his words were cut off; he made eye contact with me and then . . .

He was surrounded by the people he loved and who loved him. I'm thankful we were able to share his last moments and know that they were filled with love. He was buried a few days later near his parents and beside little Jessie.

If it sounds like I'm doing well after losing him, I'm not. I'm a mess. A big fucking mess! I still can hardly believe it happened. I don't understand why such a wonderful person would be taken from us so early in his life. How . . . why am I even existing without him? He was my soul mate.

We had spoken about the possibility of this happening after the first event, of course. He wanted me to know, in no uncertain terms, that he loved me and that I should go on with my life as best I can; that I had a wonderful family who would always be here for me; that I should live the remainder of my life for both of us. Just writing these words has the tears running down my cheeks. I miss him so much: his smile and sense of humour, his caring, his ability to calm me, and to understand me when I couldn't even do it. I miss kissing him goodnight. I miss rolling over in the morning and feeling his warmth beside me.

I'm sure you went through the same emotions when you lost Michael. I'm so sorry I couldn't be there for you when you went through that, Jess. While I'm sure it was difficult helping Charlie through the grieving process, I feel sure the love you and he shared helped you both a lot.

Robbie had come home to see his father after receiving my letter in early October. He was here with us when it happened. We had several discussions about whether he wanted to replace his father as the town's doctor. He was up and then down. In the end, I told him his father and I understood that he was happy where he was working in the hospital. He wasn't failing anyone if he made the choice to do what would make him happy. In the end, that is what he decided to do. He stayed with me for a week after Ben's service, and then he returned to New York. Since then, he writes almost weekly. He knows that I have love and support here, but I think he feels guilty that he is not a part of that.

After Robbie left, Sabel and the family came to stay with us for a few days. The young ones are good for the spirit, and Sabel and Running Otter are just wonderful. Sabel took losing her "daddy" very hard. She and I have spent many hours remembering good times and crying over tea or wine.

Holly and Owen are expecting a baby in April. Thankfully, she told us the news as soon as she realized it this past summer. She and I spend a lot of time together, something I am thankful for. We talk, we cry, and we laugh. She is a very sensible young woman. I'm glad she found Owen. He is a strong person to lean on, and I know she needs that. She misses her father every day. Phillip has made an effort to come down to Sabel's every other weekend and spend the night, so I've been able to sit and talk to him as well. He is more of an introvert than the others and sometimes needs to be drawn out before he will share his feelings. He feels Ben's absence. He misses knowing he was there, but he seems to be dealing with it. As a matter of fact, he has started what will be a series of articles about serious/life-threatening health-related issues, why they happen, and the best emergency responses. He hopes to find a paper that would be happy to share them. I may suggest he put it all into a book.

After that day, I found myself unable to return to my bed. It didn't feel right to be there without him . . . knowing that he would never be there with me again. For the first while, I slept in Robbie's old room, but then I decided to leave the house. I've moved back into my old room at the store. Gracie offered me a larger room upstairs, but I'm happy back here. It's small, but I have all I need, and Gracie is always there to check up on me.

Holly and Owen are living in the house. It is theirs now to fill with love. She and I still work at the apothecary in the Doctor's House, for now. A doctor comes down from Auburn for a few days every week, something that will continue until we find someone permanent.

I've spent a lot of time sitting at my favourite place just thinking, remembering, and crying. It's still so peaceful there, but it doesn't offer any magical solutions . . . I don't suppose there are any.

I can't stop seeing it, Jess. Every time I close my eyes—his eyes widen, he looks at me, he falls. Every single time. When will it stop? I know the others have been suffering with this as well, but it's not something it helps to talk about really, except to know that you're not alone. We each have to deal with it on our own.

Also, I will confess only to you, I've been drinking more. I know it's not the answer, but a temporary fix is better than nothing.

Gracie has had a difficult time of it. Not only were she and Ben close since childhood, but Jimmy has complicated things somewhat as well—that's a story for another day. It's been hard to watch her suffer. We have cried together many times . . . I only wish something good came from crying. We will survive. We will go on—we have no choice.

Love Charlotte

February 19, 1848

Dear Jess,

Early February brought much snow, and a brutal coldness has settled in. I'm glad that the little wood-burning stove in my room kicks out such good heat.

My mindset is the same as last month. I am almost always sad, I cry every day. I feel scatter-brained and unable to retain things, and I feel so fucking angry. Poor Benny, and poor the-rest-of-us who miss him so much.

Anyway, I know that writing to you will take a little of the weight off my shoulders, so here is an update:

I didn't tell you in my last letter, but late last fall, Mitenah's cat had a litter. When they were old enough to leave their mother, I took one, Holly took one, and Sandy took one. So, I have another kitty companion, this one is actually Hazel's great-grandkitty. She is dark brown like Hazel, but she has white hands and feet and white fur around her little pink nose. I've named her Boots. She cuddles in at night, reminding me of Hazel and happier times. Boots is not crazy about the snow, so I don't have to worry about her wandering off when I let her out.

I mentioned Jimmy in the last letter. Tonight, as I sit bundled on my bed with Boots curled at my side, I will tell you about that. You remember when you were here, he lost the watch we brought him from 2013 during a game of cards? Well, there may have been incidents before that, I can't say, but there have certainly been some since, although we didn't realize it at the time. Things have only recently come to light.

Over the years, Jimmy has continued to travel to Auburn or sometimes Utica for supplies, depending on what we needed. All the trips to Utica required nights away from home, and depending how much he needed to carry home, he would occasionally take the store's horse and buggy. One time Gracie had molasses on her list for the store. When he returned, and the stock was counted, he was shy one barrel of molasses. Jimmy waved it off, saying they must have counted wrong as they loaded the wagon and said he'd straighten it out. Another time, it happened with whiskey, and another with some other liquor. These occasions were separated by years, and no one thought anything of it until the end of last year.

Jimmy took a cart up to Auburn with Nya and Mocha. Usually, he returns the same day or late the next morning. This time, he was gone for two nights. Gracie was worried because he always comes home the next day. She stayed here with me that evening, and I did my best to distract her. When he arrived the next morning, he was pale and looked sickly. I thought he might have some kind of bug, so I asked

a bunch of questions, made him a special brew, and sent him to bed. Gracie and I went to the stable to unload the cart where he'd left it. She said, "He doesna usually take the horses to the stable until after we've unloaded." Her forehead furrowed as she spoke. I was untying the crates and barrels when she asked, "Where's Mocha?"

Looking around, it was clear that Mocha wasn't there, only Ruby, Nya, and Oreo. I knew Jimmy had come straight into the stable, but I peeked outside to see if Mocha might be grazing out there. He wasn't.

Gracie's face turned bright pink as she realized he'd come home without one of the horses. "Perhaps Mocha is ill or injured and unable to travel home," I suggested.

Gracie gave me a "hmmf" and said nothing more.

After we'd unloaded the new stock into the store, I started putting things away, and Gracie disappeared. Shortly after, she returned with a glass of whiskey in each hand. I knew this was a bad sign, but took mine and waited for her to say something. "Charlie, I've had it wi' that man. You ken I've suspected o'er the years that some things missing when he returned to town were not miscounted or lost?" I nodded. "I canna mind that he'd be se bold as te wager Mocha in a game o' cards." I thought "holy shit", but said nothing. "He telt me the first night he lost the extra coin he'd taken wi' 'im. Tryin' te win it back, he lost Mocha." She swallowed hard, and I just knew I didn't want to hear what she was about to say. "He stayed the extra night te try te win 'im back." She looked at me with tears in her eyes and shook her head. "He didna . . . and he wagered—" She broke down then, sobbing uncontrollably.

All I could do was wrap my arms around her. I wanted to say, "Whatever it is, we'll deal with it, Gracie." I could only think of one thing that could be worse. I let go of her and asked, "Did he lose the store?"

As she shook her head, the tears continued to roll down her cheeks. "No. Not the store."

"What then?" I asked.

"The Doctor's House."

The words echoed in my ears. My world went black, Jess. He had bet and lost the Doctor's House—Ben's legacy. What the fuck are we to do now? How am I supposed to look at him again? How could he do that?! Was it even his to bet?

I sat there looking at her, horrified.

She told him she didn't want to see him there when she opened the store in the morning. She wanted him out. She wanted him gone. She spoke softly, but the determination was clear. She was finished. We sat in silence for quite some time before she spoke again. "He telt me the name o' the mannie he lost to. I suppose I'll hae te go see if I can buy Mocha back, but the Doctor's House . . ."

I suggested we talk to Clement or Owen to see if they wouldn't mind going for her.

"Aye." Her chin quivered and she added, "I wish Benny were here. He'd help look after this mess and Jimmy." I lost it then, Jess. Ben would have been able to make it right. Not only that, but I don't think Jimmy would have bet the building if Ben had been here. What a mess.

Anyway, the next day she spoke to Clement, that's Lily's husband in Auburn if you recall, and he paid the gentleman a visit to buy back our horse.

When I offered to let her stay with me that night, she accepted. We talked into the night over lavender and valerian tea, about how far Jimmy had fallen. She is still unsure what will become of them, but she knows she doesn't want to be near him, or even see him right now. His daughters have not completely disowned him, but they're keeping him at arm's length. That he would act so carelessly at the expense of the family business they've all worked so hard for, is tough to understand. He's been *staying at the inn, as I understand it. How he spends his days, I don't know, and quite honestly, I don't care.*

As for the Doctor's House, it now belongs to Mr. Harrison Brown, card-player extraordinaire. We took a couple of weeks to empty it of our things—the beds, the counter, the shelving, the chairs, and all the jars and sachets of herbs. And we made arrangements to return in the spring to dig up our plant stock, to be planted elsewhere. These items were divided between the store, the house, and my old room. What a shame. Poor Ben would be beside himself. This was definitely an occasion for a few whiskies. There have been many.

The apothecary has moved back to the store for now. Gracie moved some things around; it's a bit cramped, but it's worked out okay. Gracie and I get to spend lots of time together again, like we did in the old days, only now it seems rather than looking forward to our happy lives, the happiness is behind us.

Tonight will bring February's full moon, the fourth I've spent without Benny. God, I miss him, Jess.

Love Charlotte

April 18, 1848

Dear Jess,

It's been a couple of months since I wrote, and I thought I'd catch you up a bit. Gracie and Jimmy have reconciled. She told me that after many conversations they have arrived at the best solution they can. In Gracie's mind, his dishonesty is not the root of the problem, it's his inability to control himself when gambling. The lies follow, and she understands that part of it. In order to prevent this from happening again, one of two things will happen from now on. Either we will send someone else to pick up our supplies, or Jimmy will go with someone to do it. Simple as that. And there will be no more card playing here, or anywhere else.

So far, things between them and at the store seem back to almost-normal. I don't know if it can ever be what it was for me—I feel like he stabbed Ben in the back. I don't think I'll ever get over that, but she needs to do what is best for her, and I will support her whatever that is.

One day not long ago, she and Jimmy came to me with an idea. They want to expand the store into the front portion of my room, giving me more work and counter space, and the store more display space. Of course, that would make my room too small to live in—they offered me Hettie and Eli's house. (It's been empty since she passed away and used mostly for storage.) I told them I would think about it.

Last week, Gracie visited me one evening and confronted me about my drinking. She'd been quiet about it, hoping I would snap out of it, but apparently I haven't. She loves me, I know that, and says she hates to see me wasting away my evenings alone with a bottle. Maybe she's right. I don't know.

Holly went into labour early this month. Gracie and I were there to assist. The labour was about eighteen hours and normal, but she delivered a stillborn little boy. She was, and is, devastated. Owen can do little to appease her. Of course, she was so ready to share her world with a baby. Poor thing. I've done my best to help make her postpartum experience as painless as possible, but it really sucks to have to heal, and to wrap your chest etc., and not have an infant to show for it, not to mention having to look at the crib they had made. She knows she will get pregnant again, but she's not ready to let go of this yet. I think working with me is a good distraction for her.

The town has found two doctors from somewhere near Auburn, who will come to town for three days a week, rotating between them. That will leave us without a doctor four days a week until we find a permanent one. Lawrence has arranged with the owners of the inn, to let the doctor stay there when he's in town. In the meantime, Holly and I will do our best to help anyone who is in need and will send word to Auburn if there is urgency. She and Owen have invited me to return to the house to live many times, but in all honesty, I'm quite happy to be back here. It feels safe and cozy.

As the winter weather has turned to spring, I can feel the new life, the renewal, the rebirth. The air has warmed, and the lake has melted, the birds are chirping, and the trees and earliest flowers are in bud. This time of year holds such potential. I hope I can fully embrace it.

Once again, I write on the day of the full moon. Thankfully, the sky is clear today. I think I will prepare my altar and do a ritual tonight. I haven't done one since I lost Ben . . . It's been six months. I haven't felt like thanking the Goddess and God, because I have not felt thankful. Every minute of every single day, I miss him. Many of my days have been spent in my head, replaying images that became memories far too soon. Today, however, I feel inspired by the promise of the Pink Moon. I will do my best to let go of the negative energy I've been holding on to, making more space for positivity in my daily life and my relationships. I will celebrate the love Ben and I shared. I will celebrate my wonderful children and their children. I will celebrate family and good friends— past, present, and future. I have much to be thankful for.

I love you, Jess.

Charlotte

Epilogue

I squint against the light cascading in from behind my new curtains. I'm in no rush to get out of bed this morning. Today, Holly will work the apothecary counter until 1:00 p.m., then I'll go in for the afternoon.

I stretch, reaching back to fluff my pillow—just five more minutes.

Finally, I swing my feet over the side of the bed into my slippers and walk over to the windows to let the light in. It looks like another sunny day, something that always helps the morning mood. What else always helps? Hearing Gracie's voice as she walks into the store kitchen.

"Ah, good mornin', lass."

"Good morning, ladies," I say to Gracie and Evelyn.

"I've scrambled some eggs for you, Auntie Charlotte. And there's toast just there." She points to a plate on the table.

"It was a lovely moon last night. I'm glad I came te find ye. It's been a whilie since we've done that, eh?" Gracie winked at me.

"That is has. I'm glad you came to join me." I pour myself a coffee.

"What are yer plans teday, Charlie?"

"Today I've got some seeds to check on in my room and some dried herbs to grind before work. I'll probably have a quick poke around the garden, too, and see what's coming up."

"We'll see ye a little later then," Gracie said, and walked out into the store.

I sniff the air as I look at Evelyn. "Mmm, it smells good in here already, Ev. Is that dinner or supper?"

She smiles and answers. "I'm making some soup for dinner. What you're smelling is the beginning of meatball stew. Tonight, I'm trying something new."

"Yum! I'll be sure not to miss it!" Once I've finished my eggs and toast, I refresh my drink and head for my room. "Have a good morning, Ev."

While sipping my coffee, I reach into the cupboard for the herbs in need of crumbling and set them out on the worktable. Next, the mortar and pestle and some small jars.

Ah, good to the last drop, as they say—or will say, I guess. I slip into my apron and put a fresh pot of water on the wood-burning stove. Just as I set the small pot down, there's a knock at the back door. Startled, I splash water over the edge and hear the "tsk" sound of it sizzling on the hot surface. "Jeez, Charlotte, get a grip."

Running my hand over the front of my apron, I open the door.

My breath catches as my heart skips a beat.

"Chweh'n, Sky Watcher."

Dear Reader:

I hope that you enjoyed reading Sky Watcher's latest adventure
half as much as I enjoyed writing it.

If you can spare a minute or two, I wonder if you could leave a
short review of the book so that others might know what you
thought of the story. Just a few words can make a world of difference
to independent authors, who don't have the backing and
exposure offered by traditional publishers to help spread
the word to readers.

You can find a review link at
www.HeatherLynnBooks.com.

Thank you for reading.

Heather

Glossary of main characters

Bennet Williams -Town doctor. Son of Mabel and Alec Williams, brother of Gracie, husband of Charlotte.

Carole-Anne Crawford (aka Elizabeth Bruce) – Possible ancestor of Charlotte. Wife of Keith, mother of Maisie.

Charlotte Williams (nee Harper) - Wiccan, time traveller, apothecary, and wife of Dr. Ben Williams.

Dark Wolf (Sitting Deer) – Youngest son of Gifted Hands and Keen Wolf. Brother of Mitenah, half-brother of Running Otter..

Edmond Douglas – Part owner of the inn and tavern with his brother Oliver and sister-in-law Victoria.

Evelyn Moffatt – Youngest daughter of Gracie and Jimmy Moffatt.

Gifted Hands – Native American (Tuscarora) friend of the Williams family. Widow of Straight Arrow. Joined to Keen Wolf. Mother of Running Otter, Mitenah, and Dark Wolf.

Gracie Moffatt (nee Mary Grace Williams) – Owner of the General Store, daughter of Mabel and Alec Williams, sister of Ben, wife of James Moffatt. Mother of Sandy, Lily, and Evelyn.

Holly Williams – Youngest daughter of Charlotte and Ben.

James (Jimmy) Moffatt – husband of Gracie and part owner of General Store. Father of Sandy, Lily, and Evelyn.

Jessica Saunders – Best friend of Charlotte in the twenty-first century. Wife of Michael Saunders.

Jessie Williams – Twin of Phillip, daughter of Charlotte and Ben. Passed away suddenly in 1826 at the age of four.

Keen Wolf – Native American (Tuscarora) friend of the Williams family. Brother of Straight Arrow. Joined to Gifted Hands. Father of Mitenah and Dark Wolf.

Keith Crawford (aka Brian Oakley) – Preacher. Husband of Carole-Anne, father of Maisie.

Lawrence Southern – Town magistrate. Owner of the grist mill. Husband of Phoebe. Father of Lionel, Peter, Rebecca, and Graham.

Lily Moffatt – Middle daughter of Gracie and Jimmy Moffatt.

Mabel Williams – Owner of General Store. Wife of the late Alec Williams, mother of Ben and Gracie Williams.

Maisie Crawford – Daughter of Carole-Anne and Keith.

Michael Saunders – Ex-boyfriend of Charlotte in the twenty-first century. Husband of Jessica.

Mitenah – Daughter of Gifted Hands and Keen Wolf. Sister of Dark Wolf, half-sister of Running-Otter.

Penelope MacNeil – Daughter of Preacher MacNeil. Mother of Janee Southern.

Phillip Williams – Twin of Jessie, son of Charlotte and Ben.

Rebecca Grim (nee Rebecca Southern) – Daughter of Phoebe and Lawrence Southern. Sister of Lionel, Peter, and Graham. Widow of Ronald Grim. Mother of Winnie, Francis, and Eloise. Adoptive mother to Janee.

Robert (Robbie) Graham Williams – Son of Ben and (late) Sussannah Graham.

Running Otter (Running Cub) – Son of Gifted Hands and late husband Straight Arrow. Half-brother to Mitenah and Dark Wolf.

Sabel Williams – Oldest daughter of Charlotte and Ben.

Sandy (Alexandra) Moffatt – Oldest daughter of Gracie and Jimmy Moffatt.

Swan Song – Son of Song Bird and Burning Oak. Husband of Mitenah.